The Bangkok Blues

The Bangkok Blues

An R.P. Merlyn Boating Adventure Novel

Larry C. Watkins

Writers Club Press
San Jose New York Lincoln Shanghai

The Bangkok Blues
An R.P. Merlyn Boating Adventure Novel

Writers Club Press
an imprint of iUniverse.com, Inc.

For information address:
iUniverse.com, Inc.
5220 S 16th, Ste. 200
Lincoln, NE 68512
www.iuniverse.com

ISBN: 0-595-18416-2

Printed in the United States of America

Acknowledgments

Thanks to my wife Annette, without whom none of this would have been possible, and to the writers and artists of The Writers' Club of Whittier, for their continued encouragement and advice, especially Lucy Byard and Madeline Baker.

CHAPTER I

Leaning back into the corner of the cockpit, I steered with one bare foot on the tiller and reveled in the motion as SHIELA, a Cheoy Lee Offshore 27, broadreached under main and a striped 135 genoa.

Our destination was Ko Phai, a small riot of green jungle and golden sand dropped into the cobalt blue of the Bight of Bangkok, twenty-three nautical miles northwest from my duty station at the deepwater port of Sattahip, Thailand. The sleepy beach town of Pattaya lay eight nautical miles off our starboard beam.

Suddenly, Pen squealed, a sound of delighted surprise and practically jumped to the leeward side of the cockpit to get closer to the water. I knew what she was excited about, I'd seen them coming. A pod of dolphin swarmed around us, leaping and blowing as they filled the air with squeaks and clicks.

"Oh, Bob," Pen exclaimed, pronouncing my name in the Thai manner, with a short vowel, "I no see before!"

"Talk to 'em," I said. "They like it."

Clapping her hands, she called out, something I didn't understand, but those sea mammals moved in even closer, rolling on their sides to eyeball her.

"Look," I said, "they say *Sawaddee*."

Her hands in front of her, Pen gave the pod a deep, respectful wai. "*Sawaddee ka*," she said solemnly. The clicks and squeaks increased and they moved in closer.

An idea came to me. It was a little devious, but not mean-spirited.

"You know," I said, "they like it when you take your clothes off."

She looked at me, the disbelief plain on her exotically pretty face.

"*Ching-ching*," I said with as much conviction as I could muster, "it's true, I no bullshit. They like it, makes 'em think you *same-same* them."

I could see the battle being waged in her dark feline eyes, skepticism versus a desire to believe and for emphasis, I slipped my own shorts off. The teak was warm on my tanned bare butt.

Suddenly she stood up and in a single flowing motion pulled her shirt off over her head. A gold amulet in the shape of the full moon glinted against her butterscotch skin, then the sarong she wore slung low across her hips slid down her legs to become a puddle of colorful cloth on the weathered teak grating of the cockpit sole.

I watched her prominent nipples harden into upturned chocolate kisses as she felt the sun and wind on her naked body for the first time. An expression of guarded pleasure chased the apprehension from her almond-shaped dark eyes and as she pulled a ribbon loose her hair became a long silky black telltale in the warm southwesterly.

Sitting on the deck with her legs under the leeward lifelines, Pen dipped her feet in the warm water and gasped as one darted in almost close enough to touch with her big toe. With a shriek of delight, she grabbed me and I felt myself lifted with her contagious joy. She thrust both legs out, far over the edge, the closeness of the animals wiping from her mind her fears of falling overboard, of being lost at sea, of being sick, of the boat in general and I thanked the Skipper upstairs for bringing this show to us now. I had talked about safety, sailing skill, righting moment and navigation until I was blue in the face and it didn't have anywhere near the effect that these sea mammals were having on her right now.

They stayed with us for twenty minutes. Pen laid on the deck, talking and cooing to them while I snapped several pictures, then as quickly as they had come, they were gone.

The boat rose to a wave then settled. Pen's eyes flared, but only for a second. Confidence surged through her and with a cat-like grace, as if she had been doing it for years, she scrambled onto the cabin top, went to the mast, hopped onto the boom and leaned back into the taut curve of the mainsail. Spreading her feet, she raised her arms over her head and gently shook her round, sloping breasts for me.

"You *sway-mahk, ching-ching!*" I called to her and the kiss she blew to me was heavy with promise. She was beautiful up there, but I knew she didn't think so. She thought her skin too dark, her lips too full and the bridge of her nose too broad, but I couldn't get enough of her.

"I do for you, *Tilok-cha,*" she said. A melting, enigmatic smile, the one that can mean so many things in Thailand, shaped those luscious lips. I shot a whole roll of film as she played and cavorted naked on the cabin top.

Gibing onto a starboard tack, I was able to lay the southern end of the island on my port bow and we slid around the point and up the east side of the island to a large natural cove that offered shelter from the prevailing southwesterlies. The anchor went down in thirty feet of water so clear I could watch it dig into the sandy bottom.

Pen slipped her sarong back on and readied the go-ashore bag while I inflated the small dink. Ashore, I wriggled my toes in the golden sand and tied a stern line to a palm tree. I had three days off before reporting back for duty aboard the army tug in Sattahip and I wanted the boat secure.

One more time, I thanked the fates for Brian Fellows, an Aussie civilian and refrigeration engineer, who had left the boat in my care when he'd returned to Sydney for a family emergency.

Scooping a hollow in the sand, I laid a fire while Pen quickly cleaned the small tuna I'd caught earlier.

"I feel just like Gardner McKay!" I said as I hugged her.

"Gar' who?" She smiled, pressed herself to me and the natural sandalwood and spice scent of her skin made me dizzy.

"*Mai pen lai*," I said, "just know I'm glad you're here with me."

Not so far away, other guys were dying in a hot, fetid jungle or shivering under a central highlands rain, but I was on a deserted tropical island with a beautiful girl and a trim little craft anchored near-by. I almost had to pinch myself. There was only one small pebble in the pudding of my elation, but I was working on a plan that would take care of that.

Wanpen Sirikit Prathorn had been my *tilok*, my live-in lover, for five months now. Our bungalow, known as a hootch in the vill' by all the GIs who had one, was small and simple but adequate in the tropical climate.

The Gulf of Thailand was a sailor's paradise of warm clear water and generally good weather and with a good boat and a loving woman, I could be happy here for a very long time. If Pen would go for it, that is. I almost blurted out what was on my mind, but with an effort held it in. I couldn't have dealt with another rejection right then, not since last week when she'd stunned me with the news that she didn't want to go to the United States. Be very careful, I told myself.

After a dinner of grilled fish, rice and fruit, we sat on a blanket with a fallen log for a backrest and watched the waxing moon climb into the ultramarine blue sky of early evening.

She turned her head, brought her face close to mine and kissed me in a spontaneous gesture of affection and happiness, which only made me shake my head.

"What's the matter?" She asked. It came out Whassamatta?

"Look," I said, pointing at the picture postcard view of the scimitar of golden sand with the boat anchored in the cobalt bay, "is this beautiful or what?"

"*Chai, sway mahk.*"

She fingered the gold amulet and pointed at the moon.

"I love moon," she said softly, "I like to go there, with you. No have Bangkok cowboys, no numba ten GI, you and me, can do, *naa*?" She followed this with a rapid stream of Thai that I knew wasn't for my benefit, or even my understanding.

The recent Apollo missions to the moon had captured world-wide attention, but I knew she wasn't talking about space exploration.

"What did you say, just now?" I asked her.

She cut a quick glance at me, giggled like a small girl, and said, "I ask man-in-moon, what is happy?" She said it HAP-py. "He can know, can tell me, happy, yes or no?"

It was a spike through my heart for her to ask the man-in-the-moon if she was happy or not. This girl was confusing and confounding me in ways I'd never experienced before and I felt like I was running through thick, clingy mud every time I thought about it, so I changed my line of thought, to something more pleasant.

I told her again about how I used to dream of having my own boat in a tropical paradise and a beautiful woman to share it with. Throwing a satin smooth bare leg over me, she laughed, a low throaty gurgle of pleasure that made my spine tingle. A smile lit her face from within as she brushed her fingertips along my jaw.

"What?" I strained to keep my voice calm.

"You make me happy."

In the very last of the day, when the light has gone beyond golden, her eyes still glowed and her smile was so wide that the tiny dimple in her cheek showed.

"Really? How?" I caressed the dimple and she grabbed my finger and kissed it.

"You talk a lot when you happy, yes?"

"No I don't," I said, embarrassed somehow.

Yes," she replied, "you do. You talk a lot. I like hear you talk, say any's-ing, I don' care."

Her fingers played in my chest hair and my heart soared to Polaris that now rose above the horizon.

"I love you eyes," she said as her lips brushed mine, "*sway-mahk*. You hair, ver' nice. You *sway-mahk GI!*"

I pulled back to look at her. I didn't consider myself all that good looking. A shade under six feet, a hundred and seventy pounds with light brown hair, regular features and a strong nose, I held my own, but I did have my black Irish daddy's killer blue eyes.

"You're very beautiful, too, Pen," I whispered. She'd put on a pound or two in the months we'd been living together and in the gathering moonlight she was achingly beautiful.

Pushing me flat onto my back, she lightly dragged her stiff nipples over me and let her hair drift across my face as her tongue darted between my lips.

"You know, Bob-*cha*, wha' I like?"

I knew what she liked, all right. "You want?"

"*Chai*," she said as she pulled me on top of her, "I want *mahk-mahk!*"

Her breathing, quick and urgent, spurred me on as she wrapped her slim thighs around my waist and guided me to her gate. Taking her plush lower lip between my teeth, I pushed a little. She purred, then splashed, hot and copious as I entered her in one long single thrust.

Starting slow, I watched her, and when her round little belly started to tremble I began to bang her, hard and fast. With her eyes squinched shut, veins and cords stood in relief as she pinched and pulled both nipples. Our flesh slapped wetly together, like the small surf that lapped at the shore only yards away.

A low trembling moan came from deep within her, the signal she was very close. I gave it all I had. She gripped me spasmodically and her hips pumped a powerful rhythm that tripped me over the edge. A growl of pure animal pleasure resonated inside her, grew into a rising howl and as she writhed and moaned under me, I bubbled up and shot her full, my own wild cry ringing in the moonlit stillness of the deserted cove.

We collapsed into a gasping pile of spent energy and long moments later, as my own pulse and breathing slowed, I became aware of a sound, one I had never heard before.

I raised my head to listen, and was just about to call it to her attention, when I felt her body shudder under me and realized, with a deep shock, that it was her crying.

"*Cha,*" I said softly, the endearment sounding very natural and right, "what's the matter?"

I jiggled her butt, hoping she was really laughing, but knowing it wasn't so.

Without seeming to she pushed me off to sit up and hug her knees tightly to her chest. She gazed at me for a second, then her fantastic lower lip trembled and she burst into tears that were twin trails of glittering despair in the moonlight.

This was not the reaction I had hoped for after such a wonderful joining of our flesh and spirits. Huge racking sobs shook her body and trembled her hair and when I tried to put my arm around her, she moved away.

"*Tilok-cha,*" I asked, "what is it?" I began to sense that all was not as it seemed.

She pulled in a deep breath, wiped her eyes with her hands, and said between sniffs, "Bhudda say, no want nos'sing, have much happiness, want som'sing ver' bad, have much hurt you heart, you know?"

Was I getting this right? It seemed like she was trying to say that wanting something very much leads only to unhappiness, and I felt my euphoric balloon of only moments ago start to implode.

This seemed like another example of religion throwing a damper on the human experience. I had always thought the pagan Polynesians or the American Indians had the right attitude, worshiping things that were close and needful in everyday life, like the earth, the sun, moon, stars, wind, water, and letting the animal that is man live a peaceful, happy, sensuous, guilt free life. Missionaries were the ruination of the world.

Gradually, the tears and sniffles trailed off, but Pen still rocked back and forth, her arms around her knees.

Maybe, I told myself, she was beginning to change her mind about coming to the world with me and she was confused about her feelings.

"You not happy?" I asked as I slid my open palm along the incredible softness of her thigh.

"Yes," she said, very low, so low I had to lean forward to hear. "I ver' happy with you. I love you *mahk-mahk*, maybe too much!"

Her hand closed over mine and she held it for a moment, then she raised it to her lips and kissed my fingertips one at a time. In the moonlight her big dark eyes seemed filled with an undecipherable longing, then her long lashes fell like the curtain on the last act. My heart began to thud in my chest.

"What's the problem then?"

"*Mai pen lai,*" she said, the Thai answer to all of life's difficult, troubling questions.

At that moment I would have given anything to have understood her conversation with the man-in-the-moon.

Before I left this exotic country, the comfortable cocoon of my own beliefs and assumptions would be shattered by deceit and death. I would never again take anything at face value. The very core of my soul would be tested and I would emerge from it bruised and battered but like steel that takes a constant beating, I would be work-hardened. It seemed like only yesterday that I had stepped from an airplane.

CHAPTER 2

As a Southern California native, I had no idea what humidity was, but in December of 1968 I found out quick enough. When I stepped off the big silver bird at Don Muang Airport, outside Bangkok, and took my first breath, I thought I'd drown right there. Thick, almost gelatinous, the air seemed to flow in and out like syrup, but after twenty-five hours of dry, stale airplane air it was at least real. Overhead, puffy white cotton-ball clouds, pushed by a steady twelve knots of wind, raced across a sky as blue as topside enamel.

The bus ride into the city of Bangkok was on the wrong side of the road but me and everyone else was too busy craning our necks to care.

The countryside slid by like a Monet painting. Green, in every shade imaginable, dominated everything, but was contrasted by a ribbon of brown water in the roadside ditch. In that water, small brown people washed cars, buffalo, and kids at the same time. Kids smiled and waved but the adults seemed more reserved, but the buffalo had no opinion on the matter.

Long rows of shacks, all perched on bamboo stilts, stretched along the road and paralleled canals, but at the edges of the city, where the green gave way to gray concrete and black asphalt, traffic started to pile up. Small cars, gaudy trucks, even gaudier buses, motorcycles, scooters and taxis all clamored for space and right of way. There wasn't a traffic light in sight, but there were many circles. I thought of the one on

Pacific Coast Highway, near Signal Hill. To make it out of that one alive you had to be quick, decisive and plan in advance, but these were race-tracks compared to that one.

After an hour of sensory overload, the bus pulled into a gate and stopped in front of an imposing building that proclaimed it to be MACV Headquarters (Thailand). Us newbies were herded into a room where a chaplain gave us the usual lecture about keeping it in our pants and told us a few things about the local culture: Don't touch anyone on the head, don't cross one foot over a knee and point the sole of the foot at anyone, and no matter what you do, don't insult the King or Queen. It was a state offense and taken very seriously.

Soon I was on another bus, a smaller one this time, without air conditioning. The winter-weight Class A uniform, so valued in the knifing winter wind of Travis Air Force Base in Northern California, became a clinging wet blanket in the steaming box of the bus, but there were other things to occupy my mind.

Joseph Conrad's narrator Marlow, upon arriving in Siam, called the combination of sights and aromas, "impalpable and enslaving, like a charm, like a whispered promise of mysterious delight". I had to agree.

Odors rushed in through the open window, the likes of which I'd never experienced. Rotting vegetation, diesel exhaust and sickeningly sweet spices combined into a heady mix that made my head spin and even though I was exhausted, I couldn't close my eyes.

Things are different here, I told myself. This might actually be fun, and besides, no one was shooting at me. Yet.

CHAPTER 3

Sunlight winked and dazzled off saltwater scuffed by a light breeze and the air was thick with the harbor perfume of diesel exhaust and low tide. I breathed it in while images of summers past wavered in my mind. Boats squatted in cradles like sea monsters out of the water in my Uncle Jack's boatyard in San Pedro, California and masts, rigging, tuna towers and fly bridges stood stark against a hard blue sky while topsides gleamed with fresh paint and new varnish.

Uncle Jack was the wizard and I the apprentice on his Colin Archer-designed thirty-seven foot gaff ketch, the CHARLIE MARLOW. On this beautiful vessel Jack had unlocked the arcane mysteries of wind and water on sails and hull, showed me how a boat could move against the wind, and introduced me to the thrill of a twenty knot wind over the quarter while the boat hummed and vibrated with power and speed.

He taught me when to shorten sail and keep punching into it, and when to heave-to and ride it out, literally and figuratively.

I almost had to take the tenth grade over again when a two-week Christmas vacation cruise to Mexico turned into a six-week sojourn around the Baja Peninsula to La Paz, where a howling norther in the Sea of Cortez had shown me that the sea was indifferent to my petty concerns and my longing for attention and nurturing took a poor second place to the state of the tide and the phases of the moon.

Before I was eighteen I could set sail, steer, reef, stand a four hour trick at the wheel, plot a course, coastal navigate, change engine oil and filters, bleed a fuel system, adjust a packing gland, tune the rig, tie a one-handed bowline in the dark, and splice three-strand line, not to mention lay varnish so it looked like deep glass, and when I was drafted I was starting to get the hang of celestial navigation.

I had swung on an anchor in every cove the Channel Islands had to offer, and had read every book Uncle Jack had, works by Melville, Conrad, Forrester, and others, most of them by the oil lamp in my quarter-berth bunk. I was at home on the water, I felt a connection between the anchor rode of my soul and the heaving salt and I knew it was where I wanted to make my life. Before she died, Aunt Chloe had told me that Jack wanted me to attend the California Maritime Academy and become a Merchant Marine officer, like he'd been before his war.

While most guys my age were drooling over hot-rod Chevys and bored and stroked Fords, I panted over Crocker sloops and cutters, Garden and Archer ketches and yawls; cars were just a way to get to the chandlery to pick up boat parts.

The high-pitched whine of an air-powered tool and the rhythmic clang of a large hammer on steel brought me back to where I stood then, on a concrete dock bound by a pretty little bay in Thailand.

"Well," Rick said, "there it is, our home for the next year."

Rick Harbiter, a tall, lanky soldier-hippie from Oakland pulled the last drag from that Pall-Mall while the cherry singed his long nonregulation moustache then flicked the butt away and gazed at the stubby vessel before us.

The LT 1975 looked pretty ragged after her tow all the way from Okinawa, but what the hell, she wasn't designed to look pretty, unless beauty was counted as a function of form, and in that case she was very comely.

The LT stood for Large Tug. A hundred feet long and three hundred sixty gross tons, she was the largest of the harbor tugs, capable of coastal work but not intended for blue water. She'd been towed by another army tug, an ocean-going hundred and forty-two footer.

"Hey, Rick," I asked out of the blue, "how'd you come to be here?"

"I guess they needed tug people here in Sattahip. The Sea Bees built this port to support the air force bases in Thailand."

"No shit, huh?"

"I wouldn't kid ya', man. The army has more small boats than the navy does."

"That right?"

"That's right. Now, let's see what we're up against."

Rick stepped off the concrete dock and dropped five feet onto the bowput, that shaggy moustache of frayed rope and truck tires on the bow of the tug.

I watched him disappear into the deckhouse, then followed. Inside, I found him drawing a cup of coffee from a gleaming stainless steel urn.

"This's a good sign," Rick said, slurping up a mouthful of the heavily sugared black brew. "A boat with fresh coffee is a happy boat." His big brown eyes closed as he sipped again.

"You guys the two new snipes?"

I turned to see a man standing in a passageway, wiping his hands on a rag. Dressed in a stained and rumpled white T-shirt, paint-spattered jungle fatigue pants and jungle boots, he had a long narrow face and nose that had been broken more than once.

"That be us, Chief," Rick said and went forward, offering his hand.

I thought a salute would be more in order, but I'd find that warrant officers rarely bothered with military protocol.

The man shook Rick's hand, then mine.

"OK," he said, "put your gear below, pick a bunk and a locker, then report to the engine room, we got a lot o' work to do."

Chief Engineer Paddy O'Sullivan, "Silky" to his friends, turned out to be a no-bullshit kind of officer who knew his stuff. The working complement on the tug was six engineers, eight deckhands and three officers. We engineers painted and greased and polished and serviced and fueled and oiled everything in that engine room and had it ready for duty in five days, six days ahead of schedule.

CHAPTER 4

The *baht* bus, a Toyota truck with bench seats and a metal roof bolted into the bed chased the twin beams of its own head lights through the damp dark. One just like it zipped past, headed the other way. These little trucks were the public transportation of the country and they traveled back and forth between the crossroads. Each one was independent and the fare was one *baht*, equal to a nickel. All you had to do was stand by the side of the road. One would be along in five minutes or less and a wave of the hand, with the palm down, pulled them to a stop.

I was very glad when we finally slowed down and pulled off the road at the next crossroad. Four of us piled out, paid our *baht*, and with a rooster tail of gravel and a lot of noise and fury, the driver turned around for the run back.

"I'm glad that ride's over!" I said with exaggerated relief. I was, too.

"That's the way they do it here," Rick drawled with the authority of experience. "Time is money." He didn't seem a bit fazed, and when he started toward the biggest building around, we followed.

Garishly lit, the building appeared to have been dropped into the jungle. A cluster of shacks had grown up around it and they all hunkered down amid a pool of blue and yellow light that was quickly swallowed up by the humid tropical night. A huge plastic and fluorescent sign proclaimed this place to be the "San Francisco Bar", and it was a magnet for horny, thirsty American GIs. Even from a distance the thin wooden walls pulsed and expanded in time to the loud music. The door opened, spilling light, noise, and two couples. The guys were air force, from the sprawling base just down the road at Utapao, and drunk as lords. They both held bottles of the local panther piss beer and were talking loud and trying to fondle the girls. The girls laughed and flirted, but they deflected the roaming hands as they stumbled off down a path.

Rick, Charlie and I were on a recon mission to check out the night life and we bravely mounted the low porch and went inside.

The bare fluorescent tubes in the ceiling showered the interior with a cold light that made the swarm of tiny tables and the multitude of chairs seem even closer together than they actually were. A seething, shifting mass of humanity stretched from the door all the way to the crude bar that ran along the back wall of the single fifty by fifty foot room.

Perched on the end of the bar was an ancient cash register, presided over by an old mama-san with skin like tree bark, who sat on a high stool so she could see everything. The thick smell of beer, stale cigarette smoke and sweet perfume overpowered the efforts of the feeble air conditioner that groaned in one window.

We found a table in the back, away from the juke box that pounded out bubble-gum rock and Motown. At least this wasn't a red-neck bar, full of GIs from Texas in boots and hats, whooping and hollering to shit-kicker tunes about trucks and divorce. Armed with our own bottle of 7-Crown from the PX, we ordered set-ups from a bored waitress.

"A short-time is three bucks, an all-nighter is ten," Charlie proclaimed smugly to display his expertise on local prices.

I had known Charlie slightly from the army school in Virginia. He was a doofus of the highest order, but he had a good heart and there wasn't a devious bone in his freckled, pear-shaped body.

The subject of prices made my heart start to beat fast and I lit a cigarette to cover.

"A beer is a buck, drinks are a buck-fifty. The beer is lousy, the drinks are watered."

Charlie had been in-country a whole four days longer than Rick and I, but in spite of his studied attitude of cool, his brown eyes were as big as saucers as he looked around.

The girls, unless seated with someone, glided from table to table, flirting and ruffling hair and teasing while our necks became sore from so much swiveling and craning around. Spontaneous whoops and hollers broke out here and there, exclamation points in the general revelry.

"Jackwow, jackwow!" some GI shouted. It cut through the din like a siren through city noise, and all the girls in the place took up the chant.

"Jackwow! jackwow!" Each of them made wildly exaggerated sexual motions, as if they possessed a three foot phallus. It was gross and obscene, but at the same time oddly compelling. All the girls thought it was hilarious and the chant went around the room, like a cheer in a stadium, then quickly died away.

"They're yellin' 'handjob'," Charlie said to no one and downed his drink in a hurry, then mixed himself another and downed half of that as fast as he could.

He fastened his attention onto every girl that went by and there was little conversation at our table because we were so busy watching what was going on around us.

Rick leaned over toward me. "Charlie's workin' up to somethin'," he said.

"How do you know that?" I already knew but wanted to hear Rick confirm it.

"Look at the way he's drinkin'. He's workin' on his courage." Rick looked as relaxed and confident as if he were on his own front porch.

"Where were you stationed before you came to Thailand?"

Rick glanced at me. "I was on an ocean-going tug out o' Okinawa for a year. I been all over Asia, man, the Philippines, Vietnam, Japan, Singapore, Guam, lot's o' places."

"I thought so," I said. Rick merely smiled, but it occurred to me that I was glad I'd met him.

Glancing at Charlie, I could see he was on the verge of something.

"Hey, Charlie," I said to him, "ask that one there to dance." I pointed to a cute one with an especially provocative wiggle going by in a tight red dress.

He watched her, the battle between fear and desire plain on his freckled face.

"Not yet," he said when fear won out, then he picked up his drink and gulped it down. The girl in the red dress must have had a sixth sense, because she zeroed in on him and wrapped her arms around his head while her fingers played with his hair. She shook her charms in his face, then favored him with her most dazzling smile.

The color rushed up his neck and into his reddish hair so that you could almost see the heat waves he was giving off. He started to choke and cough and she whacked him on the back. He stopped coughing and just stared at her. She laughed and it sounded like a wind chime and broke the tension. We all stared at her. She seemed so in control of things as she looked at each of us in turn. She faced Charlie and willed him to speak. It worked.

"*Sawadee.*" Charlie croaked out a hello, practically exhausting his vocabulary of Thai words.

"*Ah, phut Thai dee mahk!*" she said, flattering his ability with the language. She hooked a chair over and dropped lightly into it. Her unfettered breasts shifted under the thin material of her dress as she helped herself to a cigarette from Rick's pack of Pall-Malls lying on the table. Delicately, she placed the cigarette between her painted lips and looked at Charlie expectantly. He just stared back at her. Rick picked up his Zippo and handed it to Charlie and motioned toward her. Charlie came awake at last, jumped and knocked over his glass, spilling the dregs of the drink onto the middle of the table.

"*Mai pen lai,*" she said calmly, still looking at him. We would all learn that *mai pen lai* was a Thai phrase that covered many awkward or embarrassing moments. It meant never mind, don't worry about it, it's forgotten.

Charlie managed to open the lighter and flick it into life without setting any fires. When the cigarette was going, she took a tiny puff, grimaced and put it in an ashtray, not used to the strong unfiltered tobacco.

"What you name, GI?" she asked with a tilt of her head, her sing-song voice like tiny bells. Her long dangly earrings fired off flashes of light.

"Charlie." He looked like he was about to mess his pants.

"Char'ie," she said with a smile, "dance wis me."

Standing, she took his elbow. At the dance floor she turned to face him and started to sway and writhe with a graceful eroticism, in time to the thumping beat of the Four Tops.

Charlie danced like a spastic chicken, his elbows and knees going separate directions. I almost expected him to start clucking. He was aware of all of us watching him and, trying to catch the beat, he became a maniac, flopping and flinging himself around, which only made it worse. His eyes became enormous and his flared nostrils made him resemble a horse trapped in a burning barn.

She must have sensed that he was about to bolt. Moving in close, she threw her arms round him and pressed her body right up against him, slowed him down, and used her own movements to impart the rhythm to him. He calmed right down, the panic-stricken look left his face and was soon replaced by an expression of stunned amazement, like a true believer who has seen the light.

They danced slowly, oblivious to the sea of sweaty, jerky bodies that swirled around them. When the song was over, they made their way back to the table and the smile on Charlie's face was as big as the sky. They sat down, whispering and giggling together.

"Hey, you guys, this is Suzie," Charlie said, beaming around the table. Suzie flashed a million watt smile around and we all nodded. She raised her hand and called out, two quick syllables. A waitress appeared and Charlie ordered more Seven-Up. Suzie leaned in close to Charlie and whispered in his ear. The panic-stricken look came back, and he started to stutter. She whispered some more, and now he really looked sick.

Suddenly, Rick leaned over and whispered in his other ear. The panicked expression was replaced by one of gratitude as he looked back at Rick. Rick sat back and nodded slowly.   Charlie's hand dove into his pocket and came out with some bills, some of which he peeled off and gave to Suzie. She smiled sweetly and the money disappeared. The drinks arrived, with something green for her.

"What'd you say to Charlie?" I asked Rick.

He turned to me. "I had a hunch that Suzie there told him that he'd have to take her in the back right now or she'd have to move on. The place is gettin' crowded, she don't have time to coax him. I told him to order her up a green bar drink for her and to give her a couple bucks to sit with him for a while. He's happy, mama-san is happy, Suzie's happy. Charlie can have some more liquid courage, then…" Rick shrugged, tipped ashes into an ashtray and smiled like an indulgent older brother.

"Far out." I muttered. What a guy, I thought. I would come to know that Rick was one of the most selfless and generous people I had ever met, a true hippie in the good sense of the word, and I would value his friendship in the coming year.

Charlie had himself another drink, danced another dance with Suzie, and made a decision. His face was flushed, every freckle highlighted as he took her arm and announced, "Don't wait for me, guys, I'm going for the all-nighter!" With his chin high and his shoulders back, he looked like he was at parade rest, and with a last look at us, he nodded at her, and she led him toward a door. Rick and I offered lewd and obscene encouragement.

"I hope he gets his money's worth." I remarked with a laugh.

We sat there for a while and finished the bottle of Seagram's. I was getting pretty tanked, and the later it became, the more the girls flirted.

Rick grinned. "You wanna get yourself a girl?"

I felt the rush of heat come over me, my throat closed so that I had to gulp melted ice from my glass before I could say, "Yeah, I think I will."

CHAPTER 5

On a hot afternoon several of us were sprawled on the aft deck under the awning as we headed out to meet a refrigerator ship. White clouds tumbled through the sky like popcorn and the wake, white as sugar against the cobalt blue water, boiled out astern.

"When we gonna go the 'Kok?" Donnie wanted to know.

For the last several weeks, that had been the question on everyone' mind. When were we going to Bangkok? Two of the three other tugs had gone and the crews had returned with tales of debauchery and drunkenness that, even if only a little true, rang in our heads like clarion calls. Instead, we stuck it out here in Sattahip, a hundred and ten nautical miles southeast of that mystical city, mushing around in port, pushing ships on and pulled them off the dock, moving barges, or sitting around doing nothing and trying to keep busy. I was glad I was a snipe and could just go down to the engine room. It was hot down there, and noisy too, but you soon got used to that, and aside from infrequent visits by the Chief, no officers or sergeants ever came down there. We could sit under the ventilator, smoke, drink coffee and play cards for hours, no one the wiser as long the generator kept hammering out its one lone song.

"Goddamn!" Donnie groused and lit a cigarette as his big butt smothered a corner of the lazzarette hatch. "I think I've fucked every hooker in this town at least once! I want a shot at that Bangkok gash!"

"I hear that!" Charlie threw in, his head and neck sopping wet. He had just come out of the engine room and he sat on a paint bucket and mopped his face and neck with a rag.

"What about you, Merlyn, had your fill of the girls in Sattahip?"

Donnie's eyes glittered and I knew he was hoping for some kind of entertainment at my expense.

"I'm doin' OK," I said.

"Just OK? Shee-it, man, you should be goin' through whores like Sherman through Georgia!" He brayed like an ass at his own joke.

I looked at Rick, who rolled his eyes but kept quiet. I did the same. I didn't want to admit to myself, let alone Donnie Brickham of Chattanooga, Tennessee, that my encounters with working girls had not turned out to be all that was expected. They were usually cute or at least attractive but conducted business like it was a business. With so many army and air force installations near-by, there must have been ten thousand GI stationed near here. The whores didn't have to work hard and try to get repeat customers because there was a steady stream of new ones. Quantity, not quality, was the order of the day.

I also wanted a shot at Bangkok. There were more *felongs*, or foreigners, but there were also more girls and I had heard that because of the increased competition, they were more eager to please.

"OK, guys, let's get the shit together."

The Leading Seaman, a short, skinny hard-stripe sergeant named Evan Fowler, had been tagged with the unfortunate nickname of Peach, and when he tried to get the deck crew up and moving, they took their sweet time about it.

Peach stood there in his snowy white T-shirt, sharply creased fatigue pants and shiny boots and tried to keep the slow burn under control. This had been happening·more and more and everyone knew that if he didn't get it turned around soon, he'd be backed into a corner that he'd never get out of, despite his rank.

Drawing himself to his full height of about five-eight, he looked up at Kevin's stocky six feet and tried to roar,   "Trooper, you got about five seconds to get that line faked down or you're gonna find yourself with an Article Fifteen!"

That was the worst thing Peach could have said, and his best roar was about as intimidating as a kitten's meow. Kevin stepped up close to him, his big belly nudging Peach, and slowly drawled, "It might be worth an Article to smash your pretty face one time!"

To his credit, Peach didn't back up one centimeter, but he turned a whiter shade of pale. Options, of which there were damn few, flicked across his face like a parade of one. He was screwed and he knew it.

Art came around the corner of the deckhouse, took the situation in at a glance, and strolled over to where Kevin and Peach glowered at each other.

"Say there, Kevin my man," he said slowly, "you're not giving my friend here the Sergeant any kind of grief, are you?"

The only sounds were the faint whine of the ventilator motor and the slithering swish of the wake. Under my boots, the steel deck vibrated with the force of the twelve hundred horsepower main engine.

Kevin's beady eyes flicked over to Art and I could see the whirring of his brain as he tried to figure out this new development.

Art Delaplane was no Peach. Shorter than Kevin by two inches, he weighed the same and while Kevin's was mostly in his middle, Art's weight and power was much in evidence in his massive arms, deep chest and broad shoulders.

Kevin stalled for time. "What the fuck is this, huh? Since when are you on his side?"

Art reached down, opened the heavy lazzarette hatch, plucked the hundred foot coil of inch-and-a-half nylon out and dropped it on the deck. Under his copper skin, the muscles of his arms and shoulders bunched and flexed like snakes in a bag and the feat wasn't lost on Kevin.

"I'm on no one's side," Art said with a wide grin. "I just like to keep a happy ship, that's all."

Seemingly without effort, Art picked up a ten-inch shackle and
started to attach it to the eye in the line. I watched the tattoo on his
upper arm, the face and bust of a pretty woman with long hair, exotic
eyes, luscious lips and large, round breasts with prominent, upturned
nipples. It was a real work of art, done entirely in one color but with
delicate and subtle shading, the work of someone who has all the time
in the world.

"Give me a hand with this, will you?"

Art thrust the shackle into Kevin's hands and let go, then quickly
started to fake the line down on deck.

"Get the monkey fist and bend it on," Art said to one of the other
deck hands, who jumped like he'd been stung.

For the job to be done right, Kevin had to walk the heavy shackle
with the end of the heavy line forward on deck so Art could continue.
Art glanced at him and with that look, I could see, and I'm sure Kevin
did, too, that Art would just as soon take his head off as not. Kevin
moved out, dragging the line with him.

"Hey," Peach put in, as he suddenly realized that he was the one in
charge, "I don't need anyone to back up my orders for me. I can…"

"Sure you can, Sarge. I don't mean to say you can't. But," Art looked
around with that tight little grin at all the crew who had gathered from
out of the woodwork to any confrontation, "from time to time, we all
need a little hand. Co-operation gets the job done faster. Isn't that what
they teach at Leadership School?" He smiled then, his teeth white and
perfect in his darkly handsome face.

Peach watched him for a second, then went up the ladder to the boat
deck, headed for the pilot house, muttering to himself.

Finished with the line, Art strolled forward around the deckhouse.

"Awesome, huh?" I said to Rick.

"No shit. Glad we're snipes. I've never seen any one guy do up a
shackle like that."

"There it is."

"What about it, Kevvie?" I said to Kevin as he came back. "You gonna hassle ol' Peach anymore?"

I liked Kevin well enough, but he had a superior I'm-from-Boston attitude that I liked to puncture whenever I had the chance.

"You're a fuckin' snipe," he snarled. "Keep the hell out of it." His neck quivered under his damp jowls.

"Bite me, ya' deck ape," I laughed.

Snipes always ribbed the deck hands, calling them apes and mops, claiming it didn't take any more brains than God gave a monkey to do deck work. But to be an engineer, well, that took some smarts.

Kevin bristled and his eyes narrowed.

"You feelin' froggy," I said, "ya' wanna leap? Go head on, ya' fat fuck, see what it gets ya." I shifted my weight onto my back foot and dropped my right hand. I was pretty sure I could take Kevin if I had to and if he did leap, I'd bring a whistling right up from the basement, but he only mumbled something and stalked off. The rest of the deckhands drifted away.

I looked at Rick. He seemed to be deep in thought and then he turned to me.

"What'a'ya' think Art's after?"

"What'a'ya mean?"

"I dunno," Rick said. Under his damp, gray T-shirt, his thin shoulders shrugged. "Why'd he do that? I been in the army long enough to know that a guy like him doesn't do anything without an angle of some kind." Under his thick moustache, Rick's lips twitched and he went into the galley for more coffee.

The days began to roll along, each of them the same. The work was boring and tedious, tending machinery in the hot engine room, but our work schedule of two days on, two days off, three days on, three days off allowed plenty of time off.   The only problem was what to do. Guys off duty took to hanging around on the boat deck, drinking iced tea, smoking and reading and playing juvenile practical jokes on each other until Toby happened to be in the wrong place at the wrong time.

I didn't know it at the time, but that was the beginning of my association with Art Delaplane, an alliance that would have a profound and lasting impact on me.

CHAPTER 6

On our day off, Rick and I sprawled on top of the pilothouse as three of the four army tugs headed out to meet an incoming tanker. Heavily loaded with JP-4 jet fuel, the MOBIL TRADER had little freeboard and our bow was almost dead even with their main deck. As we matched their speed and approached at an angle, crews on both vessels gleefully traded greetings and insults.

A seaman caught our monkey fist and hauled in the messenger line, then four of them pulled up the three-inch nylon bow hawser and dropped the eye over a midships cleat. The engine room telegraph clanged as Skip rang down for SLOW ASTERN.

A mile later, the MOBIL TRADER was still clipping along and the pilot on the bridge called for increased power from the tugs. I could feel the vibration through the studded soles of the jungle boots I wore as the twelve hundred diesel horses in the bowels of the tug ran up to HALF ASTERN. The hawser creaked, groaned and drew bar-taut.

The petroleum pier, a spindly-looking arrangement of steel and concrete, was rapidly approaching. If the ship were not slowed considerably, the flooding tide would send the heavily-laden ship crashing into the pier, destroying it, putting the ship on the rocks there and possibly spilling tons of jet fuel into the water.

The telegraph bells clanged again. An experienced engine guy can listen to the telegraph and tell pretty much what the skippers state of mind is. If he's calm and relaxed, the bells have a slow, mellow tone, but I heard the thread of anxiety in the rapid, jerky bells now.

The main engine's RPMs rose to its maximum of three hundred and twenty-five revs per minute, very fast for sixteen inch pistons. All six of them hammered and thumped in their steel cylinders.

Suddenly, I heard Peach shouting something, then his voice faded as he ran aft along the boat deck, shouting and swearing.

"What the hell?" I asked Rick.

"Sumpins' up, man. Gonna be some people hip-deep in shit damn quick!" He jumped up and ran for the ladder. I was on his heels.

From our perch on the boat deck, we watched as four deckhands raced madly to get quartering lines ready. On our starboard, Art manipulated the heaving line. Gathering several long coils into one hand, he locked his gaze on his target and let fly.

The weighted monkey fist soared up and away, trailing the light line in a smooth arc to the deck of the ship, where waiting crew pulled up the inch and a half nylon quarter line attached to it.

As soon as the loop was dropped over a massive cleat, the skipper stopped the engine, put the spun the wheel to put the rudder the other way, and rang for FULL AHEAD.

Rick and I stood rooted to the spot. Peach, listening to a walkie-talkie, had his hand in the air, waiting for a signal. Strain pulled his smooth face into stark planes and hollows as he waited, then he dropped his hand.

"Now!"

Art stood there, the line held loosely in his hand and with a casual gesture, as if he'd been doing this all his life, he stepped to the after bitts, threw four figure-eights of line over the bitts and pulled.

Like a python, the line pulled tighter and gripped the bitts with its coils while creaks and groans rose from where it looped and snaked over the smooth steel.

The angle of the tug to the ship changed again and the lines came under more strain, the coils sliding over each other and the bitts with such friction that the nylon began to smoke. Art tossed in another coil and the snaking stopped.

"They're tryin' to slow her down."

The quartering line ran from our aft bitts to a point on the ship in a straight line a hundred and fifty feet long. I could see the line shrinking from the strain and water being wrung from it fell in glittering drops into the sea.

"Goddamn," Rick breathed, "I ain't never seen a line that tight!" His eyes were huge behind his glasses. The tug shivered and vibrated as the big prop under our fantail whipped the water to a white froth.

"If that line was to break," Rick began, but he didn't finish it. His gaze was locked on another figure that had come down the starboard side. Toby McGillis, an amiable and unassuming deckhand from Savannah, Georgia, had no idea that his life was about to change.

"Look out!" Art shouted, pointing at the line as it vibrated like a plucked guitar string.

A look of startled comprehension washed over Toby's face and he planted one foot to stop, then started backing up, too late.

With a soft crumpling sound, like a big towel dropped, a hundred and fifty feet of bar-taut inch and a half nylon line shot down from the side of the ship where it had parted and just like a gigantic rubber band, snapped toward us. In the blink of an eye, it came writhing aboard and caught Toby high on the right leg.

I heard anther noise then, like a pistol shot. Toby was knocked to the deck. Relieved of the hold from the line, the tug yawed wildly to port and crashed into the steel wall of the ship, crumbling and bending the steel pipe awing supports like so much limp spaghetti.

The GQ bell went off and along with several whistles on the ship they shook the air with urgency. Toby lay on the deck, unmoving. Shouts and screams from our own pilothouse and from the ship filtered down to us, almost lost in the din of the bells and sirens.

"Jesus Christ!" I heard Art say. I looked at him. His coppery skin, stretched across the bones of his face, seemed thin and almost translucent. He didn't appear panicked. He also didn't go to the fallen man, but instead grabbed another line from the rack and made ready to throw it to the ship.

I wondered where our people were and realized then that they hadn't seen Toby get hit. All they knew was that Art was OK and getting another line ready.

I looked at Rick, he looked at me, then I found myself dropping down the ladder to the main deck.

Toby lay on his side, his right leg bent weirdly forward just below the hip. Blood seeped from his fatigue pants, bright red against the gray non-skid steel deck. I checked his pulse. There wasn't any, nor was he breathing.

I guess training took over and I tilted his head back, reaching into his mouth and cleared his airway then pinched his nose shut and whooshed some breath into him, once, twice, three times, then put my palms together, pushed four times on his chest, then blew two more breaths into him.

I became aware of someone else there and glanced up to see Rick cutting away the fatigue pants with his army-issue knife. More blood ran out, shockingly red like a pool of spilled paint.

"Holy shit!"

The deep voice of the bos'n, a grizzled old E-6 with white hair and paint-stained fingers, came to me then but I didn't look up, busy blowing and pushing.

Toby gurgled, gasped and choked, then coughed a little and was breathing.

The deck continued to vibrate, gear rattled and I heard the squeaking sound of the line snaking off the bitts again, then, just as suddenly, it ceased.

Rick laid the pants leg open and we could both see it then. The bone stuck out of a gash in Toby's thigh like a broken white stick and his calf seemed to be twisted a hundred and eighty degrees. Rick quickly folded the cut-off piece of pants into a pad and tried to stop the bleeding. He did slow it down some.

The bos'n was barking into a radio even as another other army tug moved up beside us to add its thrust against the tide.

A work boat came alongside with medics and Toby was taken away on a stretcher.

"Get the hose," Peach said to Kevin, "and wash that deck down before it dries."

Without a word, Kevin pulled the deck hose from its reel on the after bulkhead and directed a stream of water. The last we saw of Toby was the blood he'd spilled, thin and watery as it ran over the side through the scuppers.

"I thought this duty was supposed to be a piece of cake, no danger and all of that shit," Art said, as if a promise made to him had been broken.

"Not for this poor sonofabitch," Rick replied, "but at least he's still alive and goin' back to the world."

CHAPTER 7

"Awright you guys, listen up! Skip's got a few words for you."

The bos'n glared at us while Peach stood off to one side. The skipper stepped up onto the lazzarette hatch, paused for a moment and looked around at all sixteen of us from his five-eight pudgy self.

"OK, here's the deal," his head, covered with a fuzz of thinning blond, was like a tomato, red in the heat. "As you know, the boat works pretty much seven days a week, if things need doing."

That was pretty much true. Port operations went on around the clock, although ships normally timed their arrival for daylight.

"This tug," the skipper went on, "is too small for the off-duty crew to hang around, so, what I want every man to do is to get himself a hootch in the vill'. I know, I know," he raised his hands, and his voice, as we started talking.

"I know it's against regs, but I want you to do it. You need some-place to go when you're off-duty. I don't want a repeat of what happened to McGillis."

Many of the guys had already taken that step on their own and had gotten girls to move in with them. Charlie had done it when he'd found a girl he liked in town.

"C'mon, man," he said to me as we headed back down the ladder to the engine room, "Lin will find a place for ya'. All you gotta do is give her about thirty bucks for a months rent and few basics. She'll set it all up, man!"

Charlie looked the picture of domestic bliss. He was getting fat, even after only a few weeks of conjugal living.

"I don't know," I said. "I haven't met anyone I'd want to live with yet, and besides…"

"Besides nothin'," he insisted. "You get someone to move in with ya', yer a lot less likely to catch a dose of the clap, you know?"

The clap was a presence in town and some guys had gone to sickbay with a drip more than once. It was rumored that if you got the clap more than four times, the army would send you to the chaplain for some "advice" on how to keep it in your pants.

"Well, I've been lucky so far, and…"

"Screw lucky!" Charlie was adamant. "You know," he dropped his voice, "if you get a chick to move in with you, you get exclusive rights, know what I mean?"

The grin on his face made him look like a lewdly mischievous little boy.

"Tell me about that part," I said.

He didn't need any encouragement. "You know how the hookers are really just so-so most of the time?"

I nodded.

Well," he went on as he checked the oil in the number one generator, "you get one of 'em livin' with you, and look out! She'll fuck your head off, man, I'm tellin' ya'! See, it's different when you live together. She don't have to hustle for her dinner every night. She keeps you happy, she's in the tall cotton, man, and she'll wanna protect that, believe me."

"How you know all this?"

"My *tilok*, Lin, just wants it all the time!"

"What'd you call her, tee somethin'?"

"*Tilok*," he said. "It means sweetheart or darlin' or honey or something like that. Don't worry, man, you get a chick livin' with ya' and you'll start pickin' up the lingo real fast."

With a slap on my shoulder, he replaced the dipstick.

Later that day we received word we'd be departing for Bangkok at
0600 the next morning. That afternoon, we took on a full load of fuel
and water.

At 0500 the next morning the main engine was lit off and by six we
had cleared the breakwater of Sattahip. The island of Ko Khram Yai, a
three by three mile jungle clad hill rising from a tossing gray sea, lay just
off the starboard bow.

Bangkok, ninety miles into the Bight of Bangkok and another twenty
miles up the Chao Phraya River, seemed to call to us over the water ruffled by a light breeze.

My two hour trick of throttle watch under way, two hours of listening to the main throb and pound, watching and recording temperature
and pressure readings, seemed interminable, but when I was relieved we
were just approaching the pilot station.

The barge, loaded with CONEX boxes stacked two high, was a hundred feet long and fifty feet wide. Towed on a long hawser for most the
trip, it had to be brought up close to the tug, into the position known as
"on the hip" for the ride up the winding river.

The skipper, bos'n, and deck crew struggled with bulky nylon lines
and steel cables as thick as your wrist, all done in a boisterous seaway
with a strong current and an opposing wind. Once alongside, the barge
was snuggled up tight with more lines wrapped around a massively
powerful capstan on the aft deck.

We sat on the barge and watched the river, nearly two miles wide at
that point, flow by, loaded with the goods of trade and commerce.
Strings of rice barges that resembled Noah's Ark, so loaded down as to
be almost awash, were pulled by an impossibly tiny towboat. Long-
tailed passenger boats, the buses of the river, glided by like carriages
with elaborate awnings and gilded paint.

As the river narrowed, buildings ashore slid past as if it was they were the ones moving. Temples, their roofs gleaming golden, their walls white and glowing, mingled with warehouses and office buildings and piers and wharves of every description. Smaller long-tailed boats, driven by engines mounted on a short, stout pole, zipped by with an insistent buzz that earned them the term skeeter boats. They had room for the operator, and only a few passengers. Quick and nimble, able to make instant turns, they were amazingly fast.

Three hours after picking up the pilot, we tied up at our assigned spot in the port of Bangkok.

I stood on the catwalk forward of the pilothouse and almost had to pinch myself. This was a foreign port, no doubt about it, just like in the tales I had read and those Uncle Jack had told me about.

The small rusty ship moored ahead of us looked like the archetype for Conrad's tale "Typhoon". With the grand name of OCEAN ENDEAVOR and a home port of Kowloon, it was festooned with a spider web of lines and cables. Pieces of gear were stacked on the aft deck in haphazard piles while a crane on the dock plucked cargo nets and pallets stacked with bags from deep within its holds.

We had the last space on the river-side dock and behind us was a jumbled community of local barges with low roofs, held together with an impossible tangle of mooring lines running here and there. On the dock, trucks and forklifts chuffed busily about. Stevedores, dressed in every type of rag imaginable, moved in and out of the gaping doors of huge warehouses like a colony of ants.

In the center of the river ships from all nations were anchored in the stream of brown water, waiting for their turn at the docks and watercraft of every description buzzed by, from ships and tugs to tiny little cockleshell craft loaded with steaming rice pots and good things to eat. Sculled by an old mamma-san, they were the catering trucks of the river and plied their trade from one end of the docks to the other.

Debris floated downstream. Bits of palm tree, small islands of living palms torn from the bank upriver, packing materials, trash and the occasional dead dog, all moving down to the Gulf of Siam, as they had been doing for millions of years. It took all my senses to sample the heady mix of sensations. Over and over, I told myself that I was indeed in Bangkok, Thailand!

The showers on board had been running continuously for the last two hours, and now there was a crowd of GIs on the stern deck just panting to be let loose in the city. Bathed, powdered, shaved, dressed up, smelling good, and bragging about how the girls of Bangkok had better watch it, we waited for word that shore passes were granted.

"Listen up!" It was Peach. "Everyone shut up, the skipper wants to talk!" Groans of dismay rumbled over the deck.

The skipper made his way to the lazzarette hatch and stood on it. He looked a little ragged in rumpled fatigues, his cheeks unshaven, his plump, round face tired and his blond fuzz in disarray, but he was pleased with his first arrival in Bangkok. An air of accomplishment and pride emanated from him.

He made a short speech.

"Alright, you guys. This is the first real time in Bangkok for most of you. Don't get all crazy and think you have to do it all the first night. We will more than likely be coming here many times in the coming months."

A buzz of excitement and approval ran through the crowd, and I felt a tingle down my back.

"Another thing," he cut a glance at Silky, who nodded, "there's a bar just outside the gates of the port called the Mosquito Bar."

Another buzz rippled through the crowd. We'd all heard of the Skeeter Bar.

The skipper raised his hand and the buzz subsided. "I want to tell you that the place is a typical waterfront dive, so stay out of it. There are lots of good bars in the city and taxi drivers know where they are. That's all."

Subdued groans of dismay broke out here and there but no one voiced any outright dissent. The skipper and the chief went back to their quarters to gather what they needed for their stay in the air-conditioned BOQ in the city.

Rick and I crossed the barge and stepped onto the dock, headed for the port gate, moving slowly to avoid cracking a sweat in the steamy heat.

Rick had donned his standard shore outfit of wrinkled khaki pants and a wrinkled blue T-shirt. Worn, scuffed sandals clung to his feet and the blue granny glasses he wore, combined with his luxurious moustache and too-long hair made him the hippie of the crew. Being from the San Francisco area, he cultivated it.

I wore a pair of wheat colored custom-tailored pleated pants of a light cotton/poly blend and a blue cotton shirt open at the neck with short sleeves. Thin shoes over silk socks completed the effect.

"Bob, Rick, hang on a second."

We both turned to see Art approaching. Everyone had dressed up in their best tailor-mades and was looking pretty good, but no came close to matching Art in the flash department.

He sported brand-new Levi jeans, a black western shirt with yellow piping, mother-of-pearl buttons complete with silver tips on the collar and black cowboy boots that winked under a fresh shine.

"Say, where you guys headed?"

"Why," Rick said, "you wanna make a deal of some kind?"

"You are a suspicious guy," Art said easily, a grin showing his perfect teeth.

"So what do you want?" I asked.

"Well, since Rick brought it up…" He paused while Rick snorted an I-told-you-so.

"You guys want to make some money?"

"Doin' what?"

By his tone I could tell Rick was interested.

"Sell me your ration card."

Rick and I looked at each other and both of us slowly nodded. Each man was issued a card that allowed him to buy a certain amount of liquor and tobacco every month, but the allotment was huge. Six cartons of cigarettes, six bottles of booze and six cases of beer for every man. No one smoked and drank that much. Selling your excess was worth a few extra bucks every month. Art was the first guy to think of buying up everyone's excess then reselling it in the city. He'd make more money on the quantity.

"OK, how you wanna do it?"

"Let's go to the PX. Buy the stuff and I'll take care of the rest of it."

At the port gates we piled into a taxi for the short ride to the PX and inside joined the long lines for liquor and tobacco, emerging with cartons of Salems, bottles of Johnnie Walker Red and Gordon's gin.

As we were loading the stuff into a small truck that Art had arranged for, he turned to me, a look of appraisal and speculation on his face.

"Say man," he said, "I've been thinking about something."

I kept quiet. I didn't want to get too friendly with Art. I wasn't sure why, but something, some kind of foreboding, just a feeling, told me not to.

I saw his face change as he tacked onto a more direct course to what he wanted.

"How'd you like to make some more bread?" He asked suddenly.

"Pay me for the booze and smokes and we'll be square, man."

"That's chump change," he snorted. "I'm talking about some serious folding green."

I didn't refuse right away and he took that as an opportunity to go on. I glanced around to see Rick pretending to examine some phony Rolex's on a tray held by a local who swore they were the real thing, for only ten bucks, man.

"I've been thinking about what you did, remember?"

I looked at him. "What're you talkin' about?"

"When that line caught that poor fuck Toby."

I nodded slowly, wondering where this was going.

"You handled yourself pretty good," he said as his black eyes roved over me. "You didn't panic, shit on the deck or jump overboard, just did what had to be done. You probably saved his life. If we'd'a been in combat, you'd'a got a fuckin' medal."

"Well, thanks for that, but are you goin' somewhere with this," I asked, "or you just blowin' smoke up my ass for fun?"

He laughed, a short bark devoid of mirth. "You should lighten up some Merlyn," he said, "It'd be good for what ails you."

"What'd'you want, Delaplane?"

"Well, for starters, my name is not Delaplane, it's *de la Plano*."

"That right?"

He nodded, absently waved away a street vendor and lit a cigarette with a snappy move on his Zippo. "Delaplane sounds less…"

"Ethnic?"

"Exactly."

"So what it is, man? I've got plans and we're burnin' daylight."

"OK," Art said, all business now. "Now that we have hit the 'Kok, I could use some help moving this stuff. I'll make it worth your time and effort." He waved his hand when I started to protest.

"I have locals to do the grunt work. All you have to do is just be there, just stand around."

"What'd'you mean, stand around?"

"Just be there," he said, "you don't…"

It came to me then. He didn't want to be the only white guy, wherever it was he was taking this stuff. He wanted back-up.

"No, thanks," I said, "I'm good for now."

To give Art credit, he didn't try to talk me into it.   "OK," he said and reached into his pocket to pull out a wad of greenbacks. Peeling off two twenties and a ten, he handed them over. "This should cover the ration card."

Fifty bucks was actually less than I could get myself, but I'd have to schlepp it around, load and unload it. It was worth it to get rid of all at once.

"OK," I said, folding the money into my clip.

Art gave Rick his money and we caught another taxi back to the port.

"What was Art bendin' your ear about?"

Rick didn't look at me, just blew smoke out the taxi window into the heated damp of the gray day.

"Offered me a job, can you believe it?"

"Watch your ass with that guy, man," Rick said and snapped the butt out the window. "I hate the monsoon season," he said, wiping his neck with a kerchief.

I didn't think anymore about Art's offer, right then anyway, and by the time I realized I was in way over my head, it was much too late to think about getting out. Survival was my number one concern by then.

CHAPTER 8

At the Skeeter Bar, our whole crew, everyone who was off duty, anyway, sat around a big table downstairs, where Silky O'Sullivan regaled us with tales of his navy days.

Situated hard by the dock gates, the Mosquito Bar actually catered to the merchant fleets of the world and other GIs were rare. We were generally younger and our short hair and clean-cut appearance was in high contrast to the merchant seamen, who tended to wave their freak flag high and defiant. That gave us an edge with the girls, one that we exploited to the fullest.

The sidewalk cafe/curio shop that was the downstairs never closed and there was no door. The front and side of the corner building was open to the whole cosmic life force that teemed in the street. Taxis, private cars, scooters, bicycles, *tuk-tuks*, those open-air, sputtering, popping three-wheeled contrivances that were so much easier to negotiate traffic in, buses, trucks and thousands of pedestrians made their way along the broad avenue in a jangling, honking flow of life that practically never ceased. Even in the wee hours, a man could get something to eat or drink, buy a carved teak elephant or ivory chess set, or simply sit and watch it all go by.

Rick and I joined the crowd at the table and ordered heaping plates of *khao phad*, stir-fried rice with pork, chicken, beef or shrimp.

Tales of danger and conquest flew around the table, most of them outrageous lies without even a kernel of truth, but who really cared if your ride back in the world was a Firebird or a Mustang.

Art was the only one that could back up claims with pictures and he laid two of them on the table, of a British racing green Sting-Ray with Arizona plates.

"This could be anyone's car," Donnie declared, tossing them onto the table.

"Sure it could, but it is mine."

A kind of certainty rang in Art's voice, like he didn't care if anyone believed him or not, but he didn't stick around long enough to argue. Spotting someone or something in the street, he scooped up his pictures and tucked them away.

"Gentlemen," he said as he stood up, "you all have a good time, and the next round is on me." He dropped twenty bucks on the table like it was a quarter and strode away.

While everyone goggled at the crisp bill lying there, I watched Art make his way out through the wide-open side of the bar and climb into the back seat of a car with two other guys in the front. Both of them were locals, what were called cowboys, street hustlers, or numba ten *poochai! Poochai* was Thai for man, boy, male, while *pooying* was the word for female.

With a clash of gears and spurt of rubber, the car shot away from the curb.

Promptly at 2000 hours, the upstairs nightclub opened and we trooped up the stairs like a squad of soldiers storming a hill.

Taking a table as far away from the bandstand as we could get, we prepared to show everyone and anyone that we were a force to be reckoned with, so, fueled by alcohol and the powerful local weed, we tried not to look like newbies.

Girls wearing sarongs to their ankles, cotton shirts and no make-up took drink orders and then gave them to the wrong people and couldn't have cared less.

Silky had gone back to the boat to change and true to his nickname, was now turned out with style and flair. He wore a loose Hawaiian shirt of bright yellow, with shocking pink and purple flowers on it, and a pair of custom-made yellow sharkskin pants that fit his lean athletic frame just so. Expensive-looking ventilated leather shoes over silk socks adorned his feet. A gold medallion hung from a gold chain that looked like it could anchor the tug in the river and his brown wavy hair was carefully combed and held in place with a scented pomade. He was ready to boogie and looked it but unlike most of us, he seemed comfortable and relaxed.

Donnie had on a pair of nondescript jeans and a dark blue T-shirt, outside his pants so his big belly didn't show as much. At least they were clean.

Charlie and Donnie must have shopped at the same place, except Charlie's T-shirt was tucked in.

"Well, what'd'ya think?" I hollered over the throbbing juke at Rick. He sat there, sweat beading his lip and forehead, his eyes big behind his glasses.

"'Bout the same as anywhere else, I guess," he replied. "Change the language and it could be Saigon, Manila, Hong Kong, Okinawa, lots of places."

Come to think of it, he was right. But to me, it was foreign, exotic, the mystery of the Orient all rolled into one. I expected Lord Jim, dressed in an immaculate white suit, to stroll up the stairs from the street level and order a drink at the bar.

The table next to ours was occupied by a group of Swedish merchant sailors. Loud and boisterous, they spent money like water, grabbed at passing girls and shouted their guttural lingo. Many of the girls answered in what sounded like the same language, but with more of a sing-song lilt while skillfully deflecting the hands.

Charlie was quiet, not drinking and I noticed he kept glancing at the door.

"You expectin' someone, Charlie?"

He nodded. "Lin's comin' up on the bus, we're gonna meet here."

Donnie heard what he said and started going off like a schoolboy. "Charlie's got a girlfriend!" Over and over.

"Shut yer fat face!" Charlie said.

Donnie laughed, the high giggle of the bully. He repeated the mantra several more times in various tones and cadences, like he was trying to get the rest of us to sing along, but no one did.

"If you weren't such a fat pig," Charlie said to him loudly, "you could get a girlfriend, too."

Donnie guffawed. "I can get a piece of ass any time I want it, all it takes is this!" He waved a fistful of cash.

"You think yer not payin' for it, too? Hahaha!" Donnie's voice rose into a drunken screech. "The only dif'ence is I pay up front, an' you pay…"

"Brickham."

That's all Silky had to say. Donnie shut up.

Suddenly, Charlie lit up. I turned to follow his gaze and through the fog of cigarette smoke and maze of tables, saw two girls headed our way.

One of them wore a tight dress and had her hair up. She was like a walking jewelry showcase of necklaces, earrings, bracelets and rings. Attractive in a thin, angular way, with high cheekbones, thin lips and big eyes, she made a beeline to Charlie. When she ruffled his hair and kissed him on the ear, he seemed to almost melt into a puddle on the floor.

"Everyone," Charlie practically yelled, "this is Lin, and she's my main squeeze!"

Most guys didn't introduce girls to a table full of crew mates like that, but Charlie was so happy to have a girlfriend that he must have blocked out the fact that she was a working girl.

The other girl stood there, looking around the bar like this was only a brief pause in her busy day. When she finally did glance at us, at me, she caught me looking her up and down. Her expression changed then, from resigned boredom to a teasing challenge that, without a word, asked me if I liked what I saw.

I did. She had a face that was more oval than round, glowing dark skin, dark exotic eyes and a nose that was slightly broad in the bridge, but what I couldn't stop staring at were her full and luscious lips. She wore little jewelry, only a pair of gold hoop earrings, something gold on a thin chain around her neck, and a watch that seemed huge on her delicate wrist.

I hooked a chair over from the next table and with a gesture invited her to sit down. She seemed to think about it for a moment while I examined the smooth, dark expanse of her midriff between the knotted tails of her yellow silk shirt and the tops of her white bellbottom hip huggers that showed the flare of her hips.

When she decided to sit down, she settled into the chair like a ballet dancer, bending at the knees and hips. With a flip of her hand, she pulled her long shiny black hair in front of her to drape it over her shoulder.

"Hi," I said to her. She nodded very slightly, held my gaze for an instant, then looked away, her gold hoop earrings sparkling in the shattered light of the rotating mirrored ball that hung from the ceiling.

Lin whispered to Charlie. He leaned toward me.

"Bob," he said, "this is Pen. Pen, this is Bob. Him number one GI." He gave a thumbs-up endorsement, then turned back to Lin.

Pen smiled, small and quick, and held out her hand. I took it, and she shook twice, firmly, then tried to let go. I held on and felt a shiver run up my spine.

"Buy me one drink, can do?" she asked in a small but assertive voice.

"Try this," I said, and poured a stiff shot of Seagram's over some ice and splashed in some Seven-Up. She picked it up and took an experimental sip.

"Good," she said, setting it down. "Drink later. Buy me one drink, *naa?*" I realized she needed a Bangkok Tea to get points with the mama-san.

For something to do, I asked her to dance.

On the floor, she moved and swayed with a supple, feline grace while I did my standard routine of bending my knees with the beat of the base drum and after the song ended, she pointed back to the table.

"Where from, United States?" She asked when we were seated again.

I was so busy watching the way her lips formed the words that it took a second to realize she'd asked me a question.

"California," I said quickly.

Unlike many of the girls, she didn't seem too impressed by that.

"You know," I added, "Hollywood, movie stars?"

She only nodded, clearly unmoved.

"What's your whole name?" The girls like to tell us their whole name and I liked to hear it, the tones and trills like a small musical piece. Pen was no different.

"Wanpen Sirikit Prathorn," she said, with a touch of pride.

"How old are you?"

A flash of annoyance crossed her face, but only for an instant. I also liked to hear what they said, but not for the sounds. Many girls were not girls anymore, but women, but it was hard to tell. They could look sixteen and actually be closer to thirty.

"I eighteen," she said.

"Really?" I must have sounded dubious.

"*Ching-ching*, I no bullshit GI."

"What year were you born, come on, quick now?"

It was an old bartender and liquor store clerk's trick. If they answer quick...

"I don' know how you say..." She said something in rapid Thai, then brightened. Dipping her finger in my drink, she wrote something on the table. "That year, GI."

"*Mai-dai* call me GI. Call me Bob, can do?"

Like everyone, I was falling into the *patois* of bargirl Thai and English.

"OK, Bob," she said with a smile. Like all Thai people, she pronounced it with a short vowel. They always put a Thai spin on English words, placing the emphasis on the last syllable. When they said "later" it came out la-TER. "Hungry" became hung-GRY, and so on.

A waitress came by and Pen stopped her, spoke to her rapidly for a moment. The waitress was not a working girl and not available to GIs, turned to me.

"*Sawadee, khap,*" she said with the deep *wai* of a female addressing a male.

"*Sawadee,*" I replied, giving her one too, only slightly smaller.

"My name is Thoni. I attend University of Bangkok?" She nodded encouragingly, to make sure I knew she was a college student..

"Pen asked me to tell you, this," she pointed to the squiggles Pen had written on the table, "this is Thai writing, it says nineteen fifty."

"Ah, OK then. Pen is eighteen years old?"

"Yes, eighteen," Thoni said. She and Pen exchanged a few more words, then Thoni gave me another *wai* and left.

"OK," I said.

She nodded. "How old you?"

"I'm twenty, *yeesip-ha.*"

Her eyes lit and she smiled. "You speak Thai *dee mahk,*" she said and in a spontaneous gesture placed her hand on mine. It felt cool and warm at the same time and it somehow made me feel much more connected to her than if she'd grabbed my thigh under the table.

Rummaging in her purse, she pulled out a cigarette. I reached for my lighter, but she shook her head and stood up.

"*Monee,*" she said, motioning in the Thai way, her palm down, for me to follow her.

Skirting the dance floor, she made her way to the far corner of the room, pushed aside a hanging curtain and opened a door. I felt the flow of warm moist air and saw stars, then she was out the door. I followed.

We were on a landing for the back stairs, and we were not alone. Three or four other girls and the same number of guys stood around or had gone a few steps down. The fresh air smelled and tasted great after the smoky bar and now Pen put the cigarette to her lips. For a second, I wondered why she bothered coming outside to smoke, then I snapped to it.

Striking a wooden match, she lit it up and I caught a whiff of it. She smoked it like a cigarette, even though it was a Krong-Thip, a Thai menthol cigarette. The tobacco had been removed, mixed with finely chopped, potent Thai weed and carefully placed back into the paper tube of the cigarette and gently tamped down.

She pulled another hit from it then passed it to me. I preferred my weed unadulterated in joints or a bong, but, what the hell, when in Rome… I smoked it the way she did, not expecting much of a buzz.

Back at the table, she turned to her friend. I watched as they spoke in whispers for a minute, then Pen turned to me, an expectant look on her face. Somehow, I knew this was it. Yes or no. Now or never. Put up or shut up. Fish or cut bait. Jump off the board or go back down the ladder 'cause she had to move on if I wasn't up for it. With the speed of thought, these things went through my mind and I was surprised to realize I didn't want her to leave. I decided to go for an all-nighter.

"Pen, you want to go with me?" The thought that she might turn me down rippled through my confidence. If the girl didn't like you, she could and would say no. It was rare, but it did happen, but Pen looked me up and down then smiled.

"OK, Bob," she said, "I go with you."

Slowly, I let out the breath I'd been holding while Pen said a few words to her friend, then, taking my hand, she led me down the stairs.

We crossed the boulevard, dodging trucks, taxis and tuk-tuks, then headed down a little side street lined with small shops and vendor carts, stopping before a shabby-looking three-story building.

Her room on the second floor was typically small, with a big bed, small mirrored dresser and chair, and a free-standing closet. A few pictures, cut from magazines, were tacked here and there and high on one wall, in isolated splendor, a portrait of the King and Queen of Thailand gazed down on us.

A small lamp on a nightstand and a fluorescent fixture in the ceiling provided light while a fan perched in the window washed a stream of warm moist air back and forth.

Looking around, I wondered how many other men had been in this room, how many others had…. I shook those thoughts away, angry at myself for analyzing everything to death.

Cooking smells, sharp and pungent, drifted in to tantalize for a moment, then were gone. We sat on the bed. To try and avoid the awkward moment, I asked her about the watch and she took it off to show it to me. It was Swiss and very heavy. Links had been removed from the bracelet to fit her tiny wrist.

"Dutch officer give to me," she said with a trace of pride.

She flicked the small bedside lamp on, turned off the harsh overhead light and returned to sit very close beside me. The dimmer light made it somehow easier to drift into the purpose of being here, but in the middle of the horrible silence as she waited for me to get going, I told her she was very fine. With a tiny smile and a thank-you-very-much, she graciously accepted the compliment as her due. I told her she spoke good English, and she again said thanks very much. "Speak English, Danish, German, *nit-noy* Norwegian, *nit-noy* others."

I was impressed and told her so. She smiled, dismissing it, then stood up and pulled her shirt off over her head, undid the short zipper and stepped out of the white bellbottoms, which followed the shirt onto the chair. Lying on the bed, she stretched out in her bra and panties.

For some reason, I noticed that the bra and panties didn't match. Her bra strap was held with a safety pin and there was a small hole near the waist seam of her panties that allowed just a bit of flesh to protrude slightly. It somehow looked tawdry. Perversely, I thought of her bra and panties as part of her uniform, and I wondered why she didn't keep it in better shape.

I was immediately sorry for such a mean-spirited thought, and while I was sitting there pondering all this, she rose up onto one elbow and started to unbutton my shirt.

Suddenly, I was apprehensive and breathing hard. What if the Great Disappointer didn't rise to the occasion? I would look like a fool. I'd had more than a few drinks and that Krong-Thip had snuck up and hit me harder than I would have thought. I could tell things weren't happening at all. The street noises became very loud and I could hear other distractions, *tuk-tuks* rattling and wheezing by, people laughing and shouting, cafe noises and the deep, rumbling note of a ship's horn from the nearby docks.

Standing, I stripped to my boxers and stood there like a goof until Pen took my hand and pulled me down on the bed next to her. She made a motion, and in the dim light I noticed that her bra had disappeared. I caught my breath at the sight. Surprisingly full, her breasts fell away from her in roundly sensual curves that culminated in dark, succulent, upturned nipples. I stared.

With a tiny laugh, she placed my hand on one. Smooth and taut, it felt like a well-filled water balloon, only so much warmer and softer. Nothing happened for me and I was starting to sweat.

"Take off," she said, plucking my boxers.

Somehow, I got them off and stretched out beside her, my heart pounding in my chest.

When I didn't roll over on her, she must have sensed something was wrong and reaching behind her, she clicked off the light. The soft, humid darkness seemed to close in around us and the room was suddenly smaller and much more intimate. The street noises seemed to fade away.

It seemed completely logical then for me to roll over and kiss her breast. Small noises of encouragement welled up in the dark and I felt her nipple swell up and become firm in my mouth, a first for me. The spicy sandalwood scent of her skin flooded my senses and with my head spinning, she made more noises, low in her throat that seemed to vibrate though me.

"*Dee*," she said, "*Dee mahk*." Good, very good.

Her breath, sweet and spicy with a touch of alcohol, came to me. Booze on a girl's breath always did it to me, and it was like a valve suddenly opened. Things started to happen very fast.

With a low chuckle, she pulled me on top of herself and spread her legs. I could feel her thighs, unbelievably smooth, hot and cool at the same time as they slid up along my waist.   Subtly, she took charge. I was more than willing to allow her complete control. I felt her hand slither between us. She held me for a moment, then slid me up and down her soft furrow and with a gasp I was at her gate.

With her arms around me and both hands on my back, she let out a long tremulous breath, whispered, "Push now," and rose up to meet me.

I entered her in one long incredible glide. Absolutely astonished at the sensation of soft, tight, warmth that gripped me like a boneless fist, I held still.

"Do like this," she whispered and began to undulate her hips in a slow, powerful rhythm that pulled me toward the crest.

This was just the most mind-blowing thing I had ever felt. I wasn't a virgin. Hurried, awkward encounters, full of anxiety and disappointment with girls who did it simply to be able to say they had done it during the Summer of Love were nothing like this.

Skilled and knowledgeable, young and giving under the right circumstances, Pen was a revelation.

"*Dee, naa?*" She asked as her hips continued to heave and surge under me like a long ocean swell.

"*Dee mahk!*" I gasped, unable to say any more.

She giggled happily and with one hand squeezing my bicep and the other on the small of my back, she urged me to plunge into her.

When she took my earlobe between her lips and nibbled it, my dick seemed to suddenly expand and I rocketed to the crest, bubbled up and detonated while she writhed and moaned under me, matching my every thrust with one of her own all the way down the long slide back to earth.

I must have dozed for a while, how long I couldn't tell, but I started awake, lying on my back. The bedside lamp dropped a cone of soft yellow light on us as Pen lay beside me. Propped up on a pillow with an arm behind her head, she smoked a cigarette, an ashtray on her naked belly.

Seeing I was awake, she smiled, reached over and held the cigarette to my lips. It was the most intimate gesture that I'd ever had from a member of the opposite sex and it thrilled and delighted me with a sense of sharing. I took a huge drag, felt the pleasant bite of the nicotine and blew a cloud of smoke to the ceiling.

"Oh, man!" I had to exclaim.

"Good, *naa?*" she said, a playful tone in her voice while she held the cigarette for me again.

I looked sideways at her. Her smile was a light in her eyes.

"*Dee mahk.*" I said, and reached to cup one breast. With a purr of pleasure in her throat she closed her eyes and stroked the back of my hand. I was struck, again, by the simple intimacy of the gesture.

"Hungry, you want eat?" She asked. I nodded that I was. She mashed out the cigarette and got up. "You want shower?"

I thought about it. This would me the Thai shower of a big clay pot of water and a pan in the bathroom down the hall, but what the hell, when in Rome... I loved that expression. Those few words made even the most inconvenient hassle an exercise in cross-cultural exploration.

I nodded yes. She handed me a towel, took one herself, and we wrapped them around ourselves and headed down the hall.

In the bathroom, she closed the door, hung the towel on a hook, and stood there, unselfconsciously naked. I pulled my towel off and hung it too.

The bare bulb hung from the ceiling. Leaning forward, Pen gathered her long hair on top of her head, put a clip in it and straightened. Her eyes, hidden in deep pools of shadow, seemed to watch me from the darkness while the top of her head, her shoulders and swaying breasts glowed with highlights. As she poured a pan of water and soaped herself, I watched the shifting patterns of light and dark, the bright streams of dripping water, with total fascination. She didn't mind me watching, either, until I started to get turned on again.

"*Del nit*. Eat firs." With a teasing laugh she told me to wait a little. I realized I was famished.

In the street we ate crispy fried dim-sum from a smiling, mama-san's vendor cart. Pen laughed, musical notes in the warm, wet air, as I wolfed them down, joking that I was stoking up for another round.

"*Chai-see*," I said, agreeing with her.

"*Dee mahk*. I like," she replied as she delicately nibbled one of the flaky dough balls.

An old mama-san, her face seamed and wrinkled, shuffled slowly down the street toward us and approached the table. Timidly, her gaze cast down, she held out a small wooden bowl. A beggar.   I thought Pen would shoo her away, but I was wrong.

"Bob," she said, "give me five *baht, naa*? I give you back."

I gave her the five *baht*, twenty-five cents. She put it in the old woman's bowl, then shook out a few of her Salems and put those in the bowl, too. The old woman raised her head a little, made a sound and shuffled off while Pen watched her go for a second or two.

Five *baht* and three American cigarettes was an incredible act of generosity and I looked at Pen for an explanation. She said nothing about it and I didn't ask.

Finished eating, I plucked a Marlboro from my pocket and she slipped a Salem from her pack. I realized that she had waited for me to finish before she smoked. I had my Zippo out in a second and lit us both up.

Taking my wrist in her hand, she admired the lighter. "Ver' nice. Zippo *ching-ching, naa*?"

"Oh yeah," I said, "Real Zippo."

Japanese-made fakes were a dime a dozen, but a real Zippo was a status symbol among the girls of the Mosquito Bar. An idea came to me. "You like?"

"*Chai*," she said. "I like ver' much."

When she let go of my wrist, her red nails traced a line up my forearm that set my hair on end.

"Here," I said, "It's yours." I put the lighter on the table in front of her.

Her eyes lit up like sparklers and her whole face blossomed into an expression of wonder and gratitude, then a deliberately lewd smile appeared.

"*Kop chai mahk*," she said.

"You're welcome," I replied, thrilled at what I was sure was to come my way.

Back upstairs, she again took control as we lay down on the bed naked together, and this time, she left the bedside lamp on. I watched her butterscotch legs rise up and felt them close around my waist while she whispered deliciously filthy things, felt myself slide snugly into her, and told myself that Zippos were cheap in the PX. I planned to stock up.

The next day, Charlie and I had the engine room watch. The tug almost always stayed two days and two nights in Bangkok, so everyone got at least a day and a night in the city. At 1630 hours, I snagged a glass of iced tea from the galley and headed up to the boat deck for a smoke and a breeze.

The wet, heavy air carried the reek of low tide and the threat of rain. Charlie, Brett and Silky O'Sullivan were there. Silky was spinning tales of his navy days to kill an hour before he headed into the city.

"I'm tellin' you guys, it works. Here, try it."

He took a piece of paper from a pocket. Folding it into squares, he looked around for a volunteer. Brett was closest so he was drafted.

"Hold your thumb out, like this." Silky said, demonstrating.

Measuring from the cuticle to the tip of Brett's thumb with the folded paper, Silky tore the corner off, unfolded it, and there was a ragged circle. "That's the diameter of your crank, believe it or not."

"Get the hell out!" Brett exclaimed. Everyone laughed and I think Brett was secretly gratified to see that the hole in the paper was of a respectable size.

"I ain't kiddin'," O'Sullivan laughed. He liked a joke at someone else's expense, knowing that the other guys will circle around the chosen victim like wild dogs, biting with verbal bites until the victim either lashes out in defense, or tucks his tail and runs. Tom Brett, a lean rangy guy with dark, curly hair, was from Camden, New Jersey and was a master of the put-down. He could also hold his own in a scrape, too.

Donnie ambled down the deck from the pilothouse and plopped his big butt onto the lifejacket locker. He had a look in his eye and one hand behind his back. What happened next was as inevitable as the tide.

"Hey, Charlie," Donnie said slyly, with a wink at the rest of us, "there's a Swedish ship anchored out."

Charlie visibly tensed up and it was all he could do to keep from jerking around and looking for himself. His beady little eyes cast about the circle of faces for a glimmer of truth and support, but stony silence and impassive gazes were all that met his silent appeal. I could sense the circle starting to form.

Charlie couldn't help himself and spun around. Sure enough, there was a Swedish ship anchored in the stream. Under his ruddy color, Charlie turned white. We could all see the Jacobs ladder hanging from the stern of the ship, the acknowledged signal to mama-sans to run a skeeter boat load of girls to the ship. Those girls could scramble up a Jacobs ladder like monkeys climbing trees and they'd stay all night in the cabin of whoever wanted them and had the cash, then scramble down the ladder at dawn to the waiting skeeter boat.

"Hey, Charlie, I can see Lin goin' up the ladder!" Donnie said excitedly, and slyly glanced around at the group, looking for the smirks and chuckles that reinforced his mean little game. A sudden gust of wind enveloped us with the smell of rotting vegetation and stinking mud.

Charlie strained to see, but the only thing visible on the ladder at this distance were dots of color. But maybe…

Charlie looked at each of us sitting there in turn, near-panic distorting his pasty features. What if Donnie was right? Charlie turned to Silky.

"Mr. O'Sullivan," he used the correct form of address to a warrant officer, hoping for a little more sympathy, "can I go to Lin's hootch and see if she's there?" The fear that Lin might be plying her trade made his voice crack.

It was all Silky could do to keep from laughing in his face. He shook his head. "Don't you have the watch tonight, Charlie?"

"Yeah, but late watch. I can go there and be back in an hour!" His liquid brown eyes made him look like a whipped puppy.

Silky shook his head again. "Army regs, Charlie, if you're on duty that night, you can't leave the vessel."

Charlie looked around wildly, searching for ideas. No one had any. There was little sympathy for him, either. Imagine that, in love with a Bangkok whore! No one would admit to that, even if it were true. Charlie hadn't admitted anything, but his actions spoke loud and clear.

"I gotta go check on her!" Charlie suddenly bleated.

I could see the embarrassment and fear fighting for domination in his face, and it made me want to look away or reach over and slap him, the way you slap a hysterical person, I couldn't be sure which. Charlie didn't even notice. He ran into the pilothouse, and we could see him looking at the ship with the binoculars, scanning it from stem to stern.

Silky leaned over, and in a low voice, said to us, "I've heard that kind of talk before. It's what makes guys miss ships and go AWOL."

I said nothing, not wanting to commit either way.

"Charlie," Silky hollered.

Charlie ran back, hope lighting his face.

"See if you can trade duty days with someone." Charlie brightened. That is, until he looked around. Everyone who is off duty is already gone, with the exception of Donnie. Charlie looked at Donnie. Donnie shook his head, his joy at the pain he was inflicting obvious in the way his beady eyes gleamed in his fat, sweaty face. We all squirmed in embarrassment for Charlie, but no one left. The pack mentality again, like watching a car accident or a house on fire.

The cloudburst came then. It blotted out the river, the ships in the stream, the dock, everything. The world shrank down to the size of our boat deck, and the only people in it were us.

"C'mon, Donnie, you'll get a whole day off just for doin' my late watch!" Charlie nearly begged.

Silky had another idea from his navy days. "Charlie," he said, a touch of pity in his voice, "try and pay someone to take your duty for you. But remember this," his tone hardened and his face became still. "Don't leave this vessel without a replacement." He went forward into the pilot-house, leaving behind the implied threat.

Charlie, breathing hard, was starting to sweat. His eyes landed on me.

"Charlie, I'm already on watch, I couldn't make it to tomorrow morning."

He barely heard me, the search for a way off this boat taking on colossal importance.

"Donnie, I'll give ya' five bucks to take my watch tonight."

"Five bucks? What, I look cheap or somethin'?" Donnie leaned back, enjoying himself, the sweat on his face gleaming in the watery after-noon light.

"Alright, ten bucks, ten bucks for six hours of watch time. C'mon!"

I could hear the murmurs. Ten bucks! That's a lot of money just to go check on a hookers whereabouts. I leaned over to Brett and said, real quiet, "That Donnie's an asshole!"

"Think so?" Brett replied with a laconic shrug. "Maybe. I think Charlie's lost his head. Can't feature bein' whipped in this place."

Brett doesn't like Donnie anymore than I do, in fact, probably less, but he had a point. He was used to the concept of the strong preying on the weak. It was just the natural order of things and would never change.

"Alright, how much you want?" Charlie was through wasting time.

"Twenty bucks, up front, right now," Donnie said flatly. I felt a warm rush come over me and I wanted to wipe that sneer off Donnie's face with a quick left-right combination, and I told Brett so. He just grinned, but shook his head and lit a cigarette.

If Donnie's fat face made me want to smack him out of anger, then the look of agony that washed over Charlie's face made me feel sorry for him.

"Let me owe it to you, man!" Charlie bleated, his mask of despair becoming deeper as his voice rose higher.

Donnie laughed, the low, chuckling humorless giggle of the bully that has his victim right where he wants him. He shook his head slowly, savoring it. "Right now, in advance."

"Ten now, ten later. C'mon, I'm good for it!" Tears gathered in his eyes, from frustration or fear I didn't know but he didn't seem to notice.

"Take the ten now, Donnie!" I heard myself say as rain rattled on the awning and deck.

Donnie turned to glare at me and I could see the malicious cunning in his eyes. He was trying to figure what he could get from me, what stake I might have in this.

"You keep out of this, Merlyn," Donnie said. His tiny eyes glittered in his beefy face.

Silver threads of lightning sizzled through the dark clouds on the horizon. They were coming toward us, rolling and tumbling together in shades of gray over the green of the jungle and the brown of the river.

I told myself I could take that Donnie, and I must have stood up. I felt a hand on my shoulder and jerked around. Brett was shaking his head.

"Don't, man," he said in a low voice, "it ain't your fight."

I had to admit he was right. I sat down and lit a smoke and welcomed the bite. The rain let up for a moment, then returned with a renewed vigor.

"I guess you're SOL, Charlie," Donnie gloated and slapped his meaty thigh in glee. I made up my mind to give Charlie the money and was starting to stand when I heard it.

"Maybe not."

Everyone turned to see who had said that, except me. In the instant it was said, I knew for a certainty who it was. I was right.

Art strolled around the stack, fresh from a shower, wearing a different cowboy outfit and smelling of talc and aftershave. Reaching into his shirt pocket, he pulled out a fat wad of cash, peeled off a twenty, and handed it to Charlie.

Charlie stood there with his mouth open, staring. Art must have heard what was going on through the ventilator and listened, waiting to see what the outcome would be. I was getting to know him, and knew he would never make an appearance until he had figured an angle.

"Thanks, man." Charlie managed to blurt out, then thrust the bill at Donnie, who looked at it morosely. This wasn't supposed to happen. He was supposed to get to watch Charlie suffer for hours, or watch him do something really stupid over his girl. Now Art had gone and spoiled all his fun, and he wasn't happy at all. He started to back up. In the same moment, Art and I both took a step toward him.

"Take it Donnie." Art said softly, his white teeth showing in a ghost of a smile against his coppery tanned face. Donnie looked from Charlie to Art, then glanced around wildly. He was trapped, and he knew it. He reached out to snatch the bill, but Charlie let go so it fluttered to the deck.

"There's your money." he said, then spun around and was down the ladder, over the empty barge and on the dock, running through the rain, still in his fatigues, looking for a taxi.

Donnie muttered, but picked up the wet twenty and went forward, trailing curses.

Brett shook his head, went to the railing and blew smoke into the falling rain.

"That was pathetic," he said, flicked the butt into the river and ambled off.

Art looked over at me.

"How are you?" he asked with a grin.

"So," I answered, "what do you figure you can get out of Charlie, now that he owes you?"

The grin disappeared. "Charlie doesn't owe me." He emphasized the *owe*. "He kicks out the twenty on payday, we're square. No vig, no charge, just doing a favor for a friend."

He took a rag from a back pocket and flicked it over his polished boots.

"You know," he said in a conversational tone, "I was offered two hundred bucks for these boots by a local the other day. Turned it down. You know why?"

He paused and looked at me like a professor waiting for the student to come up with the right answer in response to the proper stimulus.

"Because I didn't need the two hundred. I did need these boots. They make me feel good." He flicked more imaginary dust from the polished leather and slipped the rag into a pocket.

"Money is only good for how it makes you feel," he said. "Money by itself has no value, it's only what it can do for you that counts." He grinned very wide, his perfect teeth almost glowing in the wet gloom.

What did Art need, I wondered, and what would he do to get it?

"That offer I made yesterday still stands."

"And my answer's the same."

Art smiled, like he knew something I didn't.

CHAPTER 9

At 0700 the next day we depart Bangkok in bright sunshine. A strong flood opposing the fresh breeze raised a vicious little chop and by the time we dropped the pilot at 1000 hours, the bank of clouds that had been piling up on the northeastern horizon swept over us to blot out the sun.

I was in the engine room, bending a long piece of brass brazing rod into a watchband. Without heating it, I was having trouble getting just the right shape, when, over the hurried thumping of the main engine, I became aware I wasn't alone.

Looking up, I saw Art standing there, watching me impassively.

"So how did you like Bangkok?" Even though he hardly raised his voice at all, I heard him clearly over the racket.

"I liked it fine," I said, wondering how long he'd been standing there.

"Meet anyone interesting?"

I looked up. Art gazed back at me with the bland innocence of a child asking why is the sky blue.

"You mean," I said as I examined the bent and twisted piece of rod, "did I get my hambone boiled?"

A real laugh showed his perfect teeth, startlingly white against his coppery skin.

"They talk like that in California?" He offered me a smoke, then sparked his lighter for both of us.

"No, but all my cousins in Texas do, and yeah, I met someone I plan to see again."

"Outfuckingstanding." He paused for a moment while he looked around. "Say," he said then, "let me ask you something."

Standing there in nothing but boxer shorts and flip-flops, his thickly muscled legs spread slightly, he didn't seem bothered at all by the heat and noise of the engine room. That was unusual in a deckhand and I wondered, What could Art want to know about the workings down here?

"Well, what?"

"You have any metal down here, that you can make things out of?"

"Depends," I said, "wha'd'you wanna make?"

Art's gaze, flat and frankly appraising, seemed to lay my insides open for inspection.

"A throwing knife," he said.

"No," I said, turning away, "we ain't got anything."

I tweaked the brass rod some more, trying to get it to hold the shape I wanted but it kept springing back. I ignored Art and hoped he would go away, but he didn't. Instead, he stepped up and pointed at my bent and twisted hunk of shiny metal.

"You know," he said, "if you bend that around a smaller radius it will hold its shape better."

I looked at him for a long few seconds. There was not a trace of smarminess, of I know more than you, of anything other than the facts as he had stated them.

"How do you know that?" I emphasized the "you".

He shrugged. "My people have been making tools and weapons for thousands of years. I know a little about it."

"Oh, yeah?" I said with a smirk. "And who's your people?"

"Chiricahua Apaches." His voice was flat and without brag. "See this?" He held out his wrist. "I made that band in…high school."

I looked. The watch itself was only a Timex, but the band that held it was a work of art. Finely wrought silver with turquoise inlays, it was complex and beautifully shaped.

I looked back at him. Why hadn't I seen this before? I asked myself. The wide face, coarse hair black as a crow's wing, the copper skin. I remembered the 'Vette with Arizona plates.

"Geronimo's people," I said, a touch of awe creeping into my voice in spite of myself.

Art looked at me and nodded, a certain something in his black eyes.

"My great grandfather rode with the U.S. Army into Mexico," I said, "lookin' for Geronimo. My grandaddy said the Apaches were without doubt some of the finest warriors that ever threw a leg over a horse. They could live on sand and cactus for weeks and travel at a pace that would kill a white man."

"Where did your grandfather live?"

"Farwell, Texas," I replied, "near the New Mexico border, it's…"

Art nodded slowly. "You know your southwestern lore, then."

"I've got cousins in Ft. Worth, Austin, and Lubbock."

"So," Art said, with a small laugh, "you have any metal down here?"

"Hell, yes!" I said. "Here, check this out."

I pulled a sheet of silver-gray metal, about twelve inches square, from a rack and handed it to him. He looked it over in a cursory manner.

"This make a good knife?"

"Pretty good," I answered, "it's three-oh-four stainless, very tough, but not impossible to work. Takes a lot of time, though, man. Why don't you just go to the vill' and buy one? There's plenty to choose from, ya' know."

The scorn on his face was plain, as if the subject was beneath contempt.

"That's all junk and crap from Hong Kong, made for Bangkok cowboys to flash around. If push comes to shove, I want something to stand up."

He nodded his head, slowly, while he turned the sheet in his hands, figuring form and line.

"Will a hacksaw cut it?"

"Yeah," I said, "but you'll have to go slow. If you try to rush it, you'll break the blade."

"Thanks." He nodded while he looked at me. I felt something else coming, but he shook his head, just a twitch, then stuck his hand out. We shook.

I went around the main engine to check the oil in the generator but he stood there, oblivious to the heat and noise, turning the sheet of steel in his hands.

I could see him standing on a ridge in the desert, the sun setting behind him, long hair blowing in the wind, examining a piece of deer antler, turning it, feeling the tool or weapon that is in the antler waiting for the right hands to bring it out. I wondered too what kind of push or shove he had in mind, then realized I didn't want to know. As it would turn out, that would be both a mistake and a blessing, one that would ultimately save my life.

CHAPTER 10

True to her word, Lin had found a place for me and I went with Charlie to have a look at it.

"Yer gonna love it, man," Charlie enthused as we rode a *baht* bus to *Kilo Song*, the second crossroads east from the town of Sattahip.

"What's it like?"

"Well, don't expect an apartment like back in the world, but it's, well, you'll see."

Hopping down from the bus, Charlie practically skipped along a graveled path that wound beneath a stand of trees. Here and there trash lay piled where it had been tossed from other bungalow windows, dogs slept in the shade, their legs in the air and tongues in the dirt. Wide-eyed toddlers, what the Thais called *dek-dek*, scampered along behind us without a scrap of clothes on. On a wooden deck that was like a courtyard for a group of three modest bungalows, a man took a shower without removing his sarong, the unisex tube of cotton cloth that could be worn a dozen different ways. The sight of two tall *felongs* strolling up the path didn't seem to faze him a bit.

"Here it is," Charlie said.

He was right, it was no apartment back in the world but it was a little more substantial than many of the ones I'd seen. Built on a slab, it consisted of a Thai bathroom that was a hole in the ground surrounded by a molded concrete footpad and a large earthen water jar with a few hooks and small shelves for sundries.

Separated from it by a thin wooden wall of slats was a very rudimentary kitchen that was really only a *hibachi* and a sink.

"Where's the water faucets, man?"

"What water faucets?"

"Exactly!" I said. "There's no running water, how do…"

"I told you, man. Dig it, this's Thailand, not the world. You buy water from a tank truck comes around once a week, fills up your jar, there." He pointed.

"What about dishes, cookin'…"

He laughed. "Man," he said, "you ain't gonna be doin' any cookin'. You just buy whatever you wanna eat. A big plate of pork-fried rice is ten cents, man. Papaya and egg breakfast is another ten cents. One o' these kids'll run get it for you for a nickel. Besides," he went on in a knowing tone, "once you get yourself a *tilok*, she takes care of all that."

"I don't know, man, it…"

"Listen," Charlie's face was starting to turn red with exasperation, "the old man said to get away from the tug. You gotta go somewhere. Get a place, and get yourself a *tilok*, a live-in babe. She'll take care of everything, man, don't worry."

"You seem to like it."

"Man, I love it! Lin feeds me, gives me a massage, a shower, then fucks me 'til I can't stand up anymore. You don't have to go blowin' bread in bars, pickin' up a different chick. Get one to stay with you, she'll bend over backwards to keep ya' happy. This's a fuckin' paradise, man, get with it! Didn't you like that chick from the Skeeter, Pan, or Ping or…"

"Pen," I said, "her name is Pen, and yeah, I liked her all right."

"So there you go!"

Charlie's enthusiasm was infectious, but I wasn't ready to commit yet. "What's it gonna cost me?"

"Peanuts, man! Twenty bucks for the first month. That'll cover rent and a few incidentals, like sheets, some towels, that kind of thing. Bring some canned stuff from the boat if you want, hell, we're payin' for it, right?"

"Right." Tug crews received COLA pay, Cost Of Living Allowance, and bought our food from the commissary in Bangkok. We had Skippy peanut butter, Welch's grape jelly and Star-Kist tuna, not army food.

"All right," Charlie said. "Check out the upstairs, man."

An outside staircase led upward to a screen door that sported a hefty hasp, beyond which was a kind of screened porch. A simple wooden table, a kind of sideboard thing, two chairs, a cooler and a hammock strung from two beams made up the furniture.

"This's the living room. You can get a better couch, buy it from a GI rotating home, and a fan, too, gotta have a fan. One thing you don't need, man, and that's a heater!" Charlie laughed at his own joke but he was right.

"So you live out here on the porch, then, right in front of everyone?"

"Well, yeah, but look around. You don't have any neighbors except those," he pointed, "and they're on the other side of that big ass tree."

That was true. I couldn't see anyone's porch from this one and the tree would provide valuable shade, making the whole hootch much cooler.

"Here's the important room, man, the bedroom." There was no mistaking the lewd expression on Charlie's round, open mug as he opened a door at the far end of the porch.

The bedroom was the only room with real walls, and they were only thin slats, but the door actually closed and locked.

"Check the bed."

The bed, a typical Thai affair, was big, low and firm, solidly built of some dark wood, maybe teak. It had the Thai pillows, long and round, and a thin coverlet over two sheets.

Against the wall a free standing closet stood, doors open, ready to receive all my worldly goods.

"You'll have a lot o' fun here, man. Make sure the hammock is tied up good, you don't want it to break, if you know what I mean." Wink-wink.

Twenty bucks seemed like a small price to pay for so much happiness, but joy is like sorrow, both difficult to measure.

A week later, the tug made another run to Bangkok. We'd left Sattahip at 0600 and rode the flood tide all the way up the gulf and up the river, too. Making good time, it was only 1330 hours when we tied up to our place and as usual, the off duty crew hit the dock running, first stop, Mosquito Bar, now known simply as the Skeeter.

"So what're you gonna do?" Rick wanted to know as we sat downstairs scarfing jumbo fried prawns and sipping those little Pepsis.

"Wha'd'ya' mean?"

"Man, it's early. The girls don't come around until at least five, usually later, till the bar opens. You might miss her, she might not show up. A lot of these girls have steady customers on the ships, you know. They watch the shipping news and know when they're comin' in. Pen might be booked up."

A long jagged icicle formed in my gut. I hadn't thought of that.

"Hell with that," I said as an idea began to form, "her place is across the boulevard and down that little street, somewhere." I wasn't so sure I could find it but was anxious to try.

"Don't do that, man." Rick's eyes grew very large and his voice rang with alarm.

"Why not?"

He shook his head and his long hair trembled. "'Cause, man," he said. "The girls ain't ready for customers now. They ain't got their make up on, they wearin' old clothes and doing laundry and shit, man. You gotta wait 'til tonight, man."

"Tonight?" What the hell would I do until 2000 hours? "Too bad she hasn't got a phone," I muttered.

A shoeshine boy came by but when he saw our sandals and sneakers, he set his box down and brought out his pad of paper and two pencils.

"*Mai ow,*" I said. I didn't want to play tic-tac-toe for one *baht*, a nickel, a game. I had other things on my mind.

Rick was game though and laid four coins on the table. Quickly, the boy, about twelve or thirteen, with big dark eyes and long lashes, laid out the squares and insisted on first move.

Within seconds, Rick was down four *baht*.

"You know what he's doin', don'cha?"

"What?" Rick asked, losing another game.

"By goin' first, he can nail down three corners."

Rick glanced at me. "I know, man," he said quietly, "but I don't mind losin' a quarter or so to these guys. They're workin' for it, not beggin' it. I consider it a worthy cause."

While Rick lost another dime, two *baht*, I watched and suddenly had another idea.

I laid ten *baht* note on the table. The shoeshine boy thought he had another mark, but I held up one hand.

With a combination of English and fractured Thai, I asked him if he knew of the *pooying* named Pen who worked out of this bar. He said he did, and knew where she lived, too.

"Pretty damn good," Rick said, nodding his approval as he sparked up a Pall-Mall.

"You tell her," I said to the shoeshine boy, "a *felong*, a GI, American, wants to see her and ask her if she'll come here as quick as she can."

Tearing the bill in half, I slid one piece toward him. "Half now," I said, "the rest when she gets here, OK?"

He raked the torn half off the table and leaving his shoeshine box disappeared into the crowded street.

"Pretty slick, man." Rick tipped ashes into an ashtray and chuckled.

"Hope it works."

Ten minutes later the kid was back and said Pen would be here. He pointed at my watch and showed the hands going around one time. One hour.

Rick stood up. "Looks like your plans are made, man. See ya' later." He ambled to the street and disappeared into the teeming traffic there.

I sat and smoked and sipped Pepsis.

I saw her first and watched her come in. Everything else seemed to drop out of sight, to blend into a static mass of gray cloud and gray shapes along the edges of my vision. In the center, she became a dazzling, moving spot of color and brightness.

I watched her look around. She probably wondered who sent that message. All *felongs* probably looked alike to the shoeshine boy and Pen and I had only been together for one night over a week ago.

I waved. When she saw me and smiled, I felt a rush of air out of my lungs and realized I must have been holding my breath.

She approached slowly and stopped at the end of the table. Wearing a sarong tied around her middle so that it fell to her ankles and a short sleeved cotton shirt with flips on her feet, she was dressed for daytime with her hair pinned up and little jewelry, just small earrings and that amulet, peeking from her shirt.

"Hi," I said as calmly as I could.

"Hello, Bob."

She remembered my name! Her low husky voice sent a thrilling ripple down my spine. I puffed up with pride a bit and the grin must have spread across my face.

"How are you?" I asked her.

"Fine."

"Would you like to sit down?"

Slowly, watching me, she moved around the table. She lowered herself to the chair, her back straight and her eyes steady on me. With the shaded daylight on her face I could see she wore no make-up, just a subtle eye treatment. Large and dark, they looked me over candidly. I saw too that even without lipstick, her beautiful, full lips were smooth and luscious looking. She looked every bit as good in the daytime as she did at night.

"Are you hungry, you want to eat?"

Slowly, languidly she shook her head no, then crossed her smoothly contoured forearms on the table, leaned forward and looked at me.

"*Ow ali?*"

I was taken aback. What do I want? What kind of lame question is that, I wondered. What the hell does she think I want?

"I want you," I said matter of factly, looking her straight in the eye.

Suspicion made her eyes narrow. "You come Mosquito Bar daytime, find me?"

"Yes."

She laughed, a warm three-note musical scale. Her teeth glowed white in her dark face. "*Sattahip mai mee pooying?*"

I laughed too, a little too loud. "Lots of girls in Sattahip," I said. "Not same you."

She laughed again and leaned a little closer. "You nice guy. Numba one GI."

I nodded my agreement to that. "*Bai, naa?*" I said. Can we go?

"*Bai nai?*" Go where?

"Your bungalow. Can do?" I said it bun-GA-low.

It must have just dawned on her that I wanted her now, because as I watched her I saw her face, that inscrutable, unreadable Asian face, go through surprise, pleasure, doubt, appraisal, and acceptance. Maybe I convinced myself it was so, but whatever it was, I was happy.

She nodded once and stood up. "Come on."

My heart skipped a beat, then made up for it with hammer blows to my ribs.

We crossed the street, dodging the traffic and pedestrians. I walked beside her, not touching her.

We entered the narrow street that I remembered from our first time, then her building. Once we were off the street, she laced her fingers in mine, and we went up the stairs hand-in-hand.

In her room, she moved around and picked up a few things while I stood there, feeling awkward and out of place.

Opening the ditty bag I carried, I took out the two cartons of Salems I'd brought for her and laid them on the table. I'd decided on the smokes instead of the Zippos. After all, how many lighters can a person use? I had been planning to spring them on her when I left, but had suddenly changed my mind. Giving her the tip first might work out best for me, too.

Glancing at the cartons, then at me, she paused, the question on her face. "For me?"

"*Ching-ching.*" I replied.

"Oh, Bob," she said, her eyes alight, "you numba one!" Moving up close, she hugged me to her. When I tried to kiss her, she allowed a very light kiss on the corner of her lips, then she stepped back.

Tilting her head back, her dark feline eyes slowly and deliberately appraised me. In the natural light, I could see the firm line of her jaw blend into the soft curve of her neck and the small hollow at the base of her throat. I wanted badly to kiss her there.

Well, now's the time to fish or cut bait, I thought. I picked up her hand and slowly ran my palm up the inside of her forearm, marveling at the velvety softness of her skin. She let loose another small laugh, amused at my wonder.

"You like, huh?"

"I like a lot."

Slowly extending her smooth, round arm out straight, I stroked it from wrist to shoulder with my fingertips.

Moving in on her I watched her cherry lips and told myself that, one day, she would offer them to me. How could anyone with lips like that not want to kiss? It was like having a precious gift and keeping it hidden away.

I tried two or three times, but those lips eluded me. She didn't get mad, but she turned her head and urged me to go elsewhere.

The shirt disappeared. Her braless breasts shook deliciously when she tossed the shirt over the window shutter and I paused for a moment to savor their shapely perfection, the way they both fell from her in sensual curves and the way her dark nipples pointed slightly up and away from each other.

She pulled the sarong off over her head and flipped it onto the other shutter, cutting the light a little more. Reclining onto the bed, she held her arms out to me. My clothes flew off and I stretched out beside her.

In the semi-dark, she rolled away slightly and I heard the faint clink of tiny bottles, then she rolled back and flung a leg over me.

Sliding my palm over her hip and thigh, I was again amazed at how silky smooth she was. I'd never experienced skin like this and I drifted the back of my hand over her.

"You like?" Her voice lilted.

"You're so incredible," I replied. "I love it!"

"You funny guy, Bob," she laughed. "Come on."

Pulling me on top of her, she lifted her legs around my waist, put me in position and whispered "Do now."

Her hips rolled up and I sank into her.

I was able to slow down this time and make it last a little longer, until I caught a whiff of her sweet, spicy breath and suddenly, trying to hold back was like trying to hold back a tidal wave. The forces gathered and all I could do was ride it and whip it to her in a lust-driven frenzy that set the wooden bed frame creaking while she gripped my biceps with both hands.

"Oh!" I heard her gasp and it set me off. I felt like I was being turned inside out.

Just like the first time, she held a cigarette for both of us and kept the ashtray on her smooth naked belly.

I watched the play of light in the fine sheen of moisture on her skin as she moved and with a pleasant surprise, I realized I was enjoying this part of it almost as much as the sex. This closeness and sharing was totally new and stirring in a strange and bewildering way and I found myself gazing at the ceiling, reflecting on it.

She reached across me to set the ashtray on the nightstand and tendrils of her hair brushed across my arm, soft as a butterfly wing.

I turned to her. Her dark, bottomless eyes searched my face. Impulsively, I reached over and tickled her. She shrieked with laughter and attacked my ribs with a surprising strength. We wrestled, tangling in the sheets, until I pinned her shoulders and stuck my tongue in her belly button.

Her laugh, high, clear and genuine, ricocheted around inside the room and in my head. I decided then and there to take her back to Sattahip with me.

Later, much later, we went out to get something to eat. It was so hot the air seemed to boil spontaneously and the low clouds laid on me like a weight, a presence that had to be dealt with.

Pen pinned her long hair up to keep it off her neck and we went to the same vendor cart as before. The smells of the city, rotting vegetation, grilling meat and exhaust fumes, were everywhere, made even more pungent by the moisture in the air and the low atmospheric pressure. Smoke from the vendor carts barely rose, but drifted sideways in a swirling bluish mass of greasy piquant aroma.

There were no snickers or catcalls that I could hear directed at us. People had to eat, and the Thai people are among the most tolerant in the world. We sat at a table and ate *khow-phad*. Mama-san gave me some extra shrimp, and I thanked her with a deep *wai*, which she returned.

People came by, girls with customers, and Pen chattered with the girl a bit while the customer and I exchanged nods. Pen smiled and waved, called greetings to people. I felt great, happy to be here, to be spending time with her, knowing we would go back upstairs soon. That is, until I saw her face change from happy and relaxed to a mask of fear and hate in the blink of an eye.

CHAPTER 11

Her dark exotic face seemed cast in wax. Her skin became tight and shiny and her full, luscious cherry lips, the ones I wanted to taste so badly, became a harsh, grim line without color. Her eyes, feral and intense, pulled the light in and let none out.

I looked to where her gaze was focused, and saw a guy ambling down the street, one hand in his pocket, the other jingling keys.

Short, stocky, with olive skin and long, light brown hair, he was dressed in cream colored pegged pants and a green knit shirt. Swaggering down the street like a bantam cock in his own barnyard, he was sure in the knowledge that he was king of all he surveyed, and any chicken he wanted was his for the taking.

I looked back at Pen. She was still watching him intently, as if he were a large poisonous spider to be avoided. I was puzzled. What kind of problem could she have with a *felong*?

By his appearance, I took him to be a merchant seaman, not GI. He was no more than ten feet away from me when he looked right into my eyes, held for a second, and swiveled away. I didn't exist for him. When he saw Pen, his face changed.

A kind of glee came into his features, like this was just the person he was looking for. He sauntered right up to our tiny table and stood there, grinning. My first thought was that he was an old customer of hers, and that he wanted her back right now.

Dread and disappointment crashed over me like a wave. I waited. He said something to Pen. She answered in the negative, her voice hard as flint. For some reason, I was sure he had said Dump this guy and meet me later.

They had some words back and forth. This guy, I thought to myself, must have lived in-country a long time, he's really rattling off the lingo, and not your typical bar-girl talk, either.

It was common knowledge that many Scandinavian merchant seamen retired in Bangkok for the pretty girls, cheap living and relaxed lifestyle. I figured him for one of those.

I didn't catch what was said, but it wasn't hi-hello-how-are-ya-I'm-doin'-fine. He wanted something, and it was plain that either she didn't have it or didn't want to give it to him. He kept going on and on, it seemed to me, even after Pen had indicated me sitting there and asked him to bug off.

I'm as polite and reasonable as the next guy, but there are limits.

"Hey, you," I said, loud enough to cut him off. "What's your problem? She's with me now." I nodded up the street. "Hit the bricks!"

"Bob, plees, I can do, *naa?*" Pen's voice seemed to tremble a fraction and her eyes became large and luminous as she looked at me. "I can do," she said again.

When she turned back to face him, her eyes went to narrow slits again.

He turned his head to look at me. For the first time, I noticed that his eyes were as green as shallow sea water. He made a noise, like a small laugh, then said,   "Keep out of it, GI."

His English was very good, hardly any accent at all.

He started yakking at her more, his voice harder, his body language more threatening, punctuating his words with a pointing finger at her, considered very bad manners among Thai people. Her eyes glittered but her tone remained neutral, neither defiant nor subservient.

He didn't look that tough. I'd faced guys that looked tougher and meaner than this one. I wished I had hard shoes on because I had no intention of allowing this strutting low-life to screw up my plans. I had three days off and I was going to take full advantage of them all.

I stood up suddenly. The chair scraped back, the noise loud in the street. I was aware we were drawing attention. Pen turned to me, her face drawn and her eyes dark shimmering pools, her mouth a startled O, searching for a clue as to what I was about to do. I had height, weight and reach advantage on this guy.

"Hey!" I barked at him. "You're botherin' me now. Take a hike. *Bai lao. Loo, mai*?" With just four words, I told him to get lost, and fast, then sarcastically asked him if he understood.

I felt the adrenaline rush of the challenge made, the odd time-warping of slow motion, the hot flush of oxygen-rich blood into muscles. My peripheral vision fell away, replaced by the diamond hard intensity of total concentration on his next move. I waited.

His gaze slowly shifted over to me, like a heat-dazed lizard as he looked me up and down across the table.

He had the brown hair and green eyes of a *felong*, a foreigner, but the shape of his face and the lay of his features said Thai blood pulsed in his veins.

He said something to Pen, contempt curling around the snarl in his voice. He turned and walked away, slowly, to show me he wasn't worried about anything I might be able to do.

I turned to Pen. "Who was that guy?"

She was watching his' back, her face twisted in anger, muttering things, vile things I was sure, in a low, intense voice. Spots of color dotted her cheeks and her breasts rose and fell with her breathing.

"Was that your pimp?"

She looked at me, incomprehension plain in her face.   "Peemp?"

"Yeah, you know, like a mama-san?"

Her face changed, and she looked at me like I was really stupid. "I no have, what you say, peemp! I'm biz'niz girl, mysel,' no peemp!"

She snorted, light and delicate, to show me what she thought of that idea.

"Oh."

How was I to know that? It's not like I'd been here for a real long time and knew all the ways and means of the place. I later learned that girls who worked out of bars and clubs split the take on the hustled green drinks and simply paid the mama-sans a flat fee for use of the bar. Street pimps didn't really exist.

Dragging in deep breaths of the moist air, I tried to calm down. "Well who was that guy?"

"He, ahh, I don' know you say, he give *baht* to biz'ness girl, get more *baht* back, *loo mai*?" She pantomimed giving a small amount, and receiving a large amount back.

I thought for a second, then it hit me.

"A loan shark?" Oh, shit!

I was thinking about that when I turned to Pen, and the look on her face, as she watched me, made me stop. It was as if she were trying to make up her mind about something, but it was gone in a flash. She smiled, and with a little coquettish tilt of her head, said, *"Bai, naa?"*

I nodded, glad to be away from there.

Later that evening, as we lay naked on the bed, our legs tangled, smoking the cigarette, I asked her if she would like to go to Sattahip and get a place with me.

She looked at me, her face suddenly blank and unreadable. "No can do, Bob," she said.

"Why not?" I asked her, stunned to hear the whine in my voice.

Her eyes seemed to bore into me.

"You want me all time?" she asked, as if she had heard it all before and still didn't believe it.

"Yes, all time."

"You say you want now, but later, you no want no more, I know…" she cut a glance at me and I watched the black silk curtain of her hair ripple with light as she nodded her head in affirmation of her own statement.

She lit another Salem, blew smoke to the ceiling and shot another glance at me. She held my gaze. It dawned on me that she was throwing out objections to test my resolve, to see if I were serious. I kept telling her I was serious, that I wanted her, not only for her physical charms, but to have someone to hang out with, to spend time with, to laugh and talk with.

"I like you, Bob, I wan' go with you, but…" Her hands fluttered in her lap as she took a short, angry puff on the cigarette.

What the hell now? I wondered, annoyed. "What's the problem?" I asked her.

She looked up at me, gave me a melting smile, and then looked away. "*Mai pen lai*. Not you problem. My problem."

"What the hell you mean, no problem, it doesn't matter? C'mon, out with it!" An idea came to me. "It's that guy, isn't it, the green-eyed cowboy, right?"

She sighed, fidgeted, looked me in the face again, then away, like she was trying to make up her mind about something. Stubbing out the cigarette, she said, "Yes. I owe him much money."

"Well, how much?" How much could she owe this guy, anyway? How much would it take for him to threaten her. Not very much, I concluded.

She named a figure, in *baht* and I did a quick mental calculation. Two hundred bucks? Nearly two months of disposable income for me. A chunk of change, all right.

Ignoring accepted protocol, I looked her in the eye. "What did you need two hundred bucks for?"

She raised her gaze to me, and I could almost see the thought train in her head. Should I tell this *felong* the truth, or make up something? At least, I told myself I could see it so when she said her mother was sick and she'd borrowed money for the doctor, I chose to believe it.

Her head on my shoulder, she raked her nails through my chest hair. "I like," she said, gently tugging a handful.

I palmed one of her dark nipples to feel it bud up. "I like this, too," I said.

We laughed together.

"You know, I might have a way to work something out. That green-eyed cowboy, he likes money, yes?"

"*Chai*," she replied, "Him like *baht mach-mach*."

"Good deal," I said slowly. Anyone who loves money can usually be counted on to make a deal. It was people who did things out of passion that you had to watch out for.

Either she didn't know him that well, or he had other demons after him, but that green-eyed cowboy needed watching in the worst way.

CHAPTER 12

The tiny skeeter boat skipped across the black water of the Chao Praya River like a flat stone. Small bamboo and timber landings and other vessels, barely perceived in the sodden, rushing darkness, whizzed by. The engine buzzed and howled.

Glancing sideways, I barely make out the dark, slouching form of Art as he sat beside me. I envied his apparent calm and held on with all my might as the boat went into a sliding, skittering turn. In the narrow confines of the klong, the driver barely slowed and when the moon broke through the low clouds for a moment he gave it even more gas.

For this midnight mission Art and I had happened to wear the same thing, olive T-shirt, jungle fatigue pants and jungle boots.

After five minutes of jerking turns that tore long pale furrows in the water, we slowed some and came to an intersection of another klong. Another skeeter boat, piled high with boxes, emerged from the damp gloom.

A signal was exchanged, low whistles in the dark, then we were moving, heading further into the back country, away from the river, but in the cloying darkness it was impossible to tell. I had no compass, no flashlight, no matches, only my Zippo lighter.

The klong narrowed until the jungle merged overhead and became a tunnel. A wet something brushed my face and I jumped. Suddenly, I couldn't stand it any longer.

"Where the fuck we goin'?"

"Be there soon, man, be cool, OK?"

Art's voice, smoothly confident, seemed to calm me down some. Thoroughly lost, I longed for a smoke, but if Art didn't light up, neither was I.

Was this worth two hundred bucks? I was beginning to wonder and told myself over and over that it was. Art had assured me that we would do nothing illegal and I clung to that glimmer of delusion like a pilgrim clings to his beliefs.

Left turns, right turns, hairpin turns, so many that I lost track. The engine slowed. Art and the driver conferred in low tones as we drifted, then I was surprised to realize that I could see something ahead, a faint shape, lighter than the water and the jungle. By using the night-vision technique of not looking right at it but just to one side, I could tell it was some kind of wharf or small pier with a ramshackle building on it.

Art stood up and had a look around. Satisfied, he grunted and we made a landing on a tiny floating dock. The driver tied us off while Art continued to stand in the boat and look around.

A voice from above made me jump. I didn't understand the words, but there was no mistaking the tone. Low and sneering, it also carried a harsh reprimand.

Suddenly Art spoke up. He had apparently understood every word because he answered with a long stream of Thai, his tone imperious and challenging.

I heard the click-scratch of a lighter. The weak yellow flame of a tiki torch atop a pole showed a couple of *poochai* on the wharf, neither of them looking too friendly.

"Come on, and remember what I told you." Art murmured as he stepped onto the float and went up a rickety bamboo ramp to the wharf. I followed.

I found myself face to face with one of the *poochai*. Slowly, he eyed me up and down, and even in the weak light I could see his curled lip.

His jaw stuck out and he said something too fast for me to catch. His breath smelled of the cheap local whiskey, but his eyes were still focused. He wasn't totally shitfaced, not yet at least.

I expected him to move back and give me room. When he didn't, I knew he was fishing for some kind of confrontation, probably to make sure I knew who was in charge.

"You got a problem?" I asked him in bargirl Thai, using a neutral tone. Dressed in the flashy cowboy thug style of narrow pants, slim shoes and silk shirt open to the naval, he appeared about my age but it was hard to tell. Several ounces of gold gleamed on his smooth chest. Thai people almost never put their savings into banks, preferring to buy gold jewelry as a hedge against inflation.

Slowly, arrogantly, he continued to look me up and down, muttering things and sneering as hard as he could.

"Merlyn, don't take any crap from that cowboy punk," Art said. "He gets in your face, cold-cock him. He's an asshole anyway."

"These two the only ones here?" I kept my gaze on the cowboy's face.

"Ha!" Art barked that short little laugh of his. "Don't sweat it. Fire him up if he gives you any shit."

I couldn't let the cowboy think that he was going to put anything over on me, and keeping my hands loosely at my sides, I said, "Excuse me, boy."

He did the fake turnaway and I knew this was it. Stepping back and to the side, I let his punch go by and when he was off balance I put a fist in his gut. That would usually end it, but he kept his feet and staggered backwards, sucking air hard through his open mouth, then he telegraphed the kick.

These local cowboys all considered themselves to be badass kick boxers, and maybe they were, to some extent. This guy went five-eight and a hundred and twenty pounds and was clearly fighting out of his class.

Uncle Jack always said to have a plan and carry it out. Jack had been a reluctant barroom brawler from a long time ago while in the

Merchant Marine and the navy. On my first day of junior high school, when I came home with a bloody nose and bruised face, he had taken me into the backyard and showed me a few things. Some basic boxing, some wrestling moves if it went to ground, plus a few assorted dirty tricks for emergency use. He made me practice and lightly rang my bell sparring with him until he was satisfied that I had it down.

Now I just let the kick go by, then stepped up and popped this cowboy in the nose with two stiff jabs. Blood spurted out of his face, dull red in the yellow light, and the look of surprise and pain that flashed through his whisky-clouded eyes was gratifying as hell.

"C'mon, man," I said to him in English, "you're overmatched, just let it go."

Pride, stubbornness, and whiskey, the triumvirate of an ass-kicking. There was no way he was going to think about it and then decide to just give up. I'd already given him all the slack he had coming, and if he came on now, I was going to end it quickly.

On he came. I feinted right, and he fell for it. An open-palm slap to the side of his head stunned him silly and a left to the jaw spun him halfway around. With my right foot on his butt, I shoved him forward. Arms pin wheeling, legs running, he went off the wharf and with a splash, the black water closed over him.

I looked at Art. With a kind of Well, that's that gesture, he turned away, toward the building. "OK," he said, "let's get to work."

A door to the shack opened and four locals emerged. Without a word or a glance at me, they formed a line and started to unload the boat. Amid a lot of thrashing and blowing, the guy in the water surfaced, then stood up. The water was up to his chest, and when he made the floating bamboo dock, he pulled himself up and laid there.

Coming to stand next to me, Art offered a smoke, which I gratefully accepted. Two huge drags later, my pulse had slowed enough so I could speak.

"What now?"

"Like I said, just stand here and you'll earn your money." With a look at me, Art clapped me on the shoulder. "Wait right here," he said and went into the little building.

From inside, I heard a burst of words, then Art's booming laugh. He came out, nodded at me. "OK," he said, "Let's hat up."

Clapping his hands, he said something in Thai that I didn't catch. The boat engine started. I looked again. The driver was already there and I couldn't be sure if he had ever got out.

Art hustled down the ramp and I felt the whole rickety structure shake. "Come on," he snapped, "let's shake it!"

Jeez, I thought, the job's done, what's the hurry? But I put a spring in my step and scrambled down after him and practically jumped in the boat, too. It's a good thing I did. The boat was already moving when I hit it and I barely had time to get a grip before the driver nailed the throttle. We took off out of there like a scalded cat and when I looked back, the torch was out and the darkness was total and perfectly complete.

Christ Almighty! If I thought we had boogied coming up the klong, that was nothing compared with how we went down it. We were low-level flying, barely touching the water and the banks, black and indistinct on both sides, streamed by with a rushing closeness.

"What the fuck?" I shouted at Art.

He turned to me. Even in the pitch darkness, I could see his teeth bared in a grin.

"*Mai pen lai*," he said calmly.

Gritting my teeth, I put my head down and hung on against the sudden, violent lurching of the speeding craft. What are we runnin' from?

Skipping and sliding, the skeeter boat careened down the klong as if the devil himself was on our tail.

"What the fuck we goin' so fast for?" I had to shout to be heard.

Art only smiled, his teeth white in the gloom, then the driver threw that boat into a slithering S-turn that had my fingers aching as I held on.

Suddenly, he cut the throttle and whipped into the bank. Art appeared to be looking for something.

"What are you doing?"

"Hang on," he replied. "Look for a white rag right around here."

I heard it then. In the near distance, the banshee whine of another skeeter boat coming down the klong behind us, moving fast.

Time to find that rag.

"Is that it?" I pointed at a white blob of something that appeared to hang in space.

"Yeah!"

Grabbing the rag, Art yelled something and the driver ran the boat across the klong and nosed softly into the opposite bank.

From up the klong, the whine was getting closer, turning into a growl that sent shivers along my spine.

Art clambered over the small deck to the bow and his arms and hands moved around.

"OK," he said, "watch this."

He shoved us away from the bank and we shot into a turn, down the klong to just before another bend, where we turned to look back the way we'd came.

The growling whine grew louder, rose and fell, held steady, changed pitch up and down, until, pushing a sonic wall ahead of it, the pursuing boat skipped around the bend. The three-quarters moon broke the cloud, just enough to see the shape of the boat.

I heard a twang, like a big guitar string being plucked, a splash, the skeeter boat yawed wildly off course and jammed itself into the bank with enough force to shove its bow into the dense jungle. The engine screamed, then abruptly sputtered to a stop. I heard voices calling.

The hair along my arms stood up. "Was that what I thought it was?"

"Could be," Art said, "then again, maybe not."

"You strung a wire 'cross the klong, didn't ya?"

Art shrugged.

"You mighta cut someone's head off!"

"They should have thought about that before they tried to rip me off."

Clouds closed over the moon again and I was grateful for the dark so no one could see me tremble.

CHAPTER 13

Two days later in Sattahip I was awakened for routine late watch and at 2400 went down the steep steel ladder to the engine room to officially relieve the watch. Everything was normal, as it usually was. I made an entry in the rough log and headed for the galley.

A thick hunk of ham, two slices of cheese, mayo and mustard, all of it on toast with a cup of tea set me up for the six hour watch, then I went topside for a smoke.

My personal favorite place was the starboard after edge of the boat deck. Propping a lifejacket into the curve of rail above the locker made an almost perfect lounge chair. A night breeze off the land brought the stinking sweet smell of drying tapioca over the deck for a minute, then it was gone.

"How's it going?"

Shit! I nearly swallowed the cigarette in my surprise and turning, I saw Art standing there, his expression bland as vanilla.

"You fuckin' Indian," I said, "why you gotta sneak up on people all the time?"

Without a visible change of expression, he took a hit off the joint he held in his right hand then offered it to me.

"Pass," I said. "It'll put me to sleep."

"Good thing your only on watch, not guard duty. I could have offed you in a blink."

I looked at him, wondering if he was trying to tell me something or merely making conversation.

"If I'd'a been on guard duty, you wouldn't'a got within fifty feet of me, Chief." I threw that in to irritate him because I knew he didn't like it, but he made no reaction, merely sucked the last hit from the joint and flicked the roach over the side.

"How's that knife comin'?"

"Good," he said. A flare of interest lit his face. "Havin' it polished at the Batty."

The Batty Company was an Australian outfit, contracted to build and maintain the humongous freezer and refrigeration plant at the port. There were three or four Aussies in charge of two dozen locals running the place. They had an impressive maintenance shed in the port complex and a floating machine shop anchored in the bay.

"Here you go."

Art held a wad of money out to me. I took it, counted it out. Two hundred.

"OK," I said. I felt a tingle of accomplishment tempered with apprehension. "We're square."

"Right on. Say, if you want to make some more bread, I might have some..."

"No thanks," I said quickly, "once is enough. You and your friends play too rough for me. I got what I needed."

He laughed a little. "There's playing rough, and then there's playing rough," he said, "those guys were out of their league, that's all."

At 0600 the next morning my watch ended. I had three days off and was headed for the Kok.

A brief stop at my hootch for a nap and a shower, then I packed a bag, hitched a ride to Camp Samesan and caught the daily army bus to Bangkok. A taxi from the Bangkok HQ to the Skeeter, and by 1430 hours I was paying the same shoeshine boy to deliver the same message to Pen.

She showed up in less than an hour, looking cool and fresh, wearing a sarong tied around her waist and a white cotton shirt. She sported a little eye liner, and had her hair piled up and pinned.

When she sat down and looked at me, I tried my damndest to act cool, but there was no fooling her. Sharp as a tack, she spotted something was up immediately.

"What you do?" Her voice held a trace of suspicion but also a lilt of amusement.

"Let's go to your place, I wanna show you something."

She looked at me, the questions in her eyes, but, nodding her assent, she rose and we headed across the street.

Once in her room, with the fan watching that tennis game again, I reached into my buttoned shirt pocket, brought out the wad of Thai money, took the rubber band off, and laid it out on the bed for her to see.

"*Mach baht,*" she said. A light clicked on and her eyes started to glisten.

"Damn right, it is a lot of money."

"What you do?" Her gaze clicked from me to the money and back again while I had tried hard to keep my studied cool together.

I couldn't stand it anymore. "It's for you," I said fast, "so you can pay off that cowboy…"

Her lips formed a startled "O" as I went on, "…and come to Sattahip and stay my bungalow with me!"

"Oh, Bob!" Covering her face with her hands, she sagged onto the bed. "Oh, Bob!" she said it again, then picked up a handful of the money.

"How you get?"

"No biggie," I said. "I did some work for a guy, that's all. Now you can come stay with me, right?"

With a glad cry, she flung the colorful bits of paper to the ceiling and we watched as they flew around like multi-colored snow, caught in the frantic wash of the fan.

With grin on her face and her eyes snapping, she pulled her shirt off over her head. With a twitch of her shoulders, she set her gorgeous breasts to shaking then slipped the knot of the sarong. I wasted no time and kicked off my sandals, peeled my shirt off, unbuckled my belt and let my pants drop. I'd long ago dispensed with underwear, preferring to let the boys just hang in this climate.

Pen came right up and pressed herself to me.

"Umm," she murmured. Closing her eyes, she rubbed her nose lightly in my chest hair. "You *hohm dee mach.*"

No one had ever said anything like this to me and I nearly fell over.

"Oh, you sweet thing," I gasped out, "you smell so good, too." I plunged my face into the juncture of her neck and shoulder and breathed in her scent.

Rolling around on the bed, I tickled her lightly again, loving the way she laughed, and she counter attacked. The money stuck to us like postage stamps, as if we were going to mail ourselves somewhere.

Carefully, I placed her hands over her head.

"Stay like this," I murmured. Very lightly I stroked her from her fingertips, down her wonderful arms, over her tiny, delicate sea shell ears to the very tips of her ruby red toes. A soft, sibilant purr escaped her as she locked her fingers together and closed her eyes. The silky touch and spicy, foreign scent of her made my head spin.

Then I realized something and in the natural light flooding in the open window, I checked and was amazed.

Except for the magnificent mane on her head and her long, straight, luxurious bush that was shaped like an ace, her body was completely hairless. Her arms were bare and there was not a trace of hair or stubble on her legs. Even her armpits were as smooth as peeled eggs.

"Damn," I breathed.

"*Ali?*" What, she wanted to know.

"You," I said breathlessly and slid both hands up her legs. She laughed, a low, self-assured sexy chuckle and pulled me to her.

When she placed me at her gate, I paused. Leaning down, I kissed her. She allowed only the lightest, briefest touch, then she steered me to her breast and her hips rose up to take me inside her.

Twice more I attempted to kiss her and each time she deflected me. When I touched my lips to the hollow at the base of her throat she pulled in a quick, gasping breath that set me off. Whispering, moaning and pumping her hips, she took everything I could give her, matched me thrust for thrust and when I collapsed on top of her, she wrapped her arms and legs around me and held me tightly.

"You ver' good, Bob, *dee mahk*, I like a lot." Her lips and tongue, hot and moist on my neck, made me tremble.

We laid there in the dampness and, just like before, shared a smoke.

"I know, you hungry, *naa*?" She said it hun-GRY.

"Hey," I said, an idea taking hold. "We have to celebrate! What's the best hotel in the city?"

"Bes' hotel? The Oriental. *Mach baht!*" Her eyes rolled.

"Don't worry 'bout money, baby," I said. "I'm like a drunken sailor. When my Uncle Jack got into port, he used to go the best hotel in the city to have dinner and a drink in the bar and that's what we're gonna do! Put on your best dress and let's boogie!"

"No, Bob," she said with a laugh. "You crazy. I like, but no do, *naa*? Wait, we eat here."

She stood up, tied her sarong over her breasts and went out the door. She was back in less than a minute.

"OK," she said, "Food come, better than Oriental, you see!" She dropped the sarong and laid down next to me.

One leg over my waist, her head on my shoulder, she said, "When you wan' talk cowboy Duke?"

"Tell me about him," I said.

"Him name Tok, but he like call him Duke, same-same movie man, you know?"

"John Wayne, the Duke?"

"*Chai*! John Wayne. Duke." She pronounced Duke with a short vowel and pantomimed a six-gun. I would find out that she loved western movies and the more gunplay the better.

"How come Duke has green eyes and looks like a *felong*?"

"Him fadda seaman from Sweden. Him madda biz'ness girl. She dead now, long time. Duke numba ten!" She practically spat the words out. "What you say him?"

"Loan shark," I said. He was also a blackmarketeer, a dealer in stolen property, a Murphy artist and a certifiable wacko, but I didn't know this at the time. I wish I had.

"Well," I picked up my watch from the night table. "Let's meet him at eighteen hundred, downstairs at the Skeeter. Can?"

I looked at her. She sat up, her knees drawn up under her chin, hugging herself, her liquid dark eyes troubled.

"What's the matter?" I asked.

"Duke ver' bad *poochai*." She sounded almost frightened.

He might be a number ten sonofabitch, I thought, but I've never found a guy that was too bad to handle, one way or another. Everyone has at least one weakness, all you had to do was find it. I didn't know the depth and breadth of Duke's weakness, but even if I had, I probably would have done the same.

The food came. Pen sent word via the delivery girl to Duke to meet us later, then we spread the food on the dressing table.

When she opened the banana leaves and newspaper wrappings, clouds of fragrant steam rose in the already moist air. Each package contained some colorful delicacy, carefully prepared and artfully arranged. Forks, chopsticks and those funny spoons were included, along with four ice cold seven-ounce Pepsis.

"What you like?"

"Surprise me," I replied, and surprise me she did.

At 1745, Pen and I sat downstairs at the Skeeter. My carefully thought out plan was to butter him up with flattery, soften his hostility, and let the money do the talking.

Pen spotted him first, and nudged me. He wore a black silk Hawaiian shirt with pink flowers splashed on it, with pleated tan pants and soft shoes.

As before, he strutted like a bantam cock. I wondered if he did that on purpose or that was just the way he moved. I decided the former. Under the table, Pen took my hand and squeezed it.

Walking right up to the table, he stood there for long seconds without saying anything. I knew what he was doing and I stared right back at him. Pen broke the silence with a stream of impatient Thai. Tearing his practiced stare from me, he glanced at her.

"So," he said in English, "we meet again."

Extracting a pack of Salems from his pocket, he lit up and set the lighter, a gold Ronson, on top of the pack, without offering either of us one. A deliberate snub, and if smoking a cigarette could be made into an elaborately stylized insult, he did it.

"We've come to pay you your money," I said pleasantly.

"Oh you have, have you?"

This guy spoke English better than I did and I congratulated him on it.

"So what?" he said, "Don't you think people can learn your language?"

"No, no," I said, "it's not that. It's just that you're so good at it, that's all." I smiled, the most winning and amicable smile I could make.

He looked off into the distance, and I noticed that he rubbed his knuckles.

"The Catholic sisters make sure you get it right." The words, like hot metal through a die, sounded like they had been drawn from his very being.

I glanced at Pen. Her eyes smoldered but she didn't say anything and I assumed she was letting me handle it.

"That's a great shirt," I said. "Is it silk?"

The look he gave me could have could have pierced armor.

"Cut the flattery and let's get down to business, OK?"

I could think of no reason for the hostility, other than he was just an asshole.

"All right," I said, "the sooner the better."

I pulled the pre-counted roll of notes from my pocket, stripped off the rubber band and fanned them out on the table like a deck of cards.

"Four thousand *baht*."

Try as I might, I couldn't keep the trace of So there! out of my voice. Under the table, Pen's hand found my thigh and squeezed.

Duke glanced at the money, then at me. When he didn't reach for it my trouble alarm went off.

His eyes, hard and flat as green slate, stayed on me for a moment, then his gaze flicked sideways and landed on Pen like a lash. I felt her flinch.

Stubbing out the cigarette, he spoke slowly. "Excellent," he sneered, "but I think you forgot one thing."

My stomach jumped, then fell. Pen stiffened.

"What would that be?"

"The interest. She owes me eight thousand *baht*, not four thousand."

Under the table, Pen's fingernails, those ruby red talons I loved to feel scraping over me, now stabbed me like cat's claws.

Keeping my calm, I smiled. "You didn't say anything about that before."

He nodded at Pen. "She knew. *Pen mai dai mai mee simong hee!*"

It surprised me to realize I understood every word he said. "*Chai-see*," I agreed through clenched teeth, "she's no dumb twat, but…"

Pen fired a barrage of words at him, but he ignored her and kept his flat green smirk on me.

"Listen," I said. It took every bit of self-control I possessed to keep from cold-cocking this strutting Third World punk, "you're a business man. How 'bout this? You take this money here," I pushed the pile of bills a fraction of an inch closer to him, "you take this as a down payment, and I'll get you the rest, but Pen comes with me now."

"You must really enjoy her charms to pay that much. Bangkok has plenty of girls, prettier than her, a better fuck than her. Why don't you keep your money and find another girl, eh GI?"

"I don't want another girl," I said, surprised at the conviction in my own voice. "Money's not important, except for what it can do for you." Art was having more influence on me than I had counted on.

I'd thought I had Duke figured out, but now I wasn't so sure. Pen had said he loved money, but apparently he didn't love it that much. What did he love, I wondered. The answer to that would come as a painful surprise.

CHAPTER 14

Rick, Charlie and I sprawled on the fantail like landed fish as the tug headed out to meet an in-bound refrigeration ship. Watching the wake boil out astern was like gazing into a fire, hypnotic and soothing as I savored the delicious ache in my groin.

"Glad yer back, man," I heard Brett's voice as he flopped down. "I'se startin' ta' think you'd gone AWOL in the 'Kok."

I had to laugh a little, but I didn't say anything.

"What'd ya' do all the time? See the sights, check out the zoo?"

I couldn't tell if Brett was kidding me or not.

"No," I said, "me'n Pen stayed in her room most o' the time, smokin' stick and gettin' it on. We only came out to eat and hit the head."

"All right!" Brett's thin lips cracked his narrow face into a grin. "That's my idea of three days off. Who'd'ja do this with?"

"Bob's got hisself a *tilok*," Charlie announced as if he were the prospective best man.

Brett's face showed surprise. "That right?"

I nodded and fished out a smoke.

"Who is she?"

"Pen, from the Skeeter."

Brett tossed his ice tea dregs over the side, wiped sweat from his neck with a rag. "She cop yer joint?"

I started to snap back an answer, then stopped. I didn't want to admit to anyone that she did not suck my dick, yet, nor did she kiss much at all, but I hoped to remedy that soon.

"We get along real good." I left it at that.

"So she doesn't," Brett replied deadpan, "Don't worry, she will if you insist enough. Watch out for the tricks, though, man, those *tiloks* are full of 'em."

His flat New Jersey accent and his cynic's manner made his words seem matter of fact, devoid of any leer or prurient interest at all, as if it was purely a matter of anthropological interest.

"Oh, yeah," I said, "the moanin' and groanin', the faked nut. I know about that shit. I didn't just fall off the truck yesterday, ya' know."

Brett's brown eyes showed nothing. "Good for you."

I knew that was all he'd say. I was glad in a way, but I also had a nagging sensation that I was missing a vital piece of information.

"Remember what happened to Moose?" Rick threw out.

A general chorus of "Oh, that poor SOB," broke out.

Moose was a great and trusting soul from the Midwest with absolutely no romantic experience before he came to Thailand. "Somethin' about a bank, or somethin'..." I let it trail off, hoping someone would pick up the thread.

"Yeah, I remember," Rick scooped it up like a fumble on the ten yard line and ran with it. "His *tilok* had him stashin' money in a local bank every payday. When the account got big enough, the snidely bitch took the bread out, sold all the furniture and the TV he'd bought her, all the gold jewelry, and hatted up. Poor Moose, man, they curtailed his tour, shipped his ass back to the world he was so out of it."

"How the hell could he let himself be suckered like that?"

Rick looked each of us in the eye. "They're full of tricks and voodoo shit, man, spells and chants 'n' stuff."

"Like what?" I heard myself ask.

"Don't let yer *tilok* trim yer nails or cut yer hair. Get yer laundry done by the service here, not'n the vill', an be careful what you eat at yer hootch."

"What the hell, man, you gotta eat!"

Rick laughed, lit a cigarette and snapped his lighter closed. "You never heard o' the blood trick?"

I shook my head slowly.

"Dig it then," he said and blew smoke into the sullen, wet air. "They take their menstrual blood, you know, the period," he looked around at each of us. No one spoke, twitched, or coughed. Rick possessed a well-honed sense of the dramatic and he knew exactly when to continue.

"They'll collect it somehow, dry it." Slowly, he puffed the smoke, "then sprinkle it in your food."

"Oh, man!"

"Christ on a crutch!"

"Jeez, Rick, that's total bullshit!"

Everyone handled their revulsion differently. I glanced around. Charlie looked like he was going to feed fish, while Brett and Rick exchanged a look.

"Supposed to put you in their power," Brett said. He nodded his own affirmation and gazed across the bay toward the town of Sattahip.

"I'm tellin' ya' man," he went on, "this Asian pussy is the best in the world, but it can be fuckin' spooky sometimes and cost ya' more than just money, know what I mean?"

I felt like I had a Spanish windlass around my chest. The reefer ship, small as ships went and painted a brilliant white, let loose a tremendous blast of his horn that vibrated the very clouds they were so low. It was the signal the pilot was aboard and wanted the tugs on station.

At 1630 the officers and enlisted men E-6 and above made a beeline back to Camp Samesan and the air-conned quarters there.

On the dock, I looked toward the Batty Company area and what I saw absolutely floored me. Like a moth to a flame, I was drawn to it by a force I was powerless to resist.

There, up on the hard in an out-of-the-way corner of the dock, she looked forlorn and a little shabby.

Small but capable looking, she rested with her keel on a six foot long chunk of 12X12 timber blocked and shored with wooden wedges. Four welded steel pipe supports with plywood pads, two at the bow and two at the stern held her upright.

Walking around her, I noticed work had started on her. Her rudder was unshipped and lay across two husky sawhorses, the mast lay across three more, and there was a collection of rusty metal junk in a pile.

A local *poochai,* an employee of the Batty, wielded a plastic scraper on a patch of barnacles.

A ladder, propped against the stern and tied off, provided evidence some work was being done inside the hull. I could hear the sounds, clinks and clanks, of someone working with tools.

I looked at the ladder and wondered if I should climb up there. Probably not, I concluded. I had on my jungle boots, good for a steel tug, but not for small sailboats.

Taking a stroll around her, I estimated her length at twenty-six or twenty-eight feet and she carried a low freeboard to go along with the graceful sheer line.

"She's a beauty, ain't she, mate?"

Startled, I turned toward the deep voice with the foreign accent.

"Good lines," I replied. "The full keel will make her sea kindly and the rudder's big enough for good control."

In the gray cloudy light I saw his eyes widen in surprise. "You know about sailboats then, hey, mate?"

I nodded. "I know a little about 'em."

A smile lit his face as he extended his hand. "Name's Brian."

"Bob," I said, and looked him over while I shook the hard, calloused hand. Medium height and broad-shouldered, he sported an unruly crop of blond hair that the bush hat couldn't quite control. His startling gray eyes looked steady and the deep lines from his nose to the corners of his mouth made me think he spent a lot of time outdoors. Under that sun browned nose was the most luxurious blonde mustache I had ever seen. I was immediately envious.

His ready grin revealed a row of impossibly white teeth and his skin looked like soft glove leather. He wore his khaki bush shirt tucked into a pair of tattered, multi-pocketed shorts and his muscular arms and legs were covered with a mat of fine blond hair. Raggedy boat shoes sans socks clung to his feet. I guessed he was in his late twenties.

"You work for the Batty?"

"Sure thing," he replied. "Freezers 'n' reefers and fixing up old boats is my game." He gestured. "Found this one in Sydney, practically right in me own backyard."

"Must've cost ya' to ship it here, what with…"

"Not a bit of it," he replied, "the ol' BattyCo picks up that tab, hey? Had the cradle made at the shop in Sydney, a Batty crane slung it onto a Batty ship and unloaded it just a few days ago. That's one advantage of workin' for a big outfit."

He gestured behind him at the Batty office, the shed and the concrete barge floating in the bay. "We have a complete boat yard right here, everything I need to fix her up right."

"Great," I said, not a little envious. What a set-up. "What's her name?"

"Right here," he said, and pointed up at the transom over our heads. "This's the first thing I did, back in Sydney."

I looked up. SHIELA, in beautiful gold leaf script was spread out on a carved teak transom board.

"Who'se the builder?"

"This's an Offshore Twenty-seven, built by Cheoy Lee in Hong Kong. The glass hull is sound, the house is teak, and the spruce spars are complete. The Volvo diesel needs a rebuild, took on a load of salt-water, and she needs new through hulls. The rest is just spit, paint n' varnish."

"There should be great sailin' around here, the islands and all."

"One o' the reasons I brought her here from 'Stralia, mate. When she's done, we'll take her out, how's that?"

I stared at him goggle-eyed, hardly believing my good luck.

"Outstanding!" I said.

CHAPTER 15

An endless three-day duty cycle was over. We didn't even look forward to chow anymore. Jimmy the cook had transferred away and the new cook was not worthy of that lofty title, since all he did was make mush in the morning and set out horsecock and cheese for dinner. His suppers were unrecognizable chunks of ash swimming in a gravy that smelled like diesel fuel. Everyone had a hootch in the vill' and spent as little time as possible on the tug.

All the way to my place, Pen was on my mind. Savoring this first homecoming, I conjured up images of her waiting for me, hot and ready, panting with desire.

Our driver dropped me at the entrance to the graveled alley and the other guys offered advice.

"Give her hell, man!"

"Fuck her bowlegged!"

"Show her no mercy, man!"

Not even the low gray clouds could dampen my mood as I strode up the alley and rounding the corner, I saw it.

There it is, my hootch! Knowing that someone waited for me inside made it look different now. Trying to remain casual, I hurried up the stairs. The big brass padlock stood guard and there was no sign of Pen.

Dark thoughts of mayhem or accident swarmed through my mind. No note was pinned to the door and no messenger came around. I had no phone, and besides, who would I call? Sitting on the bottom step, I lit a cigarette and fumed.

Thirty feet away a huge old tree thrust knarled, heavily barked branches into the gray sky and some of those branches passed very close to the south wall of my hootch. The cool green aura of the massive tree would provide valuable shade during the dry season.

"What's the haps, Bobby?"

I nearly jumped out of my skin.

"Fuck!" I yelled. "How come you're always sneakin' up on me, god-damnit?"

Art had abandoned cowboy outfits and was now dressed more or less like everyone else, in thin, loose fitting cotton pants and short sleeved shirts. I wondered how he had walked up the graveled alley with sandals on without me hearing him.

He stood there, his broad copper face bland, his black eyes calm. "Lighten up," he said, "you'll have a heart attack."

I glared at him but he seemed not to notice.

"Pen not here yet?"

"Would I be sittin' out here if she was?"

I lifted my shirt, hoping for a bit of breeze.

"Hot, isn't it?"

"You got that right," I said, thirsty and wishing for a Pepsi.

"Listen," he said. "You up for another little job?"

I couldn't believe it. "Are you kiddin' me? You gotta be kiddin' me, man! You are, right?"

He remained expressionless, merely turned and walked away. I thought he was leaving and was both glad and irritated at the same time, when he stopped.

Suddenly, he planted his right foot, spun around, then a silvery flash shot from him straight to the tree and stopped with a thunk. The knife handle quivered slightly.

"That the one you made?"

Without looking at me, he pulled it from the tree. "Yeah."

This time, he walked even further away, then suddenly turned and threw. That sliver of stainless steel tumbled and flashed end over end and bit into the tough bark with a solid thunk that buried its tip an inch deep.

"Can I see it?"

Art came over to me and with a flourish, handed me the knife, handle first.

"Jeez, man!" I didn't even try to keep the admiration out of my voice, "this is some great work!"

Wide, flat, beautifully formed and polished, the knife was also sharp as a razor. A carved bone handle with rounded edges was held in place with two brass studs behind a small finger guard.

Laying it across one finger, I found it was perfectly balanced, the BP just in front of the guard.

"Can I try it?"

He hesitated only a fraction of a second. "Sure."

Stepping off about ten paces, I tried it, once, twice, and on the third time got it to stick.

"Does carryin' this around make you feel better?"

"Better? No," he replied, perfectly deadpan, "it makes me feel less badly. Listen," Art retrieved his knife from the tree. "Want to make some more bread?"

I looked at him, wondering if he were psychic or something. How did he know when I needed to make some extra cash?

"Why you ask?"

"I hear you have a lot of experience around boats," he said. "I need a guy who can handle one and I'll make it very worth your time."

"What a coincidence," I said, "you offerin' some extra cash right when I need some."

Art's gaze, steady and black as embedded basalt, never left my face. "Life is like that sometimes," he said. "Are you in?"

"Tell me about it."

Art shrugged, his massive shoulders moving under his shirt like a small earthquake. "Drive a local fishing boat out to an island, then bring it back. Piece of cake."

"What's the boat full of?"

His eye twitched a little. "PX booze and smokes, cases of steaks, like that."

A deep breath of the damp air did nothing to calm me. I didn't want to do anything with Art and was on the verge of telling him so. I would pay Duke's blood money out of my army pay, but even as I thought it, I knew I couldn't do that. I had to pay him off all at once to get him out of our lives. I saw Art looking over my shoulder at something and turned to see Pen approaching, carrying several bundles.

"OK," I said to Art. I named a price and he nodded.

"I'll get back to you about the details," he said. The knife disappeared.

As he walked by her, Art said something to Pen in a low voice that made her face pinch closed, but she made no reply.

CHAPTER 16

When she turned back to me, her expression had changed. Setting the packages on the first step, she hurried to the resident spirit house, the small structure atop the short pole the spirits dwelt in. Clucking and murmuring, she picked bits of leaves and twigs from it, brushed the worst of the dirt away with her fingers and righted several small items inside.

Still muttering, she came toward me.

"Hi," I said.

"Hi yousel." She smiled, picked up her packages, took my hand and led me up the stairs.

At the landing, I clicked the lock open and pushed in the screen door, aware how different it felt now that I had Pen with me.

Dumping the load of packages she carried onto the table, Pen turned to me. "Eat now, can do?"

She set the table, a shrimp and rice dish for me, several strange things for her. It was 0900. I'd been awake since midnight on only two hours sleep. I was too amped to sleep or eat now but I nibbled and grazed and sipped the sharp, fizzy little Pepsis.

Pen plucked about a tablespoon of white, sticky rice from the bowl with her fingers, molded it into a ball and shot it like a marble into her mouth, forked up other things and used chopsticks for some other. The funny spoon came into use for a spicy coconut milk and lemon-grass soup that she gently insisted I try. I decided it must be an acquired taste.

After the food was gone, Pen cleared up, then looked at me. I'd seen that expression before, but first, a shower.

Wrapped in sarongs, hers over her breasts and mine around my waist, we headed downstairs. The water felt good, swishing away the stickiness of the morning and night before and when we finished, Pen sprinkled a sweet-smelling powder on both of us.

Ascending the stairs, I watched her butt jiggle under the sarong and felt a pleasant sense of proprietorship. That smooth round ass under there was mine now.

"***Gunsha, naa?***"

"OK." I loaded the bamboo bong. We shared a bowl and headed for the bedroom. At the door she stopped me.

"*Del nit, naa?*" Her voice was a breathy whisper and her hands were warm and dry on my chest. "Wait a little, I tell you come in, can do?" A tilt of her head suggested an erotic promise.

"OK."

She closed the door. Nervous apprehension started to rise and I flopped into the hammock and lit a cigarette. I had a vague feeling that I was not the one in charge here.

The smoke finished, I was still waiting and knocked on the door.

"Wait, *laa*," I heard her call out.

I listened at the door for a moment but heard nothing, then her voice startled me when she called me to come in. My gut quivered for a second and I took a deep breath to calm myself.

Opening the door, I saw her standing near the foot of the bed with her arms at her sides and hands slightly behind her. The shutters were closed and the room was dark.

"Let's open this a little." I opened the louvers of the shutters to let in some light and air and when she objected, I pointed outside.

"Look," I said, "there's no neighbors close, no one can see. It's too dark and hot in here, come on…"

I left the shutters angled up as a compromise and turned to look at her. I let out a long, appreciative breath.

The red silk robe she wore, emblazoned with a green and yellow dragon on the left front and tied with a green silk sash, fell to her mid thigh. Her bangs, puffed into a wild profusion of soft curls on her forehead, allowed a few curly tendrils to escape and as I watched, she reached up and pushed them back from softly shining eyes that had the longest, blackest lashes I'd ever seen. Gold earrings sparkled under her tiny sea shell ears and her lips glimmered a dark pink.

Slowly, she slipped the knot of the sash. The robe fell open, just enough to reveal a long slice of her naked front.

Eagerly, I started to open it further, but she pulled the knot of my sarong, pushed me backwards until I sat on the bed, then she climbed up to straddle me.

The smooth, inviting curve of her shadowed breast invited me in and I cupped one in each hand and thumbed both nipples. They stiffened into stalks and underneath her, I sprang to attention. She felt it and laughed, wind-chime notes in the semi-darkness.

Those pink lips, full and ripe, drew me like iron to magnets and sitting up, I took her face in my hands. She allowed a teasing, feather-light kiss, then tried to pull away.

"Wait," I said and looked her in the eyes. "I want to kiss you now, OK? Do like this." I showed her a pucker.

"I know, but I don' like kiss."

"Well, that's cause you've never really been kissed right, then. Come on, this's no short-time, you stay with me now. I want. Can?"

She hesitated, then nodded.

By example and whispered instructions, I showed her how to move her lips a little, how to make it soft and clinging. When I pulled back to look at her, her eyes were wide and wondering.

"Good, huh?"

She smiled then and came to me. I slipped her a little tongue and she sucked it greedily, then gave me hers. We parted with a smack and she laughed.

"That's the way!" I said. "You like?"

"*Chai*," she replied, eyes glistening, "I like *mahk-mahk!*"

We fell sideways onto the bed, lips and tongues busy, then she was on her back and I was between her silky legs and inside her, pouring it into her fast and urgent.

Again, I dozed off, and when I woke, I was alone.

Stumbling out onto the porch/living room, I found her in the hammock, wearing her sarong and shirt, eating grapes and reading a magazine.

When she saw me, her smile lit my heart. I would discover that her eyes were truly a mirror of her soul and when she was happy, they shined with light and joy, when she was sad they could be lifeless and dull, but when she was mad, they could spit glittering fire.

With a motion, she invited me into the hammock, where I gratefully reclined.

Skillfully, she slit the skin of a grape with a long, ruby-colored pinkie nail, quickly peeled it and offered the naked grape to me.

The sweet fruit burst in my mouth and I told myself that this must be what the King of Siam feels like. A pretty girl feeding me peeled grapes was about as close to royalty as I'd ever been.

"Where you from, Pen?"

She glanced at me, mild surprise on her face. "Why you ask me, you no ask before."

I shrugged. "You weren't livin' with me before."

She considered that for a moment, then said,   "Chiang Mai."

All the girls said they were from Chiang Mai, like Chiang Mai was the only town in the whole country besides Bangkok, Sattahip, Pattaya and Rayong.

"You have gir' frien', United States?"

"For a while I did, but...we broke up?"

"Only one? Why no more, you *sway mahk* GI."

She explained *sway* meant physically pleasing, the *mahk* added emphasis and the term could be applied to both men and women. She encouraged me to speak Thai, added words and phrases to my vocabulary so that we started using a *patois* of bar-girl Thai and English.

I talked and talked, about sailing the Channel Islands, working in the boatyard, many things. She smiled, her eyes alight, and kept up a constant stream of peeled grapes while I stroked the inside of her thigh.

"What do you do?" I finally asked her, tired of the sound of my own voice.

"I biz'ness girl," she answered, as if that explained everything, and in a way, I guess it did.

"Well," I persisted, "what you like to do for fun?"

The blank look on her face told me she had no idea what the word "fun" meant.

"You know," I said, "what make you laugh, what makes you glad you're alive, that's fun."

A wistfulness settled over her as she gazed into an unseen distance. "No have fun," she said, her voice soft and low.

"What'a'ya mean, no fun? That's no way to live, you gotta make your own fun."

She toyed with the amulet she wore. Her dark eyes seemed to pull me toward her and at that moment I decided then and there to bring some fun into her life with me.

I had a look at that amulet. Bigger than a quarter, it depicted the full moon in amazing detail. The craters that formed the man in the moon were delicately etched and an aura of radiating lines depicted moonlight. Thick and heavy, it must have been 18k.

"Very beautiful," I said, admiring its color against the glow of her skin.

"I love moon," she said. The light spilled from her eyes again and made me glad somehow. "I wear this long time, never take off."

I nodded. I had never seen her without it, and wondered if it had been a gift. I asked her that.

"*Mai,*" she said, "I buy for mysel'. Him check-check me, you know?"

"You mean he watches out for you?"

"Yes," she said. A trace of something crept into her voice. "Him and me, we togetta, him keep me, how you say, no..." Her slim hands waved in frustration at not knowing the English word.

I took a guess. "No harm," I said. "Out of harm's way."

When she shook her head yes in an emphatic gesture, I took it as another example of some Eastern mystical thing about horoscopes, spirits, omens and superstitions and didn't think much more of it, except to think that we both shared a kind of kinship about it, but I never thought of the moon as a guardian angel or anything. Before the year was over my mind would be changed for me.

The knock at the door startled both of us and we looked at each other. Through the screen I could see it was Art.

"Come in," I said. I suddenly wished I had on fatigue pants and jungle boots and not this ridiculous sarong.

Art stepped in. He was dressed down a little in a pale blue T-shirt stretched over his broad shoulders and arms with a pair of pleated cream colored cotton pants and sandals. His black hair, gleaming with a light pomade, was slicked straight back. I had to admit it was impressive.

"Well," he said, taking us in as we sprawled in the hammock, "you are living the life now."

He nodded at his own statement and looked around. He looked at Pen and said something, a rapid stream of words that I didn't catch. She replied tersely, then he smiled and spoke to me.

"A nice pad and a fine looking hammer, too. You got it made."

I couldn't help it and had to laugh. "You got that right," I agreed. "What's the haps?"

"Listen," he said as he slipped a pack of smokes from his back pocket, "I'm having a little shin-dig tonight at my place in *Kilo Nung.*"

He lit the cigarette with a tiny gas lighter. "Why don't you and your new *tilok* there," he nodded at Pen, "come on by. We can discuss things then."

"I don't think so, man." I shook my head. "Tell me about it now, and…"

"All the details aren't worked out yet. I'll know more tonight," he said easily as he held the filter in his teeth.

"All right. About eight?"

"Stylin'," Art said, and with a wink at Pen, he left.

"What's he winkin' at you for?" I asked her.

"What is wink?" She pronounced it WEENK

"Like this." I showed her what a wink was. Suddenly, a cold dread filled me. "You go with Art before?"

"Never!" Her eyes blazed and her face suddenly seemed cast in bronze.

"What did he say, before, when you first got here?"

"He say hi, how are you."

Looking her right in the eye, I asked, "Is that all he said. He didn't say, or mean, anything else?"

"*Mai*! No," she said again, "he say *sawadee*, no more, *ching-ching*."

The meltingly sexy look she gave me wiped it from my mind, but only for now.

Art's hootch, located in the high rent district, was all on one floor and shared a stone courtyard with three others. Walking up the flagstone path, I noted the absence of litter and smoking piles of trash in this part of town, so unlike most other places that were strewn with refuse. For a country of such beautiful, gentle people, it was amazing that they had no concept of trash cans. People just threw it wherever it was convenient, and it rotted back to earth right where it landed.

I wore a loose blue cotton shirt, open at the neck with a generous collar over a pair of tan linen slacks. Both items had been custom made by an Indian tailor in Sattahip and were a perfect fit. My shoes, light brown and featherweight with a moderate point in the toe were worn over nylon socks

Pen was dressed for maximum flash in a spaghetti-strapped green silk dress with a matching bag. Except for a pair of gossamer green silk panties she was naked under the dress. Three inch spike heels lengthened and molded her smooth, bare legs and sculpted her already fine ass into a work of art worthy of Rodin.

Her hair swept smoothly up one side of her head, showing off her pretty ear, then cascaded down the other side in a bounty of loose, curly ringlets like a frozen black waterfall shot through with glittering lights.

The full moon amulet glowed at her throat and gold hoop earrings added subtle highlights. She'd left the gold watch behind and I was secretly glad. Her eyes, framed and accented with a delicate blue-green shadow, seemed huge and her lashes were impossibly long and thick, but it was those lips that drove me mad.

Carefully shaped with a shimmery coat of color called Crimson Passion, they begged for kisses and when she touched her coral pink tongue to the corner of her mouth, I almost passed out.

She looked exotic, beautiful and dangerous, like a *femme-fatal* from a *noir* movie. I couldn't stop ogling her and as we walked up the path I dropped back to watch her butt shimmy atop those legs. Looking back over her shoulder, she playfully swayed her hips for me.

"Yowie!" I said softly.

Standing on the path, the light wind rustling the trees in the dark, she waited until I came up to her. Pressing herself to me, she put her hand up behind my head and gave me a brief, clinging kiss, then skipped away.

"More later," she said.

"*Ching, naa?* You promise?"

Her smile, slow and sweet, was all the answer I needed.

Pausing at the open door, Pen beside me, I looked around for Art. Eyes fell on us and conversation lagged as we were checked out.

Seeing no one I knew, I slowly strolled in. Led Zeppelin's "Whole Lotta Love" gushed in thick waves of sound from the biggest stereo speakers I had ever seen and the air was blue with cigarette smoke.

I became aware that other GIs were watching me with hard, challenging eyes. Did I have the right place? A beaded curtain at the other end of the room parted, and Art eased through the doorway carrying three bottles of PX booze in one hand and two sixers of beer in the other, which he set on a table littered with empty bottles, ice buckets, ashtrays, half-filled glasses, beer bottles and food containers.

He walked over and put his arm around a tall, pale-skinned beauty wearing a black leather micro skirt and a shiny black low-cut top. Black spike heels and seamed nylons made her legs look incredibly long and seductive.

She turned on a million-watt smile, full of dazzling white teeth, dimples and red lips, but her eyes remained flat and dark. Tilting a glass, she drank, blinked at him, laid out another mechanical smile and cocked her head to avoid a kiss. He turned, and saw me.

"Bob!"

He rushed over, dragging her with him, and took my hand. "Come in, glad you could make it. This is Nok, Nok, Bob and Pen. Say, what are you drinking?" His voice boomed over the stereo. The pale-skinned beauty didn't even bother to turn on her fake smile.

The icy stares of the others warmed up a little. If Art knew me, I must be OK. I took a bottle of Pepsi for Pen and a San Miguel from the cooler and pried off the tops.

"You want something to give that a kick?" Art asked. I shook my head.

"Come on in here."

Art led us through the beaded curtain into a back room that was lined with low couches, on which sprawled an assortment of GIs in gaudy clothes. A few girls perched like wary tropical birds here and there and smoke curled lazily from the open bowl of a six-hose hookah that squatted on a low round table.

"Here," Art said, thrusting one of the tubes in my hand and another at Pen, "you know what to do!"

I sparked up my Zippo and took a polite hit and Pen did the same. Art rushed out to greet some new arrivals.

Sitting on the couch next to me was a GI I had never seen before. He turned to me, stuck out his hand and said, "I'm Ray. Nawlins, Looziana."

"Bob." I replied, taking his hand. "Los Angeles, California."

He did an elaborate slap-and-glide dap that he pulled off with considerable style that made us both look good. He had taken full advantage of the tailors in town and sported a colorful outfit that included a shiny vest over a puffy-sleeved shirt with a flowing collar.

"Ya'll know Art?" he asked.

The mass of inky black hair lay in gentle curls on his head, and with a straight nose, a neat black moustache and very white even teeth, he was a *sway mach felong.*

"Yeah," I said, "we're on the same tug, down at the port."

He nodded at this, took a sip of his local beer, a Sing-Hai, then held it up. "This panther piss is the worst, ain't it? I'd give a lot for a quart bottle of frosty cold Jacks right about now, yes."

"There's plenty of JD out on the table, man," I said to him.

He looked at me funny for a second, then laughed.

"No, man," he said, "not Jacks, as in Jack Daniels, but Jax, J-A-X, the finest beer in the world, brewed only in Nawlins."

Pointing at the bottle I held, he asked, "You like that dark Philippine swill?"

I nodded that I did.

"Well, I ain't gonna hold it against you, no. Each man to his own, that's what my daddy used to say, him." I noted his speech pattern, one that sounded strange and familiar at the same time.

"Yeah," I said, "you might want to think about that tomorrow when the top of your head feels like it's gonna come off. I hear that stuff has formaldehyde in it. Try some of that hookah," I suggested.

"Don't like smokin' it, man. Makes me think about home too much, yes."

"Well, you oughta be pretty used to this weather then, being from there."

"Ah, yes, yes, I am, yes. But there's no Jax, no red sauce, no crawfish, no dirty rice…"

"Man, you got giant prawns, local hot sauce, and plenty of rice. Improvise." I swigged from the beer.

His eyes opened wider. I could see he must have had more than a few of those beers.

"You know, you might be right, you." He raised his bottle in salute. "This the first time you been to Art's pad?"

"Yeah."

"Pretty nice, huh?"

"I guess." There was glass in the windows and an air-conditioner labored in one, but I liked my place.

"Pad like this ain't cheap, no," Ray observed.

I nodded.

"You see that piece o' tail he got?"

"Yeah," I said, "she's fine all right."

"That's officer material, yes. She don't do no EM, man, you know that. Am I right, or what?"

"My ol' lady's a fox, too, and I ain't no officer."

He looked past me at Pen and gave her a slow up-and-down.

"You did real good," he said, then he leaned over closer and asked, "Where's Art gettin' all this bread, huh?"

I turned to look at him. His dark eyes gleamed and for the first time I saw the white streak in his hair, just a touch, at the temple on the left side, going back to just over his ear. He saw me looking at it, and smiled. "My momma say that the angel Gabriel touched me there when I a little boy. What you think?"

"You play a horn?"

He laughed, his white, even teeth looking even whiter under his dark moustache. "No," he said, "but I can play a Cajun washboard pretty good, yes."

"Isn't that like playing the tambourine? All you got to do is rub it or tap it in time, right?"

He nodded. "Somethin' like that, yes."

"What's your MOS?" I asked him. It was the kind of innocuous question guys ask each other all the time, but it made him look at me for just a split-second too long.

"Lab tech at the hospital," he said. At that time, I thought nothing of it.

We were silent for a bit, each of us sipping from the bottle we held. Out of the corner of my eye, I saw him furtively watching me. He asked a couple questions, what kind of car I had in the world, the kind he had, what he wanted, stuff GIs yak about. "Art told me he had a 'Vette back in the world. What he tell you?"

"He showed a bunch of us a picture of a Sting-Ray, said it was his."

Ray nodded and sipped his beer. "That guy's a bullshitter from a long time ago, man. He always talkin' some trash and wavin' the cash, ain't he? How you think he gets all that dough to wave around, him?"

"Listen," I said, putting an edge in my voice, "if you're so interested in Art's money, why don't you ask him?"

He raised a placating hand, as if it were no big deal, then mumbled something about getting another beer and left.

I turned to Pen. She was talking to a girl on the other side of her, also dressed to the nines. They both looked bored but were trying to hide it.

"Go now?" she asked.

I shook my head. I'd gotten all dressed up and didn't want to leave now, besides, I hadn't talked to Art yet.

Just as I was about to get up, a tall skinny American come through the curtain and nearly crashed onto the low couch where Ray had been.

"How ya' doin'?" he asked affably enough, and swigged from a dark, square bottle. JD again.

"Fine, yourself?" I replied.

"If you gotta be stuck in a shithole, this one's better than most."

That struck me as odd. Most guys loved the duty here, and while the weather sucked this time of year, it was better than ten-day patrols, night ambushes, rats, jungle rot, leeches and being shot at.

"What'd'you mean, shithole?" I asked him with real curiosity.

"Just what I said. This place sucks. There's no excitement, no joy, no…" He let it trail off and tilted the bottle again.

"I don't know about you," I said, "but I got plenty of joy." I indicated Pen with a flourish.

He glanced over, plainly unimpressed and swigged from the bottle. "You got a zip hooker, BFD. You ever fire a shot in anger?"

"No," I said and decided to let the zip hooker thing roll on by, "and I hope I never have to, either." I knocked on the wooden table and grinned. He didn't grin back.

"Lemme tell ya', man, a firefight'll get your blood running, ya' know? Get your juices going. It ain't like bangin' a zip whore either, wham, bam, it's over. It's a high that can last for hours, man." He had a dreamy far-away look in his eye, that thousand-yard stare, I'd heard it called.

"What the hell you know about firefights, anyway?" I asked, loading my voice with disbelief. "This ain't Saigon, buddy. Ain't no firefights around here."

He turned toward me and I could see the hostility oozing from him as he said, "What the *fuck* do you know about anything?"

I'd heard that before, and tensed. When guys used the word like that, they were spoiling for a fight.

"I know there ain't no firefights around here, that's what I know."

He looked at me with slitted eyes. I knew if this kept up, we'd be out back soon. I didn't want that, so I stood up, intending to go get another San Miguel and bumped square into Art.

He put his arm around my shoulders and more or less steered me into the other room as the tall American's curses followed us. I looked back at Pen, but she was talking to a girlfriend, and Art was hard to resist when he wanted you to follow him.

"Listen," he said when we were in the other room, "there's something you should know about that guy, Matt's his name…"

"Yeah, I know. He's a blowhard asshole, talkin' 'bout…"

"I heard him. He's not blowing smoke, man."

"What're you, pullin' my chain? What the hell…"

"He's not assigned to Thailand, man. Keep this to yourself, but he's AWOL from Nam."

A little chill passed up my back, and in spite of the temperature, I felt cold suddenly.

"Whataya mean, AWOL from Nam?" My stomach slowly sank. "What's he doin' here?"

Art glanced around, then pulled me outside where the damp heat rolled over us and the smell of rot was strong.

"He won't like me telling you this, but you should know. Matt came to the 'Kok for his R and R, never went back, says he saw too much shit there."

"Man," I said, relieved. This was the old I-can't-take-it-anymore ploy, "that's bullshit. Lots o' guys saw a lot of shit there, so what. What makes him…"

"Ever heard of Pinkville?"

"No, I don't think so…".

"Well, ask him about it sometime when he's in a good mood, he might tell you about it."

I knew right then that I didn't want to know anything about it.

"But in the meantime," Art said earnestly, "cut him some slack, OK?" Art nodded, affirming his own words.

"If you say so," I replied. "But hey…" Before I could ask him about the upcoming job, a huge crash resounded from inside and Art bolted away.

Standing on the edge of the flagstone walk, I lit a smoke. Clouds hung so low it seemed like I could reach up and tear out a fistful if I wanted to, bring it to my mouth and suck the clean moisture from it, feel it trickle down my throat and cut the film of beer and cigarette smoke that clung there.

A drunk GI staggered out the front door, towing a protesting girl with him and to give them plenty of room, I stepped off the path toward the side of the hootch.

Inside, the tape ended and in the silence before another started, I heard voices, a male and a female, speaking Thai, arguing. I thought nothing of it, probably a local cowboy trying to score a free piece from one of the girls.

The girl said something, and even if I couldn't understand the words, I could hear the undercurrent of loathing in the tone. The voice was very familiar. Without knowing why, I paused to listen, strangely compelled by the immediacy of it all.

Then I heard the male voice, and it had a familiar timbre of tone, a certain lazy cadence to the words. I couldn't place it yet, but I had heard that voice somewhere. It was almost like listening to a vigorous couple in the next room. I didn't want to listen, but I couldn't help it. For several seconds I stood there, decided it was some kind of domestic dispute and turned away. Then I heard my name. Just the single syllable, short, quick, "Bob", in the middle of a rush of incomprehensible words, but my name, I was sure of it.

Riveted now, I listened while the male voice gnawed at my memory. The female voice seemed to grab me somehow, right in the gut, but I dismissed it. All the girls sounded alike, their voices sing-song and musical, that is, until she said a certain phrase, a phrase I had heard before, when Pen had been talking to Duke on the street. He had said something, and she had responded with a short, terse sound, a type of impatient curse.

"*Maa-whey!*" she had said. Now I heard it again. It sounded like Pen, alright. Then the male spoke, and again came that lazy cadence, a softly arrogant tone, and with a jump in my stomach, I knew who it was. A flush, thick and warm, spread over me like a wave.

Edging to the corner of the building, heart thumping, I listened. They spoke so fast I could catch only a few words, "*baht*", my name again, then Art's name, *ki-mhow* GI, which meant a really drunk or stoned, literally, "shitfaced", GI.

For a brief instant, I thought of charging around the corner and demanding to know what was going on, but that would make me lose face in front of both of them for showing anger.   I listened, straining to make out what was said, but could only catch the occasional word, then from inside, the stereo came back to life, drowning them out. The Doors, Jim Morrison bragging that he was a back door man and knew what all the little girls needed. I had the eerie feeling he was talking to me.

Determined to speak to Art, set our deal and get the hell away from here, I went back into the hookah room. Someone had reloaded the bowl and all the hoses were in use. Pen wasn't there and I couldn't find Art anywhere, either. Back in the front room, I looked for him, but couldn't find him and had an idea.

At the end of the hall a door showed a light under it. The bedroom. I tried the knob, but it was latched from the inside and I rapped sharply on it.

"What?" The voice was belligerent.

"Is Art in there?" I was belligerent back.

"Who the fuck wants to know?"

"I do, you fuckhead!" My voice rose, and the door jerked open, but only a few inches.

"Bob," Art peered out, "go have a brew and I'll be there in a minute. We'll talk then, OK?"

"I wanna talk now, man, I'm..."

"In a minute!"

"Now, or I'm gonna hat up!"

The door opened a little and Art's face came out. He looked at me. "Bob," he said, "work with me on this, OK? Give me ten minutes, can you do that?" The way he said it, it sounded like it was such a little thing to ask.

"Five minutes," I replied

"OK," he said, "five minutes." The door closed with a click and I was standing there with my face hanging out.

In the hookah room, the crowd seemed to have thinned, only Pen and one girl on one couch and another guy and a girl across the room nuzzled each other. In the corner, on the floor, a dark form sprawled, peaked too soon.

I sat next to Pen, and watched her. She looked composed enough, her breathing normal, but she had just a trace of perspiration on her forehead and her pretty dark eyes were still full of the fire of confrontation.

"*Ali?*" She asked. What?

I shook my head and looked her up and down.

"*My pen lai,*" I said as casual as I could, then the beaded curtain exploded inward and Matt staggered in, followed by Art.

Matt's gaze swiveled around, came to rest on me and he flopped down next to me. I heard Pen suck in an expectant breath and I tensed, sat still. Art was watching all this with an air of detachment, like it was happening on a movie screen, not in his own place. His head dropped to his chest and bounced back up. Matt was trying to form words.

"Well," he slurred, "looka here. This's the guy that knows we ain't in Saigon."

"Look," I said, "you're in a tough spot." I paused, hoping that it would sink in and he would get the idea that I bore him no malice. "You do what you gotta do, man, and I don't have nothin' to say about it, OK?"

He blinked. "Fuckin' A," he said, and blinked again in slow motion. The look on his face changed. He looked confused. "Fuckin' A," he repeated, trying to validate his own mood.

Art perched his bulk on a corner of the low table and gazed at me as his chin slowly sank to his chest.

"What about this little job, Art?"

His chin lifted and his eyes popped open. "I hear you know your way around boats," he said.

"I've been around boats all my life and can sail anything from a dink to a schooner, operate anything from a ski boat to a tug."

Art laughed. "Don't be modest now."

"There's not a boat built that I can't handle."

"That right?"

"Yeah, that is right."

"OK, you're in. I'll get with you on the details."

"You say when and where."

I turned to Pen. "Let's go," I said. The weirdness level was rising and I was anxious to be gone from here.

Before I could stand up, though, Matt came to life.

"Hey," he said suddenly in a clear voice, "what's the closest you ever come to dyin?"

What the hell was this?

"I'd like to hear the answer to that," Art said.

I thought about it for bit. The memory could still make me shiver.

"Actually," I said, "there wasn't much to it. I was sailing a homemade catamaran in twenty knots of wind twelve miles off Pt. Fermin. Capsized it. The force of it threw me into the water and the wind on the trampoline blew it away faster than I could swim for it. I clung to a cooler for hours. It was gettin' dark and cold. Commercial fishin' boat came by and a guy takin' a leak over the side spotted me. Another five minutes 'n' it'd been too dark ta see me." I shrugged, to show it was no big deal, hoping no one saw the terror of the memory creep into my eyes.

Matt took a deep breath. I knew this would be a war story, but I didn't want to listen to any macho bragging bullshit about how he or anyone else killed a lot of what was coming to be called gooks, and I was getting set to stand and leave when I glanced over at him.

He sat there, looking dazed and confused, as far from a swaggering gook-killer as was possible. He seemed to shrink, to pull himself down into a hard knot as if he were steeling himself, and in a low monotone, began to speak.

"We were choppered in'n landed on the outskirts of a little vill', a place we called Pinkville."

Art caught my eye, and nodded, just a little.

"The place was s'possed to be a VC stronghold an' a lot of our guys'd been killed around there in the last few weeks. We were gonna shut the place down, deny the enemy that resource. A whole company went in from all directions. We landed on the right flank, in some elephant grass, made it to a trail and was headed for a cluster of shacks when we heard small-arms fire up ahead. We were ready, movin' fast, when around a bend comes a group of people, old men, women and kids, maybe fifteen or twenty. None of them was armed, they offered no resistance. The LT with us said to take care of 'em, then he headed into the vill'."

Matt chain-lit another cigarette and continued. "We herded 'em off the trail, to beside a ditch and were watchin' 'em, see if they tried to get away. None of 'em did. They just stood there, eyein' us, talkin' low. The LT come back and seemed kind o' surprised to see 'em all still standin' there."

"I told you to take care of 'em," he says. A Spec4 tells him we were takin' care of 'em, we're guardin' 'em, none of 'em even tried to get away."

"The LT looks at the guy and says, No, I mean take care of 'em. The Spec says, what do you mean, take care of 'em?"

"The LT looks him right in the eye and says, Kill 'em."

No one spoke for a long time, each one of us knowing what came next, none of us willing to say it out loud, except Art.

"It wasn't your fault, Matt, you were following orders."

Matt raised his head and stared at Art with dead eyes, blasted empty of conscience and soul by the condemnation he that he heaped onto himself.

"I tried to save some of 'em," a voice, not his own, said. "I tried, really, I did. I told 'em to get in the ditch, lay down, play dead. A few did, then another guy came up and started shooting into the pile of bodies in the ditch, picking off any that moved. I didn't shoot, but a guy in the squad, he pointed his rifle at me and said if I didn't shoot, he'd shoot me, so I...I fired a few rounds, just for show, ya' see?"

His gaze swept the room, seeing no one, seeking a glimmer of understanding, but received only blank stares in return.

"I didn't kill no one!" His voice, torn from him by forces he couldn't control, broke into a screech, then his mouth opened, he twitched a few times, then slumped over onto his side. A sound, a sob or a sigh, I couldn't tell which, came from him, then he was silent.

No one moved for a long moment. Standing, I pulled Pen up with me and headed for the door.

"Hey, Bob." Art said in a low voice.

I stopped at the door. "What?"

"I'll pick you up at eighteen hundred the day after tomorrow. I hope your mouth is not making promises your ass can't deliver on."

CHAPTER 17

"Look, man, I ain't sayin' anything, just listen to what this guy has to say, that's all!"

I glared at Rick, seriously pissed that he would even suggest such a thing, but in the back of my mind, I knew what he said made sense.

The local *poochai*, a young cowboy, stood there easily, trying to cover his anxiety with a crooked-tooth grin. He shifted his weight back and forth once or twice to show his impatience, but he wouldn't say anything. That wasn't the Thai way. Confrontation was to be avoided at all costs, but like a lot of people who worked around American GIs, on the base, in the port or in the clubs and bars, he was influenced by us. He picked up ideas, attitudes and mannerisms. The one-finger salute was everywhere among Thai men and boys.

"You tell me," I said to Rick.

"Well, you probably know a lot of the girls butterfly to pick up cash, especially *tiloks* of tug crews."

It was supposed to have happened to a guy on the 2082. With our work schedule it might have been inevitable. A guy has to work for three days straight and the girl knows it. She needs some extra bread and doesn't want to ask him for it, so she goes out on his first two duty nights and plies her trade at the opposite end of town, figuring none of his buddies will see her. None of the other girls will rat her out, either.

"This guy," Rick said, "will, for a small fee, keep an eye on Pen for a couple of weeks, on your duty days. If she gets itchy and looks up some customers, he'll tell you about it and you can kick her ass out, get another one. You know she's got someone watchin' you when the tug's in the Kok, don'cha?"

That was pretty common knowledge and I looked at the cowboy. Long black hair, combed into a ducktail, pegged black jeans, and a white T-shirt made him look like an Asian James Dean. He wouldn't look me in the eye.

"What's to keep him from tell me she's a good girl and then black-mailin' her, too? He gets paid from both ends, then. I wouldn't trust this fuckin' cowboy t' tote my shit, let alone t' watch my ol' lady. Too many ways for me to get screwed. Forget it."

"OK," Rick said as if he were washing his hands of the whole thing, "sorry, *khap*," he said to the local.

The *poochai* walked away, trailing a laughing stream of Thai over his shoulder and when he looked back at me to gauge the effect, I gave him a one-finger salute. The laughing stopped, choked off in mid-chuckle.

Later, I would wonder who had had the last laugh.

Art took me at my word and three days later I found myself at the helm of a sixty foot Thai fishing boat departing out of the village of Ban Phe, headed for Ko Samet, a club-shaped island about six miles southeast in the Gulf of Siam.

The dim lights of the vill' disappeared into the misty darkness astern. Scattered rain fell from invisible clouds in drops the size of berries and the fluky wind shifted direction six times in as many minutes. The northeast monsoon's leading edge was here but seemed stalled, hesitant to commit.

The ancient two-stroke diesel in the fishing boat wheezed and huffed as the high bow shoved the water aside.

The only chart I had was a small tracing I'd taken from the large-scale chart that was under a sheet of Plexiglas in the tug's pilothouse and the only compass was the kind issued to infantry troops. Taped to the crude binnacle, it was better than nothing.

Wearing the standard garb of clandestine adventurers, jungle fatigue pants, an olive drab T-shirt and jungle boots, Art lounged on the port seat, his thick legs stretched out in front of him. I wore the same thing and passed the edge of the flashlight beam over him. He appeared to be asleep, but I knew he wasn't. Body relaxed and comfortable and his mind alert, he'd gone into waiting mode.

"Where's that other guy?" I asked.

Art didn't stir. "Back there," rumbled from his barrel chest.

Back there was the living part of the crude deckhouse, separated from the wheel by a hanging curtain.

"Is he straight?"

"Straight as he needs to be."

An errant wave slapped the hull and shoved the bow off, but Art didn't move. He seemed to almost float there, barely moving to compensate for the motion.

"For our sake," I said, "I hope he's..."

"Look, Merlyn, your job is to drive this tub, OK? Let me worry about Matt."

For the thousandth time, I told myself that this would work out, but I was afraid Uncle Jack might be right.

Soon after high school graduation, a friend and I took his boat, a beautiful bright-finished 34 foot Chris-Craft Commander to Catalina Island in a building Santana condition to see a couple of college girls who worked their Christmas break on the island.

"You're thinkin' with the wrong heads, the both of you," Uncle Jack said as we cast off.

We knew what we were doing, we said. In the middle of the San Pedro Channel, caught in forty knots of wind and twelve foot waves, we were forced to alter course and barely made the West End, headed for the protected anchorage at Catalina Harbor.

Now as the fishing boat wallowed in the building waves, I asked myself if I was thinking with the wrong head again. I told myself that I was taking a calculated risk and that it would all work out. It'll be worth it, I kept telling myself. When I'm laying up in the bed and she's stroking me with the fur between her thighs and rubbing those stiff chocolate kiss nipples on me, I'll be glad I did it. That's what I told myself.

To get my mind off that, I turned to Art.

"Where do you know Matt from?"

Again, Art looked up, one eye open, but before he could respond there was a flurry of motion behind me. Matt stood there. By the dim wash of the flashlight I couldn't see him too well, but he didn't look good. The boat lurched and he was suddenly moving fast, to the starboard gear locker, where he ended up in a jumbled pile of elbows and knees.

Raising a bottle of Jack Daniels, he took a long drink, smacked his lips, made a noise and seemed to drop off again. That was how he handled it, by staying shitfaced.

Suddenly Matt jerked as if stung, then looked at me blearily. Struggling to stand, he fell back and knocked his head on the corner of the locker. Feebly, like a stunned crab, he waved his arms and legs as he struggled to rise.

In a flash, Art was kneeling down next to him. Gently, like a father to a child, he eased him back down, murmuring and patting his shoulder and when he settled, Art took the bottle from his lifeless hand, replaced the cap and took it with him back to his place, where he resumed his waiting stance without a word.

I kept my mouth shut and concentrated on finding that small cove on the east side of the island, marked with an X on my crude chart. Operating in the dark, without lights or any real nav aids, using only rudimentary piloting and guesstimating our speed based on experience and watching a chuck of wood float by, I was more than pleased when the cove turned up at the right time in the right place.

"That's why I hired you," Art said.

I said a quick silent thanks to the Skipper upstairs.

"I'm good at it," I said to Art.

"What would you rather be, lucky or good?"

He didn't wait for a reply but roused up Matt to help handle the mooring lines.

Secured to a rickety pier, I smoked, listened to the scattered rain and waited for the unloading to be completed. Lit by the jerky beams of several flashlights, a stream of locals carried boxes of various sizes off the boat and stacked them on the pier, then they started loading crates from another stack on the boat. What the hell was this? Art had said nothing about bringing stuff back. A chill shot up my spine in spite of the warm wet air.

Where the hell was Art? I checked my watch. I wanted to be back in my hootch before dawn.

Heavy boots clumped on the deck and I turned to see Art and Matt watching as the last of the crates was lowered into the hold.

"What the fuck is this shit?" I demanded. "You didn't say anything about bringin' stuff back!"

"Don't worry about it." Art appeared perfectly calm. He'd known all along. The sense of doom and dread that I'd been pushing away for hours now suddenly loomed up and rushed over me.

"Let's go!" Matt hollered, a grin splitting his cadaverous face, "we got shit to do!" He seemed completely sober now, happy almost.

Silently, I started the engine. Matt and Art cast off. Backing away from the dock, I wondered what he was so glad about, and what was in those boxes.

Before the night was over, I would find out. I would also know the answer to the one question I had been dreading for a few years now.

CHAPTER 18

That tiny compass gleamed dully in the beam of the flashlight. I held the wheel steady, our course northwest and pushed the throttle against the stops while that old engine hammered and wheezed and the wooden hull creaked and groaned in protest.

The wind had made up its mind and now seemed to be trying to make up for lost time, kicking up short, steep waves that we took on our starboard bow. The jerky, erratic motion stirred up the bilge, releasing a miasma of ancient fish, diesel fuel and exhaust that rose up like a choking cloud.

"What's in those crates?"

"Just drive the fucking boat, Merlyn."

Art has screwed me good and there was nothing I could do about it, right now anyway. "Where's Matt, gettin' shitfaced back there?"

A loud thump behind me, audible over the racketing engine, made me turn around. Matt stood there, swaying easily with the motion. Alcohol gleamed in his eye and seeped from his very pores as he looked at me. I could feel it coming and he didn't disappoint.

"Hey, Merlyn."

I made no response. Outside the crude pilothouse, rain slashed down in a sudden gust like birdshot, then let up.

"Hey, dipshit, I'm talkin' t' you!"

Out of the corner of my eye, I saw Art pull his feet under himself, ready to stand.

"Ya think yer such hot shit, don't ya?" Liquor slurred Matt's words, but there was no mistaking his tone and I turned slightly, to be able to see him if he made a move at me.

Even though he was tall, Matt weighed about as much as dried straw. His long spindly arms were like sticks and his chest had almost a concave quality and his dirty, stinking clothes hung from him.

"Fuckin' punk," he snorted. "Work on a tugboat, huh? You don' know shit from fuckin' shinola, ya' know that? Combat, that's where it's at! Fuckin' A!"

Tilting a bottle to his mouth, Matt pulled a four-bubble hit from it and glared at me, the challenge clear. The boat lurched and Matt was thrown. Grabbing the curtain for support, he pulled it down with him and I heard the dull thonk as his head smacked the deck.

Art moved to him, flipped the nearly empty bottle out the door, then folded the torn curtain into a crude pillow that he placed under Matt's head.

Standing, he came up beside me.

"Listen," he said, "don't take it personal, OK? He's like that with everyone."

I turned to look at Art. He was nodding slowly, like we were sharing some deep dark secret that had to kept tightly guarded.

A thump and a loud curse came from behind us.

"You guys talkin' 'bout me?" Matt demanded in a strident, pissed-off voice.

Art was still calm and raised a hand in a placating gesture.

"No, man," he said, too calmly, I thought, "we're not talkin' 'bout you. C'mon, let's go on outside. You got any smokes?"

With an arm around Matt's shoulders Art tried to get him outside, both of them stumbling and jerking with on the pitching, twisting deck.

It was a good effort, but Matt wasn't going for it.

"Listen," he suddenly shrieked and threw off Art's arm. "Officers said they were VC! I didn't wanna do them people! I didn't wanna shoot no women or kids! They made me, you unnerstand? They said they'd put me in Leavenworth if I didn't! They said they'd shoot me if I didn't!"

Veins and arteries pulsed in his neck and his pale, death's head face was shiny with sweat. His eyes scared me. Even though he stood right there in front of me it was like looking into the soul of a dead man.

I could smell his breath, fetid and hot. I could smell him now too, rank and animal-like, with a sour, acrid component that nearly gagged me.

By now Art was trying to calm him down, murmuring soothing words, but Matt was wound up now. His face started to twitch uncontrollably.

"They lined 'em up near a ditch," he screeched, "and just opened up on 'em!" Words started to pour from him then.

"Women and kids, little girls and boys, their faces turned up, cryin', beggin' us not to shoot, and we shot 'em! Down in the pit, there were some of 'em still alive, and we walked back and forth and picked 'em off, one by one!"

He paused to suck in a great shuddering breath, then went on, "I di'n't want to, I di'n't! They said they'd put me in Leavenworth! I couldn't go to jail again, I couldn't, I'd die there!"

Deep racking sobs drove him to his knees while Art stood there, patting his back, making sounds.

In the midst of all this I felt something, like an insect bite, and I smacked my neck, then looked at my hand to see if I'd got him. It had blood on it, a big smear. Must have been a big one, I thought, then I saw a chunk of the window casement fly away. There wasn't any glass to break, but I thought it odd that the boat would suddenly start to fly apart like that. Then I saw Art.

He must have heard or seen it, too, because suddenly he was crouched very low, peeking out the starboard door, then he whipped back around just as another chunk of wood, a big one this time, flew away with a curious silence. The exposed wood was raw and new, like a wound.

Art spun, grabbed Matt by the shoulder and shook him like a terrier shakes a rat.

"They're here," he shouted. "They're here! C'mon, let's go!"

By now I was hunkered down, too. Matt looked up and a visible change came over him. Gone was the haunted look. Exhilarated and happy, he appeared joyful even. Scuttling into the dark at the rear of the pilothouse, he returned in seconds dragging a rucksack.

Drawing a long, dark object from the sack, Matt tossed it to Art, then pulled another one out, which he kept close to his body as he peeked around the wooden doorjamb. Suddenly he sprang up to lean out the door.

Five or six long yellow tongues of fire leaped out into the dark, and I realized he was shooting out the door! More flashes come from outside, forward of the house, lighting the scene like a strobe. I realized that it must be Art shooting too.

What the hell? I didn't try to look outside but dropped to the deck and steered with one hand while I tried to bury myself into the smooth, worn wood. The house was being riddled with bullets that bit huge chunks of wood loose and sent them spinning away.

Something poked me hard in the side. I thought I'd been shot but when I looked I saw it was Matt, hitting me with something.

"Here," he shouted, "pop some rounds out that door!"

I took the Colt .45 pistol from him. The hammer was already back and without checking the magazine, I stuck it out the door, pointed it more or less behind us and pulled the trigger over and over until the slide locked back on an empty mag, then tried to steer straight away from the bullets that ripped the air over my head.

I could see Matt, prone on the deck, firing short bursts.

"I told ya' they would come!" I heard him shout, almost gleefully.

Art didn't respond but kept firing. When his magazine emptied he dropped it out, methodically locked in another and resumed firing.

There was a lull in the fire coming at us. I glanced behind me just in time to see Matt, in one fluid motion, nearly launch himself out the door and empty a thirty round magazine in three bursts, scream something, then flip himself back into the house. His eyes pulsed with a manic energy and his face was split by the widest grin I'd ever seen. He was loving this.

Jerking the rucksack toward him, he rummaged inside. "Hey!" he yelled at Art, "there's only two mags left!"

We took no rounds for nearly half a minute, and Art risked a peek out the door. Still no shots. For long seconds we waited while the engine hammered away. I realized we were probably way off course, but I kept it this direction anyway.

"I think they're gone," Art ventured.

"They've hatted up, man, and *di-di*'ed the fuck out o' here!" Matt almost crowed. "Man, did you see that?" He couldn't contain himself, and repeated it several times without a response from Art or me. Art sat on the deck, the smoking rifle across his chest, breathing hard, eyes closed. I noticed then the rifle was an AK-47.

Suddenly, I felt everything I'd eaten for the last three days start to come up. Still holding the wheel, I leaned out the door and blew a tremendous stream of vomit over the side. Even after there was nothing left, I continued to retch until it felt like my whole gut had been pulled out. My whole body, from my scalp to the soles of my feet, tingled like a struck funny bone.

"If you feel something hairy comin' up, swallow it quick, it's your asshole!" Matt shouted, and then laughed, a howling, ringing laugh that chilled me.

I managed a weak "Fuck you!" then laughed myself, a mix of chain-reacting adrenaline and relief that it was over and I wasn't dead.

"Don't worry about it," Matt shouted over the engine, "everyone blows chow the first time. You did good, kept your head and did your job. You'd do all right in combat."

I motioned to Art to take the wheel. Stripping off my shirt, I leaned over the side to wet it in the water, put it to my lips and sucked some out to rinse my mouth, then wiped my face, neck and body.

"You smell yourself?" Matt asked, his voice matter of fact.

I looked at him and couldn't help but nod.

"That's fear, man," he said. "Pure-D straight fear. Happens to everyone. Hey," he turned to Art, "I told you that steel plate would be a good idea!"

I looked at Art. He was standing now, and I heaved myself up, amazed that my legs held me. I saw the compass was still intact, and we were only slightly off course and at full speed.

"What was that all about? Who the fuck were those guys?"

Art looked sideways at me, and by the flashlight, I could see his copper mask of a face. "They're nobody anymore." He turned away.

"What's in those crates?" I shouted while I shook uncontrollably with dissipating adrenaline.

He looked me full in the face. "The less you know, the better."

"What kind of bullshit is that? I didn't bargain to get shot at! You sonofabitch! I coulda been fuckin' killed! You knew this'd happen, di'n'cha?" I dared him to deny it.

"Listen," he said, calmly, "I didn't want to take this load back, but I had no choice." He offered smokes around. Matt took one, and I started to, but I thought if I took it, it would mean that I somehow forgave him or something, so I angrily refused. He shrugged while Matt lit them up.

"Those guys," Art gestured vaguely out the door, "are a bunch of shitheads. They aren't important anymore."

"There it is." Matt said with conviction while he and Art slapped palms.

There it is, there it is. Born in the cynicism, horror and chaos of Nam, the phrase is used to express a cynical, don't-give-a-fuck attitude about everything from lousy officers who are only interested in their career to the way things work in general. In Viet Nam, the wind doesn't blow, it sucks, There it is. That LT is gonna get us killed if we don't frag him first, There it is. In a firefight, civilians sometimes get killed, There it is.

"What's your unit in Nam?" I asked Matt suddenly.

His training took over, and without thinking, he answered. "Charlie company, eleventh brig…" He stopped.

Anger leaped from his eyes like the flame from a muzzle and I felt the camaraderie of only a few moments ago shatter. He started forward, toward me.

Art stepped between us and pushed Matt down onto the gear locker.

I couldn't help myself when I said, "You were at My Lai, weren't you? You were there, killed people, women and kids, old men, huh?" Suddenly, with a startling revelation, I knew I was afraid of Matt.

The fire went out of his eyes like it had been dowsed with a fire hose. He slumped forward and his chin sank onto his chest. His shoulders heaved convulsively, but he didn't look up.

"Yes," he said in a hoarse whisper.

Slowly, like a giant redwood, he toppled over onto his side, and seemed to shrink down into a hard knot of silence and despair that no amount of whiskey or heroin could cleave.

"Man," Art said, as if it took a very great effort to get the words out, "I wish you hadn't a done that."

Me, too, I thought to myself, me too.

Suddenly, with a roar of cosmic proportions, the rain came, draining the moisture from the air and cooling it. A powerful gust of wind trembled the heavy boat, as if the whole country had sighed in relief and now looked toward the heavens for the annual washing away of the sins that the falling water of the monsoon would provide.

CHAPTER 19

I made it back to my place just as the eastern sky turned a dirty gray. My feet were like lead weights as I clumped up the stairs. The inside latch was off and I pushed the screen open to see a form rise from the hammock and come toward me.

I smelled her first, that sandalwood and spice scent, then she was in my arms, hugging me and murmuring words I didn't need to understand. We stood there, holding each other, for a long time.

Downstairs, Pen poured pan after pan of water over me but it did no good. I wanted a hot, needle-spray shower and clouds of billowing, cleansing steam to wash the fear stink from my skin, to clean away the sting of bile rising up my throat. I wanted to wipe the memory of the whole thing from my consciousness, but all I had was this cold water from a pan, so I used lots of soap instead.

Despite the shower, I felt hot, nervous and jittery. Two bong hits, usually enough to slide me into euphoric passivity, had no effect.

Pen saw the state I was in, and tried her best to interest me in a bout of hot sweaty love, but I couldn't stop thinking about those bullets flying around, and which one might have had my name on it. Had I escaped by pure dumb luck, or was it something else? I remembered what Pen had said about the moon, but there had been no moon, only rain and wind. I pushed the thought away, unwilling to speculate.

All I wanted to do for now was lie there, one arm flung over my eyes, and relive the whole horrible, scary scene. I comforted myself with the thought that now that I had enough to buy Pen's freedom, I didn't have to go out there again.

Lying next to me with her head on my shoulder, Pen laid a hand flat on my chest and flung a leg over me.

"Bob, t'ank you ver' much, *kop khun mahk*, you do for me." Her soft, full lips touched my collarbone and I turned to look at her. "No one ever do anys'ing same for me before, not my father, not mother, no one, ever."

A convulsive tremor shook her and she pulled herself on top of me. Her breasts and belly squashed warmly into my front and I felt the tickle of her bush on me and felt her sigh when I put my arms around her. Her almond-shaped eyes, shiny and moist, looked into mine, and she blinked once, twice, and pressed her face into the crook of my neck.

"Where's your daddy now?"

"I don' know," she replied, "him *bai lao* long time ago."

I felt her inner thighs on my waist as she squeezed the caps of my shoulders with her small, impossibly strong hands.

"I hear that. My mom left my father 'cause he couldn't give up the bars, racetracks and other women. He hauled ass somewhere, too. I barely remember him."

"When I fifteen year, my father sell me Chinese man *mee mahk baht*."

"No shit? Your daddy sold you to a rich Chinese?"

"*Mai go-hok, ching-ching*, one sister, too."

"Jeez! Takes all kinds, I guess. What'd your mother say about that?"

"What can? *Mai mee baht*, no food, no clothes, no have nothing. Have *song pooying*, sell, can do."

"Your parents had to sell two girls just to live?"

"No biggie, happen all time Thailand."

Her bottomless dark eyes were as calm and matter-of-fact as if we were discussing the rain that rattled on the tin roof as she nodded.

Raising herself onto her hands and knees, she dragged her chocolate kiss nipples over my chest and flicked her tongue over my lips. She felt me stir and laughed.

"Him woke now, *naa*?"

"*Chai-see*, he's comin' around."

Cooing and murmuring, she kissed my chest and trailed her satin tongue from my chin down my throat to my collarbone, and when her tongue snaked into my bellybutton I twitched heavily.

Rubbing her face in the light dusting of hair on my belly, she made me squirm with low, primal sounds of pleasure. A thought throbbed through me. Could this be it?

I'd been trying to get her to suck my cock from the first day, but she'd always found a way to get me between her legs instead.

My hands on her head, I very gently urged her down as my hips pumped involuntarily.

Reluctantly, she moved down and very lightly kissed the quivering head. It throbbed in anticipation.

"C'mon baby," I whispered, "kiss it for me, huh?"

Her lips, light as butterfly wings, fluttered over me for a tantalizing few seconds, then started back up. "Oh, *tilok*," I gasped, "suck it, come on."

"No can."

I held her head while I throbbed about, trying to keep her down there. "Suck it, come on…"

"*Maa-whey!*" She twisted loose and sprang away. "No can do!"

"Why not?" I had a new idea, and said slyly, "You like when I do for you, *naa*?"

She couldn't deny that. The first time I'd licked her between her legs she nearly broke my neck with her thighs.

She looked down at my vibrating readiness, then into my eyes.

"Buddha say no can, *tilok-cha*." Her hair flowed back and forth over her face like a stage curtain as she shook her head. As far as I could find out, Buddha had no opinion on the matter.

"Listen," I said, "I risked my fucking life for you last night, and now..." I watched her and waited. She said nothing, but pulled the sheet around herself and retreated to a far corner of the bed, where she watched me like a trapped animal looking for a chance to escape.

"You no suck my dick," I said, "you can go back to Bangkok and quick! I'll find another girl. Sattahip, Bangkok have plenty girls!" Crossing my arms over my chest, I waited.

Tears glittered in her eyes for a second, then spilled down her cheeks in twin trails of despair. I was ready for this, though, and steeled myself against the sobs.

"*Ching-ching*," I said, "*bai Bangkok, lao-lao!*"

"Why you do?" She wheedled between sobs. "Bhudda say, no can!" She snuck a look at me through that screen of pitch-black hair and didn't move.

"*Bai, lao!*" I barked with a wave of my hand.

She burst into tears. Sobs racked her slim body and her ribs appeared and disappeared as her chest heaved. I felt like I had just smashed something beautiful and delicate, something prized and valuable, and was just about to tell her to never mind, it was all right, that it didn't matter, when she snuck another look at me through her hair. My resolve came back on a flood of anger at her for trying these *tilok* tricks on me. Did she take me for a fool?

My chest felt like a steel band was slowly tightening around it and I stood up, wrapped a towel around myself, and went out onto the porch, where I lit a smoke and flopped into the hammock. The hootch creaked and groaned as I set the hammock to swinging.

Sometime later, I woke up and found myself on the bed. I couldn't remember how I got there, but the hard-on that throbbed and tingled didn't require any memory.

I felt a warm, tight envelope of sensation slide down over me and my hips twitched. I writhed about, intensely enjoying this warm pressure on my very stiff member and I reached up to open the shutter a bit to let in more light.

But then, suddenly, I was aware of another sensation on me, down near the root, one that was not so good. It felt like something hard and cool was sliding on me, it felt like...

I saw her crouched over me. Naked, her face contorted into a deranged mask I hardly recognized, she looked into my eyes. In one hand, she held my throbbing pride and joy. In the other, a long knife gleamed in the light. She was cutting my dick off!

Rage and fear collided, I bellowed a curse and, unable to believe she would do this to me, I swung at her as hard as I could.

With cat-like speed and grace, she avoided the blow and I heard her laughing. Now that she was away from my most prized possession, I looked at myself, afraid of what I might find.

Blood pumping in red geysers from the stub of my former erection, pushed by my own pounding heart. I could imagine how fast I would bleed to death, cut like that, but, there was no blood and I was still intact. What the hell was this?

I looked at her. She showed me the knife in her hand then, and mimicked what she had done. She had been running the top edge of the blade back and forth on my dick, playing a joke on me. She laughed, not her usual trilling musical sound of delight, but a low, heavy, dangerous sound of See what power I have over you?

"No butterfly, *naa*?" Her tone was mocking and serious at the same time. "I *kin kway* for you, you no butterfly, huh? *Mai-mee kway, mai-dai* butterfly, *naa*?"

So that was it. She was afraid of sucking my dick after I'd butter-flied. Well, what she said was true. If I didn't have a dick anymore, I couldn't butterfly.

That low, heavy laugh, laden with meaning, came from her again. Goose bumps jumped from my skin as I realized what she could have done at any time and relief that I was still whole turned to a surging, misty-red flood of anger.

"You bitch!" I snarled in rage, "You ever cut me, I'll kill you!" I trembled uncontrollably as I stared at her.

Pinpoints of light shimmered in her tousled hair. Her face changed, from playful amusement to maddened outrage in a heartbeat. Her wrist flicked in a blur.

. I felt more than saw it go by my head and I turned slowly. The knife handle quivered, the point imbedded deep in the wooden wall.

I turned back to her. Kneeling on the far end of the bed with one foot on the floor, she was balanced, poised, and ready for action, her dark eyes shining, muscles bunched and tight under her gorgeous skin. Her breasts rose and fell with her breathing, like a ground swell at sea reacting to a distant storm. Even though I'd been scared out of my wits and as mad as I'd ever been I thought she was the most beautiful creature I'd ever seen. I wanted her, badly.

"It been joke!" she said, her voice tight. "I no do to you. It been joke, I sorry!" It didn't sound or feel like a joke to me.

I saw a shadow in her eyes, as if she knew that we had entered a new stage in our relationship, and even though trust and affection could no longer be taken for granted, ours had been tested and hardened like steel in fire.

"No talk me that, Bob, " she almost spit, "No talk me bitch, no talk kill me, I don' like!"

A chilling flush swept over me. This was one serious and formidable woman, a woman who had survived, on her own for the most part, in a tough life where nothing was easy.

My anger suddenly vanished. I glanced away, then back to her. Her eyes were still hard as flint, but as I looked at her, they softened and her breathing slowed.

I flexed my hands and rubbed my thighs. "OK," I said and dragged in a deep breath. "No talk like that, I'm sorry, too, but, baby, I gotta tell ya', that scared the crap out o' me!"

Again I saw in my mind's eye a fountain of my own blood and an involuntary retch twisted me. I fell back onto the bed and, breathing deep, tried to calm myself.

I heard the snap of a Zippo lighter, the filter touched my lips while she held it for me a few times, then I heard the ashtray rattle as she stubbed it out.

A feathery touch, her fingertips on my chest, stomach, and the head of my dick. I felt her hair drape and brush me with tips soft as clouds as she worked what she knew.

Her tongue trailed a wet line below my bellybutton and I felt her breath on me, hot and damp. Tiny kisses, light, airy touches of her open mouth sliding around on my lower belly, closer and closer. I lay still and waited. She held me in her hand and her silken tongue slid over the head.

This was it. I knew it. Things started to happen now.

Her tongue licked a trail of liquid fire up the bottom of my shaft that flowed over the head into the warmest, wettest, most intimate satiny embrace I had ever felt.

I was no authority, the recipient of only one inexpert blowjob before, but this was beyond incredible and I had to see it.

Her long black hair flowed in waves around her face and her head moved up and down as I watched myself slide in and out of her mouth. One hand, red-tipped fingers spread for balance, rested on my stomach while the other cupped and squeezed my balls possessively.

With just a few minutes of this I was completely in her power, and she knew it. Tilting her head, she flipped her hair away, looked directly into my eyes and took me deep. I felt the pressure start to build and so did she.

"You like, huh?" Her eyes twinkled while she wrapped her hair around my shaft and jacked it.

"*Tilok*," I breathed, "I love it! Now I do you."

Ignoring her half-hearted protests, I rolled her onto her back, but before I could slide down her smooth body, she grabbed my head with an amazing strength, pulled me toward her and kissed me, her lips and tongue greedy and demanding.

Instantly, in some instinctual corner of my mind, I knew this was a test. If I hesitated for even a fraction of a second the closeness and intimacy we had gained here now would be irretrievably lost. I kissed her back and felt her hands swarm over me.

She broke loose and fell back with a gasp, needing more oxygen than her little bud of a nose could deliver. Sliding down her body, I licked her nipples and rubbed my face on the sensual curve of her smooth belly.

Her small, well-defined bush was a delicious tickle.

"Oh, *tilok*," she said as I urged her thighs apart, "*mai dai, naa?*" She didn't like me to gaze at her and one hand crept between her legs.

"You are so beautiful," I said to her. "I love to look at you." Very gently I pulled her hand away and stroked the amazing softness between her legs.

She stopped struggling. "*Sway, ching?*"

"Beautiful, really." I licked her thigh and felt her tremble.

"You are like a tropical flower," I whispered, "you know flower?"

"Yes," she murmured, her eyes glowing, "I know flower."

Right before my eyes her most delicate inner flesh erupted from her in softly convoluted whorls that blushed a luminous crimson and she opened like a night-blooming jasmine at the first hint of sundown.

I licked up her cleft. Her whole body convulsed and her legs splayed wider. I'd never seen anything like it, had never in my life experienced this. With trembling hands, I spread her open and watched as the iridescent pearl of her clitoris emerged.

"Oh, baby," I gasped out, "you are so gorgeous!"

A low groan from her sent waves of pleasure through me. I tried to remember the different techniques I'd heard about in barracks and crew quarters bragging sessions, but conscious thought left me and I simply immersed myself in her taste and scent.

Her body trembling, she clutched my head, then suddenly a new sensation, a new dimension, appeared. A silky, slippery warmth spilled from her. I pulled back to see a clear fluid bubble from her like an underground spring in the desert, then she pulled me close again and clamped her thighs around my head. Whimpering and moaning, she held me tightly while she shook and trembled to a peak that made her cry out for long seconds.

Slowly, her trembling thighs relaxed. I heard her labored breathing slow and looked up to see her eyes closed, her body sheened with perspiration.

A tremendous surge of pride and power rippled through me and when I licked her again she convulsed like she'd been shocked and grabbed me.

"Stop, *tilok,* stop, I no can…" She held me tightly and trailed off into gasping little breaths that made her tremble

as she pulled me up and guided me into her, "*lao-lao, naa?*"

Her voice seemed wrapped in a ragged urgency but she didn't need to ask for it fast because I was on the edge myself.

Holding her feet, I pushed her legs back and stroked it in and out while she gripped me with a convulsing frenzy that I'd never felt before. Her eyes glazed over, her belly twitched spasmodically and her head whipped from side to side as she begged me to pound her harder and faster.

In seconds my primer ignited and I fired into her just as her whole body went rigid. Eyes squinched shut, veins bulging and cords tight in her neck, she shouted out something that sounded like a plea, then we collapsed together into a gasping mass of quivering damp bodies.

We lay still for a long time before I slipped from her. When I opened my eyes, her face was very close and her eyes were open but barely focused.

"What you do me?" Her voice, dreamy and wondering, lilted.

"I think you've just had your very first orgasm, or two or three," I said with a grin. "I'm honored to be the one."

"I like, ver' much," she said shyly. Her eyes, darkly incandescent, looked into mine as her arms and legs squeezed me tight. Her eyes closed and her tongue came out to touch mine.

A wordless bond seemed to come over us then and I passed out wondering about it.

CHAPTER 20

I barely heard what sounded like Rick's voice shouting over the thrum of the generator and looked up. I couldn't see him or anyone and went back to slowly spreading white enamel paint on the engine room bulkhead.

"Hey, man, come outa' there, it's sixteen-thirty!"

This time I saw Rick leaning down into the engine room escape hatch, holding what looked like a wine bottle in his hand.

"C'mon," he yelled over the noise, "bong time!"

I laughed, dropped the paint brush into a bucket of diesel fuel and headed for the galley to wash my hands in the only warm water on the tug. Assembling a ham, turkey and Swiss cheese on wheat from the platter laid out and pouring a tall glass of iced tea, I headed for the boat deck.

Rick, Brett, Charlie, Donnie and two deckhands, Terry Something and I guy I didn't know at all were sitting in a circle on the side of the deck away from the port, so the stack was between us and the dock. In the center of the group, like an object of religious significance, a squatty wine bottle reposed.

"What're you guys doin'?" I asked around a mouthful of turkey and ham.

"We're gonna turn this big bottle into a kick-ass bong," Rick proclaimed. "Here's the bowl, all ready to go, all we gotta do is get it into the bottle somehow."

"Good luck," I said.

Rick reached behind him and picked up a drill motor with a small drill bit already in the chuck. "Right there."

His tone was half question and half statement and he blipped the trigger a few times. The drill spun with a raspy mechanical sound.

"You can't drill glass," I said and swigged iced tea.

"And why's that, smart guy?"

"Donnie, are you such an asshole naturally, or do you work at it?"

Donnie's beady little eyes grew brighter. "Maybe I should just kick your ass and be done with it," he said.

I had to laugh. "If you're feelin' so froggy, go ahead an' leap, ya' fat fuck."

"Knock it off," Charlie said. "Donnie, there's a grease trap with your name on it you don't shut up." Since he'd been promoted to bull oiler, a kind of straw boss of the engine room, Charlie had become very good at finding ways to get back at Donnie.

"So tell us, why can't we drill glass?" Brett always seemed to remember what the mission was.

"'Cause it's a crystal structure," I said. "It can't be cut, it shatters." Cramming a mouthful of meat, cheese and bread into my mouth, I shrugged and chewed.

"What about glass cutters, then?"

"Glass cutters don't really cut glass, they scratch a deep gouge into it, then you tap it and if you're lucky, it'll break along the scored line."

"OK, how do we make a hole in it?"

"You could maybe chip it out. Got anything sharp and heavy?"

Terry the deckhand went to the bos'n's locker and returned with a big marlin spike. Finished with the sandwich, I set to work, tapping the glass with the pointed end. Each tap knocked a chip loose and before long a hole broke though. Once the hold was made, it was easy to chip it out to the right oblong shape.

Rick inserted the bowl and stem, carved from a knuckle of bamboo the size of a thumb, six inches long, then dripped candle wax around the join.

"Ta-Da!" He held it up.

Water was added, the bowl was filled and Rick had the honor of first hit, since it had been his idea when he'd gone aboard a merchant ship to trade a bag of apples for whatever he could get. He returned with some steaks and that bottle.

"Here," Rick said to me, "you get the second bowl."

I held up a hand. "Pass," I said, "I got the late watch."

The bong went around several times and people's faces started to melt through their hands and everything became very funny. I thought I'd go check on the SHIELA.

In the corner of the port, I found the SHIELA up on her stands looking a lot better than when she'd arrived. Her white topsides, compounded and buffed, glowed with fresh wax. A local worker, and employee of the Batty Company, wielded a long-handled roller laden with dull red bottom paint

Brian himself was supervising the installation of the newly balanced and polished two-blade prop.

"Lookin' pretty good, Brian."

"Thankee, mate. Been goin' good. This jobbo woulda' taken me three months to do myself, but with help," he gestured at the locals, "it'll be done in just less than one."

"Goin' back in the water soon?"

He looked at me, his moustache twitching in the breeze. "Bet'cher backside, cobber. Gonna splash me beauty day after tomorrow. How 'bout it, mate, you up for a whacking great sail?"

"Hot damn, would I! Day after tomorrow, yeah, I'm off duty then!"

"Great! The Batty crane's gonna hoist her up about eight-thirty. Would you be wantin' to bring someone with you?" He laughed. "I thought so, I'll have a little bit o' crumpet along, too. I'm to pick her up, end o' the town pier at noon, day after tomorrow?"

"You bet! Man, this's so outstanding!" I took his offered hand and shook it. I could tell he was busy and didn't have time to talk, so I took my leave and went back to the tug.

Smoking a cigarette and reading in the galley, I didn't hear anyone come in.

"Hey, Bobby," Art's voice startled me. He was the only one who called me Bobby.

"What's up, Art?"

"Same bullshit, different day. Went up to the snack shack for a burger. Can't stomach that horsecock. Say, how's everything?"

I couldn't detect any lewd or salacious meaning in his words or tone, and he didn't seem to be making idle conversation, either. He returned my gaze, a question in his eyes, as if he really wanted an answer.

"Everything's good," I said cautiously, my senses on high alert.

"When was the last time you were at your pad?"

"Day before yesterday. Why?" My pulse jumped.

"Oh, probably nothing, but I saw that low-rent cowboy calls himself Duke coming out of the alley to your place yesterday."

"Brown hair, green eyes, looks like a Swede?" My heart thumped in my chest as I wondered what the hell he could be doing in Sattahip. Pen and I had taken the bus to Bangkok to pay him the rest of the money and I'd let him know, in no uncertain terms, that I didn't want to see him around. Now here he was. "You say anything to him?"

Art's broad coppery face was as unreadable as the desert he called home. "No," he said, "why would I do that?"

"I don't know, Art, why do you do anything? 'Cause there's an angle in it for you, that's why." I let my exasperation show.

"If I were thin-skinned that might insult me, but I'm not, and it doesn't, but what would you want me to say to him?"

"Nothin'," I said, "I don't need no one to speak for me."

He nodded and when he turned away, I caught a glimpse of his stainless steel knife in what looked like a worked leather scabbard worn on his belt.

"You been practicin' throwin' that Arkansas toothpick?"

He glanced at it. "No so much," he said. "I was always good at it, it was just a matter of getting used to this one."

I knew without a doubt that that was no idle brag.

"Listen," his manner changed slightly. "Are you up for another trip?"

"Another trip? Jesus Christ, Art! Wha'd'you think? I almost got fuckin' killed out there, and yer askin' if I wanna go back? What are you, freakin' crazy or what? Christ on a crutch! I don't believe you, man!"

I started to climb from the booth, but his hand on my shoulder stopped me. It was like being caught in a bear trap and I threw my arm up to break his grip. "Don't ever do that again."

"OK, sorry, but dig it. I'm not alone in this, there's other guys, too, guys who, well, let's just say they don't like to be told no."

I stared at him, unable to believe what I was hearing.

"Is that a threat?"

"Take it any way you like, but don't forget what I said."

He turned and started to walk away.

"And don't you forget this," I called after him. "You fuck with me I'll make you regret it, ya' hear?" He stopped and turned back.

"You know what a black flag means?" With an effort I controlled my voice, in spite of the adrenalin tremblies that were already starting to come on. "I'll tell you. It means you'll have a shitstorm on yer fuckin' head the likes of you never thought possible."

He gazed at me calmly, almost sadly, then turned and went up the ladder to the pilothouse.

Suddenly, I needed air. On the fantail, I smoked and paced, trying to work it out. What did Art mean, he wasn't alone? I couldn't imagine him letting anyone tell him what to do. Maybe, I thought, he's just trying to make it look like it isn't him putting this pressure on me. And what was Duke coming around my place for? I'd paid him off and he seemed to accept it, but now I wasn't so sure.

I went down into the crews quarters and tried to catch a few winks, but the shallow sleep I fell into was riddled with dreams of rain, bullets, and green-eyed local cowboys and I finally went topside and relieved Rick an hour early.

The rest of the watch, the next day and night dragged by like Father Time had his feet stuck in mud. I couldn't get Duke off my mind, and as soon as 0600 rolled around, I was the first one off the tug.

Arriving at my hootch, I bounded up the stairs and pushed the screen, but it was latched from the inside. After what seemed a lot of knocking, Pen shuffled sleepy-eyed out of the bedroom and unlatched it.

Entering the porch, I had a look around, not sure what I was looking for, maybe an ashtray full of butts not our brand, some men's clothes or shoes that weren't mine, all the things books and movies use for clues. There was nothing, but Pen noticed something was up right away.

"What?"

There was no use confronting her without something to back it up with, and I was so glad to see her that I pulled her close and kissed her. She kissed me back the way I liked, her tongue a quick surprise as I steered her into the bedroom.

Reaching under her sarong, I squeezed her ass and cupped one breast.

"Umm," I made a noise as I held two handfuls of her warmth. "Oh, you smell good!"

She laughed, a cute sexy chuckle, but when I tried to slip the knot of her sarong, she suddenly pulled away, jumped onto the bed and pulled the sheet up. I thought she was teasing me. When I flipped the sheet off though, she snatched it back, but not before I saw it.

There, on her thigh, obscenely purple and nasty against her butterscotch skin, like a sea slug on a china plate, lay a bruise the size of a plum. Twisting the sheet away from her, I looked at it while she squirmed. It appeared to throb with anger even as I watched it.

"How'd you get this?"

I looked at her, and for a fraction of a second, I saw something in her face. It was gone in an instant, but something had been there.

"It nothing. I hit…" She jerked her knee to indicate a rapid movement of her leg and pointed at the end of the bed. The corner post looked likely, but it was too low. That bruise was up on her thigh, on the inside, not the outside.

"Did you fall?"

"Yes," she said quickly, pulling the sheet over it. "*Mai pen lai,*" she said.

I shook my head, wondering. I knew about bruises. Boats are bruise factories and I had seen plenty and this one was a beaut. It had taken some force to create it, and it appeared to be a few days old.

I sat there, thinking. A couple of weeks ago she had had another bruise on her, this one on her upper right arm, and she had explained that one away, too, as being the result of her own clumsiness, claiming to have bumped into the door, and now this one, a few days old, right after my three-day work cycle.

"Has Duke been around here?"

"Duke? No, no see him, long time, him stay Bangkok, *laa*?"

"Someone told me Duke's been comin' around. Is that right?"

"*Mai,*" she said, "Duke no see, him…"

"Pen, don't lie to me!"

"Pen *mai lun*! I no lie! Why for I do?"

"I don't know," I said, "but…"

"Who tell you Duke come here?"

I saw no reason not to tell her. "Art told me yesterday that he'd seen Duke comin' out o' this alley."

"Maybe. Duke know many people, *mahk-mahk pooying, poochai.* Maybe he come Sattahip, biz'ness. Many *pooying* leave Bangkok, come Sattahip, *ching.*" Her dark eyes bored into mine as she nodded. I wanted to believe her and I think she could see it in my eyes.

"C'mon," she said as, she pulled me down onto the bed, "you work late, *naa*, yes, I know what you like now…"

I woke, hot, sticky, my throat parched, and stumbled out onto the porch. Pen reclined in the hammock, smoking and flipping through a fashion magazine published in Singapore.

"Pepsi in cooler, *laa*."

She'd already shopped for the day. Fishing an ice cold Pepsi from the cooler, I popped the top off and sucked it dry, all seven ounces of it, then gasped heavily. Damn, those things cut a thirst!

I always took my watch off when we made love and it was in the bedroom.

"What time is it?"

"I don' know, maybe 'leven?"

Eleven? Something nagged at the edge of my consciousness. I went in and picked up my watch from the nightstand and saw it was 1115 hours. Something, something….damn!

"Get dressed!" I yelled, "we gotta go!"

Pen dropped the magazine, startled at the yell. "*Bai?*"

"Yes, go now! We're gonna have us some fun today. We're goin' for a sail on Brian's boat!"

"Go on boat?" Pen's eyes, already huge, were getting bigger.

"Yeah, go on boat! C'mon, it'll be lots of fun!"

She protested but I ran downstairs, showered then ran back up and dressed as fast as I could.

Talking fast, I coaxed Pen into getting dressed and we hustled the few blocks through town. From the end of the small pier I could see the port, a mile and a half across the bay. Two tugs worked and strained to push a ship to the dock, diesel smoke puffing from their stacks. The two islands in the northern part of the bay, Ko Phra and Ko Tao Mo thrust green humps from blue water into a cerulean blue sky. The monsoon was taking a break today.

SHIELA, still a hundred yards away, approached the pier under power, a small creamy white wave at her bow.

"Ahoy, mate!" Brian hollered and waved. Standing in the cockpit and holding the tiller with one hand, he bent to the engine controls. Sitting on the cockpit seat, I saw a pooying, almost hidden under a big hat and very dark sunglasses.

A perfect landing on the pier just kissed the two fat fenders he had hung over and with a single line amidships he held the boat steady while I clambered down the rusted steel ladder bolted to the pier.

Turning, I reached up a hand for Pen, but she was already half-way down and dropped onto the deck beside me with a light, surefooted grace. Most women, unless they're very experienced, can't board a boat without a lot of fuss and bother.

"Good job," I said. Pen smiled indulgently and moved to the cockpit, claiming the space opposite the other girl. They exchanged a few words, probably of commiseration at the folly of us two crazy *felongs*, then Pen opened her bag and unfolded a hat as big as a manhole cover. I noted then that both girls were dressed almost exactly alike. They both wore long pants and long-sleeved shirts, big sunglasses and huge hats.

Obviously, they didn't want any sun on them. Brian wore only a pair of shorts while I wore cut off fatigues, a white T-shirt and army-issue sneakers.

Brian gave the pier a shove, pulled his line aboard and we were soon underway.

He introduced the girl, I did the same to Pen, and then I took a look around.

"Man," I said to Brian, "she sure looks good!"

He let loose that Aussie guffaw.

The deckhouse glowed under ten coats of spar varnish, the laid teak deck looked freshly scrubbed and the white fiberglass cabin top gleamed under a compound and wax job.

Stepping from the cabin top to the cockpit, I noted the teak grating on the cockpit sole. "You make that grating?"

"Nah," Brian replied, "I had one of our local boys do it. Good fit, hey?"

I spun a cushion into place and sat on it. Turning the tiller over to me, Brian prepared to raise sail.

"Gonna be a great day." Brian leaned into the halyard and the mainsail snaked up the mast, luffing in the light breeze as I held the bow into it.

"D'joo add these?" I admired the chrome Barient self-tailing primary winches.

"Oh, yeah, one of the first things I did. Makes single handing crackin' easier."

"I hear that," I replied. "My Uncle Jack has a thirty-seven foot Archer ketch, built in sixty-one, one of the last production woodies."

Brian nodded slowly and I saw his lips form an expression of approval.

As we motored-sailed out of the breakwater, Brian hauled up the striped genoa, set the halyard taut and returned to the cockpit.

"Hong Kong sails?"

"Oh, yah. Stock from the builder. I might crank up a suit of tanbarks later. Right then, cobber, fall off and let's reach toward that island, hey?"

I put the helm up and the sails filled with a satisfying whomp! Heeling to her lines, SHIELA began to glide ahead as I steered for the southern tip of Ko Khram Yai on a perfect beam reach. Brian killed the engine and in the sudden quiet, the only sounds were the gurgle of the bow wave and wake.

A gust whooshed over us. I fell off to gain speed. After so many months, it was good to feel a tiller in my hands again.

"Isn't this too freaking great?" I yelled to no one in particular. I glanced at Pen. Behind the big sunglasses her face was as immobile as the jungle-covered limestone hills around us.

"Ya' like this?"

"*Chai.*" Her voice was small and tentative, as if she didn't want to waste any energy in useless talk. I saw the death grip she had on the coaming then and the way her neck and shoulders seemed as taut as the stainless wire shrouds.

"Relax, Babe," I said, "we have attained Nirvana!"

The gust ended and I came up a little.

I noticed Brian watching me and all at once I became aware that I was Bogarting the tiller. After all that work, he must want to feel it himself, but it was considered bad form to ask for the helm.

"Here, Brian," I said, "you take it!"

With a wave and a laugh, he bade me stay there. "I wanna walkabout on deck and eyeball the rig. You keep it for awhile."

"Ya' don't hav'ta' ask me twice!" I hollered.

Brian made a complete circuit of the deck and his practiced gaze took in every detail. He adjusted a line here, scrutinized the set of the sail and tweaked the vang a little.

"Let's harden up, I wanna squint the mast, mate."

"Roger that," I said, and brought her up.

Brian cranked winches and soon we were hard on it, the apparent wind at fourteen knots, holding a steady heel angle of fifteen degrees.

Concentrating on the masthead fly and keeping her in the groove, I didn't pay much attention to Pen. Both girls sat there, silent and unmoving behind the carapace of sunglasses and hats.

Lying on the deck, Brian sighted up the mast, made a few notes on a pad, then we tacked the boat and he checked the mast again.

"Just a little off."

Plucking a tool roll from a coaming box, he tweaked and sighted, we tacked and he sighted and tweaked some more, until he was satisfied he was tuned as well as he could make it. "I'm glad you could come along, mate," he said. "This jobber goes so much easier with someone knows how to steer."

Slipping the tool roll away, he clapped his hands. "Who'se for a brew?"

"Twist my arm that's enough!" I said.

Brian laughed and ducked below, emerging with two bottles of beer and two squatty green bottles.

"The golden elixir, Fosters, for us," he said, handing me one, "and a bit o' ginger ale for the ladies, eh?"

Cautiously, I sipped the beer. Full-flavored and crisp, with no bitter aftertaste, it was light and thirst-quenching. I noticed it disappeared from Brian's bottle in no time.

"This's great beer," I said after a whacking great gulp.

"Best beer in the world," Brian said. I smiled. Everyone thinks their favorite is the best.

I noted Pen was merely sipping from the green bottle she held. "*Mai dee?*" I asked her. No good?

She shrugged. "OK," she replied.

"How you feel?" I asked her, "*Chep tenee, naa?*" I touched my own middle.

"*Mai.*" Her stomach didn't hurt. I was very glad to hear that because I planned to spend a lot of time on this boat if Brian would let me and I wanted her along.

Brian's girl chugged from her bottle and although she didn't say anything, she displayed all the signs. It was hard to see her color or expression, but she was very quiet, one hand holding her own middle.

We sailed for three hours, tacking to stay near the harbor, then about 1600, Brian announced that that was it for today.

He must have seen the disappointment on my face because he laughed again. "Don't you worry," he said, "there'll be plenty of days. The dry will start soon and we'll get some really great weather. There's an island," he waved behind him, "about twenty nautical miles nor'nor'east with the prettiest little cove you ever saw. Golden sand beaches, blue water, and deserted, too. This whole area 'round here," he threw a gesture all around, "and on up into the Bight of Bangkok, is dotted with beautiful islands just beggin' to be explored."

The wistfulness in his voice was as plain as the moustache on his face and I knew he was right. On runs to the 'Kok we passed many islands that appeared to be right out of a Robert Louis Stevenson novel. I'd never seen Ko Samet in the daylight, but I would bet it contained many golden sand beaches and green-shaded jungle pools.

Unknown to me then, a defining moment of my life, one that would shape me forever, would soon take place on a golden sand beach under the silver light of the full moon.

CHAPTER 21

A week later, after another afternoon sail, Brian laid the bombshell on me. His eldest son was in a Sydney hospital, suffering an unknown but serious ailment and was scheduled for tests.

"Oh, man, I'm so sorry..." was all I could think of to say.

"He's a tough kid," Brian said, "he'll pull through, but I want to be there. I leave tonight, fly out of Bangkok tomorrow." In his hand he held something that he gazed at.

"Listen, Cobber," he said and looked me in the eye. "Would you watch SHIELA for me? I don't know how long I'll be gone, but boats don't like to just sit, so if you'd use her some, I'd be obliged to you, mate. I watched you the other day and I know you'll take good care of her."

He held out his hand. The object was a cork float with two keys attached to it.

"Hatch and ignition," he said.

I took the keys and shook his proffered hand, recognizing the contract we were entering into was born of a kindred spirit, one that transcended the mere legal, and I was determined to live up to it. The timing couldn't have been better. I'd been in-country now long enough to be eligible for my own R&R and what could be better than five days spent exploring the emerald green islands and warm blue waters right outside our own front door?

When I told her the good news, Pen didn't see it that way.

"Come on," I said, "it'll be fantastic! We'll sail, swim, eat, drink and fuck on the beach!"

She looked at me and must have seen something.

"Can do," she said, "but firs', go see somebody, *naa*?"

"Who?"

She rattled off something in Thai, but I didn't catch it, my mind already planning for The Trip.

That night, lost in lists of chow and trying to familiarize myself with the boat, I didn't make it back to the hootch until nearly midnight and had a hard time dropping over the edge into the tender care of Morpheus, but about three I woke, shouting and shaking, with Pen stroking my face.

I tried to tell her about the dream, but she didn't know what a lighthouse was, so I drew a picture and explained.

"It was my job to light the flame," I said, "but I couldn't find my Zippo lighter. A storm came up. A white clipper ship sailed by, looking for safe harbor, but since the light wasn't lit, they hit the rocks. The ship broke up, everyone died."

She looked at me for a moment, her eyes calm and steady.

"You worry abou' sa'lboat, *chai-mai*? You worry som'sing bad happen it. You scare' you make mistake, boat go down." She pantomimed a sinking boat, her quick, lively hand perfectly imitating a sinking vessel.

She nodded, just a little. "I t'ink so."

In spite of myself, I had to admit what she said made sense. We laid down, she put her head on my shoulder and I marveled at how she could read me like that. I also wondered what else she could intuit from my dreams.

The next morning, we both stood naked in the bath while I poured pan after pan of water over her head. A shot of shampoo and I worked up a good lather on her head, then started rubbing it all over her. It had the predictable effect on me, but she was anxious for us to go some-where and rushed us through getting dressed.

We set out, I along for the walk mostly, enjoying the morning. Pen was dressed very conservatively in a cotton shirt and one of her many sarongs around her waist so that it fell to her ankles, with flips on her feet. I had on long tan pants, a loose white shirt and sandals. We sauntered along, in no hurry, past shops and stalls that were just starting to open.

Bunches of bananas hung like frozen chunky yellow waterfalls from beams and posts. Spiky jackfruit, mangoes, papayas and other fruits were piled up artfully, while plates and platters of fish, both whole and sliced were arranged in intricate patterns designed to catch a buyer's eyes.

Mama-sans, their betel nut-stained teeth black in laughing mouths, gossiped in doorways and small brown kids scampered about, their eyes bright with curiosity and wonder.

We passed through the center of Sattahip, near the bus station, and were moving down a side street when Pen stopped in front of an ornately carved red door, knocked lightly, and waited. I looked at the heavy wooden door. Solidly built, the frame was carved with an elabo-rate dragon motif and painted a burnished gold.

"What's this place?" I asked.

"*Feng-Shui* man," she said, watching me.

"What's that?"

"Him look you later, see you..." she waved her hands, as if pushing air away from her. "See you, later...Ah, don' know word. See later, you know?" She said it la-TER.

An idea came to me. "He sees the future?"

"Yes! Him see future, can do! See many t'ings, see *kwang-hai*, see..., about boat, the SHEILA..."

She broke off and rattled a stream of Thai in frustration. I shrugged. If she wanted to consult a fortune teller, that was fine by me. Don't knock it till you try it. I tried to keep an open mind.

The door opened, and a young girl ushered us into a large room, twenty by thirty feet or so. Her eyes down, she murmured a few words, then disappeared through another door. Pen stood there, waiting, biting her lip, her hands clasped in front of her.

This room continued the red and gold theme, but to an even greater extent. The vase in the corner, the small sofa, the table that held another vase, and a hutch against the wall were either gold or red or a combination of the two. A screen painting of a gold and green dragon chasing its tail stood in the corner, the colors so bright they almost jumped from the screen. The thick, cloying smell of incense hung in the air.

Another door opened. Pen went through it and motioned for me to follow. This room was smaller, only fifteen by twenty feet and at the far end, seated at an elaborately carved teak desk, an elderly Chinese man studied a chart that was spread before him. Long white hair hung straight from his tight-skinned skull. A mustache and wisp of beard sprouted from a lined, parchment-thin, gaunt face.

Each corner of the room held large earthenware jars with domed lids set on small tables. Bits of paper were stuck to the lids while around the bases of each were mosses, sticks and rocks, artfully arranged to mimic nature. Brass lamps and tall red candles provided a flickering light.

I started to say something, but Pen grabbed my arm and made shushing noises. I was about to argue, until I saw the look on her face. Those dark eyes were full of fear and respect. I kept my mouth shut and waited.

After several moments, the old man looked up and spoke. Pen translated, and asked me my birth date. Pen told him, and he consulted one of the many books on his desk.

After several seconds, he spoke to Pen again. I caught a few words, but most of it went over my head. Pen audibly gasped and turned to me, her eyes wide and wonder-struck.

"Him say, you are close to wind and water."

I was impressed, a little anyway. It wouldn't be hard to know who I was. This was a small town, after all, and there was only one sailboat in the whole harbor. It was probably common knowledge who sailed on it.

Again, he consulted his books and charts and stroked Chinese characters onto a piece of thick, heavy paper with a deft, quick hand that was perfectly controlled, without a hint of waver or shake.

I was getting tired of standing there and started to wonder about a place to sit down when the old man looked up and pinned me with a stare. I stared back.

In a low voice I could barely hear, he spoke directly to me, but I understood none of it. When I turned to Pen for an explanation, her expression nearly knocked me out. She stood there, her lips opened slightly, eyes wide, not breathing, pale under her butterscotch color.

The old man uttered a long stream of words, and these had a calming effect on her. She visibly relaxed, and started breathing again.

She made a very deep *wai*, gave him some money, and hustled us out.

Back in the bright sunshine, we walked down the street. Everything seemed normal. Birds twittered, insects buzzed, children laughed, people shopped and gossiped.

Stopping at a sidewalk cafe we had a Pepsi and a smoke.

"What'd the old guy say?"

"*Feng Shui* man," she said sternly, "him say you been sa'lboat man long time."

I nodded, pleased, glad my lifelong association with boats showed in my spirit, or whatever the old man had looked at. I thought Uncle Jack would be pleased, too.

"He tell me som'sing about you, ah, what you say, you later?"

"You mean the future?" I repeated for her.

"*Chai*! Future! Him say, someone want do you bad t'ing, some numba ten *poochai*!" The intensity of her expression made me look closely at her. Her dark eyes, bright and searing, seemed to look into my very core.

"You mean someone's lookin' to do me in?"

"Him don' know, some man, no like you, you check-check, *loo-mai*?"

"Yeah," I said, wondering if the old man was tossing in some grief just to round things out, "I'll be careful, *ching*."

"Him tell me too," she continued, "you no die in water. You no die in boat." Relief seemed to pour from her eyes over this bit of fortune-telling, and it stirred me in a way that I wasn't entirely comfortable with, but I didn't know what bothered me about it, only that she appeared to really believe in what had just happened. I knew I wouldn't die in a boat. It wasn't my karma, I could feel it.

As I sat there in the shade, I flashed back to the day we'd found the body of the Thai paratrooper who had died in a night jump into water. It occurred to me that he probably didn't think it was his karma to die in the water, either.

CHAPTER 22

"OK," I said, "I think we're about ready."

I thought she was bringing way too much stuff but kept it to myself. Better to let her find out herself.

"You remember what time?"

The look she gave me said much more than her simple reply of "Yes, I rem'ber."

"All right then. I'm on my way. See ya' then."

She puckered up for a good-bye kiss and I was surprised at the intensity of it. Jeez, I thought, I'm only going back to the port to get the SHIELA and bring her to the town pier, where Pen would be waiting.

My driver, our regular guy, waited downstairs and I picked up Pen's duffel, a big make-up bag that I'd tried to tell her she wouldn't need but she insisted on bringing anyway, and another bag of miscellaneous stuff.

For the ten minute drive from my hootch to the port, I went over mental lists. Fuel and water, check. Ice, check. Beer and soda, check. Groceries, check.

Several weeks ago Brett had found the spare key to the tug's freezer that the thieving cook had hidden. Inside, we'd found cases of steaks, chops, roasts and seafood and ice cream we were never served for chow. Cook was undoubtedly wheeling and dealing. I liberated several steaks and a slab of pork chops and put them in the reefer aboard SHIELA where they would slowly defrost and be ready for the grill.

From the tugs pantry I helped myself to several cans of green beans and corn, boxes of crackers, cheese, cookies and fruit, all the necessities of eating well on a six day tropical cruise. Brian kept some dry goods like rice, beans and boxes of Aussie pasta aboard, too.

When I boarded the SHIELA, my own pulse beat a fast rhythm against my eardrums, but the familiar ritual of getting under way soothed me and by the time I dropped the line to the mooring, I was serene.

Approaching the town wharf, I saw Pen. The light breeze fluttered her hat brim and her loose clothes rippled like a flag. The sight of her sent a wave of pleasure through me.

Up into the wind, I placed the boat right next to the wharf, Pen tossed her bag to me then dropped lightly on deck, using the shrouds as handholds. I let the wind blow us off the pier, gave her a shot of throttle and we were off, bound for the narrow northern passage out of the Bay of Sattahip.

"Good job gettin' aboard, babe," I told her.

She smiled and settled into the port forward corner of the cockpit. Flattery and compliments are powerful spirit-raisers and can make an uncomfortable or even reluctant crew feel better.

"*Cha, monee*," I said, making the palm-down motions for "come here".

"I wanna teach you to steer." I pointed at the tiller.

Her face became stiff. "*Mai ow*," she declared.

For safety's sake it's important for her to know how to steer and it would also free me up to handle the sails and other deck work.

"Well, I want you to. Come on," I cajoled her, "it's easy, lemme show you."

Reluctantly, she moved over next to me and for the next half hour we worked on getting her familiar with the tiller and throttle, showed her what "fall off" and "head up" meant, and had her bring the boat up into the wind. She picked it up quickly.

"Good, *dee mahk*!" I said, rubbing her shoulders. "You *mahk simong pooying*!"

Telling her she was a smart girl gave her confidence and she turned her head to plant a quick kiss on my cheek.

We passed Ko Tao Mo to port and headed out into the Bight of Bangkok. A small swell increased our motion.

"I'm gonna raise sail now. Bring it up," I said.

With a firm and decisive motion, she put the tiller over and brought the bow up into the wind. I heard the engine as she nudged the throttle open a little more and was pleased.

I raised the main and genny, winched the halyards taut, and looked at her. "OK," I said, "just like I showed you now, fall off."

Her pink tongue just peeking from her lips, Pen put the tiller up, the bow fell off and I sheeted in. As the boat heeled and accelerated, the force of the wind was palpable and thrilling.

Shutting down the engine, I grinned at her. "You have it," I said, "you're the captain." The grin on her face lifted my spirit.

She kept it for a while then asked me to take over, which I gladly did.

Settled into the leeward corner of the cockpit, I steered with one foot and pulled her to me. We sailed on a close reach in the perfect conditions of bright sun with sparkling seas lightly textured by the warm breeze. The northeast monsoon was ending and the humidity was down some. Our latitude was almost the same as the Caribbean and the nearby islands were a handful of green gems scattered across the cobalt blue ocean.

Tying off the tiller with the lazy sheet, I tinkered with sail trim and had the boat steering herself. Grabbing a beer for me and a Pepsi for her, I returned to the cockpit and settled back against the cushions. This was perfect sailing and I was in heaven.

After a while, Pen glanced behind us. "*Maa-whey!*" she said, "*Sattahip bai-nai?*"

I laughed. "The town didn't go anywhere," I said, "we've sailed a ways out. Sattahip's that way." I pointed and with the binoculars was able to make out the range finders for the approach to the port.

She had those huge sunglasses on and I couldn't see her eyes, but I felt her stiffen up. Maybe, I thought, it would be a good time to tack and head for the first nights destination, the cove on the northwest corner of Ko Khram Yai.

The boat was well-mannered and easily single-handed, so I just let Pen relax and tacked it myself.

"It's so beautiful out here!" I said.

"Ver' nice," she agreed, but I think she was keeping something inside.

Late that afternoon, I rounded up into the wind and dropped the anchor in a pretty blue cove surrounded by a picture postcard scene of golden sand beach and parallels of slanted palm trees. Sparking up the BBQ, I cooked up a nice boat dinner for two of baked potatoes, corn on the cob and grilled steaks, that we ate in the cockpit. Pen couldn't believe how much she put away.

After dinner, we washed the dishes then sat in the cockpit, watched the stars and listened to Armed Forces Radio. It wasn't long before the sound and motion of the water, the food, the beer and the stress of the day caught up with us. I turned to say something to Pen and saw her eyes were closed.

My last thought, before I crashed too, was to tell myself how lucky I was.

The next day, I woke at dawn, refreshed and ready. A quick swim, a breakfast of some leftover steak cooked up with eggs and hash browns, and it was time for a walk on the beach.

The foot pump had the small inflatable dink up and ready in minutes. We climbed in, I took up the little plastic oars and paddled twenty yards to the beach. Wearing nothing but a pair of shorts, I welcomed the morning sun, but Pen had a different idea. She avoided the sun and hid under hats and long sleeves. She thought I was crazy foreigner for liking the sun since it was her ambition to be as pale as possible. She didn't believe me when I told her I loved her skin color.

The cove was almost a perfect U shape, with the eastern side twice as long as the western. Beyond the eastern headland, I could see the ocean wrinkling in the building breeze while here in the cove the water was calm. Sheila's mast barely moved. I dragged my bare feet through the warm golden sand.

Up ahead, a clump of palm cast a deep pool of shadow over the beach. A blanket on the sand and a fallen palm bole provided the perfect lounging area to have one of the beers I'd brought in an insulated bag of ice.

"You know," I said, sipping the brew, "I used to lie awake at night and dream of stuff like this." I waved the bottle around at the cove and beach.

"Good breezes, a tropical beach, warm water, golden sand, a good boat, and…" I looked at her. The shade was dark. I took off my sunglasses, then reached over and removed her hat and glasses. "…and a beautiful island girl to share it with. You wanna be my beautiful island girl?"

Her smile blossomed so wide that for the first time, I saw a tiny dimple in her cheek.

"*Chai-mahk*," she said, "I wan' be you *sway mahk pooying*!" She snuggled close and sipped from my beer.

"A guy could get used to this," I said. "Plenty of fish in the sea, fruit in the trees. Rice is cheap. It could be done, all right." I nodded my own emphasis and pulled a long drink.

I droned on about it, then she sat up and turned to look at me. She put out a hand, cupped my cheek and trailed her fingertips along my jaw. It left a tingling track of sensation that I could feel spread out, down my neck and through my shoulder, to trickle out over the rest of my body.

"So," I said, "are you havin' fun yet?"

"Yes," she said, and pulled the pin from her hair, spilling it down around her shoulders. She looked at me and smiled.

I touched that dimple and she grabbed my finger and kissed it. "You talk a lot when you happy."

"No I don't," I said, embarrassed somehow.

"Yes," she replied, "you do. You talk a lot. I like hear you talk, say any'sing, I don' care." With her head on my shoulder, her fingers tangled in the hair on my chest.

"Go 'head, say som'sing, I wan' hear you talk."

Pen would say almost the same thing to me many times in our time together and I was thrilled to think that here was a woman who just liked the sound of my voice.

"I want you to be my beautiful island girl," I said. She shifted to look into my eyes for an instant before her eyes closed and her lips captured mine.

The next day, we headed out of there and sailed to the next island, Ko Phai, fifteen nautical miles nor'nor'west. A warm fourteen knot wind sighed over the port quarter. The striped genny, round and sensuous as Pen's butt, pulled the boat straight and true through the water.

I heard Pen shriek, a spontaneous sound of delight and scampering to the bow, she knelt down into the pulpit to gaze at the water. I knew immediately what it was

We were surrounded by a huge pod of dolphin. Pen squealed as one made a long leap, then another and another, and when several of them came in close, jumping and blowing, to ride our bow wave, Pen almost came completely unglued. I grabbed my camera from a coaming box.

Squealing and laughing, clapping her hands, she stayed there long enough for me to get several shots of her and the friendly mammals.

I had an idea. It was a little devious, but not mean-spirited. I'd tried to get her to take her clothes off before, but out of modesty, insecurity and fear of the sun, she had refused. It was late afternoon now, the sun lower in the sky, and besides us, there wasn't a person for miles.

"You know what they like?" I asked her.

"*Ali?*" She didn't look at me, but waved and clapped her hands like a child.

"They like it when you take off your clothes."

She looked at me then, doubt and suspicion plain on her face, but I saw the maybe there, too.

"*Go-hoke mahk*," she said matter-of-factly.

"No," I replied, "*mai go-hoke*, no bullshit. They can tell, they like it." I nodded as earnestly as I could and still keep a straight face.

Her adult common sense was cracking and the child in her wanted to believe. "*Ching-ching*, huh?"

"Yes," I said, "*Ching-ching*. What for I bullshit?"

I could see she was considering it, then in a blink of an eye she made up her mind. She pulled her shirt off over her head, hesitated briefly, then dropped her long pants and stepped out of them. Apprehension and belief fought for dominance.

Right on cue, two of the bigger ones swooped in close, their dark rubbery bodies gleaming. They seemed to roll over slightly and stare up at her and their permanent grins made her laugh.

"Look, look, *Cha*, they check me!"

All inhibition was gone now and she forgot her fears of the boat and its motion. Holding to the pulpit, she leaned far over to laugh and wave for fifteen more minutes, then, as quickly as they had appeared, the dolphins were gone.

"*Bai nai?*" Pen demanded.

"They must have found some food or something. Don't worry," I said, feeling like I was comforting a kid, "we'll see 'em again, today, tomorrow, some time."

She seemed to accept that their appearance was a gift from Mother Nature and their disappearance shouldn't be regarded as something taken away.

Climbing up onto the top rail of the pulpit, Pen leaned back onto the forestay and put her hands over her head to hang on. The yellow light of the late afternoon sun lit her blowing hair and fired it into a dusky halo and burnished her butterscotch skin to a glow like it had been hand rubbed. Dark nipples taut and breasts thrust forward, her legs spread for balance, she unconsciously rode the motion of the boat now as if she had been born to it.

After many minutes of staring, I was finally able to scoop my jaw off the deck, get into position and take some pictures.

Too soon, we scooted into the cove at Ko Phai and the anchor went down. Thirty feet down, I could see it bite the sand bottom.

"C'mon," I said, plucking a coil of line from the stern rail, "I wanna get a line to a tree ashore. I'll race ya', you go first."

Pen eyes lit up at the challenge. She stepped over the lifeline, set herself on the gunnel, then executed a perfect dive off the boat. She surfaced, pushing her hair from her face.

"Come on," she said, "what you wait?"

She struck out in a strong, even stroke that pulled her quickly through the water. I watched her legs flex and bunch and her ass work for a minute, then tied the line around my waist and dove in after her.

I was a good swimmer, good enough for competition if I'd had the discipline and I thought I'd catch her easily. Very soon, I realized I might be wrong. I gave it everything I had, to no avail. That beautiful dive of hers should have told me something.

When I stumbled onto the beach and caught sight of her, I just had to stare. She stood there, legs slightly apart, shoulders back and hips thrust forward as she squeezed the water from her hair. Her breasts rose and fell as she caught her breath and the sun lit each drop of water as it rolled down her body and fell to the sand.

I noticed then that her tits seemed fuller, rounder than ever and her nipples even more taut and prominent than before. Her hips, butt and smooth belly seemed to have taken on a depth of flesh that I'd never seen. Must be the heat and sunlight, I thought. Every time I turned around, she looked more gorgeous than ever.

"Where'd you learn to swim so well?"

"I don' know." With her hands over her head tying up her hair, her tits swung and trembled. "I like swim." She said it SWEEM.

I whipped a bowline around a tree trunk then went and took her in my arms. We hugged wetly, kissed a little, but when I started to get serious, she pulled away.

"Let's go boat, take shower."

On the way back she swam slowly, lazily, her arms and legs caramel flashes in the sun. Climbing up the stern ladder she waved off my helping hand and came over the rail like a naked pirate princess streaming saltwater. On board SHEILA, we dumped buckets of fresh water over each other.

"No need to get dressed," I said, "there's no one here."

After a nervous glance around, Pen agreed and sat on the cushion while I rigged the sun awning. That done, I sat down with a beer.

I almost had to pinch myself. I'm living a dream with her, I told myself. I realized that I didn't want this to end and, even more shocking to me, I realized that time was a thief of our happiness as my rotation home date sped closer and closer.

I went below, brought out the Zenith short-wave and found Armed Forces Radio. The Beatles were asking about love, wanting to know if it would grow. If you would only stick around, it might, but there were no guarantees, they sang. A strange and eerie feeling swept over me then and as the guitar cried and moaned out its confusion I asked myself the same question.

The song ended. War news was next. I didn't want news of any kind intruding now and I spun the dial. Thai music spilled from the speaker but I passed it by, all the way to end of the dial, through all the local stations without hearing anything of interest, then started back down the dial.

"Bob *Cha*," Pen said, "check *nit, naa?*" Swiftly, she spun the dial back and with a cry of delight, found something.

The Bangkok Blues

A thin, quavering voice floated from the speaker like a wisp of fog. Thai or Chinese music, clinking bells, screechy strings, an eastern rhythm. Closing her eyes, Pen seemed to hum along with it.

I picked up a book, opened it, and started to read, but the words on the page swam together in an impossible jumble. An idea kept banging around inside my head.

I lit a cigarette and tried to read again. I read the same paragraph four times and still didn't know what it said. That thought in my head just wouldn't go away, but I blamed my lack of concentration on that tinny music.

"Can you turn..."

Her expression stopped me cold. Pain, despair, longing and suffering etched her face and it was so intense that I stared at her, never having seen such emotion before. She appeared on the edge of tears, and I was mesmerized by the power of it.

When the song was over, Pen caught my eye and smiled. She perked up, but a quiver of emotion trembled her full lips and she couldn't hold that smile and before she turned away, I watched it crack apart. Had I imagined that look, those quivering lips, the longing in her eyes? Even turned away, there was no mistaking it when she wiped a tear away.

"What's the matter?" I asked.

Her long hair shimmered.

"Nothing," she said, "song make me sad *nit-noy, loo-mai*?"

I understood she could be a little sad, all right. Music can bring tears to the eye, and anyone who denies it has never really been in love, or never really listened. The fact that a song on the radio could move her so made my heart go out to her. It scared me and made me glad, all at the same time.

That same idea popped into my head again, the one I had turned on the radio to get away from. I was amazed that such ideas would occur to me. I thought about it, became lost in it, so lost, in fact, that Pen asked me what I was thinking.

"Nothin'," I said. I avoided her eye as I watched her move to the cooler for a Pepsi. Her naked body rippled in the light.

What the hell was I thinking, I asked myself.

Standing, she rubbed the cold bottle over the back of her neck and across her forehead, down her throat and over her breasts. I watched them swing and sway and that thought jumped into my mind again and suddenly, I knew she was watching me intently.

Quickly, I turned and pretended to gaze at the scene of blue sky and water, golden sand and green jungle. It could have been a Monet painting, but I saw none of it. Could I really do it? Could I really take her back to the world with me?

Charlie's pitiful face, contorted by heartache as he tried so desperately to get off the tug and check on his *tilok*, swam before me. Was that my future? The thought made me shudder.

What was actually wrong with it, anyway, besides the social criticism and the scorn and derision that would surely come my way.

So she had known men. OK, lots of men. Did that make her a less desirable person, less honest, less giving, less concerned with making me happy? I didn't think so, if only I could get over the fact that I was falling for a hooker!

I turned back and looked right into her eyes and as I watched I saw the cloud roll across her face. She knew something was up and that it might not be good for her. Was she going to be dumped or loved even more?

"What you t'ink abou'?" she asked, trying hard for a light tone.

"How would you like to come to the United States?"

God, had I said that? I couldn't believe it. Still, it was a once in a lifetime offer for a girl in her position. Go to the US? Who would pass up such an offer to get out of this bug-infested, hot, humid, stinking poverty-stricken country?

I watched her, expecting the rushing intake of breath, the glad, wild rain of kisses she would pour on me as she joyfully accepted. OK, I thought, you can accept any time now. Come on, any time. She said nothing and wouldn't meet my eye.

Suddenly, I couldn't tell up from down, left from right, black from white and in a whirl of conflicting emotions, I waited.

"Well?"

Her gaze fell on me. I put my hand flat on her belly, moved up and cupped a breast. Slowly, she disengaged my hand from her, then moved to the far end of the cockpit and crossed her arms over her breast.

"You ask me, marry you?" She sounded dubious, vulnerable and tough at the same time, as if she did and didn't want to hear the answer.

It struck me that that would indeed be what I was doing. What did I think, that I could just put her on the big bird to the world and we could get a place and live happily ever after, like it was still in Thailand? Doubts and worries have no place in a lover's world, but this wasn't only a lover's world, it was the real world butting in.

The army seriously discouraged GIs from marrying locals and placed a mountain of paperwork, red tape, bureaucratic screw-ups, earnest and sincere talks from the appropriate clergy and everything else they could think of in front of you as obstacles to be overcome. Most guys simply gave up in the face of it, and that was the plan.

I looked at her, started to answer and hesitated for a fraction of a second. That was all it took. She knew. It occurred to me then, a girl as gorgeous as she was, she had probably been in this situation before.

With a toss of her head that set her hair to glittering, she said, "No want go United States. Why I go? My frien' here, my fam'ly here…"

Was she really turning me down, or was this a test? I didn't know. Confusion reigned.

"Why you do this?" She asked as she pulled a towel around herself. "You no wan' marry me, I know. We happy now, yes? You go United States, have American girl, no want Pen no more. I no want go United States."

Gazing off at the horizon, she went on, "I know biz'ness girl, my frien', she marry GI, go United States. Him fam'ly no like, she been biz'ness girl. She no happy, no frien', no fam'ly, want come back Thailand, no can do, too much money." An emphatic shake of her head summed up her argument.

I couldn't believe it. She turned me down! Hurt, mad, embarrassed, I started to say something that would hurt her back, something that would put me back on top, when she looked at me, her eyes brimming.

"Bob," she said, "we have good thing, huh? We been *tiloks*, long time now, yes? No talk United States, can do? I am biz'ness girl, I know." Her voice, sad and resigned, was a soft cutting lash across my heart.

That was a line she used a lot, as if in the act of defining herself as a "biz'ness girl" she negated the need to discuss anything further, as if, Why bother? I'm only a "biz'ness girl".

When I started to protest, she quickly put two fingers over my lips. "No talk now, can do?"

I kissed those fingers and didn't say anything, but my mind raced with alternatives. I wouldn't give up this easy. Maybe she was just a "biz'ness girl", but what you know is not the same as what you feel. I felt I would die without her.

For four days we sailed from one island to another and rarely saw another human being. An occasional ship, bound for Bangkok or the deepwater port at Sattahip, reminded us that a war was going on but they were too far away to seem real.

We rarely wore clothes and while I turned a little browner, Pen stayed the same smooth butterscotch color all over. She liked to go up to the bow, hold to the headstay, stand on the pulpit with her hair flying and feel the warm wind lave her naked body. If dolphins appeared, she cried out with the delight of a six year old.

For our last night, we returned to the cove at Ko Phai, the most isolated and our favorite. For dinner we wore a type of very wide, loose silk pants that were wrapped and tied around the hips. Pen tied a vaporous square of blue silk around herself that criss-crossed and cradled her breasts. The effect was even more alluring than total nudity.

I caught a five pound snapper and cooked it in a wire rack over a dying driftwood fire.

Lying on the blanket on the beach, a folded towel and a piece of driftwood for a pillow, I stoked up the fire a little, we had a bong hit and watched the moon rise. I swore I could see moonbeams shine through the water like cosmic rays, then it popped over the horizon and rose into the heavens like an orange celestial lantern.

Awe and wonder that I was in exactly the right time and place to see it, and had someone to share it with rolled over me. As the bottom edge cleared the horizon, Pen leaned over, blew her sweet spicy breath in my face and laid a kiss on me.

"A moonkiss for you an' me, *Tilok-cha*," she said and held up her amulet for me to see.

I hugged her close.

She laid her head on my shoulder. "I love moon," she said in a dreamy voice. "I wan' go there, with you. No cowboys, no numba ten GI, only you and me, can do, *naa*?" She followed this with a rapid stream of Thai, one that I knew wasn't said to me.

At this time the Apollo missions were capturing imaginations all over the world with moon landings, but I didn't think Pen was concerned with that. She wanted to get away from here, now.

"What did you say?" I asked her.

She cut a quick glance at me, giggled like a small girl, and said, "I ask man-in-moon, what happy?" She said it hap-PY. "He know, can tell me, happy, yes or no?"

It bothered me a little, her having to ask the man-in-the-moon if she was happy or not. After all, I did my best to make her happy, but what did I know, and why didn't she want to go to the world with me?

This girl confused and confounded me and I felt like I was running through thick, clingy mud every time I thought about it.

Pen rummaged in the bag and handed me my camera.

"Take picture," she said and skipped to the water's edge, where she pranced and posed with the moon, its spangled trail and the anchored boat in the background like a lonely sailor's postcard dreams.

I quickly shot several frames with an electronic flash, then turned the flash off, opened the lens all the way, slowed the shutter speed and shot several frames of her illuminated by the moon and firelight while she posed.

When I ran out of film she came and laid down beside me again.

"I been you island girl, *naa?*" Her voice, a barometer of her emotions and feelings, was a low tremolo now. A change of some kind was coming.

"You are my *su-sway mach island pooying tilok-cha, ching-ching mai go-hoke*, and I never want this to end!"

She sighed and snuggled closer.

After the flaming shootdown of her coming to the world with me, I had been examining alternatives and decided if I couldn't take Pen back with me, I would come back here.

This was a sailor's paradise and I could be happy here with her for a very long time. There were hundred of islands around here and we could spend years exploring them all, then, after that, there was Australia, Honk Kong, the South Pacific! Tahiti, Bora-Bora, Moorea, Tonga and Fiji! Thousands of tropical islands in warm, tropical seas and steady trade winds, all just waiting for the two of us to see them together.

If she would go for it, that is. I decided to keep this plan to myself for now. I wanted every detail worked out so there could be no possible objection.

All that talk of hot, humid, stinking country before, well, that was just talk, used to justify the moment.

Lost in these thoughts, I snapped back when Pen said, "*Tilok*, I wan' tell you story, can?"

"A story about what?"

"Abou' Thai people, long time ago, many year, OK?"

"Like a folk tale, a legend, like that?"

"Thailand, many year go by, OK?"

"Yeah," I said, "great. I like folk tales and stuff."

"Story abou' a *naga*, you know *naga*?"

"No," I said.

"It..it...I don' know, how you say..." With a driftwood twig she drew in the sand, a long sinewy shape of a snake, with huge eyes and wings.

"A magic serpent?"

"Yes!"

Sitting on the blanket, she began her tale.

"There been man, *mai-mee baht*, but have *tilok su-sway mahk*." In the firelight her eyes came alive with the telling of the tale of the poor man with the beautiful wife.

"The king, him numba ten, want man's *tilok*," she paused, looked to see if I understood, then went on.

"The king, him tell the man, have fight, uh, *gai, loo-mai*?" She made clucking noises and her expressive hands moved together as if they were fighting. She looked like a folk dancer dancing out the tale.

"*Gai*," she repeated and clucked again. Then I got it. *Gai* meant chicken. A cockfight! The king and the man would each field a cock. I nodded, and she went on.

"Man win, he be king, if he lose, him give wife to king." I listened intently, hooked on the passion and intense emotions that are the basis of most folk tales. Themes of good versus evil, and what people will do for love transcend race, creed and religion and become universal.

"They have fight. Man win, but king say, do more t'ings, hard t'ings. Fight with buffalo, elephant, but man, he win, king ver' mad, *mee moho mahk*." She giggled, clearly enjoying the triumph of the good and simple man over the evil king.

I laughed a little, too. The king was getting pissed because his buffalo and elephants were getting their asses kicked.

"King say, have boat race." Pen pointed at the SHEILA, lying serenely to her anchor amid a spangled silver trail of moonlight. My interest rose a notch.

"The man, he no have boat, can not find anywhere, him ver', what you say?" and she put her hands on both sides of her head and shook it back and forth, making noises, wringing her hands, and it came to me.

"Man worried, *naa*?"

"*Chai-see*, worry *mahk*. OK, day of race, a *naga* come, make himself into boat for the man. Race start, king's boat ver' fast," she zoomed her hand in front of her, "but *naga*-boat fast, too. King's boat turn over, him die, man win race, him be king, live long time with *sway-mach tilok*, be good king, because *naga* help him."

I cheered the win of the noble and decent commoner over the vile and treacherous king with a drink of beer and a round of applause. Surely, I thought, there must have been more to it than that, but Pen had probably told me a simplified version of it. She beamed and took a bow.

"Great story, *Tilok*." I said. I thought she might be trying to tell me something, to prepare me for some kind of contest or showdown and I looked for parallels to our own situation.

Later, I would come to regret that I didn't think longer and harder about it, but right then her hand slithered down my belly, slipped inside the silk pants and squeezed me in a loving, familiar embrace.

"Do you have a *naga* of your own, to look out for you?"

"You my *naga*, yes?" She looked into my eyes.

"I'll look out for you, I promise."

She kissed me, hot and urgent, trailed her satin tongue down my chest and belly and as she took me into her mouth I pulled her hair up and let it slip and slide over me.

"Man," I said to myself, "you are one lucky sailor-boy and that's a fact!"

While I watched her hair ripple in the light, she sucked me voraciously. Since the day she'd fired the knife into the wall it seemed she couldn't get enough. I watched as her mouth took me in, felt the ring at the back of her throat open as she breathed through her nose, then she rubbed her nose in my hair. The vibrations of her moaning made me see stars, and not the ones scattered like jewels on velvet above us. Telling the tale of the *naga* had really turned her on.

Opening my eyes, I saw she was on her hands and knees, still working me. With one had full of her hanging tit, I pulled her closer and stroked the damp, soft heat between her legs with the other. She twitched, popped me from her mouth and turned the rounded cheeks of her ass toward me.

I knew what she wanted and moving into place, I stroked her hips and thighs while she quivered to a series of tiny explosions that went off deep inside her. In the silver and gold light of the moon and fire, her smoothly rippled spine was like a range of low hills. Placing myself at her jade gate, I whispered to her how much she turned me on.

Spreading her elbows like wings, she dropped her shoulders to the blanket and lifted her butt, twin mounds of tenderness hungry for sensation. I smacked one cheek smartly.

"Oh, *Tilok*," she breathed, "I want!"

With a long sigh, she covered her face with her hair, her signal she was ready. Holding her hips, I slowly but firmly entered her warm, moist center and pushed it to the hilt. Holding her to me for a five-count, I pulled back until she barely held me, then plunged back in, found my stroke and started to bang her.

"Harder, *Tilok*."

Taking a new purchase on her hips, I slammed into her harder. I could see the shockwave of our meeting run through her cheeks and up her back. Small grunts and gasps burst softly from her.

"*Dee*," she said, her voice muffled by the blanket, "*dee mahk*."

At first I'd been reluctant to pump her that hard, but she asked, then demanded that I do her as hard as I could, as if she wanted to show me that she could take all I could give her.

I pounded her for a dozen strokes and watched her hair ripple with the force of it. Spreading her knees, she pushed back against me and I whipped it to her just as hard and as fast as I was able, until she started to gasp out loud.

Position change. I fell away and separated from her to lie on my back. Quickly, she scrambled up to straddle me. In the firelight her skin, sheened with effort, glistened like melted caramel.

Reaching between us, she held me in place for a tantalizing moment before she sank down to impale herself on me. With her eyes closed and her head back, she purred out her pleasure and I thought of the Rolling Stones lyric about the Siamese cat of a girl being the best pet in the world.

"I love being here with you," I said as she leaned forward to rub her nipples on me. I caught one and pulled it into my mouth. I'd never seen or felt them like this before, so achingly stiff and swollen.

Gripping her hips, I pulled her forward and smacked her ass. She squealed and wiggled and with each slap on her butt, her moans became longer and deeper and her breathing became ragged, urgent gulps of breath.

With her upper arms she pushed her tits together and shoved them both into my face. Working a nipple into each eye, I pressed her to me, then spread her boobs apart with my hands and let them swing back to softly plop against my face, again and again, while she twitched and moaned. Her tits were definitely bigger, heavier and firmer, I thought.

"I love you touch me, *Tilok-cha*." Her voice was a tearing whisper as I licked and sucked her.

Pushing them together, I licked both nipples at once. They stiffened even more, a powerful shudder racked her and amid the soft crackling of the fire I heard her gasp.

Carefully, I took both of her swollen nipples into my mouth at once and gently bit them. Her belly jumped and I felt a hot trickle on me. She felt it too.

"What you do?" she whispered, eyes wide and wondering.

"This," I answered, and again pushed her breasts together and lightly scraped my teeth over them. Her whole body convulsed as a flood of liquid heat gushed from her.

The fire, reflected in her eyes, seemed to be inside her and I pulled her to me, sucked and bit her a little harder.

Fluid burst from her in a hot torrent that poured over my balls. Her eyes were wide and staring into mine and her face was taut and strained as she suddenly jumped into a squat and rode me.

Holding her hips in both hands, I met her every downward thrust with a frantic push of my own and we locked into a wet, flesh-slapping rhythm that pushed moans and gasps from both of us.

Suddenly, she ground herself onto me, held it for a second while she sucked in a breath through her teeth, then her demanding body took over and she trembled under multiple powerful spasms that she was powerless to control.

She nearly always cried a little when she came, but this time she threw her head back and howled, a long feral scream of ecstasy that knocked me over the edge and I felt my own shuddering expansion erupt as she greedily pulled it from me.

"Yes, *Tilok*, yes!" Tendons stood out in her neck as she screamed out her need in the night.

More spasms shook her, one after another in a rolling series that slowly became smaller and less intense until finally, with a last gasp, she collapsed on top of me. The only sounds were the swish and slap of small waves on the beach, the faint crackle of the fire and our labored breathing.

We stayed like that for a long time. I thought she might have passed out, but when I turned my head a bit, I saw her eyes were open, gazing into mine. Her tongue came out to lick inside my upper lip.

"You eyes *sway mahk*," she whispered.

"Your eyes are beautiful, too, *Tilok-cha*." The endearment sounded natural and right. "That was really incredible! How you do that?"

"I don' know," she said, "I no do before." Her gaze, dreamy and languid, drifted from me then came back and locked with mine again.

Her smile was slow and sweet. "Good, huh?"

I stroked her hips and thighs, brushed her lips with mine, kissed her closed eyes. "The best, the very best, my beautiful Island Girl. I love you."

Her thighs squeezed me once, then she slowly rolled off and collapsed beside me on the blanket.

Tomorrow I would tell her of all my plans for our future together. I shivered with the unexpected joy of it all.

I thought I heard something then, a sound that seemed so out of place I thought I must be hearing things.

I raised my head to listen, and was just about to call it to her attention, when I felt her body shudder, and realized, with a deep shock, that it was her crying.

I was ready to swim oceans, to dive into volcanoes, jump canyons for her if she asked me to, if it would keep us together.

"*Cha*," I said softly, "what's the matter?"

Playfully, I jiggled her cheeks, hoping she was really laughing, but knowing that it wasn't so.

Sitting up, she drew her knees to her chest, wrapped her arms around her legs, looked at me with tearful eyes, and bawled.

This was not the reaction I had hoped for after such a truly wonderful piece of lovemaking. Great wrenching sobs shook her. Cracks appeared in my fantasy bubble as I wondered what could be so wrong.

"What's the matter?"

A fresh round of tears fell but her hand found and squeezed mine.

Gradually, the tears and sniffles stopped, she took a deep breath, wiped her eyes and looked at me. "Buddha say, no want nos'sing, have much happiness, want som'sing ver' bad, have much hurt you heart, *loo-mai*?"

What the hell was this, more words of wisdom? Bhudda always seemed to have something to say that fucked up my plans. It seemed like another example of religion dropping a damper on the human experience. I'd always thought the pagan Polynesians or the American Indians had the right attitude. Worship those things that were close and needful in everyday life, like the earth, the sun, moon, stars, wind, water, and letting the animal that is man live a peaceful, happy, sensuous life, free of guilt over some offense to God, Bhudda or whoever.

Pen still rocked back and forth, her arms around her knees, the tear tracks on her cheeks bright trails of unhappiness in the moonlight.

I couldn't understand it. What was there to be unhappy about? We had just had the most profoundly lovely joining of our mutual flesh and spirits that we had ever had, and this was just the beginning, I was sure of it.

"You not happy?" I asked her, as I slid my fingertips along her thigh.

"Yes," she said, very low, so low I had to lean forward to hear. "I ver' happy with you. I love you *mahk-mahk*, maybe too much!"

Her hand closed over mine, stilling it. Bringing it to her lips, she kissed my fingertips, one at a time.

Her eyes, huge and dark and filled with an undecipherable longing, slowly closed, her long lashes falling down like curtains on the last act.

"*Mai pen lai*," she said, the Thai answer to all of life's difficult, nagging, troubling questions.

I would have given anything then to know what she had asked the man-in-the-moon, and what his reply had been.

CHAPTER 23

The next day, after an early morning swim, we left Ko Phai at 0800 and motored for three hours on a rhumb line course that would take us west of Ko Kram Yai. The southwest wind came up, settled at twelve knots and we had a great five hour sail through shimmering seas and around green islands, arriving at Sattahip Bay at 1600 hours.

Pen kept a smile on and seemed to be having a good time, but last night I'd awakened about three. She wasn't in the bunk with me and I slipped on deck to find her sitting on the cabin top, gazing at the moon that hung like a lantern in the sky.

I watched her for several minutes before slipping back into the bunk and when I woke at dawn, she was asleep beside me, murmuring in her sleep.

Approaching the northern entrance of Sattahip Bay, I glanced at her as she sat in the cockpit, watching the green line of the shore approach.

"What's the matter, Babe?" I asked her.

"Nothing the matter." The smile she flashed didn't reach her eyes, but opening her shirt, she flashed her boobs and shook them for me. I laughed, she kissed me, quick and fiery, then settled against the cockpit coaming again. Very soon, that haunted look returned and stole the joy from her eyes once more.

Maybe she was just tired after a week on the boat. I wondered if I should tell her about my plans now, but decided against it, wanting the details in place before I said anything.

Dropping Pen at the town wharf, I motored the SHEILA back across the bay to the Batty dock and just before I finished cleaning up, Brett came by.

"D'ja' have a good time?"

"Man," I said, looking him in the eye for emphasis, "if I was to dial up a fantasy cruise, that woulda' been it. It was perfection on a stick. I don't know what could have made it better."

"That good, huh?" Flicking an invisible speck from his custom tailored belled and cuffed pants, he pulled the leg up a bit, propped a multi-colored thick-soled shoe on a bollard and asked, "Heard what happened?"

I looked at him. He looked back calmly, his wavy brown hair just lifting in the breeze.

"What?"

"Art's been busted, man. CID got him at his pad, early yesterday morning."

My stomach rose into my throat and I couldn't breath.

"Yeah?"

Brett nodded and popped out two perfect smoke rings that the afternoon sea breeze quickly shredded.

"What'd they get him for?"

Brett shrugged. "I don' know exactly, but he had a dozen angles goin', coulda' been any one of 'em."

Flicking the butt away, Brett gazed off across the wind-dappled water.

"Seen anything of that 'Kok hustler, Duke?"

Brett's gaze slid across the bay to the town, then came back to me. "No," he said, "he's a punk, but check this…"

Extracting another cigarette from the pack in his pocket, he placed it in the corner of his mouth and said, "Ever heard of a GI named Burke," he asked, "hangs out in shitkicker Patpong bar called Tumbleweeds?"

"Can't say I ever did, why?"

"That Matt guy, the burn-out from Nam, you know the one?"

I nodded that I did while my stomach pulled down into a hard knot.

"He came around, askin' about you, where you was, like that, mentioned Burke's name once, like it was supposed to mean somethin'."

"Who is this Burke, anyway?"

"Another Nam AWOL, livin' underground in the Kok. This guy is bad news, man, with a capital B. Runs a bunch of other AWOLs like his own little crew. Black marketeering, stealing from the army, smuggling, like that."

It came to me then. "That must be what Art meant when he said he wasn't alone in this. Burke, huh? I'll hafta remember that name. Say, how come you know all this, anyway?"

Brett grinned. "I must have a real friendly face," he said, "people just come up to me an' tell me things, ya' know?"

I guffawed. "You kill me," I said.

"Careful what you say out loud, man."

Brett was too cynical to be superstitious and I couldn't tell if he was kidding or not, but before I could ask him about it, he waved, said he had to catch the water taxi and hustled off.

I snapped the heavy brass padlock into the cabin hasp, caught a deuce'n'a'half to the port gate and shared a cab to town. By now it was dark and I ran down the graveled alley and up my stairs with my heart pounding, visions of blood and mayhem filling my head. Knocking the screen back, I burst in, ready to flatten anyone I came across.

Pen nearly fell out of the hammock.

"*Maa-whey*," she barked, her eyes hot, "what you..." She looked at me and stopped. "Bob," she said, "what matter?"

I sagged into a chair, weak with relief she was still here.

Dropping the magazine, she swiftly rose and came to me.

"What?" she said again. Her inquiring gaze swept over me and her hands felt my arms, looking for what, I don't know, blood maybe.

"You OK?" I asked her.

"I fine," she said. "What matter you?"

I glanced through the open bedroom door. "No one here?" For some reason, I went to the screen and latched it on the inside.

"No body," she said. Her eyes grew brighter as she watched me. "*Tilok-cha*, what problem?"

"Nothin'," I said. I felt my heart slowing down. "I heard...nothin', forget it, OK? It was nothing. I..."

The knock on the door startled me. I'd heard nothing on the stairs.

"Who is it?" I demanded in a hard tone.

"It's me," said a voice. I looked at Pen. Her face, pale and drawn, seemed to contract around eyes that were suddenly flat and lifeless.

"Who the fuck is it?" I was in no mood for games.

"It's me, Art. Open the door, man, I don't like standing out here."

What the hell was he doing here?

"Come on, man, I need to talk to you."

His voice was full of bonhomie, but it sounded slightly off, with a hurried quality that made me wonder.

I started to tell him to get lost, but Pen put her hand on my arm and completely surprised me by saying we should at least talk to him! In a stunned silence, my mind whirling, I snicked off the latch and opened the door.

Art sauntered boldly in and right behind him came someone else. I felt a flush rise and every hair I had stuck straight out at the sight of that Fu-Manchu moustache under a hooked nose. The thin, unshaven face had a deaths head quality to it but what made the tingle run all the way down to my ass was his bright, predatory eyes. I looked at Art.

"What'd'you guys want?"

"Hey, Bobby, what's the haps? Have a good time messing about on those islands?"

"Nice place," the deaths head remarked as his dark eyes took everything in.

I looked at him. "Who the fuck're you?" I had a gut feeling I already knew the answer.

His shadowy gaze fell on me like a range finder.

"Bob," Art said, "this's Burke. Burke, meet Bob, boat driver extraordinaire."

He didn't offer to shake and neither did I.

"I heard CID busted you," I said to Art.

"I was guest of theirs for a little while, then I left."

"How'd you manage that?"

He shrugged, but Burke laughed. "Faked havin' a fit in the lock-up, then clocked that red-headed stepchild of a CID cop then strolled out. My buddy Art can think on his feet." He put a hand on Art's shoulder and squeezed. Art tolerated it for a second, then moved away. A look passed between them then and I knew they'd had arguments about something. Art didn't want to be known as Burke's buddy.

Burke turned his attention to Pen. He grinned. Without a word, she rose from the hammock and went into the bedroom. I thought she'd stay in there, but she came right back and slipped into the hammock. I noticed she kept her feet on the floor.

Burke said something to her in what sounded like Vietnamese. She glanced at him for a second. Her softly sensuous face became a carved hardwood mask and her eyes were like two black buttons. She turned away without a reply.

"Is that any way to treat your friends?" Burke asked her.

She ignored him.

Suddenly, I found myself right in front of Burke, right up in his face.

"I asked you nice once," I said, "and you spoke to my ol' lady instead of me. Now, what the fuck you want here?"

He tried to look around me at Pen but I moved to block his view. I suddenly wished I had on my heavy boots instead of these lightweight sandals.

Burke looked me up and down. "Back the fuck off," he said very low.

I feinted with a right and stepped sideways to hook him with a left to the belly, but Art had a jump and caught me so fast my actions looked like nothing more than a nervous twitch.

"OK," Art said with a laugh as he gently but very forcefully pulled me away. "Here's the deal. Burke and I," he nodded to Burke, "want to talk a little business. We're getting' another run out to the island ready and we need a driver again. You…"

"What are you guys, fuckin' stupid or what?" Adrenalin kicked in and I felt almost giddy, but Art kept an iron grip on my arm.

"Yer not too fucking clever your own goddamned self."

Burke spoke matter-of-factly but the edge in his voice was clear.

"What the fuck…"

I tried to jerk away, but Art was just too strong.

"Easy, man!" he whispered fiercely in my ear and gave me a little shake. There would be no way I would get loose from him until he was ready, so I took a deep breath and tried to calm myself. Uncle Jack always said an angry fighter is a beaten fighter. Keep your head and look for opportunities.

"Look," I said to Art. "Let go of me, goddamnit!"

He did, and I resisted the impulse to rub my arm.

"I told you guys I ain't interested. I got a good thing goin' here and I don't wanna fuck it up. Get someone else."

I couldn't understand why they were so insistent on me doing this. They could have got a local guy for peanuts. There had to be something else in it, and I was convinced that I didn't want any part of it.

I was about to tell Art just that when I noticed Burke. Kneeling down, he spoke to Pen in a low, insistent voice. She wouldn't look at him and then, very slowly, he reached out, took her jaw in his hand and turned her head toward him. She tried to jerk away, but he gripped her harder, forced her head around and put his face very close to hers. I couldn't make out the words, only a low, savage rumble and I was moving before I was even aware of it.

"Hey motherfucker!" I yelled. "Take your filthy paws..."

That Art was fast. Twice now he had intercepted me and I'm not slow, but like a good linebacker, he could read the offense and put himself in the right place at the right time. He held me tight, my arms behind me, elbows cocked, and it was like being held by a bear. I could not move.

Still holding her jaw, Burke spoke to Pen, then he stopped and very deliberately his tongue came out, shockingly pink amid all that black hair and stubble, and licked her cheek and eye.

Quick as a blink, Pen had that flick knife out and laid the open blade against his carotid artery. Her eyes burned a hole in him.

"Let me go," she said tightly.

For a long second, nothing happened, then I heard it. So did Pen and we saw it at the same time. In his right hand Burke held a slim black automatic pistol. With exaggerated care, he pressed the muzzle against her forehead. I twitched hard and Art's grip on me tightened.

"What's it gonna be, bitch?"

I was convinced he wanted her to try something so he could pull that trigger. I held my breath.

Slowly, Pen moved the knife away, then flipped it so it stuck in the floor. Burke straightened up, keeping the pistol pointed at her, then he laughed, a short maniacal hoot, and decocked the pistol. It disappeared.

"You're a smart girl," he said, all traces of the laugh gone now, "a number one business girl, so don't fuck up."

He turned to Art. "Alright, Artemis, let's *di-di* on out o' here."

Slowly, Art let me go while Burke grinned at me. "Hang loose," he said, jerked the screen open and went out. Art started to follow.

"Art!"

Art stopped and looked at me like he knew exactly what I was going to say. He was right.

"What was he sayin' to her?"

Art glanced back and forth between Pen and me. His big shoulders rippled in a shrug under his loose shirt.

"Ask her," he said and went to the door.

"Wait!" I just had to know something else.

He stopped and looked at me.

"What was that about old friends, then?"

He must have seen something in my face because he laughed, a real, genuine laugh.

"Don't worry," he said, "I was never a customer of hers, neither was Burke, but dig this. Back when you two first got together, Duke didn't want to sell her debt to you, so I leaned on him a little and to sweeten the deal, I told him to double the price." He shrugged again.

"No big deal," he continued, "but listen, don't ever throw down on Burke unless you're willing to go all the way, because he is. Don't forget it."

I turned to Pen in the hammock. She looked up at me. Her eyes, darkly luminous like she was willing herself not to spill tears, seemed to reach out and grab my soul. She had never looked so beautiful, so desirable, or so vulnerable as right then, and I wanted to gather her in my arms and squeeze her, hold her, whisper things to her and tell her everything was OK, but all I said was, "Is that true?"

In Thailand, the truth is whatever you want it to be at that moment, and the past and the future are transcendental things that only matter if you let them.

She didn't turn away or even blink. She nodded yes. My heart fought with my mind for control. I wanted to believe her and looking at her I felt like I could dive into those eyes and knew then that whatever had happened in the past was in the past and didn't matter any more. Tears slipped down her cheeks and I felt the breath flow out of me like a dam bursting.

Art coughed, a reminder that he was still here.

"Listen here," I said. I looked him in the eye so there would be no mistake. "I ain't gonna do what you're askin', and that's final. Don't come around here no more, you got it?"

Art looked at me hard. If he forced me, I'd back up every word I said, no matter the cost, and I think he knew it.

"You are making a big mistake, my man," he said and lit a cigarette. He took a long, slow defiant drag on it. Smoke dribbled out his nostrils and rose sluggishly to swirl around his head in shifting, nebulous patterns, then he jabbed the cigarette into the ashtray with tremendous force, crushing it into a pile of torn paper and shredded bits of tobacco.

Turning on his heel, he jerked the screen open by the crossbar, pulled the screen loose from the frame, then stomped down the stairs.

Still in the hammock, Pen watched me, her eyes shining as I went to her. Leaning down, I pulled the knife from the floor and held it up to the light.

"Would you have, really?"

"*Chai-see.*" Her emphatic, affirmative reply was instantaneous and I had no doubts she meant it.

Closing the knife, I tossed it onto the table, where it clattered to a stop against a shopping basket.

"Pen, tell me what Burke was saying to you before."

"*Mai pen lai,* him crazy GI, I don' know what he want." she said and started to tug my shirt off over my head.

"No *mai pen lai*!" I burst out. "Not this time! Tell me!"

"Bob," she said, very slowly. Her black hair rippled as she shook her head and took a deep breath. She paused for a moment as if she were making a decision.

"Him tell me talk you," she said, "do job for him. I say *mai dai,* no can, you *mai ow,* no want, I can not tell you. He say, he hurt my mother I no do. I ver' mad, say I kill him, and do with knife, you see?"

I nodded but I could hardly believe it.

"Why's he want me? There must be some locals who can handle that boat. Why me?"

"I don' know," she said, "him do gun, you see?" She pantomimed the way Burke had held the gun to her head.

"No t'ink abou' numba ten GI," she said. I allowed her to pull my shirt off. "T'ink abou' you, me." Pulling me to her, she kissed me hard then tried to get my pants loose.

"No!" I pushed her away.

She turned her head away and I saw her shoulders shake. "*Tilok* no wan' me no more?" A single shining tear slid down her cheek.

Insects found their way inside the broken screen to whine and buzz around the light. The small green lizards quickly appeared to take advantage of the bounty, darting back and forth in a flurry of miniature strikes. They rarely missed.

I wondered if they ever got enough, if they ever just stopped hunting and feeding, or if, driven by nature, they prowled and struck and gorged until they died of too much, the victims of their own skill and instincts.

"Come on now," she said and pulled me into the bedroom. She whipped her shirt off and pushed me down on the bed. I allowed her to pull my pants off.

"Is this your answer to everything?" I asked sarcastically. "*Mai pen lai,* everything OK, let's fuck, is that it?"

For an answer she dropped her sarong, flung herself on me, mashed her tits on my chest and planted her lips on mine. Her tongue, strong and mobile, snaked into my mouth.

Keyed as I was, when she kissed me like that...

"Make love now, talk later, can do?"

Before I could answer, she swooped down, pulled the head into her mouth and tugged on it strongly.

I tried to resist, I really did, but then she slid a wet kiss up and down the bottom of the lengthening shaft, raked those ruby red nails along my sides and took me deep into her throat. I forgot about Burke, Art, everything. This room, and us in it, was all that mattered.

She sucked me until I was achingly stiff, then had me bite her nipples until she splashed. Dropping her shoulders to the bed, she lifted her ass in the air.

"Come on *Tilok-cha*," she said, the words muffled into the coverlet. "Come on now, do for me, *naa*? I want."

Her whole gorgeous body writhed and twitched as she looked at me with one eye through the curtain of her hair. She had me and she knew it.

Moving into place behind her I slapped her ass, one good smack on each cheek, enough to leave a glowing red hand print on her. She yelped and wriggled her butt. Panting, she urged me to hurry and once at her gate I shoved it into her already dripping twat.

Holding her hips, I set myself and went at her hard. We'll see who has who, I thought. She started to moan, spread her knees wider and lifted her ass. I gave it all I had and the silky smooth evidence of her arousal poured from her.

All my anxiety, all my frustrations and all my insecurities bubbled up and I jetted stream after stream into her just as she reached her own crashing, bone-bending peak. We shook that hootch until its beams creaked like a square-rigger in a hurricane and her moans and howls floated out into the darkness, until we collapsed into a heap and slid around on each others damp skin until the fan dried the moisture from our spent bodies.

"See," she said, "I tell you, make love now, talk later." When I groaned my agreement she purred in satisfaction and cocked her hips to keep me inside her.

"I never want this to end."

The conviction in my own voice startled me, but I knew I was right. No *tilok* trick on earth could fake the splash of love and I wanted hers for me for all the time I had left on this earth.

A silent squeeze brought an answer in kind. My R&R was up tomorrow at 0600. I would tell her everything, how much I loved her and wanted her always, all of my plans for our future together, everything, when I saw her next, in two days.

It never occurred to me that Pen might have be working her own plan. I saw her life as an endless series of symbiotic relationships like ours had started out to be and had assumed her happiness depended on me. Though often they see, fools never comprehend.

Chapter 24

"Shit, man, let's go!"

Rick looked sideways at me, flicked the Pall-Mall butt into the swirling brown river and tossed coffee dregs after it.

"Take it easy, man," he said mildly, "gotta wait for slack water. The moon's nearly full, flood tide's too strong…"

"Screw that!" I said and tossed cup and all into the Chao Phraya River.

"You'll be gettin' it wet pretty soon…"

"That ain't it, man." I took a deep breath to calm myself.

"What is it, then?"

"I dunno."

"What'd they say at HQ?"

"No dice. Can't prove Bangkok was my home before I was drafted. I'll…"

"What's that about Bangkok bein' home?"

Brett perched his lean frame on a gear locker and sipped iced tea.

"Bob here's tryin' to get his army discharge in the 'Kok," Rick said, "but it ain't happenin."

"That right?" Brett's lackadaisical demeanor perked up a tad. "You that short?"

"I'm down to two digits and thought I'd get the paperwork started, but they won't go for it. Seems…"

"Pen's got your cap wide open, huh?"

Brett's deadpan manner was devoid of any leering smirk.

"I got plans for the two of us," I said, chain-lit another smoke and flicked the butt away.

"Those plans include that sailboat?" Rick asked.

"Or one like it. I figure I could find one in Hong Kong, Darwin or even Sydney. I think I could get a job with BattyCo an' Sattahip's a perfect base for sailin' this area. Cost of livin's low, my ETS pay would see us for a year, even with takin' discharge back in the world."

On the river, traffic moved rapidly upstream and slowly down, the colors of the ships and boats bright under a high sun. Across the river, the jungle drew a thin green line between the brown river and the blue sky. Popcorn clouds marched in from the southwest and the air was soft and as dry as it ever would be.

"Guess who came aboard last night on my watch?"

Rick's eyes became very big as he turned to look at me.

"Who?"

"Our ol' buddy Art Delaplane."

"He came aboard?" Even Brett was impressed by this display of brass.

I nodded and pointed at the deck. "Right here. Hell, man," I said, "he was at my hootch the night before we left Sattahip. He's got a car or motorcycle stashed somewhere, they way he gets around."

"Pretty fuckin' bold for an AWOL!"

"What'd he want?"

"Wha'does Art always want?"

"To make a deal," we all said in unison and laughed.

"The fucker's still after me to drive that fishin' boat out to Ko Samet again, and check this," I said to Brett, "he had that dude Burke with him. Man, that is one scary-lookin' motherfucker! Pulled a piece on us."

"No shit?" Brett and Rick both said, their eyes big and wondering.

"No shit."

"You better watch your ass, man! Goddamn! Right in your hootch?"

"Yeah," I said. "He was talkin' some shit to Pen. She said he threatened to hurt her mama-san if she didn't get me to do that job for him. She pulled a pigsticker on him, one o' those butterfly jobs, and he stuck a little black automatic in her face."

"Ya' know," Brett said slowly as his eyes took on a shine, "there's gotta be another reason."

"I don't know what'd be. I've lost fuckin' sleep over it, man, and can't…"

The GQ bell clanged, everyone to stations for getting under way. Through the engine room skylight, I heard the telegraph rattle its message, Stand By Main Engine.

"All right!" I dropped down the starboard ladder to the main deck and ran around the deckhouse and down to the engine room. I had the first engine watch.

Before the tug even touched the dock in Sattahip, I leaped ashore and caught the last water taxi across the bay to the town wharf.

Moving swiftly up the alley, I looked up at the waxing moon as it gilded scraps of cloud with a pale silvery light. Turning the last corner, I looked around. Alarm rippled up and down my spine and goose bumps sprang out all over me. Not a single light showed. Overhead, palm fronds rattled and whispered amongst themselves and the silver-edged leaves of the banyan tree shimmered in the warm land breeze.

At the bottom of the stairs, I looked up. My stomach lurched. The screen, always closed against mosquitoes, stood open. Slowly, carefully, keeping to the edges, I climbed the stairs. Pausing at the top, I listened but heard nothing, no stereo, no sounds of any kind.

"Pen!" I whispered.

Reaching inside, I found the light switch, flipped it. The dark that resulted was overpowering in it's dread. Sweat popped despite the dry air.

Enough moonlight light leaked in through the screens so that I could tell the place hadn't been trashed. The hammock still hung in the corner, the table and chairs were neatly arranged and at the sideboard, I checked and found that the cash I kept on hand was still there. I put it in my pocket.

"Pen!" I said it out loud and felt the alarm turning to anger at her for going off and leaving like this. She knew I was due back today. It occurred to me that she might be mad that I was late and had gone to a girlfriend's, but I dismissed that right away. She wasn't like that.

The bedroom knob turned easily and I pushed the door back. The window shutters were open and moonlight, filtered through a cloud, fell onto the bed. Dimly, I saw the form there and breathed a sigh of relief. She must have dozed off waiting for me. Leaving the light off, I sat on the bed.

"How ya' doin'?" I asked in a low voice in case she had awakened.

I became aware of a peculiar smell and sniffed, but this country was full of powerful odors and I thought nothing of it.

When she didn't respond I guessed she might be a little sulky. I found her foot and shook it.

"Hey," I said, "sorry I'm late, the flood tide held us up."

Her warm butter soft skin felt strange, cool and almost rubbery.

Leaning back to kick off my sandals my right hand dropped to the bed. What's this? I rubbed my fingers together, sniffed. Something cool and clammy, slick, sticky and black in the moonlight.

I jumped up and hit the light switch by the door. The fluorescent tubes strobed once and lit the scene for a split second. Dense black shadows and harsh white highlights were like a news photograph. My stomach clenched. The light strobed again. My heart jumped into my throat as the after-image burned into my eyes, then the light caught and held. I stood there, paralyzed with shock, unable to breathe.

In the frosty white light Pen lay naked, spread eagled on the bed, a knife hilt-deep in her chest.

Blood had flowed thickly down her body, split by the soft pillow of her right breast. Some flowed down her body to pool in her bellybutton, then spilled onto the bed. I could see where I had put my hand down in it.

Her pubic hair was a dark smudge on her butterscotch skin and her chocolate kiss nipples were now flat and dull. I don't know how long I stood and stared, unable to get my mind around this horrible scene.

The smell hit me again, stronger now that I knew what it was. With a jolt, I saw that the knife was hers, the one she had pressed to Burke's throat that night.

I tried to look away but a force pulled me closer and locked my gaze on her. There was something different about her, something missing, but I couldn't put my finger on it.

Faintly at first, then suddenly brighter as the cloud moved away from the moon, I could see a luminous, pearl gray mist rise from where the knife met her flesh. It spiraled up to the ceiling, there to swirl around and around inside the room, swooping and diving with the rapid, jerky motions of a trapped bird.

I watched it for several seconds, thinking it must be an illusion of some sort, brought on by shock, anger, fear, disbelief and a trick of the moonlight.

Her open eyes held a frieze of terror and defiance, and wildly, hopefully, I thought she might still be alive. Falling to my knees by the bed, I touched her neck. Her softly smooth satin skin, once so warm and inviting, was now very cold.

"Oh, *Tilok-cha...*"

Random images of our time together swam onto the screen of my mind. I saw her on the beach, splashing in the gentle surf, laughing as she mugged for my camera, then on the bow of the SHIELA, holding to the forestay as the warm spray sparkled about her ankles.

Regret over our last moments together swept over me like a tidal wave, especially the morning I'd left for Bangkok. She'd tried to coax me back to bed, but out of a strange need to show her I could resist her, I'd pulled away. Now I would never feel her warm, sleepsoft body next to me again, never breathe her spicy scent, never again hear the lilt of her voice. All that was gone, stilled and hushed in one blinding moment. I closed her eyes, bent and kissed her full lips, now cold and unmoving.

"Don't you worry *Tilok*," I said aloud as a scalding conviction grew in me. "He won't get away with this. I know where that bastard hides and…"

I became aware of a sound, a piercing warble that rose and fell over and over again. What the hell was that? I had never heard a siren in this country before, but there was no mistake, and this one was very close.

A vehicle skidded around the corner of the alley, showering gravel and noise everywhere. An angry, pulsing red cop light pushed the silver moonlight from the trees outside. More cars skidded to a halt, doors burst open and shouted orders rang in the soft tropical air.

Touching her cheek one last time and without knowing why, I leaped through the window into the darkly welcoming leaves of the banyan tree. Moving higher into the sheltering branches, I watched Thai cops in elaborate uniforms pound up the stairs, their flashlights narrow beams of quick, probing light.

It was time to hat up. Gliding through the branches, I gained the other side of the massive trunk and dropped to the ground. As I ran down a narrow, twisting path the moon flicked through the trees and mocked me with his silent, accusing stare. Who and why, who and why?

Somehow, I knew the key to everything was in Bangkok.

CHAPTER 25

At the crossroads north of town I stayed in shadow, waiting for the distinctive lights of the northbound overland bus. I didn't have to wait long and found a seat next to an old mama-san who carried on a lively conversation with the two ducks in her lap. With their feet bound and their beaks taped shut, they didn't have much to say. I could empathize.

At a stop in Pattaya, three *poochai* cowboys vacated the rear seat. I grabbed it, stretched my legs out and leaned back into the corner to close my eyes, but as soon as I did, an image of the scene in the bedroom stormed into my mind. I shook my head but it was no use. Wobbly and distorted, it always came back into focus, like a reflected image in still water can be shattered but never erased. I smoked and watched the damp, darkened landscape slide by without seeing it.

At the main station in the city, I grabbed a *tuk-tuk* and headed for the Skeeter, hoping I would feel better on familiar turf.

Alighting from the *tuk*, I stayed in the street and checked downstairs. Not busy at this hour, but not deserted. A table full of port clerks, marked by their uniforms, were having a bite to eat before their shift. A group of foreign merchant sailors, big, blond, scruffy and drunk, talked and laughed in a language that sounded like it could scrape the tonsils off. Three more big blond guys at another table had the clean-cut look and white shirts with epaulets of merchant officers grabbing a meal.

Most of the *felongs* had girls with them and everything appeared normal, but there! At a table in the corner, with a clear view of the street, two guys sat by themselves and nursed beers. Carefully, moving around parked cars, I tried to get a closer look.

They didn't talk much but their eyes constantly swiveled back and forth. One of them kept looking at something in his hand, a picture maybe. With moderate haircuts, they could be anyone, but one of them, dark with smooth skin, wore his very black hair slightly long on top, trim around the ears but without white sidewalls. His buddy had red hair, a red nose and a red moustache and sported a Panama hat. Panama Red wore a T-shirt under a cotton poplin bush jacket with the sleeves rolled above the elbow and Blackie wore a tight blue T-shirt that showed off his muscular build.

I watched Blackie, hoping he would turn just a little and yes! There it was, that white patch over his ear. I knew I'd seen him somewhere, but where? I tried to get a look at their shoes, sometimes a dead giveaway, but couldn't see them and didn't want to risk getting closer. They could be civilian construction consultants, but the construction guys didn't hang out at the docks, they stuck to the big hotels. These two could be permanent party NCOs in Bangkok, but they could also be CID.

Slipping around the corner of the building, I headed for the back and climbed the fire stairs to the landing, the one the girls used to slip out for a breath of air, to escape an unwanted customer and the same one Pen and I had shared the hooter on. That seemed like forever ago now. Several steps from the top, I waited. As usual, the light was out.

I didn't have to wait long. The door opened, spilling smoke, light, music and two girls onto the landing. I vaguely recognized one of them but was waiting for Kim, a good friend of Pen's.

I watched as the girls lit up a Krong-Thep, a Thai version of a Salem with the tobacco removed, mixed with finely chopped weed and repacked. Smoked like a cigarette, they packed a punch. The two girls shared it while I stayed very still.

What did I hope to find here? I was trying to think of an answer when the door opened again and four people came out, two men and two girls. I was hard to tell, but I didn't think any of the girls was Kim.

They didn't stay long and soon went back in. Kim might have an all-nighter going, or she might be sick, visiting her mother, be in the middle of a short-time, there were many places she could be.

Twice more the door opened and people consumed whatever it was that got them through the night.

It was so dark the luminous dial of my watch glowed brightly. Upstairs closed at three, and it was getting close to that. Beginning to have doubts, I stood up, preparing to leave. The door opened. Silhouetted in the swirl of color that spilled, I saw the short, tousled hair of a girl who could be Kim, then the door closed and the Third World blackness fell into place again.

A noise, the click-scratch of a Zippo and the flame illuminated a face. Short, turned up nose and full lips pursed around a Salem. Kim, all right.

"*Sawadee*, Kim," I said, just loud enough to be heard over the bass thud of the music that vibrated the thin wall.

"*Ma-whey!*"

The lit cigarette flew out of the dark, hit me in the chest and showered off chunks of burning tobacco.

"Kim *del-nit*, it's Bob, Pen's *tilok*, *laa*?" I said quick and hoped a hat pin or worse, a butterfly knife, wasn't coming my way. Many of the girls went around strapped, especially the younger, prettier ones.

"*Ali-wha*?" Her voice, gruff and imperious, demanded to know what the hell was going on.

"Kim, it's me, Bob, remember?" I struck my Zippo and held it so she could see my face.

"Bob?"

"Yes! Kim, I need to talk to you, can do?"

"What you do, Bob? Pen *bai-nai*?"

She hasn't heard, then. That made me think it happened not long ago, late yesterday, maybe even tonight.

Moving up a few steps, I lowered my voice. "Kim, let's talk, OK?"

"Where Pen?" The wariness in her voice was plain and I couldn't blame her. Why was I standing on the stairs out back and not in the bar?

"Kim, when's the last time you saw Pen?"

"Long time no see Pen. Where she?"

"Kim, Pen's dead."

In the dark I heard the intake of breath and felt the gap between us widen as she moved a step away.

"Kim, I no do, *ching*. Somebody do, I don't know. What Pen do before, who she talk to?"

I could only hope I was making myself understood. Bar girl Thai and broken English didn't get it for serious questions, but it was all I had and I wanted to know what had been going on, maybe behind my back. Kim might or might not tell me.

"Oh, Bob," Kim said. I felt her move closer, then her arms came around me and I felt her scented softness pressing close.

"Come wis me, Bob, we talk, *laa*?"

Taking my hand, she led me downstairs and along the side of the building to a path that ran back into a warren of small dwellings, all linked together by narrow wooden catwalks.

She snicked the lock on one of a dozen doors that shared a common yard and ushered me inside. I automatically removed my shoes as she flicked on an overhead fluorescent.

"Sit dow," she said, pointing to a wicker chair. From a cooler she took a Pepsi, opened it and handed it to me. I didn't realize how thirsty I was until it hit my throat, then I couldn't suck the stinging brown fizz down fast enough.

"What happen Pen?"

Kim's eyes, like Pen's, like all the girls, were huge and dark, but now they seemed even darker, larger as she waited for the details.

"I don't know," I gasped, the fizz still stinging my throat. "I got home to the pad tonight and found her, stabbed with her own knife. Police come, I hauled ass out o' there, caught a bus to Bangkok, and here I am."

An infinite emptiness fell on me like a cloak, but there were no tears, no crying, only the sad acknowledgement and each of them stronger than the last one, that I would never see Pen again.

"You know a *felong*, a GI, named Burke?" I described him as best I could, but Kim didn't seem to know him.

"How bout a GI named Art?"

"*Chai*," she said, her little nose wrinkling, "numba ten GI!"

"Why's he number ten?"

"Art, *poochai* Duke, you know?"

When I nodded, she continued. "They togetta, do somesin' to make *baht, loo-mai*?"

"I understand, they're business partners. What kind of business?"

"*Ka-moy mahk!*" Kim's eyes rolled to emphasize the size of their thievery.

"What else, though? What…" I burned to ask her more about Burke, but if she didn't know the name she wouldn't know anything else, either.

"Bob," Kim suddenly said, a new note in her voice. I looked at her.

"You hair, so nice, you eyes, ver' boo'ful, you *sway mach poochai!*" Her fingertips touched my cheek for a moment.

I was stunned. I knew the girls all loved blue eyes, but I didn't think I was all that good looking, but what did it have to do with anything? Pen was dead, for god's sake!

"You go United States ver' soon, yes?"

What was this about, I wondered as I thought about it. My rotation date was still two months away, but Pen and I had spoken of it briefly. She didn't like to talk about it

Kim squeezed my hand hard. "No t'ink bad of Thailand, OK, when you home, can do?"

Anxiety washed across her face to momentarily cloud her pretty eyes and I pulled back to look at her.

"Bob," she said, "Biz'ness girl ver' sad, you know?" Sorrow and resignation tinted her voice blue.

"*Pooying* can biz'ness girl ten, fifteen year, you know, by'm'by, *pooying bai kin-kway, loo-mai*?"

I understood, all right. When their looks start to go, many girls faced the humiliation of working in *kin-kway* houses, blow job parlors, which was one small step from begging in the streets.

"*Pen mi simong mahk*. She t'ink abou' later, the..." Her pretty brow furrowed in annoyance.

"The future?" I put in helpfully.

"Yes! She t'ink abou' the future. She put *baht*..." More hand fluttering.

"She saved her money?"

"*Chai*! She keep for later, you know?"

Her dark eyes roamed over me, making sure I understood what she was trying to say, then she started like she'd been stuck.

"*Aiiee*," she screeched, "I mus' go.." She took my hand in one of hers and slipped the other around my neck. "Bob, you numba one GI, been good to Pen, she like you *mahk-mahk*, no t'ink bad abou' she, Thailand, *naa*?"

There it was again. Why would I think bad about her or Thailand when I wanted to come back and be with her for the rest of my days on this earth?

What could Pen have been up to that had got her killed? Was it some kind of business deal that she was hoping to retire on? As I walked down the path with the moon flickering through the trees, I remembered another thing I'd wanted to ask Kim about.

CHAPTER 26

A wave of weariness rolled over me and I nearly fell off the rickety wooden planked walkway as I headed back to the Skeeter. Panama Red and Blackie were gone, given up for the night, I guessed.

I had to go to ground, get some rest. Everyone I knew in the city was a working girl, all of them friends of Pen. I couldn't very well knock on a door and ask if I could crash on a couch, since none of them had couches. Undoubtedly, they all had customers, too.

I was leaning against a five foot high carved teak elephant that was a fixture downstairs when I remembered the small hotel around the corner. Lots of guys used it, I'd used it once or twice, when the tug came up to the 'Kok and a *tilok* wanted to come to.

A sleepy, smiling old man took my two dollars, handed me a clean towel, a chunk of soap wrapped in plastic and a key and led me up to a room on the third floor back. I slipped him a few bucks and asked him to get me some more clothes for the next day, then I laid on the bed in the soft dark, smoking and thinking.

I felt like the room was squeezing in on me and, unable to keep still or shake that feeling, I went out into the street, walking, walking, smoking and walking.

A thought nibbled the edges of my mind, peeked in and then slipped away before I could grab it. I needed something to key on, something I could get a hook into so I could drag it closer. Someone had said something to me that at the time I didn't think much of, but now… I walked and smoked until the eastern sky blushed a pinkish gray, then returned to my little box of a room.

In the head down the hall, I tried to scrub the night away, but even though my skin was clean I couldn't get the stain out of my mind.

In the room, I dropped into sleep almost immediately, but it wasn't restful. I dreamed some kind of dark force was menacing Pen but I couldn't run fast enough to save her and just as I reached her, she disappeared into a red, foaming mist that, no matter how fast I ran, seemed to recede before me.

I jerked awake, feeling like I'd gone to sleep on watch, clawed my way back to wakefulness, then wished I hadn't. A crushing sense of loss and dread fell on me and I had to groan.

Dragging myself off the bed, I went to the window.

Below me, like a storm-tossed sea frozen in time, tin roofs and tree tops spread out in irregular patterns to the horizon. In the middle distance, maybe ten klicks away, I could see the taller, newer glass and steel buildings of central Bangkok glittering in the sun.

Uncle Jack always said to Make a plan, work the plan. My plan was to locate Burke and…what? I'd worry about that when I found him.

I spent the day lying low, trying to sleep between vivid dreams. Again, I saw images of Pen and the things we had done together moved in and out of my mind's eye in a shifting kaleidoscope of color and motion. I saw her frolicking on a beach, mugging for the camera, standing on the bow of the SHEILA in the golden light of late afternoon, her bare breasts thrusting into the warm wind as sparkling drops of spray washed around her legs.

I saw her lying on the bed in floodlit clarity, the knife in her chest, her blood red as fingernail polish and that pearl gray mist hovering over her like a tortured, swirling being. Was I seeing things? What was that? I woke sitting up and felt like I was rising out of a hot rushing stream bed, the sweat falling from my face and neck in rivulets.

I waited then for the tears to come, willed them to come, to burst from me in a hot, cathartic gush, but none came. I felt like I was about to explode.

At 2100 I felt safer in the dark and went into the street. Downstairs at the Skeeter, I saw Panama Red in a dark corner, but he was alone. He and Blackie must have split forces so I'd have to be careful.

Crossing the busy boulevard, I headed down the side street toward Pen's old place, unsure why. At least I'd get something to eat.

The mama-san with the dim-sum cart was still there and when I gave her a *wai* and asked if she remembered me, she nodded and smiled, her teeth white and even.

"Yes, I 'member you," she replied and turned her cataract-clouded eyes toward me.

"*Phut English dee mahk!*" I said.

"Yes," she said. "English, Norway, Sweden..." She waved a hand as if to say And some others. I remembered Pen had done the same, spoke the Scandinavian languages, and it came to me then. Mama-san had probably retired from "The Life" herself and now ran this little cart. That would explain the good teeth. She'd never taken up the nut.

"How come you never spoke English to me before?"

I offered her a cigarette, but she refused, then conjured up a Salem from somewhere.

"*Pen bai-nai?*"

No one ever asked how I was, they all wanted to know where Pen was. I couldn't believe word hadn't reached the 'Kok yet. It had been almost twenty-four hours since I'd discovered the body, but when a GI butterflied on his *tilok* in Sattahip, the girls in Bangkok knew it in less than a day.

Mama-san's eyes seemed very bright as I asked her if she knew of a GI named Burke. It was a long shot. Burke didn't hang around the Skeeter so I wasn't surprised when she shook her head. As I watched, her eyes became even bigger and brighter, the cataracts like small cumulus clouds in her eyes.

"You know a GI named Art?" I described him.

"*Chai*," she said and let out a sound of disgust. "Numba ten GI."

"Does he come around here, to the Mosquito Bar?"

She cast those cloaked eyes on me and flicked ashes.

"*Mai*," she said, "no see him, long time. Where Pen?"

I tried to hold my face neutral and show nothing, but Mama-san could see better than I would have thought. I felt like my life was a picture window and she leaned forward suddenly. Her crablike claw of a hand gripped my wrist with a fierce strength I wouldn't have thought possible in such an old lady.

"What matta?" Her tone said I had better spit it out quick.

"Mama-san, Pen's dead."

The light went out of her clouded eyes and she sagged deeper into the wrinkles that time and fortune had etched into her face. She was very still for several long seconds. One hand strayed to her throat to finger something she wore there.

She let it go and I was able to get a look at it. It was just like the one Pen had worn, and then, like fog whisked clear by a stiff sea breeze, it came to me what had been different about Pen as she lay on the bed, bathed in her own blood.

Mama-san started to keen, up and down the scale, a sound that made my teeth vibrate and stood my hair on end.

I thought it strange that Mama-san and Pen would both have the same kind of amulet, then like a lightening bolt, it hit me.

"You're Pen's mother, aren't you?"

Her occluded eyes flew open, black and gray, then she nodded, dropped her head and banged it hard on the edge of her cart, once, twice, three times, they lay back in the tiny chair and uttered the most plaintive, primitive sound I'd ever heard. It rose higher and higher then cracked into a shriek. Chills rippled along my arms.

I couldn't stand it and had to do something to stop that noise before my head exploded. I took a shot in the dark.

I pointed at the amulet Mama-san wore, the one her knarled brown fingers had picked up again. "The amulet Pen wore, did it work for her?"

"*Mai*," the old woman whispered, followed by a long string of Thai. The words meant nothing to me, but they way she spoke, her head down, murmuring almost to herself made me wonder if she believed in it herself.

"Mama-san," I asked, anxious to keep her talking, "what you know about that cowboy Duke?"

The noise stopped. "Him numba ten," she bit off and spat on the ground.

Reaching into her cart, she brought out a bottle and two glasses. Setting them down, she poured a stiff shot in each, set one in front of me and picked up the other. The bottle was unlabeled and could have been anything, but how could I refuse this?

"To Pen, a good girl, she try ver' hard," Mama-san said.

"To Pen, a smart girl, maybe too smart for her own good."

We clinked glasses and she tossed hers back. With a deep breath, I did the same. It felt like I'd swallowed molten lava, but a deep breath and iron will kept me from choking. The bottle clinked on the glass again and I remembered what I'd wanted to ask Kim. Maybe Mama-san would know.

"Mama-san," I said, leaning closer. In spite of her clouded eyes, I could see the interest gleam there as she also leaned in close. I told her about the steam-like cloud I had seen hovering over the bed, swirling and shifting, and asked if I had just been seeing things or if it had really happened.

"Bob," she said, almost sadly, "that been her *kwang-hai*, her spirit, her what-you-say, her...?" Frustration at not knowing the right word washed over her seamed, long-suffering face.

"Like a soul?"

"*Chai*, her sou." Mama-san nodded. "*Kwang-hai* no can sleep, not now, no do, by'm'by all people see him who do..."

She fluttered her gnarled hands about in exasperation.

"I don' know you say, but people know, all people know who do, *loo-mai*?"

I understood, all right. The cold light of public knowledge must be shined into the dark recesses of humanity to find whoever did it, and the why known for her eternal soul to be in peace.

I saw the fork in the road as clearly as if I'd been standing on a sun-dappled country lane. One led to letting the "proper authorities" handle it. The other road led to the Patpong district and the Tumbleweeds Bar, where I was sure I would find Burke and Company. I hailed a *tuk-tuk*. The snapping, smoking, sputtering little engine perfectly matched my mood.

CHAPTER 27

At 2300 hours, Patpong was a teeming circus of alcohol-fueled debauchery. Glassy-eyed American soldiers in civvies staggered down the street towing tiny brown girls encased in tight glittery dresses. The skirts rode high on their legs and many showed a lacy crescent of blue or yellow panties, or sometimes nothing at all. They all laughed at the good time they were having.

The scene inside the Tumbleweeds Bar resembled a Bosch painting. Tables the size of cocktail trays were littered with bottles, glasses and overflowing ashtrays while on the tiny stage, four skinny musicians with slanted eyes and coal-black hair, wearing hats, boots and western shirts murdered a Hank Williams tune. On a stage along the bar, girls wearing big smiles and tiny strips of cloth strutted and pranced while trying to make eye contact with any *felong*.

I looked around through cigarette smoke thick as London fog. Booths along the wall were occupied by determined drinkers, each of whom had a girl hanging on him. In the corner a trio of drunken drovers was whooping and hollering, all except the one in the corner, who had a girl in his lap. Her short hair bounced like a loose cap while he jigged her up and down. None of them looked like Burke and Company, though.

"Hallo, GI, you ver' brave sojer. I luff you long time, can?" The voice tinkled up next to me and I felt a hand pass across my stomach.

I turned to see a cute little girl in a white sequined vest, short sequined white skirt, sequined white hat and white boots giving me the sloe eye. About to brush her off, I stopped. "*Felong* GI Burke *bai-nai?*"

She knew instantly I wasn't on R&R, I didn't want any long luff, and at the mention of Burke, the brightly glazed party look on her face evaporated like rain in the desert. She started to backpedal, fear twisting her elfin face. There was no doubt in my mind she knew who Burke was.

Grabbing her wrist allowed the little white vest she wore to slide away, exposing her small pert tits. "Where's Burke?" I asked her in Thai.

"*Mai-loo, mai-loo!*" Her voice rose higher with each syllable of denial.

She tried to twist away again and I gripped her harder. She squealed in pain and fright and frantically plucked at my grip on her with her other hand.

"Hey, leave her alone!"

A Galahad, thinks he's going to come to her rescue.

"None o' your business, trooper!" I barked at him. I felt a hot pain lance my hand and looked down to see the little "biz'ness girl" had taken a chomp on me. Her eyes squeezed shut, she put the bite down hard.

"Shit!" I yelled and grabbed her little button nose between thumb and forefinger.

She let go long enough to squeal again and I jerked away, just in time to avoid the drunken punch Galahad threw. He stumbled by off-balance and I helped him on his way with a foot in his back.

He crashed through a table, drinks and ashtrays flying, but his table buddies had seen him go down and over the general racket of the place, I heard the scrape of chairs. Reinforcements were on the way.

The cowgirl was quick and long gone now. I decided on a tactical retreat and picked a redheaded drunk bellowing a rebel yell to spin into Galahad's friends. They went down in a tangle of knees, elbows, beer, glass and splintered table.

I moved through the crowd, swivel-hipped and picking my openings and made the street.

The fresh air felt good after the acrid sweetness of the bar. My hand tingled. Almost afraid to look at it, I paused for half a second, then checked it out. Four thin trails of blood dripped from the top of the web where her sharp little teeth had punctured me.

Another complication. In this tropical heat, that would fester in no time if left untreated.

I ducked into another bar and ordered a shot of Leaping Deer whisky from the bartender. When it came, I poured it slowly over the punctures and pressed a paper napkin to it.

Now what? I took up a position across the street from the Tumbleweeds, right next to a mama-san with skin the color of a wet chamois and a pushcart of dim-sums. I bought two of them and a little Pepsi, but they reminded me of my first night with Pen and I sat there while the crisp, flaky crust, golden brown and delicious, turned cold and soggy.

Throwing the dim-sums onto a trash pile between two buildings, I asked the mama-san if she worked this place very much.

Every day, she said.

I asked her if she'd ever seen a dark-haired *felong* with a big moustache who looked like he was already dead.

Her eyes widened and a torrent of words rushed out at me. Slowly, I pieced together the fact that yes, she had seen him, many times, always coming and going from the same direction, and always walking, never in a taxi. She pointed, that way.

I thanked her profusely and gave her twenty *baht* and a deep *wai*, which she returned the same way.

Heading in that direction, I kept my eyes and ears open. The bars and clubs thinned out and several small alleys branched off the street as if they had sprung up by chance and need over the years, without any formal planning. Unpaved for the most part, they were muddy tracks lined with haphazard shacks and lean-tos that teemed with commerce by day but were dark and shuttered by night. Away from the florescent and neon of the Patpong, I became aware of the moon-light that made everything seem like a photo negative, dark and light reversed.

As soon as I stepped into the first one, I felt my pulse speed up. This is just the sort of thing we were warned against when we first arrived in-country. Keep together, they said, stay on the main streets, they said, don't carry large amounts of cash, they said. I was Oh-for-three. At least it was the dry season and the dirt was hard-packed and not a sea of mud.

A ripple of laughter floated from the dark, rose to an hysterical pitch, then stopped suddenly. Standing still, I listened, but all I heard was an occasional snatch of Thai TV and radio, another burst of laughter and a drunken shout.

This is ridiculous, I thought, and started backtracking. Keeping the moon over my left shoulder I turned a corner and saw the lights ahead. An querulous male voice burst from somewhere to my left, rose to a crescendo and stopped. I ignored it.

Back on Patpong, the lust and rut in the air was thicker than ever. I slipped into the Tumbleweeds again and made a slow circuit of the entire room, again with no luck. He might be out, taking care of busi-ness, or even out of the city.

The unlikelihood of finding Burke in the swirling chaos of Bangkok began to make itself plain. An idea came to me and I decided to make one sweep through another place, just a short distance away, a place called the Thai Room.

Compared to the frenzied lust of Patpong, the Thai Room was an oasis of calm. The crowd had thinned out, most of the girls were gone, already paired up or had retired from the field of battle for the night.

A quick look around. I didn't see a dark-haired American with an elaborate moustache, but I did see one thing and I looked again.

I was sure of it. At a table in the back a group of GIs with military haircuts and trimmed 'staches talked quietly, without the yelling, high-fives and purple bravado normal to a table full of drunk soldiers on Rest and Recreation leave. There was another thing unusual, too and it took a second to nail it. There were no girls at the table, but what really stood out was the head of light brown, almost blond hair, over olive skin.

Nobody noticed my approach and I was able to come up right beside him.

"Hello, Tok," I said, loud enough to cut through their conversation. The talk ceased like a switch had been thrown.

Duke turned, mild surprise on his face. "What's the haps, man?" He didn't seem at all surprised to see me.

"You got a minute? I'd like to talk to ya' for a second."

"OK," he said and glanced around the table. "I'll see you guys later." They murmured their agreement and Duke rose and pointed to another table.

He wore a black silk shirt splashed with red flowers outside cream-colored slacks. His long hair laid wetly on his skull, emphasizing the planes and hollows of his face. Half a dozen gold chains winked on his hairless chest.

"What's up?" He asked as we sat down.

He talked as if all were right with the world.

"I guess you haven't heard, then, have you?"

I left it hanging there like something rotten that neither of us wanted to acknowledge. He totally ignored the tone and just sat there, his fine-boned hands still and quiet on the table in front of him.

Fuck it, I thought, no time for games. "Pen's dead."

He blinked, then swallowed a few times. "When, how?" He seemed to look past me into another dimension only he could see.

"Day before yesterday, stabbed with her own knife." I gave him a brief rundown.

"Who the hell did that?"

"I was hoping you could tell me. Cops showed up at the hootch right after I found her, like they'd been tipped off. I jumped out a window.

Art and Burke came around a few days ago, right before the tug came to Bangkok. I wanna find that Burke and…"

Suddenly the room was spinning and the chair I sat on seemed to be slewing sideways.

"Are you alright?"

Duke face appeared, close and concerned.

"Yeah," I said, "I'm…" All the colors of the spectrum ran together in a soupy swirling kaleidoscope.

"Hey, you don't look good. In fact, you…"

I felt like I was drifting over the treetops, except there were no trees, only this club in Bangkok that was getting ready to close and I stumbled and staggered but somehow kept my feet.

"Let's go," I heard Duke say from a long ways off. I realized I was leaning on him as we walked and I shook myself and pulled away, but he stayed close.

"Where we goin'?" I wanted to know.

"My place."

We left the Thai Room and grabbed a *tuk-tuk*. The ride through the warm night became a series of blurs, of traffic, horns, pedestrians and revolving traffic circles. Other cars and taxis would come along side and race us for a while, then they would peel off and we were winning again.

By the time the little sputtering *tuk* stopped, I'd regained some senses and was able to walk more or less unassisted. I could smell the revolting, comforting odor of the river and somehow felt better.

We walked down a short alley to a nondescript building. Duke opened the door and we went up one flight of stairs, down a long hall way, to the end where he opened a pad lock on a door. He went in first, gesturing for me to follow.

Duke's room was larger than most and neat as a pin. The bed was made, the closet doors and all the dresser drawers were closed. There were no clothes on the floor, or anywhere else for that matter. It looked as if the maid had just left. A large framed poster for the John Wayne

movie "The Searchers" hung on a wall. It showed him as Big Jim holding Natalie Wood up in the air, knowing he couldn't kill her even if she
was an Indian by acclimation now. I suddenly understood Tok's nickname. He, too, was constantly searching.

Against the wall a table and two chairs held a vase full of silk roses.
Near the table a small refrigerator hummed. I was impressed. He must
be doing alright if he had this nice room and a refrigerator.

"Sit." Duke pointed at a chair and opened the reefer. Snapping the
caps off two Pepsis, he set one in front of me. With the first sip, I realized how thirsty I was and started pulling the brown fizzy stuff from the
bottle in huge gulps, welcoming the sizzle as the carbonation burned
away the taste of anxiety, loss and fear in my throat.

"What happened?"

I lit a smoke, paused a second, and told him exactly the way it had
been, starting with Art and Burke's visit the night before we left for
Bangkok.

Through it all, he sat there, still and impassive, barely moving at all,
hardly seeming to breathe, his pomaded hair glinting softly in the light.
When I finished, he looked at me intently for a second before turning
away. I felt like I had been examined and found wanting, but I couldn't
say why.

"It's that fuckin' Burke, isn't it?" I asked. "He's the one did this, didn't
he?" I gripped the bottle hard, my knuckles white.

I looked up to see Duke watching me in that calm, noncommittal
way he had, his eyes as devoid of emotion as green marbles. I wanted to
reach over there, take a fistful of his shirt and shake him, just to get a
reaction. Didn't he realize what I'd been talking about? Pen was dead!

"So," I said instead, "where's this AWOL prick hang out, huh? I wanna
have a little talk with him!"

•"Yes, but first you should rest, you look very tired."

All of a sudden, I felt very tired, deflated, like my life's energy had leaked
out and my skin was sagging on my frame. I realized I was hungry, too, but

I shook my head no. I wanted to find Burke before he faded away, and I stood up quick. The dizziness overwhelmed me and I started to topple, but Duke caught me before I went over.

"You lay down here, sleep for awhile, I'll bring back something to eat."

He was the picture of the caring friend, willing to put himself out for a buddy, and gestured at the bed. I kicked off my shoes and flopped down. Tension seemed to drain away from me in waves every time the fan swept it's cooling wash across my hot skin. Dimly, I heard the door click shut as Duke went out.

I don't know how long I laid there, but the next time I opened my eyes, the room was still dark but a hot yellow glow around the shutters told me it was well into the morning. My watch said 1000 hours. I had finally slept pretty well, but I didn't feel rested, and at first couldn't remember what I was doing here. Then it all came back in a rush and I felt the weight of the whole thing settle in my neck.

Sitting up, I rubbed my face. It felt coated with grit, like sandpaper. I remembered I had no toothbrush, no change of clothes, no nothing. That's when I saw the package on the table. I opened it, and found inside a tube of toothpaste, a new toothbrush still in the wrapper, a bar of soap and a clean towel. I threw the towel over my shoulder and headed for the shower down the hall.

As I wielded the pan, I again cursed the primitiveness of Thailand and wished for a hot, steaming shower. Back in the room, I put on the same clothes and was buckling my belt when Duke came in.

"You're awake," he said, "good. Let's get something to eat, then we can go see a guy I know."

"What guy?"

"A guy who might know where Burke is."

It sounded like a good idea to me.

A little noodle shop around the corner had three small white-painted wrought iron tables under a spreading Bo tree. Along the street, mama-sans swept out shops and homes with brooms made of reeds and children laughed and scampered. Some of the older, bolder ones came close to take a look at the strange sight of a *felong* so far from the commercial lust of the Patpong area.

The small street was paved with a slurry of some kind that kept the dust down and it was very pleasant to sit in the shade, except for…

She's gone, I told myself. Mechanically, I shoveled in the pork-fried rice with the egg in it and drank the *café nam kang*, an iced coffee, like I was taking on fuel.

Duke ate nothing but sipped an iced coffee.

People came by and spoke to him in deferential tones. He answered, laughed sometimes, joked, and once I was sure he threatened a cowboy who tried to hang tough but was unable to. The cowboy kept glancing at me, wondering who I was, what I was doing there and how my presence affected him. I looked him in the eye every chance I got and kept a neutral expression.

Girls and women came by and didn't look at me. They weren't working girls. Men and boys did look, but I felt no challenges, merely a curiosity. Two Thai soldiers strolled past, holding hands. Most GIs snickered at that, but Thai men friends often put their arms around each other and held hands. Nothing was thought of it.

We sat there for nearly an hour and finally a kid about twelve or so, a shoeshine boy without his box, sidled up, said a few words and then faded.

"OK," Duke turned to me, "the guy we want to talk to is not here now," I felt a crushing weight settle on me, "but he'll be in the she-boy bar later tonight." The she-boy bar was the fairy bar.

"What does later tonight mean?"

"Could be nine, could be midnight, I don't know."

"OK," I said, thinking, "Thanks a lot for lettin' me crash at your place, the chow, the shower, everything, but I gotta get back to my room, off the street."

"I'll meet you in front of the fairy bar at, say, twenty-two hundred?"

"All right," he said, "see you then." He surprised the hell out of me by extending his hand. I took it.

"Tell me," I said, holding on to his hand, "is it true that you didn't really want to sell Pen's debt to me and that Art Delaplane made you?"

He tried to pull away, but I gripped harder and watched his eyes. They were hidden by metal framed rose sunglasses, but his mouth scribed a thin line. By the angle of his head, I could tell he was pointedly looking at my hand holding his.

"Art did not make me do anything," he said evenly, "but he did point out how I might profit by it."

"And how was that?"

He was very subtly trying to wriggle free but I clamped harder. I was four inches taller than him, probably thirty pounds heavier, and I worked with my hands all the time while the hardest thing he ever did was light a cigarette or open a beer and the more he wriggled the harder I squeezed.

He became very still. "Profit," he said tightly, "can mean more than mere money."

"And so can losses."

I let go and stood up. "Don't be late."

I vowed then never to turn my back on him.

A three block tuk ride brought me back to the Skeeter. I knew in my bones I'd been close to the docks.

CHAPTER 28

At 2145 hours I cruised slowly past the nondescript red door in the cinderblock wall a hundred feet down an alley from the nearest street. There was no sign and no tout outside, but this was the place, no doubt about it.

Wondering whether I should go in or wait for Duke, I turned and came back again, stopping in the middle of the alley, right in front of the door.

Patience, I said to myself and lit a smoke. Slipping the lighter back in my pocket, I started to pace again. That's when I saw them.

They both wore sharply creased, narrow pegged pants, pointed shoes and shiny, gaudy shirts. The big gold medallions on their smooth hairless chests and their long, swoopy hair styles marked them like neon signs. Cowboys.

I made eye contact with the taller one. There was no mistaking the predatory glint in his eyes, the way he held his head, slightly cocked to one side, the easy, confident, sneering smile as they stopped in front of me.

"*Mee fichek, naa?*"

"*Mai,*" I replied and took in his surprised look as I drew on my own smoke. Asking for a light is the opening gambit, the move to make you drop your guard. When I said no, he didn't know what to do.

The taller one spoke again, his face twisted with a smirk as he nodded at the red door.

Uncle Jack always said, When the shit is going to hit the fan, be on the upwind side, his way of saying get the first shot in and follow it up, fast and decisive.

I had height and weight, but there were two of them. The bigger one was closest, so I addressed him. Raising my voice and using all the bar-girl Thai I knew, I told him that I was no newbie, I'd been in-country for quite a while and they were making a big mistake. Their expressions never changed and then I knew. This was no simple robbery. I'd been suckered into this alley and I thought I knew why. The taller one grinned, showing bad teeth. His hand went behind him.

Quick as a thought, I stepped up and sank a right into his middle, heard the air whoosh out and felt him fold over my arm, so close I could smell the tobacco and liquor on his breath.

Pivot and turn. Right foot in the other ones crotch just as he cleared his pocket with a flick knife. Surprise and pain twisted his face, the knife clattered to the street and I kicked it away. The first one was on his knees and retching, thin strings of saliva, shiny and wet-looking, hung from his mouth into the hard packed dirt. I kicked him hard in the side and felt something give as he fell over. A garbled moan bubbled from his lips. He was out of it.

His crime partner staggered away with a slew footed scrap-and-shuffle gait, both hands holding his package. I was out of danger and should have let him go, but I was pissed off and my blood was pumping, hot and quick.

I went after him, intent on inflicting more hurt, to try to blunt my own feelings of helpless rage with solid action onto him.

Instead, a hot, white, sizzling pain exploded in the back of my head, shot forward and flooded over my eyes, blinding me, bounced back and went down my spine into my legs, turning them to jelly. I pitched forward and fell into a black hole that had no bottom, only rows of spinning, blinking lights that spiraled down, down, down. It seemed like I fell face-forward into eternity.

CHAPTER 29

I tried to rub my aching head, but I couldn't. I thought I was paralyzed, and my mind started to panic and I tried to stand up, but I couldn't. I wanted to look around, but I couldn't.

The buzzing of a million angry bees ebbed and flowed in and out of my consciousness while I struggled to pull breath through a thick fuzzy cloud that clung to my face.

I could see nothing, even though I was sure my eyes were open. Shaking my head to clear it, I heard the buzz stop, then suddenly, the cloud went away from me and I knew why I couldn't get up and run. I was bound, hands, feet and torso, to a chair.

I looked around. A circle of light from above threw my own shadow onto a bare concrete floor. Breathing better now, I nearly gagged on a sweet, sickly odor. This was a tapioca warehouse.

A long bamboo pole slid out of the darkness toward me, a snake wrapped around the end.

The wide flat head ranged slowly back and forth and the black forked tongue licked the air. The slim body, black and yellow banded and about three feet long clung to the pole. In the harsh light the eyes were dots. Sensing me, the tongue licked faster and the moving head zeroed in like a direction finder.

The drill sergeants at Ft. Ord used to terrorize us with tales of the snakes in Nam. The worst was called a step-and-a-half, so-called because after you were bit you took a step and a half and died a horrible, twitching death strangling on your own tongue.

The pole moved closer and the snake dangled there, inches from my face, the shiny black tongue a flickering blur. I could practically feel the fangs sink into my cheek and the toxin disrupt my nervous system. I started to twitch involuntarily.

Slowly, the snake slid backwards, into the darkness beyond the light. The bees started up again, fainter this time. Desperately, I tried to work up something to swallow but came up dry.

I heard the distinctive rasp of a Zippo, then the flame touched the end of a slim dappled cigar and illuminated a long, thin face with a thick, dark Fu-Manchu moustache. The flame clicked out, the cherry flared and a long stream of blue smoke shot into the light and slowly dispersed upward.

"So," Burke said as he waved to someone behind him, "I hear you're looking for me."

Someone came out of the darkness and held a straw for me. I recognized Matt. The cold, sweet tea had never tasted so good and I pulled hard on the straw.

"What're you talkin' about?" I asked when I could talk.

"You, ya' pathetic fuck," Burke laughed. "You're chargin' around town like the White Knight, askin' questions, upsettin' people, all for a zip hooker."

More laughter murmured from behind him. Grinning, he turned slightly, feeding on it like a schoolyard bully.

Maybe I was pathetic to his way of thinking, but fuck him. I pulled in a deep breath.

"Listen," I said, "what's this shit for?" I nodded at the ropes that held me. "Untie me, we'll talk about…"

"I don't think so," Burke's shaggy head waggled side to side, "some of the boys are very nervous about you and…" He shrugged. "I have to respect that, even if I don't want to."

"Wha'do you know about respect? You point guns at women. Where is that thing, anyway?"

He never made a move, but suddenly he held that slim black automatic in his hand. "This one?"

I nodded.

An irrational hope seized me. Someone would know where I was and at the last second, just when it looked bleakest, the door would bust in and the good guys would be here, guns drawn, but as soon as I had the thought, I knew it wouldn't happen.

Conrad said that each of us lives, as we dream, all alone. For a while there I'd had somebody, but she was gone now and I truly was alone right now. No one knew where I was and there was no one coming to my rescue.

"You got stones," Burke said. "Not too many brains, but stones aplenty." The more-balls-than-brains syndrome.

He tossed a grin over his shoulder while I forced myself to stay calm and think. He wants something. What is it?

"Did you kill Pen?"

"Oh, yeah," he mocked me, "I've got nothing better to do than go around offing zip hookers. Are you as lame as that?"

"Then what was all that shit at my pad for? What were you sayin' to her, why'd she pull that shiv, and why the fuck you point that gun at her?" Unable to help it, I was starting to yell again.

"Business," Burke said, "plain and simple, business."

"What the fuck you talkin' about, what kind of business?"

Burke considered that for a moment, then shook his head. "I can't tell you right now."

"Cops think I did it!" I yelled.

Burke looked at me. "Did you?" His voice was flat as he relit that dappled cigar.

I shook my head. "Hell, no, I lo…" I almost yelled at him that I was in love with her, why would I kill her, but I choked it back.

"Why would they think you did it?"

"'Cause my prints are all over that pig sticker."

"That's too bad." Burke said, "Did you have a motive? Was she bangin' someone else behind your back, or stealin' money from you?"

I tried to think. Maybe she was, I didn't know, but I was unwilling to admit it now even if it were true. Afraid my voice might crack, I shook my head.

"Well, then," he leaned back on his heels with a smug look of satisfaction. "You have no motive that I can see, then. Did you have an opportunity?"

I looked at him. What was this? "You know I did," I said.

"Well, I hate to tell you this, but you are fucked six ways from Sunday." He sounded very matter-of-fact.

"They don't care who did it," Burke went on amiably, "as long as they can pin it on someone and you're the best bet for that. See, Uncle Sam doesn't want to piss off the zips 'cause they might raise the price for the bases, you know?"

He took a long draw on that cigar as he rotated it. I watched the cherry turn round and round as it glowed brightly.

"It's a known fact," he went on as if he were teaching a class, "that people only kill other people for three reasons, and two of those are the same. One," he stuck one finger in the air, "money. People will kill each other for money. In your case, that's not the reason. Two," another finger went up, "is sex. People will off each other over sex, usually jealousy, and three," another finger, "pride. Sex and pride and jealousy are related, with a power component thrown in there for good measure."

He grinned like he was enjoying himself.

"In a fit of passion," he said, "things happen. It's usually an unplanned, spur of the moment kind of thing, someone goes off the deep end, time shifts, things get blurry, and before you know it, someone's dead."

His voice lowered so much that at the last I could hardly hear him and he wasn't looking at me anymore, but at someplace where only he could go. After a moment, he seemed to snap out of it.

"Anyway," he said briskly, "you've got opportunity and your prints on the knife. They come up with a motive and CID will hand you over on a silver platter."

He smiled like a skull would smile. "What's one GI in the big picture anyway?"

"How do you know so much about it?" I asked.

"Burke was an MP in Saigon."

The voice came out of the dark, but there was no doubt in my mind about who it was.

"How ya' doin', Art?"

He stepped into the light. I was shocked. He looked terrible. His wide face appeared drawn and haggard and the clothes he wore, already loose, sagged on him like gunny sacks. Dark circles hung under his eyes like bags of coal and the scraggly stubble that covered his lower face might have been an attempt to change his appearance. There was no changing those eyes, though. Black and shiny as fresh tar, they still jumped out at me.

I looked back and forth between Art and Burke, trying to get a read on this, but came up empty. "Why you guys want me to do that job so bad anyway. Can't you get a local?"

Burke shook his head. "Don't trust the locals," he said around the cigar. "They're unreliable."

He chuckled a little. "Remember those Queens Cobras, or whatever the fuck they called their sorry asses?"

I remembered it. There were a lot of stories going around that Uncle Sam had bankrolled two battalions of Thai troops so that their NCOs were paid more than American officers, equipped them with better gear than our own guys had, the very latest stuff, and sent them to Nam to hunt the NVA. They found the NVA all right, and had gotten their asses kicked. Worse, they'd bolted under fire and couldn't be made to fight again. The public relations and propaganda coup that was hoped for fizzled out, and everyone said the money should have gone to fund ROK troops. The VC and the NVA were supposed to be scared shitless of Republic of Korea forces and avoided them if at all possible.

Burke stood there, blue smoke coming from him in puffs. "Tell you what," he said, "you help us, we'll help you, 'K?"

"How's that?"

"You do this little thing we ask, and I promise you, all your questions will be answered out there, on the island."

"What kind of sucker play is that? You…"

"You lame fuck," he said, shaking his head, "If I wanted to kill you, you'd be floatin' face down in the river. We'll be in touch."

He raised his hand in a signal. That snake came flying out of the dark straight at me. In the harsh light I could see, in a kind of slow motion, that forked tongue slipping in and out, then with a soft plop, it landed in my lap. I felt that long tube of muscle wriggle and squirm in its own panic and before I could utter, or even think of a prayer, I passed out.

When I woke, I was alone. It took a second to realize I wasn't tied up anymore. Silence crashed all around me and I couldn't see two feet or even two inches. The darkness was complete. I remembered the snake and jumped up so hard and fast the chair went flying and I patted myself down frantically, but couldn't feel anything snakelike.

Fumbling my lighter out, I struck it and held it up. The circle of weak yellow light showed nothing near me and I took a step. Thousands of needles lanced through my legs as the blood rushed into my lower extremities. As soon as I was able, I started looking for a door. The lighter went out and I moved forward, waving both hands in front of me like insect antenna.

I touched a wall, rough and wavy. Corrugated tin. Moving along it, I came to a wooden frame. A door, with a hook and eye. It opened easily and I staggered through. In the clean, sweet night air the smell of the river was like a perfume and I breathed it in, trying to flush away the stink of fear.

Catching a cruising *tuk*, I lit a cigarette, leaned back in the seat and watched as the eastern sky became a pearly gray. My watch said 0530 hours. I had the driver drop me a block from the hotel and slipping in through the back way, I made it up to my room without seeing anyone.

I opened the door with the key, took a step in, and froze. I could see nothing in the dark, but the reek of aftershave, sweet and musky, hung like a cloud. Before I could turn and bolt, a hand clamped onto my left upper arm like a foundry tong and probed the inside of my bicep. My arm went limp.

"Don't even think about it!"

The authoritative tone gripped as hard as the hand. The overhead fluorescent blinked on and I was jerked into the room and propelled at the wooden chair. "Siddown."

Using the force of the shove, I swerved and dove headlong out the open window and skidded on the corrugated tin sun awning of the floor below.

Scrabbling, slipping and sliding, I heard a voice shout, "Get him, get him, he's out the window!"

The tree looked close and without thinking I flung myself at the branch. It caught me in the chest, the air left me, but I had both arms around it and hung on.

My feet touched a lower branch. It felt solid and even as the blackness cleared, I let myself down to it, the another, and dropped to the ground.

So far so good, I thought. If could make the river, I could grab a long-tail and be miles away in minutes. With a glance behind me, I took off running and ran straight into him.

Calmly, he showed me the gun he held, pointed at the ground.

"OK, podna," he said in a friendly tone, "you shit is flaky now, so don't make me shoot you, no."

He grinned, his teeth very white in the pearling dawn. "That how you get out the hootch in Sattahip, by the tree, yes?" He tilted his head into a quizzical stance. That speech pattern was familiar, and so was that grin.

"I don't know what yer talkin' about," I said.

"OK," he replied, "we talk about that later, but now let's go, back to your room." He waggled the gun, a small hammerless .38 revolver.

Resigned, I headed back. The other guy ran up then like a dust devil on the prairie, full of himself but not of much consequence.

Huffing and puffing, he gasped out, "Sonofabitch!" and grabbed me. As he did his straw hat hit the ground

"Easy, easy!" Blackie said, "I've got him, he ain't going nowhere, him."

Panama Red let go of me and dropped his hands to his knees to catch his breath. The bush jacket he wore wrinkled and bellowed as he sucked in air and when he glared at me I saw his eyes. A pale, washed out blue, they seemed to float in his coarse, sunburned face. Deep trenches furrowed their way from his nose to the corners of his mouth and his lashes and brows were like red brushes. The rolled up sleeves of his jacket showed his muscular arms, covered with a blanket of coarse reddish hair. They stuck out away from his torso like parentheses.

"Who are you guys?" I asked, although I already knew.

"Just come on," Panama said, taking my other arm now that he had his breath back. They quick-marched me toward the hotel.

On the other side of me, Blackie gripped my other arm, too, but not as tight. I had an inch, maybe more, on him but he carried an easy, athletic grace and I knew he'd be quick and agile. The tight green T-shirt he wore emphasized his shoulders, arms and slim waist and the pleated slacks around his slim hips appeared to stay up by magic.

I looked and saw the white patch in the coal-black hair and his moustache, just a little longer than regulation, was thick and equally black in his smooth, unlined face. His eyes were hidden behind flight glasses, but I would have bet they were as brown as aged whisky.

"Who are you guys?" I said loudly.

"Shut up!" Panama barked and shook my arm.

"Let's get inside, and we'll talk then, yes."

"Get the door."

Blackie seemed to be in charge and Panama let go of me to run ahead and open the door. By the time we hit the third floor we were practically running and they were both scanning the area like guard dogs.

In the hallway they exchanged a few muttered words. Panama came in to the room with me while Blackie turned the corner.

"Sit down," Panama said, "smoke 'em if you got 'em."

I remembered that expression from basic training, and anyone who has ever heard it will never forget it.

I watched him as he took his hat and glasses off. He appeared to be in his mid twenties. Military haircut, military bearing, clean-shaven. When he spun the other chair around and straddled it, his bush jacket opened a little and I saw the square shaped blue steel gun butt and brown leather holster of his shoulder rig. An issue .45. These guys were CID, no doubt about it.

So this is it, I thought. I'm caught. There'll be a quick show trial, then a long stretch in either Long Binh or Leavenworth. I'll never find out who killed Pen, who robbed me of her and ruined my life.

Sitting on the hard bed, I started to tremble from exhaustion, fear, frustration and spent adrenalin. I couldn't stop shaking and falling onto my side, I curled up and hugged my knees to my chest.

Blackie came in then, just opened the door and walked in, like it was his room.

"What's with him?"

"Who knows?" Panama shrugged. Reaching into his jacket, he pulled the gun from the holster and made a big show of checking the magazine, then replaced it. Probably for my benefit, even though I couldn't have crawled from that room just then even if the place were going up in flames.

"So," Blackie said in an easy, friendly manner, "we had to call in a few markers to find you, yes."

Lost in my own misery, I made no reply.

"You OK, kid?" Blackie wanted to know.

Kid! He was all of five or six years older than me and I guess he thought that gave him the right to call me kid. It didn't seem to matter, anyway.

"All right then," Panama said and clapped his hands. "Where's Art Delaplane?"

I looked at him. Art? Who gave a shit about Art? Before I could answer, they hit me with "Where's Stephen Burke?"

I blinked at him, unable to comprehend. So Stephen was Burke's first name, but why are they asking me about those two, and not where I was on the night of Pen's death?

"When's the last time you spoke to or saw Art Delaplane or Stephen Burke? Where are they staying? Come on, kid, snap out of it!" Panama couldn't keep his impatience under control.

Slowly, through the fear and exhaustion, I began to see the forest through the trees. They hadn't taken me straight to HQ, but back in my hotel room. They hadn't asked a single question about Pen. It came to then. They had no interest in Pen at all. They wanted Art and Burke.

My fear began to evaporate and the shivering lessened. I looked back and forth between them, trying to see the angles.

"Listen," Blackie said, "you help us, we can help you, yes."

"Is that right?"

"That's right, asshole," Panama broke in, "and if you fuck with us, we'll see you in Leavenworth for the next ten years of your miserable life!" Veins stood out in his neck and his bleached out eyes popped. Blackie winced very slightly.

"All right," Blackie said, talking to Panama, "we're pros here, don't fuck it up."

He turned to me. "So where is Stephen Burke?"

"Here in Bangkok somewhere," I said which was all I really knew.

"How about Art Delaplane?"

"Same," I said, "in the city somewhere."

"You cooperate with us and we can help you, make a little matter of a dead girl go away. You stonewall us…" Panama left the threat dangling there. I wondered if they knew about my part of the fishing boat and Ko Samet.

"I didn't kill her and you know it."

"How do we know that?"

"Because," I said slowly, my mind whirling, "if you thought I did, I'd be at army HQ right now, not sittin' here talkin' to you. Somethin's up here. You guys want something from me, and want it bad, I think."

They glanced at each other and I knew I was right. Exactly what did they want? I waited while the silence deepened.

"What is it you want?" Blackie finally spoke up and emphasized the "you".

A deal was going to happen, and I knew exactly what I wanted. "I wanna know who killed Pen and why."

They both grinned. "We might be able to help you with that, provided you help us."

"I'm listening."

"OK," Blackie said, "but first, let's start over, us." He grinned and extended his hand. In that instant I knew where I'd seen him before.

CHAPTER 30

"Hey," I said as I took his hand, "found any Jax, as in J-A-X?"

He laughed, sharp and quick as he shook.

"No," he said, "no Jax here."

It took a second, then I realized he sounded different.

"Well, Ray, wasn't it? What happened to that Cajun accent?"

"You have a good ear," he said, still gripping my hand. "I'm Ray DuBois, Sergeant DuBois, Criminal Investigation Division, and the accent comes and goes. This," he let go of my hand after one more shake and pointed, "is Sergeant Harry Jones."

I turned to Harry with my hand out, but he ignored it. " "You can call me Sergeant, Specialist."

I kept my face straight. "OK, Sarge it is then. So, lemme get this straight. You two are willin' to deal away the murder of a local for two AWOL Gis, Art Delaplane and Stephen Burke. I'll bet…" I looked at them both, to see if they could tell what was coming, but they both appeared to be stone figures now. I went ahead anyway.

"Yer the guys Art escaped from, huh?"

Ray remained still and impassive but Harry squirmed on the chair and tried to hide it by scratching his ankle. I remembered something Burke had said about a red-headed stepchild and knew Harry was the one Art had clocked to get away. So it was personal, too.

"About Burke?" Ray asked.

"Well," I said, "the last time I saw him, he…"

I looked back and forth between. They both tried to keep a poker face, but their nostrils twitched, hounds with the scent again.

"How'd you find him?" Harry asked.

"I didn't. He found me," I said with a huff.

They both nodded. "Go on," Ray said.

"Like I said," I paused for the interruption, but none came. "He found me. I was looking for someone and a couple of cowboys, working for Burke, I guess, started some shit. I finished it, but someone hit me from behind. I woke up in a warehouse, tied to a chair. Burke was there, Art, Matt, maybe some others, I couldn't tell. They stayed in the dark, except for Burke."

I had their attention now and I went on.

"Burke heard I was lookin' for him all over Bangkok 'n' he wanted to know why. He's a suspicious guy, can you believe it?"

I paused to light a smoke. "In the warehouse he denied killin' her, said it was all just business. Offered me a deal, just like you guys are. If I helped him, he'd help me find out who killed Pen, then he threw a snake at me."

They exchanged a glance.

"Why you think Burke had anything to do with your girl's death?"

I got the feeling Ray already knew the answer to that, but I told him anyway. "'Cause him and Art showed up at my hootch the night before the tug went to Bangkok. I think he threatened her and Pen pulled a knife on him. He pointed a pistol at her, a black automatic, not an issue forty-five, either."

Ray and Harry looked at each other. "The Makarov," they both said.

"You know about that?" I asked, watching them both.

"OK, you deserve to know a few things. Here's the deal on Burke." Ray waved off Harry's objections and started reciting as if he were reading a government file.

"Stephen Burke came to Viet Nam in late sixty-seven as an MP lieu-tenant and was assigned to Saigon. He wanted to make a career of police work because he thought he could make a difference in the world, if only a small one."

"For a few months, he worked well, making the grade, climbed the ladder to captain. Then something happened to him. There were a lot of senior sergeants busted in a club kickback scheme, a lot of money changed hands. There was a lot of partying, round-eye women, booze, nice apartments, and somewhere along the line, Stephen Burke decided that he wanted part of it. Who knows?"

Ray lit a cigarette, snapped his lighter closed, and exhaled a cloud of smoke.

Unable to sit still, I stood and gazed out the window.

A light breeze ruffled through the tree leaves that broke the slanting rays of early sunlight into a glittering, shifting green and gold mosaic.

"In September of sixty-eight," Ray went on, his voice tighter now, "I was assigned to the case. This was gonna be my big break, the one that would get me out of busting privates with two joints in their pocket. I built a case, had a guy on the inside and was just about to make the bust when my inside guy was found dead with two seven-point-six-five bul-lets in him, the same caliber as a Makarov. You probably know the Makarov is a Russian pistol known to be carried by NVA officers. They're highly prized souvenirs."

I didn't know that, but all I did was ask. "So how'd Burke get to Thailand?"

"When Saigon became too hot, he left with forged R&R travel orders. Once here he hooked up with others like himself, AWOLs dealing in the black market, booze and stuff, then it got really serious."

"What do you mean, got serious? I thought it was already pretty damn serious."

Ray looked at me. "They started dealing in stolen medical supplies and guns."

"So," I said, "Burke is not only a thief and a traitor, he's a killer, too."

Harry nodded tersely. "That's about the size of it."

"So how come you can't bust him?"

Harry glared at me, but Ray only smiled ruefully.

"Don't think we haven't tried, goddamnit!" Harry shouted, "He's smart and alert as a coyote. He can smell cops and MPs, and he almost never sleeps in the same place twice in a row."

"Where'd Art fit into this?" I wanted to know.

Harry looked at me funny for a second and I felt my stomach rise, but he turned away and said, "Art was an accident. We stumbled on him after he hooked up with Burke. We didn't really bust him, just picked him up for questioning and were only going to hold him for twenty-four hours. We had nothing on him and were going to release him, but then…Well, let's just say he managed to get out of custody. But when he did that, we knew then he had a reason to run and was up to something."

Ray sucked the last drag from the cigarette, flipped it out the window, and turned to look at me. "You see what we're up against?"

A faint idea began to tickle the edge of my consciousness. I already didn't like it.

"So what's the plan?"

"There is no plan yet," Harry growled, "not until…"

"Listen here," I said. "If Burke was behind Pen gettin' killed, then I want his ass. If he ain't, then he can fly like a bird for all I care. All I really want…"

They looked at each other, then back to me. "I guess we better tell him," Ray said.

Harry nodded his agreement. Ray looked me in the eye and I knew there was a new wrinkle here, one I hadn't seen before. The fear of the unknown made my throat very dry.

"What are you talking about?" The words came out like dust bunnies from under a bed.

Harry gestured for Ray to go ahead. With a deep sigh, Ray glanced to the ceiling, then straight into my eyes. A flush broke out all over me.

"You know your girl had someone on the side, don't you?"

A flashing red, pulsating anger swept over me. Not that I thought Pen would butterfly on me, but at this shithead's blatant attempt to manipulate me. A great effort and I was able to look him calmly in the eyes.

"Nice try, but no points." I said mockingly. "She wouldn't do that. She had too much to lose to play around with another GI and besides, I took good care of all her needs."

I grabbed my crotch and hefted it in a show of masculine force and vigor, then flipped a hand in his direction to show that his lame attempt had failed.

"Maybe it wasn't another GI."

The calm certainty in his voice brought me up short. Even as I tried to stop it, little things started to click in my head, like a few times she wasn't there when I arrived, how sometimes she seemed very tired when she had no real work to do, and then there was the matter of those bruises on her.

Thoughts buzzed around in my head like moths around a flame, with no particular order, and I felt myself start to slide into a kind of believing that what this fuckhead said was true. With a force of will that shook my bones, I stopped it. Unless proven to me, I would not believe she had done anything to jeopardize what we had going. She just wouldn't do that and I told Ray so.

"Maybe, maybe not," he said. "You…"

Harry had a toothpick and was raking it back and forth across his teeth like a stick on a picket fence. I saw the laughter in his eyes. I looked back at Ray and was knocked over by what I saw in his eye. There was no mistake about it, he pitied me.

A thread of panic started up and wound its way through me and as I looked at them I thought how fine it would be if a searing, cleansing flame would suddenly appear and torch the both of them, right there in the room.

"Sit down," Ray said.

Now I was really shaken. What could be so bad as to bring on pity in this hardened CID cop? The room seemed smaller, then suddenly it started to spin. Ray put a hand on my shoulder and murmured calming things, as if he spoke to a panicky animal.

I slipped down onto the bed, my knees weak and pulse racing. Ray moved to the chair, straddled it, sucked in a deep breath and looked me in the eye. It became very quite.

"A routine autopsy showed your girl was pregnant at the time of her death. I'm sorry."

A terrific headache ripped through my brow and settled in my crown. The room tilted and spun faster, like a tilt-a-wheel gathering speed and a distant roaring noise grew louder and louder. I stared at Ray, shaking my head.

"No," I said softly, "it can't be, it…"

Why couldn't it be?

Quickly, I tried to think of all I knew about women and pregnancy. It took about one second.

"You guys are bullsh…" I stared at Ray and could see this was no bullshit.

"How far along?" My own voice came from very far away.

"About ten weeks," Ray said. "She wouldn't have started to really show yet."

"Why didn't she tell me?" I looked at both of them. They glanced at each other, out the window and down at the floor, but not at me. For some reason, an odd tingling up my spine told me something was up here, that the worst was yet to come.

"Why didn't she tell me?" I repeated louder, looking at both of them in turn.

Ray looked positively pained, Harry almost like he was enjoying himself. He started to speak, but with an angry gesture Ray cut him off.

"Listen," he said quickly, "life is tough for these girls. They have to watch out for themselves."

He said it with such care and genuine feeling that I had to look up at him. Kim and Mama-san had said the same thing.

I realized I was panting like a dog. Here it was, one of the things I had dreaded the most. I had always told myself that I would never bring a kid into the world if I couldn't be around to help him or her grow up. I would never do to anyone what my father had done to me.

"Didn't you notice when she stopped having her period?" Harry was sarcastic but I barely heard it and only shook my head.

"Her tits get bigger, she put on a few pounds?"

I could only nod and stare.

"Her nipples get real plump and firm?"

I couldn't believe what I was hearing. He laughed, a small mocking laugh that said he was in the know, and I wasn't.

"Did she…"

"Knock it off, Harry!" Ray said. "He's only a kid."

There it was again. I looked at Ray, hating him for tagging me as an ignorant kid, but I knew that that's what I was. I had no notion of her periods, only that she had had one or two and we couldn't make love for a few days. When they had stopped, I hadn't noticed. I wanted these guys to be gone so I could deal with this alone, but that wasn't going to happen. Instead, I looked at Ray.

"Who killed her?" I asked.

I heard his answer as if he were standing on another planet. "We really don't know. It's one of those mysteries of the East. Who knows what these people are really thinking, anyway? We don't even have a possible motive. Local cops are not real interested in the death of a working girl as long as she wasn't a communist subversive."

I knew then that they had no intention of finding out who the killer was, and that as long as their operation came off, they didn't care. Like he said, a mystery of the East, not our problem.

"What do you know about a GI, a tall, skinny AWOL from Nam, name of Matt?"

They looked at each other.

"You're right about the AWOL part," Ray said. "Came to Bangkok for R&R, never went back. He was at My-Lai, but that's not our problem. If we get him we'll squeeze him…"

"What do you know," I asked, "about a local cowboy, calls himself Duke. Green-eyed, brown hair, hangs around the Skeeter and Patpong."

They looked at each other again.

"You get around, don't you?" Ray said. "We've heard of him, but from what we can gather, he's just a local punk, strictly small-time, a nobody."

Did I just imagine a signal passing between them? Were they trying to shuck and jive me about Duke. Why?

"What's his connection to Burke and Art?"

"Like we said," Harry seemed irritated and I was glad, "he's a nobody!"

"Look," Ray said, real conviction in his voice, "I know its a shitty way to be, but think about it. We got a war to fight. We're sorry it happened, but we got a job to do. You help us a little, and you can be out of country in less than ten days, two weeks tops, ETS out, and get on with your life. We'll forget about charging you with black marketeering, too."

I must have looked surprised.

"Thought we didn't know about that, huh?" Harry smirked. "We were lettin' it slide for a while, since you didn't know you were movin' that kind of contraband. You thought you were only movin' PX stuff." He shook his head in the affirmative.

"Still," he went on, "we could charge you…" He let the threat hang there like the sword of Damocles.

"There it is," I said.

Outside, the sky was blue, the clouds were white and puffy, the leaves were green, a beautiful day, but it all seemed tarnished somehow, like there would never be any pleasure for me here anymore. Getting the hell out of country seemed like a good idea suddenly, but not before I found out who had killed her and my kid, even if she had never planned to tell me about it. A white hot conviction told me Burke and Art both knew something about it and I intended to find out what it was. I'd use these two humps here just like they intended to use me, with no qualms about it.

"What do I have to do?"

Ray smiled and Harry clapped his hands together like he was getting down to business.

"We want you to do that job for Burke," Harry said. "We'll be nearby and when the time is right, we'll make the bust."

His chin was out and I could see the intensity of his felt emotion, the passionate way he approached his mission in life. This was how he validated himself.

"OK," I said, "who else is in on this?"

Neither of them said anything and I began to get a sick feeling again. "You mean we're it? You got nobody else, no MPs, no locals, nobody?"

"We're it," Ray said, "and we don't need anyone else."

I glanced back and forth between them and it came to me then. "You guys haven't done the paperwork on Art, have you? You think you can get him back and no one will ever be the wiser, isn't that right?"

"In the army nothing exists until you have paperwork on it, you oughta know that by now." Ray hit the nail squarely on the head.

For the next hour we talked logistics and planning. I paid attention and nodded, building a plan of my own.

A few hours sleep, a shower, a plate of pork fried rice and I was fueled and ready to go.

I needed to see Duke right away, but the padlock in the hasp showed he wasn't here.

In the street, I went to Mama-san's place to get a *cafe nam kang* and have a word with her, but a sullen adolescent boy told me Mama-san had had to leave for Chaing-Mai. Someone was sick. Possible, I thought, but pretty convenient. Why would she avoid me, though?

A broad leafed tree with multiple trunks spread its canopy overhead as I sat on a circular cement bench and watched the river traffic. Finished with the iced coffee, I bounced the bag on its rubber band and lofted it with an underhand swing right into a trash can twenty feet away. A pretty little girl, maybe six or seven, watched me solemnly from the edge of Mama-sans shop.

"*Sawadee, dek-dek,*" I said to her.

Her big dark eyes lit and she quickly looked down, then back up at me, her smile radiating embarrassed delight. The same boy came out and hustled her inside. Just before she disappeared, she turned and waved. In spite of my bleak mood, that gesture lifted my spirits, until the boy gave me the one-finger salute.

This, I told myself, would be a good time to go see Kim, continue our conversation from the other night and find out what she meant by Don't think bad about Pen or Thailand.

She lived in the same building Pen had, just down the hall, but like Duke's place, the padlock on her door offered proof she wasn't home. Damn.

Moving down the stairs with the street door right in front of me, I saw Kim come in. Hitting the first step, she looked up and saw me. Her face blanched, her eyes opened wide like an iris, then she dropped her packages, turned and bolted.

"Kim!" I said, "wait! *Del nit, del nit!*"

Quick and agile, she made the door in a single leap and was gone. Jumping the last half-dozen steps, I hit the landing hard and skidded on the worn linoleum but managed to keep my feet and plunged out the door.

Up the block, I saw her. She had her sarong pulled up and her caramel colored legs flashed in a stride that, even as I watched, pulled her away fast. I lit after her, calling her name, asking her to stop.

She was fast, but I gained on her rapidly. Her short hair bounced and fluttered as she glanced back and seeing me gaining on her, she put on all she had while she screeched an alarm.

Some cowboy came out of a noodle shop and saw us. I could tell he was going to stick his two cents in and instead of trying to go around him I changed course right at him. A stiff-arm to the chest and he went down like a bowling pin leaving me a clear shot at Kim.

I didn't want to tackle and hurt her, so I caught up to her, got a grip on her elbow and started slowing down. She jerked hard, but not enough.

"Kim, Kim, *ali, ali*?" What, what? I asked her, why is she running away?

For an answer she turned quick, kneed me in the gut and raked her nails down the side of my face. I hadn't expected that and the air left me like my an emergency valve had popped. I crumpled and went down hard. As I looked up at her, the terror in her face shocked me, then she was gone.

People were starting to gather, muttering angry things, *felong* this and *felong* that. Stumbling and staggering to my feet, I lurched out of there as fast as I could, hardly breathing, my face on fire.

What had Kim been so terrified of?

Slipping in the side door of the hotel, I headed for the bathroom on my floor to wash the scratches and found someone had left a bottle of cologne there. Quickly, I splashed some into my hand and applied it. The sting made me holler, and for good measure I splashed some on my hand where the girl in the bar had bit me.

These girls were good at self-defense, Pen had shown me that and now I had more proof. I decided it might be best to lay low for awhile.

CHAPTER 31

I heard the click, loud in the warm, dark stillness. Coming awake I smelled the rank, fecund smell of the river, overlaid with bananas and whiskey. Before I could roll off the bed onto the floor a light drove needles of brightness straight at me and I raised a hand to shield my eyes. Something heavy laid across my chest and pressed me down hard and held my wrist.

"Be cool, man." The deep growl sounded sure of himself.

"What's it gonna be, hotshot?"

I recognized Burke's voice. I relaxed, the weight moved off, but the grip of iron still remained fastened on my wrist. "Lemme go, Art," I said.

The grip let up.

"You made up your mind yet?"

"Get that light outa' my face."

The light went onto the floor.

"Don't you guys ever just come on over and knock on the door?"

"What happened to your face?" Art wanted to know.

"I fell."

"You look like you shared a burlap bag with a wildcat."

"Fuck that," Burke interrupted. "What is it, yes or no?" He sounded strained.

"Tell me," I countered, "how…"

"I told you before!" Burke rasped, "all your questions will be answered on the island!"

Even in the dim light I could see the whites of his eyes and the set of his mouth. He was frying on something.

"OK," I said, "I'm in."

Burke's gaunt face split into his deaths head grin and Art glanced up at the ceiling for a second.

"Outfuckingstanding," Burke said tightly. "Day after tomorrow, be at the dock in Ban Phe at eighteen hundred."

I nodded. The light snapped off, the door closed. My stomach churned and I had to swallow several times to choke down something that tried to come up and filled my nose with a sickly sweet odor that could not possibly have come from me.

Leaning out the window, I sucked deep breaths of the warm air and looked at the moon. Three days from full it poured light down and cast the scene before me into stark blacks and whites.

Looking up at it, I was sure the man was laughing at me, mocking my puny plans, telling me that the plans I had made were worthless in the face of what was to come, that the best plan was no plan, to take the cards that were dealt and play out the hand the best way you could, and if you held nothing of value, then bluff. Sometimes a good bluff was better than four aces, but sometimes you got called.

I missed her so much, I didn't know how to tell it.

I slept fitfully for another two hours, until hunger drove me out into the street shortly after sunrise.

At the Skeeter I ordered scrambled eggs and fried rice, then sat with a smoke and cup of instant coffee, waiting for Ray. He showed up half-way through the second cup.

"You piss someone off?" He nodded at Kim's handiwork.

"Long story," I said.

He wrinkled his lips as he considered it for a moment, then said, "You had a visitor last night."

It wasn't a question and I was sure they had someone in the hotel, maybe even watching me all the time. I asked Ray about it.

"You're covered," he said. "So what did they want last night?"

I told him.

"How you feel about that?"

"Wha'd'you mean by that? Isn't this what we've been workin' toward? This is what we want, right?" When he didn't answer right away, I pressed him again.

He finally nodded affirmative, but I wasn't so sure now. He seemed to be unexcited about it, hesitant somehow. I didn't feel real good about it, either.

"In this part of the world," he said, as if reading my mind, "communication is difficult, so we have to do everything with messengers and personal contact or by radio. Without phones, we have to keep a close eye on you, but it's all unofficial, just people we hire out of our own pocket. Eyes in the street, that kind of thing. But, I've got something for you."

He reached into a gym bag and brought out a small black box, about the size of a pack of cigarettes.

"This," he said, holding it in his had, "is a transmitter. You press this button, we come running."

"You get the other stuff?"

He grimaced at me and pulled another bundle out of the bag. "Fatigue pants, T-shirt, boots."

"Listen," he said earnestly, "you gotta have some confidence here. In us, and in yourself. You got what it takes to look out for yourself until we can get there and get these goddamned traitors into the stockade where they fucking belong!"

"Spare me the pep talk, Coach. Where's the gun?"

"In the pants pocket, with one full magazine and one in the tube. It's a clean .45, no numbers on it. When you're done, get rid of it. So, got any ideas on the way it might go down?"

"We'll leave Ban Phe as soon as its good and dark," I said. "We'll probably head for the same cove as always, you know the one. There's a small dock and a shack for transshipping. They're all set up."

I told myself that it would work out, that things would go right, that I would get out of this with my skin intact.

Uncle Jack used to say that preparation was ninety percent of any job, luck was five percent, and skill was five percent, whether it was laying on a coat of varnish or getting ready for a run out to Santa Cruz Island.

Preparation, skill and luck.

In the hotel, I put my few things into a gym bag, checked out and walked around the corner to the Skeeter.

As I looked for a cab to take me to Sattahip, I noticed a guy perched on a Honda 350 wearing a helmet with a smoked plastic shield. That, I thought, might be the way to go. On a bike I could weave in and out of traffic, go around congestion and make good time. I stood on the curb looking at him, thinking all this when it dawned on me that he seemed to be looking back at me. A car slid into a space between us, blocking my view. I was imagining things. He had no interest in me, and I decided against a bike. Riding a bike in Thailand took a lot of concentration and I wanted to be able to think of other things.

I struck a deal with a gypsy cab driver and we were off. On the coast road, I enjoyed the ride, even though the car had no air conditioning. It reminded me of the first time I'd come down this road, those many months before when everything had been new and exciting.

Before long, though, my thoughts turned. What had Duke and Pen had going? What kind of financial deal had Art and Pen been involved in?

Who could tell me more about this? I had an idea.

Timi, Peach's *tilok*, was a good friend of Pen's and would probably know something.

Ninety minutes later I' was standing at the bottom of the stairs to Peach's hootch, pretty sure she would be here. Where does a *tilok* go in the morning?

In response to my knock, I heard some commotion from inside. Timi peeked out through the latched screen.

"*Ow ali?*"

No hello, hi, how are you, just what do you want?

"Timi," I said, keeping my head turned a little so she couldn't see that side of my face, "can I talk to you? I need…"

"No talk, no talk!" Her voice rose higher and higher with each word. I tried to calm her, at least enough to convince her that I hadn't killed Pen, but she kept yelling, attracting attention.

"Listen, Timi," I hissed through the screen, "I'll be at the Bamboo Palace."

All the girls from the Skeeter knew of the Bamboo Palace, a ratty little hotel in Sattahip. Many of the girls from Bangkok and lots of the tug crews stayed there from time to time. She knew where it was.

From the Sattahip wharf I took the water taxi to the port and went to the Batty office. There was no word from Brian so I went aboard the SHIELA, started the engine and headed out.

Once the sails were up and drawing in the twelve knot southwesterly, I put the wind just forward of the beam, tied off the tiller with the lazy sheet and kicked back in the cockpit. I could feel the tension, anger and uncertainty of the last few days melt away, as if the boat itself could pull the cares and troubles right out of me and dispel them all in the clean, bubbling saltwater of the wake. I stripped down.

Melville said, "…these are the times of dreamy quietude, when beholding the tranquil beauty and brilliance of the ocean's skin, one forgets the tiger's heart that pants beneath it…"

Those lines fit Pen perfectly. She'd had a tranquil beauty and brilliant skin, and there was no doubt she'd had a tiger's heart, too.

Standing up in the cockpit, one hand holding the backstay, I rode the easy motion and spoke out loud.

"Pen, my sweet, I promise on the memory of our time together that I will find out who did this to you and make them pay. Your *kwang-hai* will be free for the journey to Nirvana. I almost wish I could go with you."

I dropped anchor in the little cove of Ko Khram Yai, where Pen and I had spent so many days, swimming, exploring, lazing and making love.

It was exactly the same now as it had been then, but it wasn't the same and it was almost painful being there. Diving into the warm water, I relished its cleansing power and felt calm, relaxed, at ease, but filled with a purpose.

I hoped I had a tiger's heart too, even just a little, knowing I would need it in the days to come.

After dark, I brought the SHIELA back into the harbor and moored up.

CHAPTER 32

I heard the sound, a soft tap-tap, through a misty-smoky sleep. A halyard against the mast. I sat up, intending to go on deck and secure it, but when I opened my eyes, I was astounded to discover that I was not aboard SHEILA at all, but in my tiny room at the Bamboo Palace. 0200 hours by my watch. Again the sound came, tap-tap-tap.

In a daze, I looked around the room trying to find out where it came from. Tap-tap-tap, more insistent this time and with a start, I realized someone was at the door. Art and Burke maybe, but would they knock.

Springing from the bed, I stood beside the door, the .45 in my right hand. "Who is it?" I demanded in a harsh voice.

A muffled, indistinct answer.

That damned Burke liked to show up at 0-dark-30 and wave that Makarov around. I'd show him this time. I cocked the pistol, the sound loud in the stillness, and jerked the door open.

The gasp of fright didn't fit. A small figure stood there, lit by the bare bulb in the hall, wearing a black shirt, black pants, and a dark colored baseball cap.

"Bob, it me, Timi." The voice wavered with fright.

The breath I held left me all at once and I opened the door and stepped away from it, the pistol pointed straight up.

She entered the room like a cat, one step in, pause to look around, another step in, not committing until satisfied it was safe.

I snapped on the light and she jumped. Breathing hard, her eyes wide, she stared at the gun.

"So you came after all," I said, swinging the door shut.

She could hardly tear her gaze from the gun, as if it were an apparition of doom, so I dropped it into the cargo pocket of the jungle fatigues I wore.

The fear in her pulled lines and planes into her face that the harsh overhead light emphasized. Cautiously, I listened at the door but heard nothing.

"Timi," I said, steering her to the chair, "thanks for coming. I…"

"I wan' talk you," she said in a rush, "you come bungalow, but no can do, many people see, you know?"

I knew exactly what she meant. This whole country was full of people sticking their nose into other people's business, and spies and gossip were national pastimes.

I nodded encouragingly and wished I had something to offer her. Sitting on the bed, I simply said, "Yes."

"I tell you, Pen do, *poochai* Duke do, OK?"

This was too good to be true, and a flood of suspicion swept over me.

"OK, talk," I said, sniffing for the set up.

Taking off her hat, Timi shook out her short hair. Her fingers strayed to the carved wooden amulet at her throat. All the girls wore some kind of symbol and believed it protected them from whatever they needed protecting from.

"Duke numba ten *poochai*!" she said. Her face snapped from apprehension to lip-curling loathing in an instant. Gathering in a breath, she started talking.

"Duke fadda sea-man, *felong* officer, run away ship for *sway mahk pooying* work Mosquito Bar. Him love her *mahk-mahk*." Timi sighed, small and delicate, as if she herself could only imagine how it would feel to be the object of so much love.

"They stay togetta," she continued, "but Thai police catch him, give him…" Her face twitched in anxiety and her hands fluttered in her lap at not knowing the right words.

"To *felong* police." I put in helpfully.

"*Chai, felong* police. Duke fadda go back Swee-dan, him mother *mai-mee baht*, ver' big, what you say?" She pantomimed a big belly.

"Pregnant, *mee dek-dek?*"

Her eyes lit up at the understanding, then she went on. For over an hour we talked, using the Thai/English spoken in the bars, and gradually, with stops and starts, mistakes, and trying over and over, I got the gist of the story.

Duke's mother, a "biz'ness girl", had been pregnant with a child conceived in love. With her provider arrested and shipped back to Sweden, and unable to ply her trade, she had been in dire straits. An old Chinaman had offered to take her in. When Duke was born the old man took one look at him, saw his golden hair and green eyes, and promptly stole him. Sold to a rich family in Bangkok, Duke grew up well, went to a Catholic school, but the Chinaman had made Duke's mother a virtual slave. She stayed with him for fifteen years, suffering his use of her body and the abuse of her spirit. Her health started to fail.

Eventually, Duke came of age, realized from his looks that these were not his parents, and ran away. Being smart and resourceful, he found out what had happened and killed the old Chinaman and took his mother to a place where she could get some care.

His mother, already terminal, soon died, leaving Duke alone. He soon found he could make a good living supplying merchant seamen and GIs with the vices they craved. He carried a cracked and torn picture of his father that his mother had given him and searched the docks in Bangkok, boarding ships when he could, prowling the bars and cafes, looking for his missing daddy.

This sounded like a Shakespearean tragedy to me and I was sure Timi had added a few points of her own, but all through the telling, she had a strange, dreamy look about her, and her soft, feathery voice, wrapped with longing, convinced me that the core story was true. Unable to sit still as she talked, she paced and moved like a folk dancer, dancing out a centuries-old tale of tragedy and loss.

There was more.

Pen's story was a little murkier and I couldn't get it straight. Her mother was a housewife with a small child until her father died, or her mother was a working girl too. I believed the latter since I'd met the old Mama-san, but it didn't really matter. Pen ended up working the Skeeter, preferring Scandinavians and Americans to Thai and Chinese.

She met Duke soon after. He was about seventeen then, and he fell in love with her because of her uncanny resemblance to his mother. Unwilling to be dependant on anyone and determined to make her own way, she wouldn't stop working. It drove Duke nuts.

"Yes," I said, "but what kind of deal did Pen and Art and Burke have going?" The fear that Pen was somehow in on the smuggling deal from the start was growing inside me, but I couldn't figure out how, but whatever it was, I was convinced she was just looking out for her future.

"I don' know." Timi said, "I tell every'sing."

I thanked her for her trouble and told her she was a brave and loyal friend to Pen for coming to see me.

"Bob," she said. Her eyes, dark and serious, looked right into mine and I could feel the weight of what she was about to say. "You find numba ten *poochai* kill my frien', kill him, too!"

Not exactly according to the teachings of Buddha, I thought, but I told her I would, so help me God.

"Bob, Pen tell me, she love you *mahk-mahk*, no bullshit." Tears gathered in Timi's eyes and spilled down her cheeks. "She no wan' hurt you."

With a soft kiss on my cheek and her scent like a cloud around me, Timi wished me luck and swept out the door, her hat pulled low.

Moonlight flooded the room and I lay on the bed for hours, turning Timi's story this way and that, examining it from every angle.

Nervously, I took out the .45 again and checked it, felt
the weight of the loaded pistol and took a measure of comfort from
it's solid bulkiness. If it came right down to it, I'd match this Colt .45
against Burke's underpowered Makarov any day, but in spite of the
bravado I put out there, deep in the back of my mind I shivered.

Slipping the gun under the little pillow, I laid down on the bed and
looked out the window to see the sky in the east become streaked with
the pink pearl fingers of the dawn.

I woke as the shadows lengthened across the ground and with the
radio transmitter in the left cargo pocket and the .45 in the right one, I
went into the street.

CHAPTER 33

Thirty minutes and three *baht* bus rides later I was in the small village of Ban Phe.

The little houses on stilts, the palm trees, mangy dogs and naked kids playing made it all look normal. The danger lay several miles offshore, in a pretty little cove on a hunk of indifferent jungle.

I wasn't hungry at all but I stopped at a little noodle shop and forced down a huge plate of pork-fried rice and a mango along with two little Pepsis.

In the southwest, the sun turned the sea into a lake of golden fire. I looked for the green flash, but didn't see it. From the southeast, an eerie glow slowly spread into the sky. I watched, mesmerized, unable to even glance away and check on activity around me, as the tropic moon rose, an orange disk that peeked over the horizon to light a few scattered clouds with an ethereal light. I checked my watch. 1755 hours.

On my feet, I looked down the beach to the dock. A few fishing boats bobbed and tugged their lines but I saw no activity, and no sign of Ray and Harry. What did I expect, a navy destroyer to be sitting out there?

Slowly, I walked down the dock to the boat we used and went aboard. A few things had been added. A four-inch compass and a small fire extinguisher showed their shiny newness in the scarred wooden cabin and two army flashlights lay on top of the binnacle. A few cushions were scattered around on the long gear boxes that served as settees.

"You like it?"

Clamping down the urge to spin around, I turned slowly. Burke stood there in clean fatigue pants, polished jungle boots and a green T-shirt. A red bandanna added a slash of color around his neck and a black gym bag dangled from one hand.

"Yeah, I like it," I said. "Shoulda been done a long time ago."

"Well, it would have if I'd a been goin' out there, ya' know?"

I had to agree to that. Burke wasn't the type to risk his skin in a poorly equipped craft for anyone. He reached out and flicked a switch. A red light spread from a new fixture mounted to the overhead.

Bumps and voices signaled more people coming aboard. I heard Art's rumble, then Matt's slur. I pressed the start button, the engine turned over and, reluctantly it seemed, came to life.

Art and Matt slumped into the pilothouse. I glanced at Matt, but in the gathering dark I couldn't see much. He sagged onto a settee, pulled a bottle of local whiskey from a pocket, took a long drink from it and pulled the Airborne hat he wore over his eyes. I saw the look of absolute contempt on Burke's face and the sad pity on Art's, then I busied myself getting us away from the pier and hoping Ray and Harry were already on the island.

Once we were underway and steady on course, everyone relaxed somewhat. Matt continued to hit the bottle. Burke watched in silence for a while.

"Why don't you just crawl inside that bottle and save us all a lot of trouble, huh?"

Matt barely registered anything said to him, but this time he opened his eyes and looked Burke in the face.

"Up yours, sir," he said as he tipped the bottle again. Burke snorted a laugh as if he didn't care, but it rang hollow.

I glanced at the compass to check my course and then looked at Burke again. He had that black pistol out and was wiping it with a bit of cloth. Pressing a button, he dropped the magazine out, wiped it, blew an imaginary speck of dust from it and shoved it back into the handle of the gun. With a solid smack, he seated the mag and slid it into a black nylon shoulder rig he had put on.

Reaching into the bag between his booted feet, he pulled out a long black something and clipped it onto one of the front straps of the holster and drew from it a Marine Corp. K-Bar combat knife that he wiped with the cloth. Satisfied, he slipped the knife into the scabbard and snapped the catch. It hung handle down, ready for instant access.

With a smile, he zipped up the bag, put it in a corner and stood up, shook his rig a little to settle it, then went out the door and headed aft. Art followed him out.

I couldn't help but think that that performance had been for someone's benefit.

If Matt saw it, he gave no sign. In the red light his skin was blotchy, he hadn't shaved in days. A sour odor of old sweat, vomit, and urine came from him.

"Where you from in the world, man?" I asked him.

"Wha'do you care?" His tone, sullen and defiant, carried a thread of something else.

"I wanna know," I replied.

"Why?" He pulled the very last drag from that nub of cigarette, typical of the addict and flipped the tiny butt out the open door.

I lowered my voice. "Cause I do, that's why. You look like shit, you know that, and you smell like it, too." I shook my head. "You must have seen some really terrible stuff to have fallen this far."

I thought he might tell me to mind my own fucking business, or he might not respond at all, and I was about to give up when I heard him say, "I'm from Vermont." His voice was a thin tremolo, like it came from far away.

"Home of the Green Mountain Boys." I said, then added, "Some of your ancestors must have been at Fort Ticonderoga under Ethan Allen."

His face turned toward me and I saw his eyes open very wide. "Man," he said, "no one knows that. How come you do?"

"I like history," I said. My stomach fluttered. "Is your last name Allen?"

"Yeah," he said, his voice thick.

Oh, shit! I might have just reminded him how badly he has disgraced the Allen name and searched for something to change the subject. "How long you known Burke?"

He stiffened and looked up at me in a way that reminded me of a cornered possum I had once seen in Texas.

"Not very long," he said, very slowly.

"D'joo know him in Nam?"

A visible shudder racked him. "Yeah," was all he said, but his hands clamped onto his thighs and I could see him squeezing hard, breathing in short little gasps.

"You guys in the same unit?"

A strange sound came from him, a cross between a sob and a grunt. "No."

"But you knew him?"

"What the hell is this?" He shouted, his face twisting in anger. "You wanna know about him, go ask him yourself!"

"I don't give a flyin' fuck about Burke," I said, "but I wonder what happened to fuck you up this bad, man. Get a grip. You…"

Art came in and glanced back and forth between us. Matt seemed to shrink in on himself for a second, then he heaved himself to his feet and went out the door and forward, to his customary place on the forward hatch.

Art watched him go. "What were you two talking about?"

"Nothin'," I said. "Just askin' Matt what it was that knocked the pilings out from under him, that's all."

"Matt's trying to get away from himself. He's convinced he's done for, and…"

"All he needs is a reason to pull himself back, man. He's not gone yet, but…"

"Not your problem, man."

What he meant was he didn't want to talk about it anymore, either because he was part of the problem, or else truly didn't care. I watched him for a moment, riding the motion of the boat with an easy, athletic grace.

"Tell me what's goin' on." I said.

He turned a heavy gaze on me, but said nothing.

"What's the point of all this?" I said. "What's Burke lookin' to do?"

"Shut up," Art replied, his voice a low, thick rumble. "All your questions will be answered later, so for now just shut the fuck up and drive."

I was trying to think of an answer for that when he suddenly added, "I don't have to tell you to watch your ass out here, do I?"

That was the scariest thing I'd heard in a long time. Sweat broke on my already damp forehead. "Tell me anyway," I croaked out.

He stared out the window ahead of us, the picture of icy calm, but by the red overhead light I saw a vein jump in his neck, and he wiped a huge hand over his face.

I waited for him to elaborate, thoughts of blood and mayhem going through my head but he merely stared out the window.

Finally, I couldn't stand it any more. "What the hell you talkin' about, man?"

His large head rotated toward me like an owl. Dark eyes glittering slits, he looked positively demented in the red light and it made me tremble.

"What," he said, the contempt in his tone plain, "you think you're the only guy can drive a boat around here?"

I felt my skin expand and contract around my whole body and from a long distance heard myself say, "You got something to say, just say it, OK? Stop talkin' in fuckin' circles!"

"Everything is a circle, man. What goes around, comes around, you know?"

"Where've I heard that before?" I asked sarcastically, but he turned away.

In front of me, the newly mounted compass showed we were on course. How nice it would be, I thought, if people were like a compass. Simple, reliable, always told the truth, always gave you the answers you needed to get you where you had to go, but people were like a compass with a chunk of iron nearby. They both appeared outwardly normal, but were deceitful to the point of danger. What was Art's hunk of iron, what was making him deceitful?

"What kind of deal did you and Duke and Pen have going?"

I kept my tone pleasant because I wanted him to answer.

To my surprise, he looked at me over his shoulder and laughed.

"You think your old lady was up front and told you the truth about everything?"

That low laugh of his infuriated me, and the idea that he knew something about her that I didn't frosted my balls. My hand drifted down and touched the hard steel of the .45 with my fingertips.

"What're you talkin' about?" I managed to say without a squeak in my voice.

In an easy drawl, Art said, "Pen was playing you like a fiddle, man."

Now I really wanted to blow his head off, but instead of that, I merely waited and gripped the wheel tighter.

"She used you to set up a score, one that would get her enough bread to get out of the life."

I felt my blood start to simmer.

"That's what you say." Hard as it was, I kept my voice down. "She wasn't like that. She…"

"She must have done you good." He laughed and shook his head.

"Bob," he said, "she didn't owe Duke any money. That whole thing was all her idea and you went for it. Sure, we needed a boat driver, but what we paid you was peanuts to what we're making. We gave that punk Duke a few bucks to go along, but most of that bread went to Pen, and who knows, she might have had more than one scheme going. She was a smart girl."

The way he looked at me left me no doubt that he told the truth.

The moon had turned a silvery white and lit a spangled trail in the ruffled water right to us, like a silver road in the ocean. The breeze tasted slightly metallic, like it had blown over a vast rusty metal plate before it reached us.

I stewed in the juice of my own thoughts while the numbers on the compass blurred together. Pen had tricked me? How had I missed that?

We reached Laem Noina, the unlit northern headland of Ko Samet, in good time. Burke and I just happened to take out a cigarette at the same time. He was first with his lighter since I had one hand on the wheel, and I expected him to offer me a light, but he looked right at me, lit his own, snapped his lighter shut and turned away. I started to say something, but stopped. Fuck him, I thought, conserve your energy, you might need it later.

I checked my watch. In about thirty minutes I would start looking for Ao Phrao cove.

Plans for getting out of here with my skin intact ran through my head, without any help from Ray and Harry. I had just completed a complex scenario and had all the variables covered when Burke said something that raised goose bumps in spite of the heat.

"Turn in here."

"What?" I couldn't have heard that right, could I?

This was not the right cove.

"Turn here," he jerked his thumb toward the island, clearly visible two miles away, "right here."

I was so dumbfounded I kept going straight. Glancing around, I saw Art watching me intently, and then I knew. It was the old switcheroo, the last-second change of plans that spells deceit, danger and death. I slipped a hand into my left cargo pocket and thumbed the transmitter switch, praying the signal was going out.

Numbly, I turned the wheel and headed toward the island, knowing Ray and Harry would be waiting, hidden in the second cove, separated by thick, impenetrable jungle. Would they receive the signal? That little transmitter probably operated somewhere in the VHF band and was line of sight only.

"You guys got a dock or a pier or something in this place?" I asked.

"Shut up." Burke said. Hostility oozed from him. Did he know about Ray and Harry?

"You think you're such a smart guy, don'cha?" The mocking scorn in Burke's tone was loud and clear. My throat closed and it was suddenly hard to breath.

"What're you talkin' about?" I bluffed for all I was worth.

He snorted loudly. "You think you're dealing with a bunch of dumb fucks, or what? You really think you could waltz in here, get chummy with us, and lead us right into a CID bust?"

He laughed out loud. "Those two clowns, Ray and Harry, have been chasing me for a long time. I feed 'em a little somethin' every so often, keeps 'em from bringing in someone smarter'n they are. I stay ahead of 'em that way."

He laughed again and I knew I wouldn't make it off this island unless I did something drastic.

The acrid stink of fear became strong.

As we motored in, I could see a light blink a pattern ahead of us. Burke answered with a flashlight and a brighter light came on and held steady. A lantern on a pole, and I could see a rickety wharf on skinny pilings.

"Head for that."

Something told me that this was it. Like Burke had said, I wasn't the only one that could drive a boat, and he probably didn't need me to drive this one back to Ban Phe. As soon as we tied up, my life expectancy would be counted in minutes, and the only question I had was why bring me all the way out here in the first place?

One look at the dark jungle behind the light told me why. They could bury my body in the interior of this island and no one would ever find it. In two or three weeks, there would be nothing left to find, either.

A quick plan jelled in my mind. I had to get off this boat, and fast. As I set up for the approach to the pier, I jammed the throttle forward, stepped out the door to the rail and flung myself as far as I could.

The boat moved away rapidly as I hit the water and felt the warm blackness close over me.

Swimming under water, I headed for the beach at an angle away from the light. The plan was to make the beach, then try to escape over land to the next cove and meet up with Ray and Harry.

Under the water, I heard the engine slow as someone took control, then speed up, getting louder as it approached me. Turning onto my back under the water, I watched for the phosphorescence churned up by the prop, to see if they were headed my way. They were, but at such an angle that they would miss me completely.

Pinpricks of light pierced the water and shot downward, trails of phosphorescent bubbles like silver threads on black velvet. Flashlights and bullets, shined and shot with no real hope of hitting anything. In desperation and anger, they were hoping to get lucky. I stayed about eight feet down and could see the bullets lance into the water and peter out, the brightness die.

Frog-kicking as far as I could on one breath, I carefully came to the surface for another and to take a bearing. I could hear engine noise, shouting and swearing and I went down again, not as deep this time, and kicked a little harder. The boat made another circle toward me, but again didn't come close.

My lungs started to ache, but I stayed down, only coming to the surface for a breath when it felt like they would burst.

On the third pass, the boat came right over me, but I had heard and seen it coming and was able to go deep, maybe ten feet, until my ears felt like they were being pushed in by giant thumbs. The boat moved on. I was feeling pretty good, like I was going to make it, when all of a sudden the boat came back and stopped, nearly on top of me.

Had they somehow spotted me, or were they just guessing? Whatever it was, they parked there, obviously waiting for me to surface. Moving back toward the boat, I surfaced just under the stern overhang, held onto the rudder, and rested.

I could see lights being shined down into the water, but as long as none of them came near me, I was safe. Being on the trailing edge of the rudder, I was safe from the spinning prop. The boat started moving again, in wider circles, and I hung onto the forward edge of the rudder and let it tow me until it passed within twenty yards of the beach. I let go, stayed under, and stroked hard for the land, knowing it would take the boat awhile to come back. By the time it did, I was low crawling up the beach in sand so soft and fine it felt like talcum powder.

Reaching the jungle line, I collapsed against a thick tree, sucked in the warm sweet air and clawed the transmitter from my left cargo pocket. The light was out. I should have left it hidden on the boat somewhere, at least it would have raised the alarm.

Taking the gun from my pocket, I ejected the round in the chamber, dropped the mag out and locked the breech open. Thumbing the bullets out of the magazine, I shook it and the gun, blew it out as best I could, and reloaded it. I wasn't worried about the pistol. A .45 is tough and its tolerances are loose. It will fire and function as long the barrel is kept clear. It's the bullets themselves that are vulnerable. If the primers get wet, they're history.

From behind the tree, I watched as the boat bumped the dock heavily in an unskilled landing, then the dock swarmed with people. I thought I saw the familiar figure of Duke on the wharf and felt my chest tighten.

A group of locals unloaded the boat, with another group bringing boxes down from somewhere in the jungle. Meds going, stolen from the main military hospital in this area, and guns coming in, gathered and stolen from the rice paddies and villages of Nam to be sent to the insurgents in the north of Thailand, but that was someone else's fish to fry.

Confront Duke and then get out of here alive was my goal. Fading back into the trees and vines, I headed south. Dripping wet, I was soon slipping and sliding, falling down, getting up, but I kept moving. Unseen thorns and sharp palm fronds scraped and jabbed me, I tripped over vines and roots, but every hard fought step brought me closer to the truth.

CHAPTER 34

"You're gettin' there," I said out loud. "Just follow this beach all the way around the next headland and you're in the next cove. Stay close to the tree line, no one can see you and it's easier than bashing through the jungle."

I made good progress, for a while. The headland itself became a jumble of rocks, cast into a lunar landscape of razor sharp peaks and black holes by the moonlight.

Briefly, I considered swimming around them but gave up that idea. There might be currents that could sweep me out to sea or force me onto those devil's teeth.

Noting the moon's position, I plunged back into the morass of clinging vines, tripping roots and jabbing bushes. Every step was a small battle to stay upright and keep focused. The adrenaline rush of the escape was over and fatigue had set in, forcing my eyes closed and my thoughts to wander. Craving rest and a cigarette, I kept my arms in front of my face and pushed on.

"Do it for Pen, do it for Pen, do it for Pen," became the litany that made me put one foot in front of the other.

The moon became coy, hiding behind trees and clouds, popping out now and then to let me know where he was.

"What'd you say to Pen, that night on the island?" I asked the lunar man that question over and over but he only stared back at me without answering.

I reached a low ridge and shouted with glee. Halfway! That gave me strength and I pushed on.

I became aware of a light ahead of me and stopped. Someone or something had a huge light that shined on everything. Approaching slowly, I stopped to listen, but heard nothing, then it came to me. It had to be moonlight on a beach! I was right.

Keeping just inside the jungle line, I had a long look around. Nothing.

There was nothing here, not even a single footprint to indicate any human activity here in the last thousand years.

Maybe Burke was even trickier than I thought and had brought us in two coves too soon. It would be just like him. This cove was big and shallow, not like the smaller, deeper one I was used to.

On the beach, I kept close to the jungle line but the fine sand made walking difficult. Taking a chance, I went down to the hard packed sand at the waters edge and made good time.

Huffing and puffing along, I watched the small waves swish and slap and break into millions of moonlit diamond chips. The sand reflected so much light I could have read a chart.

It was a beach just like this one, the sand soft and warm with a warm breeze and the same moon that Pen and I had shared not so long ago, but it felt like a lifetime now.

We'd swam naked in the moonlight, I'd chased her across the sand, and we'd tumbled to it and rolled until we were dry, the moon and stars spinning over our heads. We'd brushed the dried sand from us like talcum powder. She'd laid her head on my shoulder and listened as I told her about everything except what really mattered.

What had I waited for? The perfect moment? Finding the perfect moment is easy. It's just like asking yourself Should I reef the sails in this rising wind? The best time to reef is when you first think of it. The perfect moment is when you first think of it, when the idea is fresh and new. Waiting for the perfect time will only insure that it will never come.

"Oh, baby, what were you doing that you couldn't tell me? What did you need that you couldn't ask me for, what did I have that I wouldn't have given you?"

Talking out loud, putting my thoughts into the air, flayed my emotions. A sob, unexpected and sharp, racked me, but the sound of my own voice steadied my nerves.

I reached a low sandy headland without rocks. The next cove was just around that sand spit, and moving up to the tree line, I low-crawled around just enough for a good look. There it was.

The rickety little wharf was clearly visible not fifty yards away. I wondered who had built these wharves, and why. Decoys? Alternates? Or were they old fishing wharves, abandoned now because of the war?

Keeping to the dense shadows cast by the moon I moved very carefully.

The cove appeared deserted, but between the head of the wharf and the tree line, I spotted a dark shape lying on the sand. The broad leaves of the trees, shivering in the light breeze, appeared to lights winking on and off in the moonlight. Keeping in shadow, I moved in for a better look.

"No," I thought to myself. "It can't be, no, no, no!"

There was no doubt about it. The dark lump was two bodies sprawled out, arms and legs akimbo, and with a fist squeezing my heart, I knew who it was.

CHAPTER 35

Trembling with fear, I felt for a pulse. In spite of the heat, Harry was already getting cold to the touch but I forced myself to make sure. Dead. I jerked my hand away.

I checked Ray and could detect a faint, thready heartbeat. For a second, I felt a wild exhilaration, he was still alive! But in no shape to do anything. I felt my resolve start to slip and a powerful urge to just run away up the beach flowed over me, but then I saw Pen dead on the bed.

Think, think, think! Basic training asserted itself. I was not wounded, not captured, and still had a functioning weapon and ammo. What did the captain say, what did Uncle Jack always say? Have a back-up plan. I had none, yet, but the .45 felt reassuring in my pocket, and I flexed sore muscles.

"See, I told you he would show up here."

I jumped and turned, knowing in my gut who's voice that was.

Burke, Art and Matt came out of the tree line into the moonlight. I could see the demonic grin on Burke's face. Matt moved with a shambling gait and a goofy grin softened his features. He must have fixed recently and was floating on a cloud of China White.

Art's head swiveled back and forth like an owl's, then he spotted the bodies and stopped dead in his tracks. A shout of dismay burst from him and he ran past me to stare at the forms lying on the beach, then he went roaring back to where Burke stood.

"What the fuck have you done, man?" Art bellowed.

"What?" Matt asked lazily of no one in particular.

"Burke's killed those two cops!" Art shouted at him.

"Yeah?" Matt said, still not getting it.

"You know what this means, you fucking junkie? We're accessories in the murder of two cops! Goddamn you, Burke!"

I half expected Art to attack Burke right then, and maybe Burke did to, because he made sure everyone saw the Makarov in his hand.

"Who you callin' a junkie, man?" Matt asked peevishly.

Art ignored him and, disregarding the Makarov, was right up in Burke's face.

"You crazy fuck," he shouted, "Two cops! They'll never stop hunting us, man, never! Oh, shit! Oh...oh...!"

Words failed him. Spreading his clenched fists, he raised his face up to the moon and howled, a deep, reverberating cry of anguish and desperation that ran on for long seconds.

Every hair I possessed stood out like a stiff wire. I felt hot and itchy. Art was calling on his ancestors and it was so spooky, so grounded in pre-history, that I expected to see shapes slinking down the beach, like wolves in the night forest.

"Get a grip ya' fuckin' redskin," Burke said. "We weight those bodies down and sink 'em, they'll be fish food in no time. Now..."

Art wheeled away. I could sense the turning tide, the subtle cutting of ties, and wondered if Burke felt it, too.

It came to me then that someone was missing from our party, and it didn't take long to figure out who it was.

"Where's Duke?"

Burke grinned. "You know," he said, "That guy has been asking the same about you."

"That right?" I said. It came to me then why Burke had wanted me to drive that boat.

"Yeah," Burke said, his gravely voice rising. "Seems he bears you some serious grudge for stealin' his woman." He grinned and his big yellow teeth gleamed like old ivory in the moonlight.

"What the hell you mean, his woman?"

"Oh, Duke and Pen go back a long ways."

In light of what I'd been hearing lately, that didn't surprise me.

"Where is he, anyway?" I demanded hotly.

Burke gestured airily with his left hand, the pistol in his right pointed at the ground in front of me.

"He'll be here in minute," Burke replied.

I turned and scanned the dark jungle. "Get your ass out here, you fuckin' coward!"

"You're about a bold son-of-a-bitch, aren't ya'!" Burke exclaimed, that devil grin of his in place. He sensed what was coming.

"I wanna know what the fuck his problem is!" I yelled.

"I'll tell you what his problem is." Burke smiled, the instigator, and lit a cigarette. "He's one crazy zip, that's what."

"Wha'd'you mean by that?"

"You know the story about his momma, how she had him, the old Chinaman, all that?"

I nodded.

"Well, it seems like it was all true and no bullshit, *mai go-hok*, as they say. Duke was crazy for Pen. She didn't dig him though and wanted to make her own way. In fact, that's why she took up with you, ya' know?"

I looked at Art. He met my gaze with a level stare that told me nothing.

"Anyway," Burke went on, "she had all kinds of plans going, she did. She was a biz'ness girl, all right, in more ways than one. It was her who said we could get you to drive the boat for us, after our local guy, ah, had his accident."

"Like a Makarov round in the back of the head accident?" I said, unable to control myself.

"No," Burke declared, the grin wider now, "straight in the heart, eye to eye, like this!"

With a blur of motion, he was right in front of me, the Makarov barrel hard against my chest, his eyes boring into mine. I could see the craziness in him then, and I had to struggle to not back away.

He stared and pressed that gun against me for long seconds while I looked back at him, then suddenly he lowered the pistol, the smile returned, and he went on.

"You came along and Pen was full of schemes and plans, but none of 'em included Duke. He couldn't handle that."

Burke's voice hardened again, and with a gesture, he showed his contempt for all those unable to handle it.

This was it. Here was what I had been searching for and at the same time fearing for the last few days.

Was this the reason she was dead, a jealous former boyfriend, and not some criminal enterprise? Could her death be that mundane? I shook my head, unable to believe it.

"Duke killed her 'cause she didn't…" I couldn't get it out there, but Burke had the answer.

"Jealous rage, man. It'll make ya' crazy, make even a strong man weak." He went away for a second it seemed, into his own past, then snapped back.

"See," he said, that tone of amused enjoyment in his voice again, "she was tryin' to get knocked up by you. Lot's of these girls try for a kid by a blue-eyed *felong* and hope for a boy."

I must have stared because he nodded, almost to himself while he talked to me.

"A blue-eyed baby boy," he said, "would worth about five thou' on the open market. Pen wouldn't let Duke near her anymore 'cause she didn't want him to plant one in her. His kid would be fuckin' worthless, couldn't even give it away, but yours, well," he waved a hand in my direction, "that could set her up real nice."

I felt like I'd been kicked in the gut. My head spun and I couldn't breath. Spots swirled and swam before my eyes. With all my heart and soul, I had been hoping that what Ray had told me about Pen being pregnant wasn't true, and now here it was, confirmed.

"Ya' see," Burke went on in a genial tone, "Duke didn't want her to have a *felong* kid, no matter how much she could make from it. Maybe he was afraid it would end up like him, I don't know, but hey, ask him yourself." With that, he pointed over my shoulder.

I turned slowly. Duke stood there, his loose tropical clothes ruffling in the slight breeze, a smile on his face, his agate green eyes hidden in deep pools of shadow. I wanted to jump him right there, but with an effort I held on to myself.

"Everything he says is true, isn't it?"

I only wanted Duke to confirm what Burke had said. He did more than that.

"Yes," he said. A mocking smile cracked his face and at that simple word, I felt a great stillness descend over me.

"I had her many times," he said, "She liked it rough."

As he talked, I saw the bruises on Pen's legs and arms, and heard her voice, urging me on, harder, faster.

"Yeah," I retorted. I felt a burning need to one-up him somehow but before I could Burke spoke up.

"Well, this is all very interesting," he said briskly, "but time is short, so let's get on with it."

He spoke directly to Duke. "Here he is, like we agreed."

Suddenly, Duke's hand made a move. I saw the blade, long and slim, shiny and lethal in the moonlight.

"You didn't know her at all," I shouted, heedless of the knife, of anything except my need. "You didn't know what she was really like, you didn't know anything about her!" My voice rose in pitch even as I struggled to control it.

Duke's calm, cool veneer shattered. "I knew her better than you!" A vein throbbed in his throat and another writhed in his forehead. "She loved me before you came along! She didn't need money, I have money, lot's of money!"

From his shirt pocket he snatched a big roll of cash and with a quick motion of the knife snicked the rubber band and flung it at me. The wad of cash exploded into a shower of bills that fell like confetti.

Icily calm again, he looked at me. "I'm going to stick this in you just like I did in her." Slowly, the knife moved back and forth, moonlight clicking on the blade.

But Duke had more to say. "I told her not to get pregnant, that I would take care of her, but she wouldn't listen to me! She wouldn't do what I told her! I asked her, I begged her, don't get pregnant, don't have a baby just to sell, but she just wouldn't listen to me!"

"She laughed at me, at my plans for us, told me she could never love me, and I…" he stood there, swaying as if stunned, his mouth open slightly, his features twisted with the pain of memory.

"So you killed her."

Each word scorched my throat as I said them. "You stabbed her with her own knife when she told you to get out, she didn't love you, she loved me!"

"Yes!"

In that one word he projected all his pain at me. "Yes," he repeated, "she told me to get out, that she hated me, that I made her want to puke! Now I'm going to kill you, you goddamned blue-eyed devil GI!"

Suddenly, Matt moved forward, his lanky frame wobbly and loose, his eyes barely focused, but his speech clear and precise. "Wait a goddamned minute you fuckin' zip," he said, "you can't talk to a GI like that!"

Duke turned his malevolent eyes on Matt. "I told you never to call me that, you fucking junkie!"

"Oh, yeah?" Matt said, but he sounded confused now, as if he couldn't remember what the argument was about.

Duke turned back to me and I felt the hate flow from the dark pits of stone looniness that were his eyes. Everything dropped away, and we were alone on this moonlit beach.

. This was it, I could feel it. My right hand slithered into my pocket.

With a hoarse bellow of rage and desperation, Duke drew back the knife and rushed me. I saw the knife rocket toward me in a vicious arc from behind him with enough force to drive it in up the hilt, and I was the target.

"No!"

With a startled yelp, Matt jumped forward, between Duke and I. I heard the sound of a slicing thud and Matt's body jerked as he took the blade.deep into his belly.

Duke jerked the knife free and stepped back, anger and frustration spitting from his eyes. Matt's hand came up, touched his belly. He looked at his own blood in the moonlight, then his eyes rolled back in his head and he crumpled.

Duke sprang forward. I brought my hand from my pocket, thumbed the hammer back and pointed the Colt straight into his eyes. If he saw it, I'll never know. He came straight on, his face a mask of single-minded hatred.

I pulled the trigger.

The flash and roar split the still, soft night, the hardball round blew out most of his throat and flung a bright spray of blood and torn flesh into the air. The force of the big slug stopped him cold. His face became a picture of shock, anger and disbelief, then, slowly, his legs gave out and he toppled backwards into a heap.

I flung a shot in Burke's direction and threw myself to the sand. A lick of fire and a tiny pop, puny compared to that .45, came from the Makarov.

As I rolled I saw a glittering, flickering light travel from Art to Burke and stop at Burke's chest, there to twinkle and sparkle in the moonlight. I heard Burke's grunt of surprise, saw him look down at his own chest in curious wonder. His left hand came up and pawed briefly at the handmade stainless steel throwing knife embedded deep in his heart, then the Makarov slipped from his hand, his eyes rolled and he pitched forward face first into the sand.

It was suddenly very quiet. I looked at Duke, then at Matt. Matt moved slightly and I scrambled to him. He lay on his back, both hands holding his middle.

Snatching up the Airborne hat from beside him I tried to stop the gushing flow of blood but his hands caught mine.

"No," he said, very low, so low I could hardly hear him after the explosions of the gunfire.

"I'm not gonna make it, man, I know. I've seen lots of wounds, and this one is.." he shook his head, as if the outcome was already written and there was no use trying to change it now. His eyelids fluttered briefly and I saw a light in his eye that seemed to wax and wane, like a distant lighted sea buoy on a dark, cloudy night.

His lips moved, and I leaned close.

"Am I goin' to hell, man?"

I tried to tear my gaze from him, not wanting this question put on me, but I found it impossible to look away. That light in his eyes seemed to hold me like iron to a lodestone. What could I say? What did I believe myself? What small thing could I say to him now to make him feel better somehow. This was his karma.

"No," I said to him, knowing in that instant that it was true. "You're gonna get a free ride to the pearly gates, man, 'cause you saved my life, Matt!"

His hands still held mine very tightly.

"I wanna say thanks for that," I told him. The light dimmed. "Did you hear me, Matt? You saved my life, you're goin' to heaven!" I sobbed out loud, wanting him to hear me and to know that he had not died anonymously, uselessly, on a lonely beach. The light flared, I knew he heard me, then it dimmed, and he was gone.

His hands still held mine in a powerful grip that scared me, as if he were reluctant to let go. As gently as I could, I freed myself and folded his hands across his chest, grateful that his eyes had closed.

Scrambling on all fours in the sand, I went over to Duke. He lay crumpled in a heap. Blood, black in the moonlight, pumped slowly from his shattered throat.

As I watched his life soaking into the powdery golden sand, I thought of that Creedence song, "Bad Moon Rising", and the line that ends, "…one eye is taken for an eye."

A great chilling shudder racked me, blurred my vision and choked my breath. I had taken his life in the fiery heat of self-defense, but would I have been able to take it coldly, calmly, in revenge, like I had assured myself that I would while awash in the searing anger of pain and grief? I didn't know, and I realized I was grateful that I would never have to find out.

Carefully, I felt for a chain around his neck. I found a heavy-linked gold one, not what I was looking for. His blood got on my hands as I searched, my stomach churned, but I forced myself to continue and used the fine sand to scrub it off. I rifled all his pockets, searched his wallet, and still hadn't found it.

I had an idea, and felt both wrists. One the left was a heavy gold watch, and on the right was a large gold bracelet, but this was not it, either, so I moved on.

I found it on his right ankle. The thin gold chain was looped twice around and fastened, and hanging from it, Pen's gold man-in-the-moon amulet, the one that had been missing when I had seen her lying on the bed with her blood flowing from her and her *kwang-hai* in turmoil.

Carefully, I opened the clasp. The chain snaked off smoothly. I held the chunk of gold in my hand and gazed at it. She had counted on this to protect her, to keep her from harm, and for a second, I thought bitterly what a failure that it had turned out to be.

In the palm of my hand, the old man looked sad and mournful, and I wondered if he knew he had failed. Anger and resentment became a scalding wave that almost knocked me over and choked me again, but the vision of her *kwang-hai* floated in front of me, its tortured writhing seeming to implore me to do something, to save it from an eternity of endless searching for a way to Nirvana. Maybe, I suddenly thought, that amulet hadn't failed, after all.

As if in a trance, I put the chain around my own neck, closed the catch, and pressed the warm, heavy moon to my chest.

All at once, a whirlpool swept over me and I felt as if I were being pulled down into a maelstrom of grief and sorrow.

A sudden, wracking spasm bent me double and I felt the tears come then, hot and stinging, to drop from my cheek onto the sand.

Here was the grieving and the shedding of tears that I had been unable, or unwilling, to realize until now. This island, this indifferent hunk of jungle and sand would hold elements of many of us in its very atoms, the physical presence soon gone, but a piece of each of us would remain, and whether we had shed blood or tears here, we would each of us be, if not remembered, at least memorialized in some small way in the universe.

Unable to stop it, I let it push me down and lying there, I cried for her. I don't know how long I lay on that beach, but as the spasms passed, I felt an odd rush of relief swell in my chest and I gazed up at the moon, so close I could almost touch it.

There, on that beach, the moonlight spangling off the water, I again saw Pen lying on that bed as if it floated on that silvery trail, only this time, her *kwang-hai* was no longer swirling and writhing and seeking escape, but had come together to coalesce into the shape of her face.

Her eyes, large and luminously glowing, seemed to lock with mine and I saw the look of gratitude, of love, of release, that she gave me. Her lips formed into a final kiss and I heard her voice as she said, "I love you."

I felt the breeze on my face, like it was her breath on my cheek for the last time. I felt at peace, as if I had done what I had set out to do, to free her for her journey.

As I put my hands together for the *wai*, I called out to her, "I love you!" then the image rose swiftly into the starry sky and was gone, only the man-in-the-moon left, looking sorrowful but content, as if he knew now that she too was finally at peace.

CHAPTER 36

When I turned around, I saw Art running down the beach, kicking up small puffs of sand that the tide would soon erase forever.

"Hold it!" I shouted.

He didn't even glance back.

"Stop!"

I brought the gun up and fired. A geyser of sand leaped beside him, and he stopped.

"Where you goin'?"

I pointed the pistol at him. A wave of exhaustion swept over me and I had to shake my head to clear it. The trees, their silver edges shifting and shimmering, wavered in and out of focus, and Art seemed to expand and contract as he stood on the gleaming sand.

"I'm bookin', man."

"No you're not! You're gonna answer for all the shit you been doin'!"

I wavered as I stood there. My eyelids were so heavy, if I could only sleep for just a minute...

He laughed out loud. I shook the gun at him, but it only made him laugh harder.

"I know you have a way out of here," I said, "'cause that's how you are. You get me and Ray off this island, and I'll have a memory problem about where you went."

"And if I don't?"

"Then...then..." I couldn't think of anything, and I stopped talking as he came toward me. I pointed the pistol straight at his chest, but he kept coming on until the barrel was right against him, and he just looked at me. The pressure of his bulk made my whole arm quiver.

"Then what?" he asked in a soft, low voice. I couldn't see his eyes, sunk into dark pools under his brow, but I knew they would be black and brittle like beach glass, and I knew my bluff had been called.

"Do it," he said, leaning into the barrel. I locked my elbow and pushed harder into his chest. My finger shivered on the trigger. Just a little pressure was all it would take, just a twitch, and he would be...

"You won't shoot me," he said, "'cause I'm no threat to you now. Besides, we're alike, you and me."

"No, we're not," I said hotly, pushing the gun harder, trying to make him back up, just one step, "You're a traitor and a liar, you use people, you..."

"What I meant was," he leaned forward even more, forcing me to step back, "when we see something we want, we go after it, no matter what."

We stared wordlessly at each other for long seconds and I knew he was right. The pistol seemed useless now. I flung it away from me, heard it splash.

"I'm sorry for what happened," Art said, as if from a long way off. "I never meant for things to go like this." A note of sorrow was in his voice, something rarely heard from him, but it was real, no bullshit, and I knew he was revealing something of himself for the first time.

In the end, Art did have another way off the island, and he helped me get Ray into the boat, a eighteen foot open job with a big outboard. Ray was out of it, but the bleeding was stopped, his pulse was steady and his breathing regular. He would make it.

I was putting Ray into a taxi, I turned around, and Art was gone. I was suddenly very pissed at him, because I never got to say those final things, those words that end, not a friendship, but a relationship of some kind, good or bad. I wanted those words, wanted them badly, and now I would never have them.

I went into Sattahip and sent the taxi with Ray in it to the main gate at Camp Samesan Army Base while I caught the water taxi to the port.

Crossing the bay, the eastern sky was a sea-shell pink, fading through soft, glowing purple to an inky blackness in the west. The moon was a diffuse ball sinking into the horizon, and I suspected that this would the last dawn I would see in Thailand, and the last time I would see the SHEILA. She lay to her mooring, serene and beautiful. I wished her well and thanked her feminine soul for the many hours of enjoyment she had provided.

As I was packing my gear on the tug, MPs showed up and hustled me off to their headquarters, then to Bangkok, where I told my story a million times to many different cops.

That night, large, somber MPs escorted me onto a military flight headed for the world, leaving all my gear behind. All my pictures, of Pen on the beach, of her on board SHEILA, naked and proud on the bow, a shot of her reclining in the porch hammock, her eyes full of mystery and mischief, all gone.

Other mementoes, small carved teakwood elephants, a jade Happy Buddha, a star sapphire ring, inconsequential things by themselves but of enormous importance to me as reminders of the joys I had known and the sorrows and disappointments that had been part of it, like the child I would never know, were all left behind.

In a way, I was glad. I had arrived with nothing, and I left with nothing, much like birth and death, but years later, while I lie sleepless in the cabin of my own boat, softly rocked in the cradle of the Pacific, images of our life together, only slightly dimmed by time and distance, would flicker like old home movies on the screen of my memory.

THE END

ABOUT THE AUTHOR

A lifelong boater and sailor for twenty-five years, I've always loved the sea. A two-year stint as an engineer aboard a U.S. Army tug brought familiarity with big boats and engine rooms, and the G.I. Bill made a college education possible and revived an affection for words and language.

Russel
3/03
ACAPULCO

Printed in the United States
745400002B

9 780595 184163